"I should have killed him."

She smiled wanly. "Start defending me, Cyn Malloren, and you'll have to take on the world."

He kissed her on the lips. "The first time I've kissed you in the morning. May it be the first of many."

Her heart trembled, but she said, "Unlikely," and began to ease away.

He put a hand out to stop her. "I promised not to seduce you, Chastity, and I always keep my word. Believe then that this kiss is just a kiss, not a prelude to more." His hand moved tenderly against her cheek. "Forget the past. You are a highborn young lady who finds herself taking shelter with a rascal, a rascal who is smitten with her charms into stealing a kiss. You can relax and enjoy it. Even if you feel obliged to slap him later on."

JO BEVERLEY is the recipient of numerous awards, among them the Career Achievement Award and Best Regency Author from *Romantic Times;* the RITA of the Romantic Writers of America for her Regency romance *Emily and the Dark Angel;* and the Readers Choice Award.

Avon Regency Romances by
Jo Beverley

THE STANFORTH SECRETS
EMILY AND THE DARK ANGEL
THE FORTUNE HUNTER

Other **AVON ROMANCES**

HEART OF THE WILD *by Donna Stephens*
SCARLET KISSES *by Patricia Camden*
SCOUNDREL'S DESIRE *by JoAnn DeLazzari*
SILVER AND SAPPHIRES *by Shelly Thacker*
SURRENDER MY HEART *by Lois Greiman*
TRAITOR'S KISS *by Joy Tucker*
WILDSTAR *by Nicole Jordan*

Coming Soon

COME BE MY LOVE *by Patricia Watters*
MY REBELLIOUS HEART *by Samantha James*

And Don't Miss These
ROMANTIC TREASURES
from Avon Books

FORTUNE'S MISTRESS *by Judith E. French*
THE MASTER'S BRIDE *by Suzannah Davis*
A ROSE AT MIDNIGHT *by Anne Stuart*

My Lady Notorious

Jo Beverley

AVON BOOKS ◈ NEW YORK

MY LADY NOTORIOUS is an original publication of Avon Books. This work has never before appeared in book form. This work is a novel. Any similarity to actual persons or events is purely coincidental.

AVON BOOKS
A division of
The Hearst Corporation
1350 Avenue of the Americas
New York, New York 10019

First Avon Books Printing: March 1993

Printed in the U.S.A.

RA 10 9 8 7 6 5 4 3 2

Chapter 1

The great crested coach lurched along the Shaftesbury road, over ruts turned rock-like by a sharp November frost. Lounging inside, glossy boots up on the opposite seat, was a lazy-eyed young gentleman in a suit of dark blue laced with silver. His features were smooth, tanned, and on the pretty side of handsome, but his taste for decoration was moderate. His silver lacing merely edged the front of his coat; his only jewels were a sapphire on his lax right hand, and a pearl and diamond pin in his softly knotted cravat. His unpowdered russet hair was irrepressibly wavy but tamed into a neat pigtail fixed with black bows at top and bottom.

This hairstyle was the work of his *valet de chambre*, a middle-aged man who sat upright beside his master, a small jewel box clasped firmly on his lap.

At yet another creaking sway, Lord Cynric Malloren sighed and resolved to hire a riding horse at the next stop. He had to escape this damned confinement.

Being an invalid was the very devil.

He'd finally managed to persuade his solicitous brother, the Marquess of Rothgar, that he was up to traveling, but only on a gentle two-day journey to Dorset to visit his elder sister and her new baby. And only in this monstrous vehicle, complete with fur rugs for his legs, and hot bricks for his feet. Now he was returning home, progressing like

1

a fragile grandmother back to sibling care and warm flannel.

The shouted command was merely a welcome relief from tedium. It took a second before Cyn realized he was actually being held up. His valet turned pale and crossed himself, muttering a stream of French prayers. Cyn's eyes lost their lazy droop.

He straightened and flashed a quick glance at his rapier in its scabbard on the opposite seat, but dismissed it. He had little faith in stories of highwaymen who fenced with their victims for the gold. Instead he pulled the heavy double-barreled pistol out of the holster by his seat and deftly checked that it was clean and loaded in both barrels.

A cruder weapon than a blade, but in this situation a good deal more effective.

The coach came to rest at an angle. Cyn studied the scene outside. It was late in the short day and the nearby pines cast deep shadows in the red of the setting sun, but he could still see the two highwaymen quite clearly. One was back among the trees, covering the scene with a musket. The other was much closer and armed with two elegant silver-mounted dueling pistols. Stolen? Or was this a true gentleman of the road? His steaming mount was a fine bit of blood.

Cyn decided not to shoot anyone yet. This adventure was too enlivening to be cut short, and he had to admit that the distant villain would be a tricky shot in the fading light, even for him.

Both highwaymen wore encompassing black cloaks, tricorn hats, and white scarves around the lower part of their faces. It wouldn't be easy to describe them if they escaped, but Cyn was at heart a gambler, though he rarely played for coin. He would let these dice roll.

"Down off the box," the nearby man ordered gruffly.

The coachman and groom obediently climbed down. At a command, they lay face-down on the frosty grass verge. The second highwayman came closer to guard them.

The coach swayed as the masterless horses shifted. Jerome gave a cry of alarm. Cyn put out a hand to brace himself, but he didn't take his eyes from the two highwaymen. The team should be too tired to bolt. He was proved correct as the coach became still again.

"Now, you inside," barked the nearer villain, both barrels trained on the door. "Out. And no tricks."

Cyn considered shooting the man—he could guarantee to put a ball through his right eye at this distance—but restrained himself. Others could be endangered, and neither his pride nor his valuables were worth an innocent life.

He laid the pistol beside his sword, opened the door, and stepped down. He turned to assist his valet, who had a weak leg, then flicked open his *grisaille* snuffbox, shook back the Mechlin lace at his cuff, and took a pinch. He snapped the box shut, then faced the highwayman's pistols. "How may I help you, sir?"

The man seemed stunned by this reaction, but recovered. "You may help me to that pretty box, for a start."

Cyn had to work to keep his face straight. Perhaps it was the shock of his bland reaction to robbery, but the thief had forgotten to control his voice. Now he sounded well-bred and quite young. Scarcely more than a boy. Any desire to see him hang seeped away, and his curiosity gathered strength.

He flicked open the box again and approached. "You wish to try my sort? It is a tolerable blend . . ."

He had not intended to throw the powder in the robber's face, but the thief was no fool and backed his horse away. "Keep your distance. I'll have the box—tolerable sort an' all—along with your money, and any jewels or other valuables."

"Certainly," said Cyn with a careless shrug. He took the box Jerome clutched, which contained his pins, fobs, and other trinkets, and placed the snuffbox inside. From his pockets he added some coins and notes. With some regret he slid off the sapphire ring, and pulled out the pearl-and-diamond pin; they had sentimental value. "You clearly have more need of all this than I, my good man. Shall I put the box by the road? You can collect it when we're gone."

There was another stunned silence. Then: "You can damn well lie down in the dirt with your servants!"

Cyn raised his brows. He brushed a speck of fluff from the sleeve of his coat. "Oh, I don't think so. I have no desire to become dusty." He faced the man calmly. "Are you going to kill me for it?"

He saw the man's trigger finger tighten and wondered if for once he'd misplayed his hand, but there was no shot. After a thwarted silence, the young man said, "Put your valuables in the coach and get on the box. I'm taking the coach, and you can be my coachman, Mr. High and Mighty!"

"Novel," drawled Cyn with raised brows. "But aren't stolen coaches a trifle hard to fence?"

"Shut your lip or I'll shut it for you!"

Cyn had the distinct feeling the highwayman was losing patience—a reaction he'd been causing all his life.

"Do what I tell you," the rogue barked. "And tell your men to take their time walking for help. If we're overtaken, you'll get the first shot."

Cyn obediently addressed the servants. "Go on to Shaftesbury and rack up at the Crown. If you don't hear from me in a day or so, send word to the Abbey and my brother will take care of you. Don't worry about this. It's just a young friend playing a jape, and I have a mind to join in the fun." He addressed the coachman. "Hoskins, if Jerome's leg tires him, you must go ahead and find some transportation for him."

He then turned to the highwayman. "Am I permitted to put on my surtout and gloves, sir, or is this to be a form of torture?"

The man hesitated but said, "Go on, then. But I'll have you covered every second."

Cyn reached into the coach for his caped greatcoat and shrugged into it, then pulled on his black kid gloves, reflecting wryly that any amount of driving would ruin them. He considered the pistol for a moment but then dismissed it. He wanted to go along with this caper a while longer.

Protected from the frosty air, he climbed up on the box and took the four sets of reins into competent hands. He quickly familiarized himself with the pattern on each which identified wheelers and leaders. "What now, my good man?"

The highwayman glared at him with narrowed eyes. "You're a rum 'un and no mistake." When Cyn made no reply, the highwayman hitched his horse to the back and swung up beside him. He pocketed one pistol but poked the other in Cyn's side. "I don't know what your game is, but you'll pull no tricks with me. Drive."

Cyn flicked the team into action. "No tricks," he promised. "But I do hope that pistol lacks a hair trigger. This is a very uneven road."

After a moment, the pistol was moved so it pointed slightly away. "Feel safer?" the man sneered.

"Infinitely. Where are we going?"

"Never you mind. I'll tell you when you need to turn. For now, just hold your tongue."

Cyn obeyed. He could sense the baffled fury emanating from his captor and had no desire to taunt him into firing. In truth, he didn't wish to taunt the fool at all. He'd rather kiss him on both cheeks for breaking the monotony of his days. He'd had his fill of being cossetted.

He glanced around and realized the second villain had gone on ahead. Risky, but he supposed they thought a pistol held against him would keep him in order.

It might. He was feeling kindly disposed.

Being hovered over by his siblings might have been tolerable if he'd been wounded in action, but when he'd been brought down by a mere fever . . . ! And now none of them would believe he was recovered enough to rejoin his regiment. He'd considered overriding the arranged plan and commanding Hoskins to head for London, where he could demand an army medical. There would be little point, however, for at a word from Rothgar some lingering weakness would doubtless be discovered.

Just as a word from Rothgar had procured him fast transport to the Abbey, and the best medical care along the way, while better men sweated out their fevers or died in overcrowded hospitals in Plymouth. Or back in the primitive conditions in Acadia. Rothgar could even have been behind him being shipped home from Halifax in the first place.

Damn Rothgar and his mollycoddling.

No one in his right mind would describe the formidable marquess, Cyn's eldest brother, as a mother hen, but upon their parents' deaths he had taken his five siblings under his autocratic wing and God help anyone who tried to harm them. Even the forces of war.

Rothgar seemed particularly protective of Cyn. This was partly because he was the baby of the family, but it was also his damned looks. Despite all evidence to the contrary people would persist in seeing him as fragile, even his family who certainly should know better.

He alone of the family had been gifted with the full glory of his mother's delicate bones, green-gold eyes, russet-red hair, and lush lashes. His sisters—particularly his twin sister—had frequently asked heaven why such an unfair thing should have come about.

Cyn frequently asked the same question with the same amount of desperation. As a boy he'd believed age would toughen his looks, but at twenty-four, a veteran of Quebec and Louisbourg, he was still disgustingly *pretty*. He had to fight duels with nearly every new officer in the regiment to establish his manhood.

"Turn in the lane ahead." The highwayman's voice

jerked Cyn out of his reverie. He obediently guided the horses into the narrow lane, straight into the setting sun.

He narrowed his eyes against the glare. "I hope it isn't much further," he remarked. "It'll be dark soon and there's little moon tonight."

"It's not far."

In the gathering cold, steam rose off the team like smoke from a fire. Cyn cracked the whip to urge the tired horses on.

The youth lounged back, legs spread in contemptuous ease as he tried to convey the impression of age and hardened wickedness. It was unwise. The cloak had fallen open and the slenderness of the legs revealed by the lounging position reinforced Cyn's suspicion that he was dealing with a mere stripling. He noticed, however, that the pistol remained at the ready, and silently gave the lad credit.

No fool, this one.

So what had led the young man into this rash escapade? A dare? Gaming debts he couldn't confess to Papa?

Cyn didn't sense true danger here, and his nose for danger was highly developed. He'd been a soldier in wartime since the age of eighteen.

He remembered the explosion in his family when he'd run off to enlist. Rothgar had refused to buy him a commission and so Cyn had taken the shilling. The marquess had dragged him home, but after battles of will that left bystanders shaking, his brother had given in and bought him an ensigncy in a good regiment. Cyn had never regretted it. He demanded excitement, but unlike many other sprigs of the aristocracy he had no taste for pointless mayhem.

He glanced at his captor. Perhaps a military career would suit this young rascal. Some curious thought tickled the back of his mind and he ran his eyes over the youth. Then he had it. He stilled a twitch of his lips and concentrated on the team as he absorbed the new information.

Judging from the smoothness at the juncture of 'his' thighs, Cyn's captor was a woman.

He began to whistle. A promising situation indeed.

"Stop that damned noise!"

Cyn did so and looked at his companion thoughtfully. Women rarely spoke in such a clipped, harsh tone, and the creature's neat bag-wig and tricorn allowed no possibility of long tresses pinned up beneath. Could he be mistaken?

Casually, he let his gaze slide down again and knew his suspicions were correct. She wore fashionably tight knee-breeches and there was no male equipment under them. Moreover, though the woman's legs appeared slim and well-muscled, the breeches and fine clocked stockings revealed a roundness more feminine than masculine.

"How much further?" he asked, touching the weary off-leader with the whip to get them all over a particularly rough stretch. "This track's the very devil."

"That cottage ahead. Pull all the way into the orchard to hide the carriage. The horses can graze there."

Cyn looked at the gateway, which contained a dip as deep as some ditches, and wondered if the carriage would make it. He dismissed such concerns. He was too tantalized by what the next stage of this adventure would bring.

With whip and voice, he urged the tired team through, keeping his seat with difficulty as the vehicle jarred down into the dip, then jerked up. The abused axle gave a threatening squeal but did not crack. He pulled the team up beneath the trees with a sense of accomplishment, and wondered if the wench realized just how skillful he had been. His schoolboy passion for coaching had finally paid off.

"Fair enough," she said ungraciously.

He began to think his mystery lady would turn out to be an antidote. All he could see of her features above the scarf was hard gray eyes. He guessed her lips to be set in a harsh line.

"What are you staring at?" she snapped.

"It seems reasonable to try to note your features so I can describe you to the authorities."

She pointed the pistol straight at his face. "You're a fool, do you know that? What's to stop me from shooting you?"

He held her eyes, still relaxed. "Fair play. Are you the type to shoot a man for no reason?"

"Saving my neck might be reason enough."

Cyn smiled. "I give you my word that I will do nothing to help the authorities apprehend you."

The pistol drooped and she stared at him. "Who the devil are you?"

"Cyn Malloren. Who the devil are you?"

He watched as she almost fell into the trap and answered truthfully; but she caught herself. "You may call me Charles. What kind of a name is Sin?"

"C-Y-N. Cynric, in fact. Anglo-Saxon king."

"I've heard of the Mallorens . . ." She stiffened. "Rothgar."

"The marquess is my brother," he acknowledged. "Don't hold it against me." He guessed she fervently wished she'd left him by the roadside. Rothgar was not a man to cross.

She made a good recover. "I'll judge you on your own deeds, my lord. My word on it. Now, unhitch the team."

Cyn saluted ironically. "Aye, aye, sir."

He climbed down and stripped off his greatcoat and tight-waisted frock coat. He tucked the foaming lace at his cuffs out of harm's way, and went to work.

The sun had set, and there was little light. A damp cold bit into him despite the hard work. The task took some time and she didn't help, just sat there, pistol at the ready. At one point she looked behind him and said, "Go back to the house, Verity. Everything's all right. We'll be there in a while."

Cyn looked around and saw the glimmer of a pale gown turn to go back to the cottage. He'd lay odds that had been the other highwayman. Everything about this situation in- triged him.

What were two young women who appeared to be of gentle birth doing in this cottage?

Why had they turned to thievery?

And what, in God's name, did they want with the coach?

He rubbed the horses down with wisps of dry grass and covered them with the blankets Hoskins kept ready for a wait. "They could do with some water," he said.

"There's a stream down the end of the orchard. They'll find it. Let's get up to the house. You take the loot."

Cyn gathered up his coats, not bothering to put them on again. He went to the coach and collected the trinket case. He considered the pistol thoughtfully. It would be ridicu- lously easy to pick up the firearm and shoot his captor. As he left it there, he wondered whether he would regret his foolishness.

Within half an hour, the answer was yes.

From where he lay spread-eagled on a brass bed, hands and feet tied to solid corner-posts, he glared up at the three hovering women. "When I win free, I'm going to throttle the lot of you."

"That's why you're bound," said the one who still pre- tended to be male. "We wouldn't know a moment's peace if you were loose."

"I gave my word you had nothing to fear from me."

"Faith, you did not. You said you wouldn't turn us over to the authorities. You might intend other mischief— against my sister and nurse, for example."

Cyn looked at her thoughtfully. 'Charles' was proving to be a fascinating enigma. She had shed her cloak, hat, and scarf on entering the cottage. Soon, almost absent- mindedly, the wig had gone too. He sympathized. He'd never liked wearing a wig and preferred the bother of his own hair.

Even stripped of disguise, she made a tolerably convincing young man. Her suit of braided brown velvet fit neatly, and if a bosom swelled beneath, the lace frill of her shirt hid it well enough.

Her head was not shorn, but her hair was a sleek cap of light brown dusted with gold, with just the ripples of a wave. It was an extraordinary hairstyle for a female, but it did not look as outrageous as it should, perhaps because she was not a soft-featured lady. She made a handsome youth.

She was smooth-skinned, of course, which made her look about sixteen, though he would guess she must be closer to twenty. Her voice was rather low-pitched. Her lips might be charming if she relaxed them in a smile, but she kept them tight and angry. He didn't know why the devil she was so angry with him.

Her companions were equally mystifying.

Verity, presumably the sister, had long, lustrous wavy hair in a shade between honey and gold, and a soft, feminine mouth. In contrast to Charles, she had a lush figure. Presumably Charles had her breasts bound, but iron bands wouldn't obliterate Verity's generous shape, which was well-displayed by a low neckline and wide fichu. The outfit she wore, however, was more suited to a serving maid than to a lady of quality.

Verity appeared to be the epitome of a womanly woman. To prove it she was much more nervous and kindhearted than her sister. "We can't keep him like this indefinitely," she pointed out.

"Of course not, but it'll keep him out of harm's way while we eat and prepare to leave."

"But La . . . But Charles," said the nurse fretfully. "you're not allowed to leave, you know that."

This woman was old, very old. She was stooped and tiny, with half-moon spectacles and soft, silvery hair. She had been Cyn's downfall. When Charles had ordered him onto the bed to be bound, he'd refused. The old woman had obeyed the order to get him there, however, and he'd been so afraid of breaking her bird-like bones he'd ended up helpless.

He noted the slip. The old lady had almost called the chit Lady something. Very highborn then, and yet one was dressed convincingly as a male, and the other as a servant.

"I don't care a farthing whether I'm allowed to leave or not," said Lady Charles. "Up till now I've had no reason to go anywhere, and good reason to skulk. Now everything's changed. I suppose I'll come back in due course. Where else have I to go?"

"You will stay with Nathaniel and me," said Verity.

"Perhaps," said Charles with a softening of her features. "But he's going to have enough trouble looking after you and William, dearest." A squawking noise came from upstairs. "There he goes again. Hungry little beast, ain't he?"

Verity hurried off up a set of narrow stairs, and Cyn absorbed the fact that one of his highwaymen was a mother and, he suspected, a recent one. It explained the rather excessive lushness of her figure. Discomfort and annoyance gave way again to fascination. He looked forward to telling this tale to his fellow officers. A good yarn was always in demand in the winter billets.

The older woman disappeared into the kitchen, the only other room on the ground floor. Cyn supposed there was a room under the eaves above where the sisters and the baby slept. This room, the old lady's bedroom, was being used as a makeshift parlor and also contained a number of bundles, boxes, and portmanteaux.

Why were the sisters here, and why was Charles not allowed to leave?

The girl was digging in a chest, ignoring him. "Am I going to be fed?" Cyn asked.

"Eventually."

"What do you intend to do with me?"

She straightened and came over to the bed. She raised one foot on the frame and rested her elbow on her knee.

He had the distinct feeling she was enjoying the position of power. "Perhaps we'll just leave you here like this."

He met her angry gray eyes. "Why?"

"Why not?"

"I haven't done anything to hurt you. I did my best to be sure my people don't start a hue and cry."

"Why did you do that?"

He was startled by how much she distrusted, and, perhaps, feared him. That explained him being bound like this. Not out of cruelty, but out of fear. With his deceptively delicate appearance Cyn was not accustomed to women being so wary of him.

He chose his words with care. "I sensed you were not evil, that you intended me no serious harm. I don't want to see you swing. In fact, I'd like to help you."

She lowered her foot and took a betraying step backward. "Why?"

"I suspect you have a good reason for your actions, and I am overdue for an adventure."

She looked nothing so much as exasperated. "You're overdue for Bedlam."

"I don't think so. I just have a low tolerance for tedium."

"Tedium has its attractions, believe me."

"I have never discovered them."

"Then consider yourself fortunate."

For the first time he wondered if she was in real trouble. He'd been thinking more in terms of some girlish prank, but he doubted this formidable young woman would look so sober over a trivial matter.

"You're in danger, aren't you?" he said.

Her eyes widened, but she said nothing.

"All the more reason to trust me and let me help you."

Her chin came up sharply. "I don't trust—" After a caught breath she said, "—people."

He knew she had almost said, *I don't trust men.*

"You can trust me."

She gave a short, bitter laugh.

He waited until he could catch her guarded eyes. "There's a loaded pistol on the seat of the coach. I didn't use it earlier because your sister was covering my men. I didn't use it when I collected your loot because I didn't want to. I'm an excellent shot. I could have disarmed you, crippled you, or killed you at my leisure."

She frowned at him, then spun on her heel and left. He heard the outer door slam and knew she had gone to check.

A few minutes later the old woman tiptoed in with a spouted invalid cup. "I'm sure you'd like a drink, my lord," she said, and proceeded to carefully feed him a cup of startlingly strong, sweet tea. It wasn't as he usually drank it but he was grateful for it all the same.

When he'd finished she dabbed up a few drips with a snowy cloth. "You mustn't worry," she said, patting one of his bound hands. "No one's going to hurt you. Ch . . . Charles is a little edgy these days." She shook her head and real anxiety shadowed her eyes. "It's all been quite terrible . . ."

Again he had the feeling they were not addressing trivial matters here.

"What should I call you?" he asked.

"Oh, I'm just Nana. That's what they all call me, so you may as well too. Are your hands hurting? I didn't tie you too tight, did I?"

"No," he assured her, though his hands were pricking with pins and needles. He didn't want Charles to come back and find him free, or she'd suspect he'd just been trying to get her out of the house. He probed for a little more information. "And what should I call Miss Verity?"

"Oh," said the old lady, who was clearly no fool, "Verity will do, won't it? You must excuse me, my lord. I have the meal cooking."

* * *

Chastity Ware hurried through the gloom of the orchard to the shadowy shape of the carriage. She had stopped in the kitchen to pick up the dueling pistols and musket. It was past time to return them and the horses. But her main purpose, she acknowledged, was to check her prisoner's words.

Her mind seethed with dark thoughts. What had possessed her to kidnap Cyn Malloren?

There'd been a point to keeping the coach, though it had been a sudden inspiration. Verity and the baby would travel much better in a private vehicle than on the stage.

And there had been a point in making him drive it. She hadn't wanted to take her attention off the men long enough to drive it herself. She had little faith in Verity's ability to shoot anyone in any circumstance.

But even if she'd had him drive a little way, she could have left him in a deserted spot. She'd driven a gig. Surely driving a four-in-hand was not very different.

A rogue male was the last thing they needed.

In truth, it had been his insufferable male arrogance that had goaded her.

He'd stood there in his blue and silver with foaming lace, too beautiful to be decent, and not at all awed by her pistols. When he'd offered her a pinch of snuff she'd thirsted to puncture his self-assurance, to see him lying in the dirt. As he'd guessed, however, she hadn't been able to shoot him over it. Then he'd turned the tables by making that gracious little speech to his servants. If it worked, it would delay and perhaps prevent pursuit.

She wished she knew what game he played, but at least now she had him safe for a while. And how he was hating it. She smiled grimly to herself as she opened the carriage door.

The inside of the vehicle was dark and Chastity had to feel for the weapon, but she found it just as he had said. She pulled the pistol out, and in the uncertain light of a quarter moon confirmed that it was primed and loaded in both barrels. He'd been boasting, of course, when he'd said he could have disarmed, wounded, or killed her—she'd been armed too—but she acknowledged he'd had a chance if he'd cared to take it.

What made her tremble was how careless she'd been to give it to him. She closed her eyes in despair. Perhaps she wasn't equal to the task she'd set herself, to get her sister and nephew to safety.

Verity had arrived only yesterday, though her problems had started some time before. Her middle-aged husband, Sir William Vernham, had died nearly two months ago, only days after her son's birth. This had triggered a battle for the guardianship of the child between the babe's uncle, Henry Vernham, and his grandfather—Verity and Chastity's father, the Earl of Walgrave.

Henry had won the first legal skirmish, and arrived at Vernham Park to take control. Verity had soon come to fear that her child could be in danger, for Henry was an untrustworthy fellow who stood to inherit a title and fortune except for this one small life. Her fears had heightened when Henry tried to keep her from her family and friends. She had fled with her baby and made her way here.

Now she feared Henry, but did not want to seek the protection of her father. Lord Walgrave would certainly keep her safe, but would immediately plan another marriage to suit his convenience. Having endured the misery of life with Sir William, Verity was determined her next marriage would be to her childhood sweetheart, Major Nathaniel Frazer. Chastity had resolved to help her sister to this end.

The difficulty was that the sisters had virtually no money, and the hunt for Verity was already intense.

Henry Vernham had visited the cottage two days ago to question Chastity and Nana—Chastity had barely had time to scramble into female garments. They had easily convinced him they were ignorant of Verity's whereabouts, for she had not yet arrived. Their bewilderment and anxiety had been genuine.

Chastity's fists clenched at the memory of being thus confronted with Henry Vernham, for he was not just her sister's tormentor, but the man who had destroyed her own life and led to her being here, shorn, and in men's clothing. She had refused even to speak to him—it was that or gut him—but he'd managed one parting volley that had almost broken her resolve.

"I'm sure you regret your rejection of my offer of marriage, Lady Chastity, but it is too late to reconsider. You are quite beyond the pale now, you know."

She'd been filled with hot rage; if she'd had a pistol at that moment, she would have shot him. When Verity arrived and told her story, however, Chastity's rage had cooled and focused. Vernham would not ruin Verity too.

There had been no time to make careful plans, or to think things through, for he could return at any moment. But they had known they had to have money to survive, and would have to steal it. This latest twist of taking the coach had also been an impulsive decision. Now she saw it could get them all killed.

Damn Cyn Malloren. Why couldn't he have been the fat and timorous merchant they'd been hoping for?

Now, looking at the ornate, gilded Malloren crest on the carriage door, she muttered some dire wishes as to the fate of the owner. Then she grinned and wrenched a sharp stone from the orchard wall. She took great satisfaction in using it to scrape away the paint and gilding on both doors.

When she'd finished, however, the satisfaction left her and she hurled the stone away. Removing the crest had been the right thing to do—tomorrow the whole country might be looking for the Malloren carriage—but her feelings were twisted and wrong. She rested her head against the vehicle, fighting tears and silently cursing the men who had made her so bitter.

Her father, her brother, and Henry Vernham.

She let a curse escape into the quiet dark of the country night. "To the lowest pits of hell with all men!"

But then she controlled herself. She would need a cool head and vigilance in order to thwart them all.

She made sure the safety-catch was on the pistol and dropped it in the pocket of her coat. She considered the rapier, then left it there.

Leading the riding horses, she walked up to her true home, Walgrave Towers. The great house was dark, for none of her family was there. Her father and older brother spent most of their time in London, and now were presumably hunting Verity; her younger brother, Victor, was at school. She left the mounts in the stables and slipped in a side door.

Silence reigned except for the ticking of clocks in deserted rooms, but for Chastity the place rang with pain and bitter memories. Recent memories. She had not been unhappy as a child here. Her father had generally been absent, and their timid mother had never looked for trouble. But this was where Chastity's father had brought her not many months ago. This was where he had tried to force her to marry Henry Vernham.

Chastity made her way to the gun room without illumination, and once there, used flint and tinder to light a candle. She unloaded and cleaned the dueling pistols and replaced them in their velvet-lined case. Her older brother would be beside himself to think his indulgent training of his little sister had enabled her to pursue this plan. Chastity's hands stilled as she remembered the last time she'd seen Fort—his rage, his cruel, hurtful words . . .

She stiffened her lips and continued her work, cleaning the musket and setting it in its rack. She was not particularly surreptitious. The servants doubtless knew she was here, and what she was doing, but they would ignore it if they could. She liked to think it was because they cared for her a little. Cynically, she supposed they didn't want to become involved in such a bitter fight among their betters.

The atmosphere of the house pressed in on her, and she needed to escape. She blew out the candle and hurried down cold dark corridors to the West Tower door, and out into fresh air and freedom. She strode back to the cottage, consciously using the manly stride she'd perfected.

She'd better get back soon, before her softhearted sister and nurse made fools of themselves over that pretty, sweet-seeming viper they'd trapped.

Chapter 2

Chastity found Nana innocently occupied in the kitchen.

"The meal will be ready shortly, dear," said her old nurse. "Are you going to let him free, or will I have to spoon-feed him?"

Though Nana's tone was mild, Chastity heard the disapproval in it. "We can't trust him, Nana, and we all have too much to do to be watching him every moment. He could escape and lead the magistrates straight here."

Nana looked up from the pan. "You should perhaps have thought of that before you brought him here."

Chastity raised her chin. "I needed a coachman."

"Ah." The old woman took plates off the dresser and began to lay the table. Chastity noted that she was laying four places, and at two months old, Verity's baby was not yet ready for table meals. "I think you can trust him, Lady Chastity," said Nana.

Chastity sighed. "Remember, my name is *Charles*."

She went off to confer with her sister. She passed through the front room without acknowledging her prisoner except to place his pistol on a box there, then ran lightly up the steep stairs. Verity was dressing her baby after a change, talking nonsense to him and tickling him.

Chastity snapped, "I don't know how you can act like that when you think of his father."

20

"I don't think of his father," said Verity simply. She tied the last lace on the sleeping gown, picked up the babe, and placed him in her sister's arms. "Look at him. He has nothing to do with Sir William Vernham."

Chastity settled the soft burden in her arms, unwillingly captivated by the magic of a baby. "He *is* Sir William Vernham," she pointed out as she made the faces the child seemed to like.

Verity stopped clearing away the soiled clothes. "I know. But he's a different one." She added fiercely, "He won't be the same kind of man. I'll make sure of that. And now that Sir William's dead it will be a great deal easier."

Chastity looked up sharply. "Be careful not to say so in front of anyone but me, Verity, or your brother-in-law will think to raise a cry of murder."

Verity blanched. "How could he do that? William died when his heart gave out in the arms of his mistress."

"True, but men are capable of anything in pursuit of their ends, especially Vernham. The magistrates would probably credit you with a poison too subtle for human detection."

"Not all men are cruel," said Verity gently. "Nathaniel is a good man."

"I suppose so, but if the world was just, you'd have been permitted to marry him."

"Oh, Chastity . . ."

"Father *knew* you loved Nathaniel, and yet he forced you to marry Sir William—a fat old squire with more money than taste." She put the baby up to her shoulder and patted his back.

Verity bit her lip. "It is a daughter's duty to marry where her father wills."

"So 'tis said, but it would be pleasant to at least see the purpose in the sacrifice. Father not only married you to Sir William but also tried to make me marry his brother. What could he gain from such an alliance?"

Verity put soiled cloths in a bucket. "I don't know," she confessed.

"One thing is clear," said Chastity. "You have done your duty. You are not even to consider obliging Father again. You are to marry Nathaniel."

Verity nodded. "I am determined on it, though my conscience plagues me. I wish I had your resolution."

"Faith," said Chastity with a shudder, "it was seeing your marriage that gave me the strength to resist Father over mine. Sir William was a vile man and his brother, though smoother on the outside, is cut from the same cloth. I can certainly believe he would plot to murder an infant."

"But I don't know how you found the courage to stand up to Father. Look at me now. The only way I can try to thwart him is by running away."

Chastity stood and placed the sleepy baby gently in his bed and covered him with a blanket. Then she wandered over to the tiny gable window to look blindly out at the garden, illuminated only by the square of light from the kitchen window. "I honestly don't know if I would have been brave enough, Verity, if I'd known . . . I never imagined he would go so far. But once I'd started to resist I somehow could not stop . . ."

Verity gathered her sister into her arms and the two young women clung to one another. "Only two years ago," said Verity, "we were happy and full of hope. What happened?" But then she pulled herself together. "We must go down to supper." She picked up the bucket and glanced at her sister. "Don't you think you should change into a gown, dearest, with a man here?"

Chastity wiped away her tears and stiffened her spine. "Assuredly not. It wouldn't be wise to let him know he's dealing with three females."

"Oh, Chastity," Verity protested. "He's a gentleman."

"How the devil can you think that a recommendation? Sir William was a gentleman. Henry Vernham and Father are supposedly gentlemen. And besides being a *gentleman,* our prisoner is a *Malloren.* They're handsome men, and have a fascinating air, but they'd all cut your throat before they'd step aside on the road. Don't be taken in by Cyn Malloren's lovely lashes."

Verity chuckled. "Amazing, aren't they? I really can't fear a man who looks like that."

Chastity's tone was curt. "I'm sure a lot of people have made the same mistake. A fatal one."

"Really, Chastity. You can't think him deadly. Shooting pheasant is probably the closest he's come to bloodshed in his life."

Chastity shook her head. "He's dangerous, Verity. I can sense it. Please try to call me Charles at all times, or at least Chas. And don't reveal our full names. Rothgar and Father have been at daggers drawn for years. Let Cyn Malloren know we are Wares and all hell will break loose."

Verity shook her head at this but made no objection. She checked William, then blew out the candle and led the way toward the stairs. She hesitated at the top of the steep flight. "Chas, what if he tries to marry you off again?"

"Father?" Chastity laughed harshly. "That's the only blessing. My defiance pushed him into ruining me with absolute thoroughness. No man is ever going to want to marry the Notorious Chastity Ware."

Cyn watched her stride through the room and go upstairs. She had found the pistol, and so he assumed she was convinced of his good intentions. She didn't appear particularly mellowed.

He wanted to see her smile. He wanted her to talk to him, to tell him her problems so he could shoulder her burdens. He was surprised to find that on very brief acquaintance he had developed a warm appreciation for his captor's spirit, and for her unconventional appearance.

That sleek, otter-fur hairstyle was extremely strange, but

it showed off a beautifully shaped skull. Why had he never realized the potential beauty in a skull? He relished the notion of stroking that sleek head as much as he would anticipate running his hands through a mass of silken curls.

That hair also pulled into focus the clear strong lines of her face—the smooth, high forehead, the straight chiseled nose, the firm jaw. Even those ordinary blue-gray eyes, when properly framed, were unforgettable. She was decidedly not in the common style of women, but then, he had never favored the common.

She carried herself with the fluent pride of a male—shoulders straight, stride purposeful. He found it surprisingly erotic, and regretted that the male attire had presumably only been put on for the robbery. He wondered how she would appear in a gown.

He wasn't to find out. She still wore breeches when she came down the stairs.

As the two sisters passed through the room to go to the kitchen, he said, "Are you convinced I will do you no harm, Charles?"

She turned and looked at him. "As long as you're tied to the bed, my lord, I'm entirely convinced."

"Afraid to deal with me at liberty, are you?"

She set her hands on her hips. "Not at all. But why should I bother to try?"

She was wonderful. "Fair play," he said amiably. "I have done nothing dishonorable."

She smiled. "Helping highwaymen is not precisely honorable, my lord."

He smiled with equal insincerity. "My apologies. I didn't realize you wanted your neck stretched. I'll see to it at the first opportunity."

"I know. That's why you're spread-eagled."

He bit back a laugh. Fencing with her was the best fun he'd had in months. What a woman. Which gave him a new weapon. "Strange way to tie a man, this," he said.

"You the sort who likes to ogle other men's bodies, young Charles?"

Prodded by his words, she looked him over and her color flared, ripping through her disguise. She looked totally female, and an innocent, flustered female at that. The situation was giving him an erection.

"Stop it, both of you," said Verity, coming at him with a carving knife. She took in the bulge in his breeches with a mere quirk of her eyebrows. "I think the man's quite right," she said to her sister. "He's done nothing to warrant such treatment. He can come and eat with us."

"Verity, stop that!" snapped Charles. But Verity had already cut the strips of cloth tying Cyn to the bed, and he gratefully swung up into the vertical, working the numbness out of his wrists.

"My dear sir," he said, delighted to be able to fence from a position of equality, "I appreciate your sister's kindness, but if you are the master of this house, shouldn't you be able to control your womenfolk a little better?"

Her eyes flashed. "With a whip, perhaps?"

Cyn winked at Verity. "Is your sister so unruly?"

"Oh, do stop it, my lord," said Verity, though she was struggling not to laugh. "You're taunting just to strike sparks. If you carry on this way, I'll tie you up again."

He raised his hands in a gesture of surrender, and followed the sisters into the aromatic kitchen. He wondered how long it would be before someone made an irremediable mistake and revealed Charles to be . . . what? Charlotte? He eyed the frosty-faced girl. 'Charles' suited her much better than 'Charlotte.'

Nana beamed to see him free, and tried to settle him at the head of the table. "No, no," said Cyn, gesturing toward Charles. "This must surely be your seat, sir, as head of the family." He smiled at them all, blatantly using his considerable charm. "Am I to be favored by the family name?"

"No," said Charles bluntly, taking the place. "Be grateful you're getting your food."

Nana placed a large pan of rabbit stew on the table.

"Wonderful food too," Cyn said with a blissful smile.

Nana beamed. "It's so satisfying to feed a man."

Cyn turned a quizzical look at Charles. "But you stripling lads in the peak of your growth are usually voracious eaters."

Charles turned red. "I am not a stripling lad."

"My dear sir, my apologies. I know some men are slow to grow a beard . . ."

"Let me serve you, my lord," said Verity hastily, and heaped a large portion of stew on his plate. "Potatoes?"

Cyn nobly forbore to tease for the rest of the meal.

"Now," he said as they sat with cups of tea, "why don't you tell me what you're up to so I can help?"

"Why should you want to?" asked Charles stonily.

"I told you, I crave adventure. I cannot exist without it. I've always wanted to be a knight-errant."

It was Verity who responded. "But why do you think I am a damsel in distress, my lord?"

He looked at her. "Are you not?"

She smiled sadly. "Damsels are usually maidens, and I am certainly not that, but I *am* in a certain amount of distress . . ."

"Don't, Verity!" said Charles sharply. "Don't trust him. *Why* must you always be so trusting? If you tell him, he'll side with the rest of them."

"What else are we to do?" Verity asked. "We need someone to help with the coach, and I'd feel better with . . ."

Cyn could hear the words *with a man to help us* hover in the room, and saw the glare in Charles' eyes. Was it simply a case of one of those tedious hoydens who wanted to be a man? He hoped not.

"You'd feel better with someone older," he supplied smoothly. "My dear Charles, don't poker up. It's clear you are doing your best to support your sister in whatever trouble has befallen her, but it is never wise to refuse a genuine offer of help. I must be close to ten years your senior, and have experience you lack. If you tell me where you wish to go, I will do my best to get you there safely."

"Maidenhead," said Verity firmly. "My promised husband, Major Nathaniel Frazer, is stationed there."

Was he the father of her child? Cyn wondered. She wore a wedding band, but that could be false. "That should present no problem. I must admit," he hazarded, "it doesn't appear to present any problem at all."

"Except money," drawled Charles.

"Ah. Hence the highway robbery."

"Quite."

No one seemed ready to offer him more information, so Cyn probed again. "I understand the appeal of traveling in my very comfortable coach, but acquiring it presented certain risks. Wouldn't it have been wiser to settle for the stage, or even those two thoroughbreds you were riding?"

"The horses weren't ours," explained Verity, "and if we kept them the fat would be in the fire. I do agree, however, that the stage would have been more prudent."

"Yes," said Charles abruptly. "You're right. Tomorrow we'll use his lordship's coach to take us into Shaftesbury, and we'll purchase seats on the stage." She turned cold eyes on Cyn. "If, that is, we can trust you thus far, my lord."

"You can trust me to hell and beyond," he said simply, "but only if you allow me a place in your adventures. I will not be denied."

"This isn't a damned game!"

"Is there real danger then?"

"Yes."

"From where?"

But she shut her firm lips on that information.

"I do think we should tell him, dearest," said Verity.

"We'll talk about it later." Charles put an end to the discussion by rising to her feet. "For the moment the question is, where does he sleep?"

Cyn couldn't resist. "Why not with you, sir?"

Charles froze, and Verity choked on her tea.

"It presents a problem?" Cyn asked Charles. "I assure you I don't snore."

"But I do," she said hastily.

"Ah. Tell me, sir, where *do* you sleep?"

"Upstairs," she said unwarily. Her color betrayed her agitation, and she added, "We have divided the space with a curtain."

"Your sister and the baby being fortunately very sound sleepers." At her blank look, he added, "The snoring." Cyn held back a grin with considerable difficulty. Heavens above, if eyes really could spit fire he'd be a cinder. Those flaming eyes, those pure, firm lips, and the flush of anger in her cheeks all conspired to create astounding beauty.

A wave of pure lust surprised him, a desire to strip her here and now, and find the feminine secrets beneath her masculine appearance; to see those eyes flame with passion instead of rage, those cheeks heat with desire. It was a good thing he was not still spread-eagled or his body would give her fits. He hastily shielded his eyes with his lashes but determined again to see this adventure through.

It was quickly decided that he would sleep in the kitchen, but only one spare blanket was available to cushion the stone floor. Since it was clear they had to trust him, they allowed him to go to the coach to collect his trunk. With some of his clothes and his greatcoat he made a tolerable bed, far better than he'd had many a time with his regiment. The kitchen was, after all, warm and dry.

Nana and Verity were clearing away the supper dishes. Charles went out and brought water from a well, then sat to read a book. Cyn made himself comfortable too.

He pulled off his boots and cleaned them with a rag. Who knew how long they'd have to go without Jerome's loving attention? He hung his jacket and waistcoat on the back of a chair. He untied the ribbons in his hair and combed it. After a slight hesitation—being in the presence of ladies—he removed his cravat and unfastened the buttons of his shirt.

Nana and Verity paid him no attention, but it was Charles he watched. He saw one flickering glance up from her book, but no particular reaction. He'd have to try harder.

Nana retired. Verity fussed over Cyn for a minute or two, then went upstairs. Cyn yawned and slipped into his makeshift bed. He waited to see what the wench would do.

She closed her book and came to stand over him. Being unbound, Cyn had no problem with her looming over him if it made her comfortable. He put his hands behind his head and smiled up at her with all the seductive power he possessed. "Do you want to share my sleeping quarters after all?"

She caught her breath and stepped back, but collected herself immediately. "I just want to make it clear, my lord, that I'll kill you if you play us false. The other two are softhearted, but I'm not."

Not a wanton then, alas, alas. "Have you ever killed anyone, Charles?"

Her lips trembled with betraying weakness. "No."

"I have."

"I find that hard to believe."

"Do you? I'm a captain with the 48th."

She gaped slightly.

"I'm invalided out at the moment, but I've seen my share of death. It's not as easy to kill as you think unless you have overwhelming cause."

Any trace of weakness disappeared. "Then I should have no trouble at all." She blew out the candles and left him with only the banked glow of the fire for light.

Cyn was sobered. He stared up at the shadowed beams of the dark ceiling. Who, he wondered, had hurt the girl so deeply that she wanted to kill? Who was responsible for her being here penniless, dressed as a man, and afraid? Without knowing the answers, he embraced her cause.

He had found his damsel in distress, but it wasn't sweet Verity. It was the difficult, angry, beautiful Charles.

Chapter 3

Nana woke him the next morning as she tiptoed about the kitchen, putting water on to boil and bringing in eggs from the henhouse. "Don't feel you have to rise yet, my lord," she said quickly, but he was already up from his makeshift bed and bundling it out of the way.

He discovered he'd grown soft in his months away from the army. Once he'd thought nothing of sleeping on the floor wrapped in his cloak, then rising to do battle. Now he was stiff and poorly rested, and he longed for a warm bath and clothes he hadn't slept in. The sooner he returned to his profession the better.

"Can I beg a little hot water so I can shave?" he asked, and the old lady happily provided it.

He worked before a small, cracked mirror on the kitchen wall, giving thanks that his beard was not particularly heavy or coarse, for he was unused to this task. Jerome always did it, even when Cyn was with the army.

Jerome was the only indulgence Cyn had allowed Rothgar to provide when he joined his regiment. In six years of soldiering Cyn had made his own way. He'd won his promotions rather than buying them. Rothgar had seriously proposed buying him a regiment, but Cyn had refused, and proved to himself and his brother that he could stand alone.

Until now.

He grimaced at himself in the mirror, still disgusted that the lung-fever had won.

He remembered the struggle to keep going, feeling sicker and sicker by the day, but denying it. After that, the memories grew hazy: the rough care of his men; the rough-and-ready military hospital in Halifax; a hellhole on the ship where he'd decided he'd rather be dead . . .

And then suddenly, dream-like, he'd been at Rothgar Abbey in the care of his family—Rothgar, Brand, Bryght, and, most concerned of all, his twin sister, Elfled. Weak, and wondering if he were going to die, he'd taken comfort in his home and family, in tastes, sounds, and faces from his childhood.

As he'd recovered, however, he'd chafed at his siblings' cossetting. Lord, he didn't know what they considered good health, but it seemed to be a state too perfect for a mere mortal to achieve. There'd been talk of him selling out and taking up another profession.

Not bloody likely.

His hand tightened and he nicked his chin. He bit back a curse and grabbed a handkerchief to dab at the blood. He finished the job without further mishap, however, and hoped that augured well for the whole adventure. When he turned, pressing the cloth to the bloody spot, he found Charles had come into the kitchen. He caught her looking at him. She colored, looked down, then boldly looked up again.

"Hand shaky this morning?" she mocked.

"My valet always shaves me. I don't suppose you have this problem yet. Be grateful. It's the deuce of a bore. I sometimes long for the days of beards."

With wicked intent, he tossed the blood-spotted cloth aside and went to his trunk to take out a clean shirt. With his back to the girl, he casually stripped off his old one.

He stretched, turning slightly to watch her out of the corner of his eye. Her color was betraying her again, and she knew it. She concentrated on cutting slices from a cottage loaf. Either she wasn't very good at it, or her mind wasn't entirely on the task, for the slices were coming out as scraps and wedges.

He discovered he could observe her in the mirror and made a pretense—still bare from the waist up—of studying the small nick on his chin. He saw her glance up cautiously, then look at him through her lashes. He stretched again, knowing this had gone beyond teasing. He was showing off like a peacock spreading its tail.

Now she was frankly looking. He could bring out the big guns. He had a scar across his chest which it seemed no woman could ignore. It came from a minor wound, a long shallow saber cut, but it looked dramatic. With Nana in the room, however, this was not the moment to try its effectiveness on his damsel.

He pulled on his clean shirt and turned. Charles was intent on buttering the slices she had cut.

"Good of you to help your womenfolk," Cyn said approvingly as he fastened fresh ruffles at his wrists. "Many young men would think it beneath them."

Her busy hands faltered, but then resumed the work. "Many young men are asses."

Her hands, he realized, were just angular enough to pass as those of a youth, but only just. She was wise to wear gloves when adventuring.

"How true." He looked for some reaction to him and saw none. He shook his head. She was the most guarded young woman he'd ever met. "I'll just use the necessary."

By the time he returned Verity was in the kitchen too, with her babe in her arms. Nana was frying eggs and bacon at the stove. He suspected Charles would normally be helping the old lady. She certainly didn't look too happy with a passive role. Being a lazy male took a certain amount of practice.

Cyn strolled over to admire the baby. He had some experience after his visit to his older sister, Hilda, and her new pride and joy. He realized with surprise that this babe was almost as young. "He must be only a couple of months old."

"Nine weeks," Verity said, running a protective hand over the babe's soft blond fuzz.

"A bit young for traveling."

The hand faltered. "It was necessary."

Cyn found he couldn't badger gentle Verity. Instead, he badgered Charles by going to assist Nana, handing her the warm plates and then carrying them, filled, over to the table. After a moment, Charles came to help. She filled the teapot from the boiling kettle, and found pots of marmalade and jam, and a jug of milk set on the cool windowsill. Her actions had the ease of familiarity, but he didn't mention it.

As soon as everyone was eating, Cyn spoke. "Well? Are you ready to tell me your story?"

After a moment of silent communication with her sister, Charles said, "We'll tell you what you need to know." She fixed him with a stony look. "I suppose you think Verity's child was conceived on the wrong side of the blanket."

It was the obvious explanation. "He isn't?"

"No. He's fully legitimate, born two years after a Hanover Square wedding, the true son of his father."

Cyn didn't rise to the challenging tone. "That must be a great comfort to everyone."

"His father is dead."

Cyn surveyed Verity, who wore no mourning and was anxious to reach her betrothed. He raised his brows.

"Lud," said Verity, "I don't know why you two find it so difficult to tell a straight story." She faced Cyn. "My husband died nearly two months ago. My brother-in-law is my child's guardian. When he arrived to take responsibility for us, I realized I do not trust him, and so I am seeking the man who will protect us both."

A number of questions leaped to mind. Cyn asked the most puzzling one. "You described this protector as your betrothed. How can you have a betrothed husband so soon after your widowing?"

Verity's color rose. "Nathanial and I were pledged to each other, though my father did not sanction it. There has been no impropriety, but our pledge still holds."

Charles broke in. "So you see, it is merely a matter of transporting Verity and William safely to Maidenhead."

Cyn doubted that. "And the matter of the guardianship?"

"Once Verity and Nathaniel are married, they will petition to have Nathaniel made the child's guardian."

Cyn sensed a great deal more to this than he was being told. "And what if the court decides that this precipitous flight and marriage shows that both Verity and Nathaniel are unsuited to the care of an infant?"

Verity paled and held her child closer. "They wouldn't!"

"They could. I'm pointing out that it might be wiser to return home and send word to your Nathaniel to come and help you in a more conventional manner."

The sisters glanced at each other; Cyn could feel the anxiety flowing through the room. It was Charles who spoke. "Verity wouldn't be allowed to marry Nathaniel, and she thinks Henry V—" She broke off, then continued, "She thinks her husband's brother will kill the child."

Cyn saw from Verity's eyes that Charles spoke the truth. "Why?"

"Because then he will inherit everything."

Cyn let the silence settle as he considered. Greed could be a powerful force, and he supposed it must be galling to an ambitious man to have one small and recent life stand between him and everything.

On the other hand, he gathered some women were a little strange after having given birth.

He addressed Verity. "How did your husband die?"

She looked down. "His heart gave out."

"What was his name?"

"Don't answer that!" broke in Charles. She turned on

Cyn. "What right have you to cross-examine her? We've told you the essentials. Help us or not as you choose."

Cyn made his decision without difficulty. "Of course I'll help you." He hardly expected it to be much of a task. It must be little over a hundred miles. An easy three-day journey. "I guarantee to deliver you all safe to Maidenhead. I would like to know, however, what pursuit we should expect. Is Guardian Henry even now scouring the roads?"

"Yes."

"But hasn't thought to look here?"

Charles glared at his audible disbelief. "He came three days ago. We convinced him we knew nothing because it was true. Verity had to make her way here on foot. She arrived after he'd left."

Cyn looked at the young mother with new respect. Seeing her soft gentleness he would never have imagined her capable of such a grueling journey, babe in arms, in November. He began to doubt his complacency. Verity, at least, clearly believed the danger was real. He saw now the touch of desperation with which she held her baby close.

"Does he know about Maidenhead?" he asked.

Charles answered. "We don't think so."

Cyn turned to Verity. "So where will he think you've gone?"

She shrugged. "I hope he doesn't have the slightest idea. He clearly thought I would come here. He might think I'd go to London. He can know nothing of my life before I married his brother."

"What of your family?" asked Cyn. "Can they not help?"

Another revealing look passed between the sisters. Charles answered. "What would I be doing here in this cottage if we had a useful family?"

"In disgrace?" Cyn suggested. "Sent down from school perhaps?"

That hit a mark, though she concealed it well. "You have it, my lord. We do not want to seek help from our family because they would not allow Verity to marry Nathaniel."

Cyn had a rule of survival which had served him well: act as if the worst was true. He rose and paced the small room. "The child's guardian has the law on his side. He'll doubtless have left word, even posters, at tollbooths and major inns. Even if he doesn't know about Maidenhead, the toll roads will be closely watched. You wouldn't get far on the stage."

Charles said, "We had planned on a disguise."

"Of what kind?"

Another uncomfortable glance between the sisters. "Verity is going to dress as a nursemaid," said Charles. "We're also going to darken her hair."

"And you?"

"I don't need a disguise."

Cyn leaned forward on the table. "Horrible Henry is going to come back here to check again. When he finds you gone, he'll know to look for you."

She met his eyes. "We'll be in Maidenhead by then."

Now that Cyn could escort Verity, the obvious solution was for Charles to stay behind, but apart from the fact that the chit wouldn't agree, Cyn didn't want that. He had a lot of exploring of his damsel yet to do.

He paced again as he weighed the options. "So Horrible Henry is looking for a fair-haired lady with a child. As soon as he checks here, he'll know he's looking for said lady plus youthful escort." He waited for the correction that never came.

He considered Charles. "What a shame you can't act the part of a lady . . ." He ignored Verity's twitching lips and a strangled sound from Nana, and pretended to study the girl. "No, I don't think you could pull it off. I can't see you simpering."

Color flushed her face. "Thank the stars for that!"

"Well then, could you play the groom?"

With a spark of interest, Charles nodded.

"Are you sure?"

"Yes. I know how to care for horses. Will you be the coachman, then?"

"No. I'll ride into Shaftesbury and hope Hoskins is still at the Crown. He can drive us."

"He'll ask a lot of questions."

"He certainly will," said Cyn. "Especially when I tell him I'll be in petticoats." He gazed benignly at the three thunderstruck faces. "We'll outfox any pursuers for sure, for I'm going to be the baby's mother."

"You're going to play the woman?" Charles said in disbelief.

"Unless you insist on the honor." Cyn fluttered his lush lashes. "But I think it wiser this way. I'm prettier than you, and *I* know how to simper."

He loved the battle which raged across her features. A very natural pique at having her looks disparaged was chased by a flash of malicious amusement—doubtless at the thought of seeing him in a stomacher and petticoats.

In that he was quite correct. Chastity was bemused and frustrated by this damn male who had invaded her life, and seemed well on the way to taking over. She hoped he hated the lacing, and looked ridiculous in a gown.

As for being plain and unable to play the part of a lady, devil a bit he knew about it. Both the Earl of Walgrave's daughters had been drilled and disciplined into perfect ladies, mistresses of all the feminine arts. How else could their father hope to strengthen his political web through their marriages?

Lord Cyn, she told herself crossly, was *not* prettier. Chastity had been declared a belle during her time in London. She'd had half the Town at her feet, including—in his cool way—Cyn's brother, the Marquess of Rothgar, the matrimonial prize of the decade.

Abruptly the humor of the situation hit her, and she bit

her lip against laughter. She as the handsome boy. He as the pretty lady. She wished she were alone with Verity and could let the laughter out. It was far too long since she'd laughed.

Cyn saw the tremble of her lips and the twinkle in her eyes. He wished she would express her amusement. He suspected she would be beautiful when she laughed.

He set to persuading his kidnappers to allow him to ride into Shaftesbury to deal with his servants and buy some women's clothing. Charles grudgingly went to obtain a mount—presumably from the nearby big house which was these ladies' rightful home.

When she returned she brought two riding horses.

"You are accompanying me?" Cyn asked. "Do you think that wise?"

"I think it wise to keep an eye on you, my lord."

"You surely will be recognized so close to home."

She looked amused. "Why do you think that would be a problem? *I* am not the fugitive. Verity is."

"Still," said Cyn, "it might be best if no one realizes there is any connection between you and me. Let's begin your metamorphosis to groom. Do you have any less elegant clothes?"

"No," she said unhelpfully.

"Then let's see what the coach has to offer." He set off for the orchard at a brisk pace. At sight of the mutilated doors, he stopped. "Was that really necessary?"

"I thought there would be a hunt for it." Chastity hated the tremor of nervousness in her voice.

He looked at her coolly. "You are a hellion, aren't you? Was this supposed to be a hit at me? This is my brother's coach, not mine. You won't sit for a week if Rothgar finds out." He considered the vehicle. "We'll buy some paint, and you can cover the damage. A plain coach will cause no comment; a brutalized one will."

Without waiting for her response, he climbed up and reached into the box under the seat. He pulled out a bundle and dropped it down. "Harry's," he said as he returned to earth. "The real groom. He's a mite taller than you, but not much." He undid the bundle and produced a rough shirt, a pair of patched breeches, and a neckerchief. "All quite clean too," he remarked as he tossed them to her. "How fortunate. You'll have to keep your own coat, hat, and boots. If you're wise, you'll rough 'em up a bit."

"That will be a pleasure." Chastity turned. "I'll go back to Nana's and change."

Cyn leaned against the coach, arms folded. "Are you just naturally modest," he asked, "or do you harbor nasty suspicions? I assure you, Charles, that my taste in bed-partners is . . . conventional."

Chastity felt her color rise again and damned it. "I never thought otherwise," she said, beating a retreat. "As you say, I'm just modest."

His voice floated after her. "Are you *sure* you've been to school?"

Chastity marched into the cottage and slammed the door. "I *wish* I'd left that man by the roadside!"

Verity looked up from the box she was packing, a distinct twinkle in her eye. "I think he's going to be an asset. No one will be looking for a brown-haired older lady, with her baby and wetnurse."

"I could have played the mother."

"You wouldn't look old enough not to be me, and your hair is a problem. Wigs are so chancy. Many men still shave their head and wear one, but not ladies."

Chastity's hand went to the silky fuzz where so recently there had been lustrous curls.

"Oh, Chastity," said Verity, rising to come to her. "I'm sorry for mentioning it. And it will grow, dearest."

"It's already growing," said Chastity, "but I can't forget how it felt when Father shaved it off. And the things he said . . ." She shuddered, then shook off the memories. "But see. Father's done me a favor. I look ridiculous as a woman, but I make a fine boy and no one suspects. Who would think a woman would cut her hair this short?"

"Father will come around—"

"No," said Chastity sharply. "Don't mention his name. He's as good as cast me off, and I have renounced him."

Verity sighed. "I'm sure he meant it for the best."

"I'm not. I'm sure he wanted his own way, as always."

"But he is our father, dearest . . ."

"Then why haven't you rushed into his loving arms?"

Verity picked up a pair of stockings and rolled them. "I confess, I cannot feel as I should toward him after the way he treated you."

Chastity hugged her, knowing how hard this unfilial behavior was for conventional Verity. It had taken a great deal for her own trust in the mighty Earl of Walgrave to be destroyed. "You are doing the right thing. Believe me, Father is not infallible, nor is he the Incorruptible he is called."

Verity surprised her. "I fear you may be right. I have been thinking about what you said yesterday. My marriage to Sir William does make little sense, and when matched with Father's attempt to marry you to Henry, the absurdity is made clear. Do you think perhaps he is becoming feeble-witted with age?"

Chastity cracked a laugh. " 'Struth, I do not! Father is as shrewd as ever, and doubtless had his reasons—as always, linked to his thirst for power. You know how obsessed he's been since Prince Frederick died ten years back."

She smiled grimly at the thought. The Earl of Walgrave had been of an age with Frederick, Prince of Wales, and his close friend. He had pinned all his ambitions to him, just waiting for the old king to die and Frederick to assume the throne. However, Frederick had inconsiderately died before his father, leaving his young son the heir. That young son, now King George III, was firmly under the influence of his mother, the Princess Augusta, and the handsome Scot, Lord Bute.

The Earl of Walgrave was out of power.

"Poor Father," said Chastity with spurious sympathy. "He really should have paid more attention to Augusta, shouldn't he?"

"Instead of making her his enemy by taking so much of her husband's time. But then, Father has always tended to discount women."

Chastity frowned over the matter. "With all his plans in the dust, I suppose it is not strange that Father has become . . . extreme in his manner. But that doesn't explain an alliance with the Vernhams. I suppose Sir William must have had influence to barter."

Verity tucked the stockings into the box. "With whom? Influence with Augusta would not help. Her enmity runs too deep, and she is sincerely attached to Bute."

Chastity raised her brows and grinned. "Some would say immorally attached."

"Chastity!"

"Don't you think so? You're alone in the fashionable world, then. And Bute is a fine figure of a man, even if he does have the spirit and brains of a rabbit."

Verity fought a betraying giggle and lost. "Really, Chastity. But I have to confess that Father's outrage that such a man is adviser to the king is understandable. Bute could be disastrous for the country and yet seems to have the young king and his mother in his control."

"Which situation Father would do anything to shatter . . ."

"But Chastity, how could Sir William or Henry possibly help him with that?"

"Not likely, is it?" said Chastity. "I did once hear Father say he was looking for evidence that Bute had Jacobite sympathies, that he had supported Bonnie Prince Charlie in 1745. It is said a great many people flirted with the Jacobites when it looked as if they might succeed in returning the Stuarts to the throne."

Verity curled her lip. "And then became staunch Hanoverian supporters when the rising collapsed. I detest such self-serving hypocrisy."

"Wasn't Sir William one of the Special Investigators set to ferreting out those hidden English Jacobites?"

"Yes," said Verity with a shudder. "He used to tell gloating stories which made me pity even those wretches. He positively enjoyed wielding power and terrorizing people, and I suspect he made a pretty penny from turning an occasional blind eye. He certainly rose from a petty squire to a rich local lion at about that time."

"Loathsome man," said Chastity, her mind on other matters. "Perhaps that's it! Perhaps he had evidence against Bute, and Father used us as bribes to obtain it. Bute is a Scot, after all."

Verity stopped her work to consider it, then shook her head. "Really, Chas, I doubt it. Bute is rather stupid, but very loyal. He is a Scot, but not all Scots are Jacobites, no matter what people say."

Chastity sighed. "I fear you may be right." She passed Verity a pile of nappies. Something firm crackled within. She pulled out a heavily sealed document. "What on earth is this?"

Verity looked a picture of guilt. "Oh, that."

Chastity inspected the document. It appeared to be just a couple of sheets of paper, folded and sealed four times. She looked at her sister.

"I didn't know what to do," Verity explained nervously. "Some time ago, Sir William showed me that, and where he kept it, and made me swear a solemn oath that when he died I would take it straight to Judge Mansfield, the Lord Chief Justice. William made me swear on the Bible . . ."

"Verity," said Chastity firmly, knowing her conscientious sister well, "you are not going to London until you are safely wed to Nathaniel."

"Of course not," said Verity, but uneasily. "I tell myself I am going *toward* London after all."

"Exactly." Chastity looked at the document. "What do you think it is?"

"I don't know. But as Sir William did not seem to want his brother to have it, I have wondered if it might be an amendment to his will . . ."

"Cutting out Henry as guardian?" asked Chastity sharply. "Let's see—"

Verity snatched it. "We mustn't! Oh, Chastity, I'm sure it will invalidate it if the seals are broken."

"But . . ." Chastity broke off. "I don't suppose it makes much difference. The main thing is to get you to Nathaniel. Then we can decide what to do about this."

"Perhaps we should ask Lord Cyn."

"Lud, no," said Chastity. "Who knows what this document is? We don't want to put ammunition into the hands of a Malloren. Keep it well hidden. Now, I'm going upstairs to change."

When Chastity had gone, Verity tucked the paper away safely and sighed over her sister's predicament. Verity had hopes that her own situation would turn out right, but nothing on earth could mend Chastity's life.

That the Earl of Walgrave should order Chastity to marry Henry Vernham was peculiar; that he should be willing to ruin such a valuable pawn as his daughter in the attempt defied belief.

Verity had been in the country, in the last weeks of her pregnancy, when the scandal had occurred. She had heard the story from her husband, however, spiced with rage and foul humor. Sir William had been furious that Chastity had scorned his brother, and had painted the worst possible picture. Now Verity had heard the story from Chastity.

Henry Vernham was ten years younger than his brother. Where William was coarse and greedy, Henry was smooth and calculating. He was not ill-looking, but had only a small competence and a minor court post. He was, in effect, a nonentity who could hardly have expected even to encounter Lady Chastity Ware except for his family connection.

He had, however, not just met her but been so bold as to offer for her hand. And the mighty Earl of Walgrave, far from laughing in his face, had ordered Chastity to accept.

She had refused, scarcely taking the matter seriously at first. The earl's rage had corrected that impression, but Chastity had still refused. She had stoically accepted petty restrictions and lectures on duty, not even bending when he forbade her to attend the Wares' annual grand rout if she would not do so as Vernham's partner.

Chastity had remarked that she had been more relieved than anything to be locked in her room if the alternative was to have Henry Vernham pawing at her all evening.

She had gone peacefully to sleep, but had woken near midnight when her father burst in on her with half a dozen guests in tow. She had sat up in alarm, and only then realized that Henry Vernham was lying in the bed beside her, stark naked. She had realized immediately that the trap could only have been accomplished with her father's full compliance. Her door had been locked on the outside.

He had doubtless expected her to give up all resistance to the match. What else could a young lady do? Chastity, however, had loudly protested her innocence and continued to refuse. The matter had then become highly unpleasant, with the whole world believing the worst, and the earl losing all control of his temper. Even whippings and starvation, however, had not changed Chastity's mind.

In the end the earl had given up. He had washed his hands of his daughter and banished her here to this cottage. He had made sure she would stay in her exile by providing no money, only the coarsest clothing, and by shaving off all Chastity's beautiful hair.

It had hardly been necessary, for where else could the Notorious Chastity Ware go? The Earl of Walgrave's daughters were not trained for employment, and no respectable man would offer her his name. And that was a shame, thought Verity, for Chastity had always been a joyous girl, made to be a wife and mother.

Chastity reappeared, transformed. She'd cinched the loose frieze breeches with a belt, and they added bulk to her legs. The moleskin shirt also disguised her shape, while the spotted neckerchief hid her slender neck, her most betraying feature. She wore the mouse-brown bagwig, covered by a battered flat-brimmed hat.

"It's marvelous!" exclaimed Verity. "A much better disguise than more elegant clothing. Lord Cyn was right."

"You *would* think that," grumbled Chastity, but with a smile.

A new problem fretted Verity. "Chas, do you think Father knows I'm missing?"

Chastity looked at her sister sharply. "He's bound to, unless Henry Vernham has hushed it up for his own nefarious reasons."

"Oh, lud. What reason would Henry have to do that? All he wants is William so he can control the estate. Or perhaps worse . . ." Verity shuddered. "Horrible Henry! That sums him up so beautifully. I like Lord Cyn."

"You like everyone," said Chastity grimly. "Here, is there space for my suit in that portmanteau?"

Verity took it. "I do not like everyone. I dislike Henry intensely. But I like Lord Cyn, and I feel very secure knowing he's an officer. Our plan is full of hazards, dearest, but I'm sure he can carry it through if anyone can."

"He's in it for amusement, Verity!"

Verity shook her head. "You must learn to look beneath the surface a little. Remember he's a military man, like Nathaniel." She paused in her work of pushing the brown suit into the full bag. "But Father worries me, Chas. He knows about Nathaniel and will have no trouble discovering where he is stationed . . ."

"And with his connections," said Chastity quietly, "he could virtually raise the country."

"Chas, we *have* to tell Lord Cyn who we are, and what he's embroiled in. Father could ruin him with a word."

Chastity's eyes widened in alarm. "But that would mean he would know who I am! Oh, what does that matter next to your safety—"

"No," said Verity quickly. "What would it gain us?" She knew how Chastity dreaded facing anyone as the Notorious Chastity Ware.

They looked at each other. "It shouldn't matter," said Chastity. "I'm sure we can reach Maidenhead without tangling with Father . . ."

"I'm sure we can," Verity said firmly, then bit her lip. "But what of Nathaniel? If Father is a danger to Lord Cynric Malloren, he's even more so to Nathaniel. His career could be ruined. Officers have been thrown out of the army for merely voting against the government in an election . . ." Verity's hands clenched on Chastity's. "And what of the baby? Do you think they *could* take William? I'd die first!"

"I'm sure they couldn't," Chastity soothed. "Nathaniel would never allow it. And you've forgotten his true nature if you think he would not sacrifice his career entirely for your happiness. But it will never come to that," she added hurriedly, knowing Verity would immolate herself before hurting her beloved. "Nathaniel is a highly regarded officer, and this is a time of war. Once the knot is tied, no one will be able to make a case for taking away your child."

In truth, she wasn't as certain as her words implied, and her own knees were turning to jelly at the prospect of challenging the Earl of Walgrave's will again. But what choice did they have?

What they needed was an advocate as powerful as Walgrave. They might as well wish for the moon.

Chapter 4

C hastity rode into Shaftesbury with Lord Cyn, alert for any sly move he might make. Despite his professed eagerness to help them, she didn't trust him one iota. He had too frivolous an attitude to life, and a way of making the most outrageous things sound reasonable.

Such as them coming into town in the first place.

And her giving him back some of his money.

After all, he'd said, he did intend to buy clothes, and it would look strange for the groom to be paying the shop-keepers. It had sounded too reasonable to deny, but Chastity was fretted again by the feeling that matters were being cleverly slid out of her hands.

They left the horses at the Crown and found Cyn's coachman there in the taproom. Hoskins was a barrel of a man with the ruddy, weathered face of one who had spent a large part of his life on the box.

"Sent the others on to the Abbey, milord, since there were spaces on the up-traveling Exeter Fly." He drained the ale Cyn had purchased for him and wiped his mouth with his sleeve. "Reckoned I'd best stay, though, in case you needed 'elp. 'Sides which, I can't go 'ome without me rig, can I?" He gave Chastity an unfriendly look, but there was no hint in it that he thought she was female, or a true villain.

48

She took as large a swig as she dared from her own tankard, and worked at looking like a cocky young rogue.

"Then you'll approve of my plan, Hoskins," said Cyn. "I want you to drive us."

"That's me job, milord," the man agreed, but with narrowed eyes. "That, and keeping you out of mischief."

Cyn grinned. "And how do you think to achieve that?"

"Lord only knows. Gallows bait, you are."

Cyn slapped him on the back. "Cheer up. It's not as bad as you fear, certainly not a hanging matter. The first thing you should do is hire yourself a horse so you can ride back with us. Then," he added blithely, "purchase a pint of paint to match the coach color as close as you can. It has been a little scratched. Be ready to ride out with us in an hour or so. My friend and I have some purchases to make."

Cyn then dragged Chastity out of the room before the man could splutter his alarmed questions. Chastity pulled against Cyn's hand on her arm, but his grip was like steel. He did not let her go until they were well clear of the inn.

"Believe me, lad," he said, "you don't want to be the one to describe the damage to the coach. Especially as it was your doing."

"It's only a few scrapes."

"I've seen Hoskins fret over a bird dropping on his varnish. He's going to want blood when he sees what you did."

"Then why are you adding him to our party?"

"We need someone to drive the coach. Don't worry. If he tries to flog you, I'll defend you to the death." He looked at the street name painted on a building, and plunged down an alley.

Chastity had expected to derive amusement from his lordship's attempts to procure ladies' clothing at short notice in a strange town. Her own ignorance, not his, was exposed.

The Walgrave ladies had only ever patronized one

dressmaker in Shaftesbury, and Miss Taverstock had only been entrusted with the simplest garments. Cyn had made inquiries of the innkeeper, and now had the direction of the town's secondhand clothes dealer.

Chastity was fascinated to venture into parts of Shaftesbury which were strange to her. There were alleys with small shops, and narrow, winding streets festooned with lines of washing. There were houses as dark and forbidding as the Fleet, and others which turned smiling faces to the world. In front of the former lurked scabrous, dirty rogues; in front of the latter sat women preparing food or knitting, while watching children and chatting with their neighbors.

Some streets were dry and wholesome, others noisome from the sewage pooling in the central gutter.

A junk shop full of fascinating bits and pieces distracted Chastity, then an herbalist's that looked as if it still operated according to the rules of Gerard's Herbal. Cyn drew her away, even from a delightful bookshop.

"We're hardly in a hurry," she protested.

"I told Hoskins we'd be back in a hour. If we're not, he'll probably decide you've done away with me. Look, here we are."

Mrs. Crupley's Emporium presented a narrow, faded front at the entrance to a particularly dismal alley. Chastity took in the foul mess lying in the middle of that dark passageway—including a dead cat—and gave thanks they didn't have to travel it. They had obviously reached the edge of respectable Shaftesbury. She doubted they would find much of use in such an establishment.

They pushed through the door, and Chastity's nose wrinkled at the musty smell of damprot and stale sweat. The place was packed with garments, headgear, footwear, and accessories. Items lay on shelves against the walls and in boxes on the floor. Most of the clothing hung from ropes stretched across the room.

Mrs. Crupley sat near the door in a rocking chair by a

stove. She had a cat on her lap, and a mug in her hand. Chastity feared it held gin.

She had to smile, though, when she saw the way the plump middle-aged woman clearly enjoyed her stock. She wore a gown of opulent yellow silk and lace that was at least twenty years out of fashion, and hopelessly stained. On her wiry gray curls sat an elaborately dressed lace cap of the style of Queen Anne.

"Good day to you," the woman said. "What can I do for you, dearies?"

Mrs. Crupley knew her stock well. When Cyn told her, without explanation, that he had need of good-quality ladies' garments for a woman of above-average height and sturdy build, she put down her cup, tipped off the disgruntled cat, and headed toward the back of her shop. Chastity and Cyn had to fight their way through after her, like battling through endless lines of washing.

"Keep the good stuff back here, I do," said the woman, "well away from sneak-thievery."

Once they reached the dim and musty depths of the place, she began pulling down samples, extolling their virtues. "Lovely, this is," she said, dangling a blue lutestring silk, her eyes darting to catch their every reaction. "The highest lady in the land could wear this as it is, or it'd cut up a treat."

More likely the latter, thought Chastity, for the gown was shredding under the arms and badly faded in many places. It was certainly large, though. Huge, in fact. Cut up, it probably could make a passable gown for a slim lady. She, who had never considered such things, became intrigued by the possibilities of secondhand clothing.

After all, it seemed very likely that she would have an impoverished future.

She expected to be asked for her advice, but Cyn ignored her. She remembered then that he thought her a youth. He didn't seem to need help anyway. He rejected various items of evening wear, and some shoddy garments which Mrs. Crupley obviously thought all the go, and chose two ugly gowns of excellent quality.

One was a brown Brunswick traveling dress with beige braid; the other was an open sacque of Prussian blue figured cloth to be worn over a quilted gray petticoat and a stomacher of blue and black braiding. He added a dark blue hooded cloak, and a plain straw villager hat.

Mrs. Crupley clearly didn't think much of his choices, and pitied the poor lady who would be forced to wear such dull stuff, but she made one last attempt. "Look lovely with new ribbons, this will," she crooned, stroking the flat hat. "Yellow or bright green, I'd think. Have to have at least sixpence for this, I will." She glanced at Cyn slyly. "A guinea and a half for all this, I'd say."

He ruthlessly beat her down to eighteen shillings and sixpence, and had her throw in a shabby black wig and a huge cloth muff as well. Chastity was amazed to see the woman look content when she took the money.

When they were out in the alley she said, "Eighteen and six for all that! You diddled the poor old dear."

He laughed. "I paid her more than she hoped for. She'd have been suspicious if we paid much over the odds. People poor enough to buy castoffs watch every penny." He flicked her an indulgent glance and dumped one of the large, newspaper-wrapped bundles in her arms. "You don't know you're born, do you, young Charles?"

Chastity snarled at him, but he was already off at a brisk pace back the way they had come. Chastity quickly followed and had to admire his command of geography. She would have been hard put to find her way back to the Crown unaided.

Suddenly he stopped in front of one of the shops that had fascinated her, a tiny haberdashery crammed with goods—threads, ribbons, caps, and ready-made ladies' undergarments. She followed him into the intimate establishment.

Showing a shocking expertise in such matters, and no

embarrassment that Chastity could see, Cyn purchased a nightgown, a lace-trimmed chemise, two pairs of cotton stockings, and garters threaded with pink ribbon.

Eyes twinkling, he held the garters up before Chastity. "What do you think, Charles? Will these please my sister?"

Chastity knew she was blushing. "As long as they keep her stockings up," she said, "I suppose they'll please her well enough. What else are such things for?"

Cyn winked at the girl behind the counter. "These bashful young lads." The girl giggled. Chastity gnashed her teeth.

Cyn looked around the shop where sample garments were hung on display. His smile widened. "I see you even have silk stockings. Let me see a pair of those, my dear."

The young woman climbed a small stepladder to reach down a box, and opened it to reveal stockings in a range of colors, some even striped. "They are of the finest make, sir," the girl said, all rosy under his attentions. "See the quality of the embroidery."

Cyn held up a pair admiringly, a very racy pair of pink silk with fancy red stripes. "Oh, I don't think one should be cheese-paring about such matters," he said lovingly, and grinned at Chastity.

She glared at him.

"Goodness," Cyn said to the shop-girl, "I've offended the lad. He must not approve of fancy stockings. Tell me, my dear, what do you think of the matter?"

The girl, thought Chastity in disgust, was incapable of thoughts that were other than lustful. And how any man could so shamelessly flaunt intimate apparel in front of strangers . . .

"Oh, sir!" gushed the shop-girl. "I do think them ever so wonderful."

Cyn admired the stockings again. "I'll take this pair. And five yards of wide yellow ribbon, if you please."

Chastity choked. Cyn looked at her and back to the

shop-girl. "I don't think he cares for the yellow. A young man of Puritan tendencies. Perhaps you'd better make it that striped fawn."

When they left the store he laughed.

Chastity glared at him. "You, sir, have no decency!"

"True. Do you not approve of striped silk stockings? They make the most of a well-turned ankle."

"It is not a matter I give any thought to," Chastity said frostily. She stalked ahead in what she hoped was the right direction.

He caught up, laughter in his voice. "You give no thought to ladies' ankles? 'Struth, but you're a strange young man."

Chastity decided it would be wiser not to pick up that gauntlet. Anyway, she had to let him lead again, for she was lost.

Despite the brisk pace he set, very little escaped Lord Cynric Malloren. As they approached the Crown he entered another shop, one advertising soap and beauty agents. This was a different type of establishment altogether, and one with which Chastity was familiar. Walgrave Towers had been ordering its soap and unguents from Travis & Mount for years. What the deuce did Cyn Malloren want here?

Again without embarrassment he purchased a pot of rouge, a box of pale powder, and, after sniffing at a number of samples, a small vial of perfume. From the ecstatic look on the face of Mr. Mount, Chastity knew it was expensive.

Once outside, she said, "Why are you wasting all this money if you truly want to help us?"

"It's not a waste. It's important to be thorough in a deception and we have ample funds, I assure you. You must learn not to worry so, Charles." He smiled at her in a beguiling way. "Perhaps you're hungry. Surely even such an unnatural youth as you must have a sweet tooth?"

What else could Chastity say but yes, and in truth she

did love sweet things. Her heart gave a little leap when she saw where he was headed. Still, she had to protest. "We don't have time or funds for pastries."

He was already within the establishment of Dunn and Carr, Confectioners and Pastry Cooks. Chastity decided that, all in all, the aroma of the bakery surpassed even that of the perfumier's.

They emerged in a little while with a damson pie and a bag of crisp biscuits. He juggled his parcels and took out two Shrewsbury biscuits. Walking backward down the street, he popped one into her mouth.

Chastity took it. He reminded her of a schoolboy on a pleasure outing, and for a moment she felt his equal—the same sex, the same brash confidence, the same carefree approach to life. She grinned as she arranged her own parcels so she could hold the biscuit and enjoy it. It was delicious, still warm from the oven.

He took a bite of his, still walking slowly backward. She took a bite of her own. He trapped her gaze and she found herself watching his lips as he bit again and chewed. He had beautiful lips, with a perfect bow-curve . . .

The muscles of his throat moved as he swallowed. His tongue slid out. He slowly licked a trace of golden crumbs away from those lips, leaving the gloss of moisture behind.

His eyelids lowered sleepily, sensuously, and he smiled.

Chastity felt her heart thump, and she gaped.

She realized they'd arrived at the inn and were standing there like statues, gazing at one another. She knew she should move but felt trapped in a web—a sticky, warm web. She had only taken one bite of her biscuit, but the sweet tingly taste lingered on her tongue.

"Taste, texture, heat," he said softly, seeming to dare her to take another bite. "Life offers such beautifully simple yet rich pleasures for our delight. Taste them with me, Charles . . ." He slowly put the last of his biscuit into his mouth.

Chastity realized she had obediently taken another bite

and was chewing in synchrony with him ... She almost choked. A dizzy heat reminded her sharply that they weren't the same sex. Nor did they have the same approach to life.

He was the enemy. He was a man. He was supposed, damn it, to be her prisoner!

She swallowed the mouthful in a lump, looked helplessly at the remaining biscuit, and dropped it in the dirt. Then she marched into the inn.

Cyn watched her go, dismayed but not daunted. For a moment he'd glimpsed the fire he knew was in her. She would be a wonderful woman to take to bed, but for some reason she feared men. Perhaps a lover had betrayed her.

Skill and patience would bring her to hand; he had both, and three days in which to use them.

As he followed her, he admitted that the game might be simpler if he put an end to this masquerade, but that would erect new barriers of propriety between them. The opportunities would be greater and more amusing as things were.

As they prepared to leave, he contemplated making inquiries about an estate five miles out of Shaftesbury, set to the north of the road. He could have the family name in minutes. He desisted.

Part of it was caution. If questions were ever asked, he didn't want anyone remembering he had been interested in his damsel's family.

Part of it was quixotic. He wanted Charles to tell him the whole truth herself one day.

Preferably in bed.

Chastity, Cyn, and Hoskins arrived back at the cottage to find Verity in a fret, sure they had been caught, or at least seen, by Henry Vernham. Chastity set to soothing her sister, and Cyn took Hoskins down to the coach and horses.

The four horses were doing well enough on grass and

water, though the coachman muttered a bit about it. He was dumbfounded when he saw the damage to his coach.

"Who the 'ell did this?" he asked, running a pained hand over the gouges.

"I'm not sure," Cyn lied. "If I explain what's going on, it may help."

Hoskins listened, unappeased. "If that young 'ellion did this to me coach, I'll take me whip to 'im."

"No, you won't. You'll leave him to me."

The man shook his head. "And what're you goin' to tell the marquess? You can't just up and disappear."

"Yes, I can. I'm not a child, Hoskins. If my orders were obeyed, my brother will think I'm off on an adventure. As I am."

"An adventure that stinks of trouble. Who is this young woman who needs to get to Maidenhead so urgent, and all underhand?"

"I'm not sure," Cyn admitted, "but she's a lady and I feel chivalrous. Now listen carefully, Hoskins. I don't know whether the pursuit will be serious or not, but I intend to take it seriously. I don't want any careless words of yours spilling anything."

"I can keep me peace, Master Cynric, as well you know."

Cyn knew he was in Hoskins' bad books when he called him Master Cynric. "I know you can," he soothed. "Now, for the journey, I'm going to pass as a woman, the mother of Verity's child. Verity will be the wetnurse. Charles will be the groom."

Cyn had expected an objection to him playing the woman, but the coachman's mind was on other matters. "That rascal's not comin' near me rig," said Hoskins truculently.

"Plague take it, man! He won't do any more damage, I promise you."

"I don't want him near me rig, or me cattle," Hoskins

repeated, and again ran his hand over the scars on the glossy coach.

Cyn sighed. He could force his will, but he feared Hoskins would take out his anger on Charles. After all, the man didn't know she was a girl. "Very well," he said. "He can travel as my brother. But it'll leave you hard-pressed."

"I'll manage," grunted Hoskins. "Where's that paint?"

Cyn left the coachman doing his best to repair the damage. When he entered the cottage and found the three ladies in the kitchen, he said, "I'd keep out of Hoskins' way, young Charles, if I were you. He's after your gizzard."

She colored. "We could hardly traipse around the country with the Rothgar arms emblazoned on the side."

"Why not? I'm along willingly, and no one connects me to you."

She had the look of one determined not to admit to a mistake. "How can I stay out of his way if I'm to be the groom?"

"You're not anymore. You're my young brother. You'd better hunt up more good-quality clothes."

She shot to her feet. "Need I remind you, my lord, that you are our *prisoner*? Will you kindly stop giving us orders?"

Cyn sat. "Very well. I leave it all in your hands."

She glared at him. "I will travel as the groom."

"As you will. As the groom, however, you will be under the authority of the coachman, and Hoskins is not known as a tender man at the best of times. He's always been remarkably proud of the perfect finish on his coach."

She swallowed but kept to her guns. "You will give him orders not to touch me."

"Will I?"

"Yes."

He shrugged. "Very well, but he's my brother's coachman, not mine. He taught us all to handle the ribbons. He cuffed us if he thought we needed it, and he'll do at least as much for you. I suppose it doesn't matter really," he added carelessly. "You'll have had many a beating at school, and I don't suppose Hoskins will do any worse."

Verity quickly said, "Charles dear, please reconsider. It would serve no purpose to upset the poor man more."

Charles threw herself in her chair. "Oh, very well." She impaled Cyn with stormy eyes. "But I give the orders on this journey."

Cyn bit back a sharp retort. Where was the charmer who had glowed over a warm biscuit? Then he reminded himself she was wounded, and probably afraid. He must control this lamentable tendency to tease her.

"As you will," he said as moderately as he could. "But I have a great deal more experience of the world than you, and Hoskins, I'm afraid, will only take orders from me. I would have thought Verity too should be consulted, as this is her affair, and she is surely some years your senior."

"Of course I will consult Verity. How would you think otherwise?"

"Young men often disregard sisters," he teased, then winced. So much, he thought, for good intentions.

"*I* do not," she responded, and stood. ''I will acquire a few other items of clothing." At the door she stopped and grudgingly asked, "Can you think of anything else we might need? Weapons, or something like that?"

He gave her credit for swallowing her pride. "I can think of nothing. We have the coach pistol, and my rapier. That should be sufficient. We are not, after all, going to war." Then he added, "Wait! One thing I don't have for my disguise is feminine trinkets. Can you acquire any?"

"I'll see what I can do."

She returned in an hour with extra shirts and a pair of top boots. She also had a leather-bound jewel box. It was a handsome piece with a solid lock, clearly intended for expensive ornaments. When opened, it proved to contain only a sparse selection of cheap trinkets.

The obvious explanation was that they were destitute,

and had sold anything of value. It did not satisfy him, for it left unexplained the men's clothing of fine quality, two thoroughbred horses, and a pair of silver-mounted pistols. Cyn's curiosity itched him like a bed full of fleas.

Chapter 5

Early the next morning they prepared for departure. Hoskins went off to ready the horses. Cyn began to struggle with his female garments. Charles dressed in her good-quality clothing and assisted her sister until Cyn slyly questioned the propriety of this. Then she came reluctantly to assist him.

He took care not to offend her modesty, and when she came into the kitchen he was wearing his drawers. He also wore the striped stockings and lacy garters. She took one look and burst out laughing. It was very feminine laughter, but he did not remark on it, merely enjoyed it.

She looked delicious, flushed with humor. Despite the clothes and the hair, he could no longer see her as anything but supremely female. Which was very dangerous. He turned his attention to his shift.

When he looked up again, she was no longer laughing, but was staring in horror at his scar. "What on earth caused that?" she asked.

"A saber," he said casually, interested to see what her reaction would be. The livid scar ran across his chest like a bandolier. All the women who had been favored with a glimpse of it had been impelled to touch it. Most had traced it, some with a finger, some with their mouths. "Fortunately it was only a glancing blow, and the cut was shallow."

61

He saw her hand twitch upward and be controlled.

"So you really are a soldier," she said.

"Did you doubt me?"

"You don't look like one."

He sighed humorously. "I can't help my beguiling charms."

She was still fascinated by the scar. She took a step closer. "It must have bled a lot."

"Like a slashed wineskin. Made the devil of a mess of my best uniform."

Since she seemed stuck, he closed the gap between them with a casual step. After a moment he had to acknowledge with regret that she wasn't going to give in to temptation and trace the scar's path from left shoulder to right hip.

He dropped the lawn shift over his head and tied the laces at the low neck, then struggled into the Brunswick gown. Designed for comfort and simplicity when traveling, it was made all in one piece. When fastened, it would have the look of a loose sacque gown over a braided corset, but in fact the stomacher was part of the bodice, kept snug around the body by laces beneath the loose back. It was appropriate traveling wear, but its chief charm for Cyn was the lack of whalebone.

He tried to tie the laces himself but couldn't find them under the heavy, wide skirts. "The laces elude me. Your assistance, please, Charles."

Her reluctance was visible, but she came over to stand behind him. She pulled up the back of his skirt. "I can't see them. They must have fallen to the front."

She fished around the sides of his torso, and the fleeting touches sent shivers through him. "Got them," she said, "but they're knotted at the front, I think."

Her hands followed the laces to the front. She suddenly jerked back. "I can't untie them," she said in a strangled voice. "You'll have to take the gown off."

"Oh, I'm sure you can," Cyn said casually. "Far easier

than struggling out of all this." His voice was strained too, but with the urge to laugh. Did she know just where her hands had been? He suspected she did.

A silence made him think she would refuse, but then her arms encircled him again. They met in front, took hold of the knotted laces, and began to work at them. She made no attempt at all to guard where her hands touched.

Cyn took a deep breath. Hoisted with his own petard, by gad! The minx knew exactly what she was doing.

She'd pulled his skirts up all the way at the back and her belly pressed against his buttocks. Her arms encircled his waist and her hands brushed against him again and again as she worked at the knots . . .

The first wisps of lust fevered his brain. He could imagine turning slowly within her arms and kissing her; sinking to the ground to explore her mouth, her breasts, the warmth between her thighs; the dark intensity of her eyes when he slid into her . . .

His own shudder warned him he had almost gone too far. His erect penis struggled against his drawers as if seeking the comfort of her hands. Those hands froze, loosely cradling him. He could feel her rigid panic.

Unless, he thought in desperate optimism, it had been a deliberate seduction, and her tension came of desire?

He pulled out of her arms and turned. No. She was scarlet. Horrified. Frightened.

Cyn forced himself to relax, struggled to control his breathing. "Don't look so aghast, my boy. Perfectly natural reaction to all that fumbling about. Nothing personal."

He turned away and raised the front of his skirts to finish the job. "We should have realized I could do this at the front myself." He pushed the laces toward the back. "There. If you can just knot them, we're done."

She looked as enthusiastic as someone putting her head into the mouth of a hungry tiger, but she came back behind him, raised his skirts again, and took the laces. In a moment they were tied and she had retreated. He just wished the feelings she'd roused would retreat as quickly.

What was he to make of her, bold at one moment, prudish the next?

"Tell me," he asked lightly, "are you a virgin, young Charles?"

"Yes!" Her color flared again, even deepened. "Not that it's any business of yours!"

"Of course not," he soothed. "I merely thought to offer my services to amend the matter."

She gaped. He knew she had temporarily forgotten her disguise, but was all too aware of the state of his body. "What on earth can you mean?"

He smiled kindly. "Just that an older man often takes a younger under his wings and shows him how to go on. Introduces him to the right kind of female. If we're going adventuring . . ."

He watched her come back to reality with a bump and, he hoped, a *soupçon* of disappointment. A layer of frost settled. "We are engaged in a very serious business, my lord. It will not allow time for visits to brothels."

"But if it does?"

He saw the mischievous gleam before she hid it. "I might be interested. But for now, we are supposed to be readying you."

Cyn loved the touch of naughtiness. She was too sober, and he knew it wasn't her true nature. She was surely a wild creature at heart, kin to himself, but for some reason afraid. He really must stop tormenting her.

"How do I look?" he asked, twirling before her.

She grimaced. "Flat, top and bottom."

Cyn looked down. The skirts hung limp, and the bodice sagged away from his flat chest. It had clearly been made for a lady of generous endowments. No one would ever think this gown had been made for him.

"The gray petticoat will serve to fill out the skirts," he

said, "but I don't know what to do about the bodice. Could it be altered?"

"Undoubtedly, but not in an hour. Wait a moment."

She left, and Cyn took the time to force control onto his body. He took some calming breaths and thought cold, unlustful thoughts.

As his body returned to a more passive state he reflected with satisfaction upon the encounter with his damsel. They progressed, indeed they did. Was she really a virgin? That would present problems, but not insuperable ones. She was clearly no conventional miss.

It was perhaps a little unsporting to let her think him unaware of her gender, but she had just shown she wasn't above trying to exploit the situation too, the hussy. He grinned with admiration and anticipated her return.

He began to struggle into the gray quilted petticoats. By the time he'd tied the laces he felt smothered in all this material. He kicked the skirts out of his way as he tried to pace, thinking that perhaps hoops were preferable after all. They'd keep the material from tangling about his legs.

He had no intention of trying to wear secondhand shoes, and so he slipped on a pair of his own. They were his evening shoes—black kid with high red heels and silver buckles. Though ladies rarely wore such shoes anymore he would merely be thought old-fashioned.

He walked a bit more, growing accustomed to the garments, to the way they moved as he walked, and the way to walk within them. Had Charles had to go through this performance when she first put on men's garments? She'd certainly learned to move with manly confidence.

His damsel returned with a big basket and held out a neckerchief. "Put this on."

It was a coarse, plain triangle of material, not at all like the filmy, ruffled ones his sisters wore. He obediently draped it around his shoulders, wondering what to do with the loose ends.

She clucked with exasperation. "Oh, sit down." When

he sat in a chair, she deftly tucked it into his neckline at the back, crossed the front points at his collarbone, and tucked them behind the stomacher. He refrained from commenting on this expertise and simply enjoyed her touch.

When she'd finished, he looked down. The bodice still hung loose. "What do you suggest? Handkerchiefs? I'm not sure I have enough for this vast cavern."

"No. They would be too lumpy anyway."

"My dear Charles," said Cyn coyly, "who precisely do you think will be feeling my bosom?"

She cast him a disgusted look. "Everyone, if you behave as a woman like you do as a man. You're a bold piece, Milord Cyn, and aptly named. Look." She indicated her basket which contained unspun wool. "Nana's next blanket," she explained, and passed him a handful. "Push it behind the stomacher."

He sat down and pulled out the bodice. "I think it will have to go inside the shift to be secure." After a couple of handfuls he said, "It would work better if you stuffed it in and shaped it. You'll be able to see what you're doing."

She gave him a suspicious look, but dutifully came over to push the soft gray wool down against his skin, handful after handful. She stopped every now and then to ease and adjust it to the shape of the bodice.

Cyn knew it was unwise to have her touch him like this, but being unwise in such matters was second nature to him. He relaxed back in the chair, studying her serious features.

Gad, but she was beautiful. Her skin was as smooth as cream satin, and the lines of her nose and jaw were as perfect as a marble statue. Her lashes were not as thick or long as his, but the purity to their dark curve was the only possible frame for her clear gray eyes.

He felt a cad for having lustful thoughts about such a pristine being, such a madonna.

Then she was concentrating. Her lips parted. Her tongue

came out to touch her upper lip with moistness. He caught his breath.

She looked at him. "Did I hurt you?"

"No," he said, swallowing. "It tickled."

She considered him warily. He caught the revealing flicker of her eyes toward his crotch, but any physical response was safely concealed beneath quilted silk and heavy cloth. He smiled blandly, and she went back to work.

Cyn didn't know why he was hell-bent on having this torture continue. He'd be a wreck before they finished.

Chastity watched nervously for a return of Cyn Malloren's lust, but then she realized it was not him she should be wary of. Each touch of his skin against her hands was like fire to her nerves. Each breath she took carried a musky smell that dried her mouth and made her lick her lips . . .

This couldn't be happening to her! Men were animal creatures, easily stirred to lust. Women were more refined. They didn't come into heat just from stroking a man's chest!

She sternly commanded her foolish senses to behave, and pummeled his bosom into shape.

Cyn worked at appearing bored. It wasn't easy. His damsel was pressed against him, breathing unsteadily, lips full and moist with the need to be kissed.

And he'd go odds she didn't even know it.

Her hands trembled against him, and she looked into his eyes for one lost, revealing moment . . .

Then she caught herself and moved away. "There. I think that looks true to life."

Cyn sighed for what might have been, then he looked down. " 'Struth!" he exclaimed. "I'll cause a riot!"

Chastity's mind was fogged by unruly longings, but his remark dragged a laugh from her. "Not if you thrust it forward and glare," she said. "Then they'll call you a battle-ax. And you better had. If anyone does feel your tits, they'll know they're not real."

He looked at her with a wicked glint. "I think you've been leading me on, young Charles. How do you know what tits feel like?"

Chastity could not think of a clever answer. "You know the problem with this?" she said quickly.

"No."

"We'll have it all to do again tomorrow."

She saw the hilarity in his eyes before he stood. *"Il faut suffrir pour être femme,"* he drawled, and twirled again. "Now. Will I do?"

And, heaven help her, she too would enjoy playing this game again tomorrow. She was undoubtedly mad.

She pulled her mind back to work and looked him over. "Somewhat," she said with a frown. "But I don't think you make as pretty a woman as you thought you would."

"Want to change roles?"

She remained silent and he smiled.

Cyn peered into the small mirror. "I forgot to buy a cap. A matron should have a cap."

"I'll get one," she said, and left.

Not pretty? Cyn realized she was correct. His jaw was a little too square, his cheeks too lean. He carefully applied rouge to them, and was heartened to realize that for once he looked too masculine.

He dusted his tanned neck, chest, and face with the pale powder, then rubbed some rouge onto his lips and pouted into the glass. He pulled the ribbon from his hair and combed the russet waves so they hung about his face. He teased curls out around his temples as he'd seen his sisters do.

Then he took up the perfume and dabbed a little by his ears. It was a musky, sultry fragrance that would distract the senses of any man who came close. That, along with his tremendous bosom, would have him defending his honor ten times a day.

He'd mainly bought the perfume, however, in the hopes that eventually his damsel would wear it for him. He indulged briefly in thoughts of her, naked and damp with lusty sweat, her body perfumes mingled with this artificial one ...

When he heard her return, he turned and pouted his reddened lips. "Kiss me, sailor?"

Chastity was startled by how feminine he looked. He'd fluffed out his hair and rouged his cheeks, but it wasn't simply the cosmetics and the figure. It was something in he way he stood, in the slight droop of his neck, and the coy use of his lashes. He was a gifted mimic.

Again, she knew he was dangerous. As she handed him the plain cotton cap, she swore off all future skirmishes.

He took it between two fingers and considered it as a disdainful lady would. "No frills? No lace? How terribly dull," he drawled in a husky but feminine voice. "I suppose it does match the equally dull neckerchief, however. To whom do these drab items belong?"

Chastity didn't want to answer that question. "That's all there is," she said bluntly. "Verity has scarcely the clothes she stands up in. If its plainness bothers you," she added sweetly, "you can embroider it in the coach. 'Twill be a suitably matronly occupation."

" 'Twould be disastrous," he said, matching her tone. "I'm sure even you could wield a needle better than I, sir." He turned away to put on the cap in front of the mirror. It was designed to cover all the hair, but he managed to set it back on his head so the front hair showed. When he'd tied the strings under his right ear, even that dismal headgear looked almost fetching.

Chastity discovered that high-minded resolutions didn't always work. She had sworn off skirmishes, but was still under assault. She and Cyn weren't touching, they weren't even looking at each other, he seemed more like a woman by the moment, and still she felt light-headed.

It was impossible that she feel like this. She had never

in her life reacted to a man in such a way, and these days she hated all men. She wondered if women *could* come into season, like horses. That was what it felt like. As if she were a giddy mare scenting her first stallion.

But he was hardly the first male she'd met.

She'd encountered all kinds of men, especially in London. There had been ones who quoted poetry, and ones who made sly, unseemly suggestions. Ones who reverently kissed her hands, and ones who groped at her body under the concealment of the dance. Then there had been Henry Vernham, who had thought he had the right to put his chilly hands all over her until she'd shown him his error by stabbing him with a pair of needle-sharp scissors.

None of these men had made her feel at all as Cynric Malloren did, and he wasn't even trying.

It was unreasonable.

It was impossible.

It was incredibly dangerous and could not be allowed.

For heaven's sake, she'd even enjoyed a brief flirtation with Rothgar without this effect, and he was the kind of man mothers warned their daughters about. As handsome as Cyn was beautiful, he carried an aura of dark power which had its own magnetic quality.

She remembered one encounter in a dim arbor of a garden during a ball. She'd known it was bold to go apart with him, and had been curious as to what he would do.

Smiling, he'd put a finger under her chin and merely touched his lips to hers. She'd felt singed—wickedly, deliciously singed, in a far more potent way than during the few groping full kisses she had permitted from other men.

Chastity had enjoyed the excitement of touching on something so dangerous, and yet she had felt nothing in particular for Rothgar, and had been secure in the knowledge that he felt nothing in particular for her. There had been none of this obsessive awareness of the man's every move, this dizzying vibration from the slightest touch.

She made a silent prayer that Cyn never find out she

was female, for then he might unleash the full power of his wiles against her, and she'd surely be lost.

Cyn grimaced as he put on the plain, coarse cap. He guessed cap and kerchief must belong to his damsel, but what could possess her to choose such ugly pieces? They were more suitable to the inmate of a house of correction.

When he put these garments together with her masculine dress, he wondered if she hated her very femininity. Look at her now. Her face had all the warmth of a marble deathmask.

Why on earth was he drawn to such an oddity? Why was he stirred by her more than he'd been stirred by the most skillful whore, or the most fetching lady? It must be abstinence. He'd not had a woman since before he became ill. Perhaps this reaction proved he was fully recovered.

In that case, all he needed was a lusty, willing wench and his obsession with his damsel would disappear.

But he found he had difficulty imagining being aroused by any woman other than this one. That was alarming in the extreme.

He sifted through the pathetic collection of trinkets and clipped a pair of earrings of painted tin on his lobes. He dismissed the rest and demanded his own jewels. He sprinkled them about the sober garments, then turned his attention to the flat straw hat.

He wound the yards of fawn ribbon around the low crown and then formed a great deal of it into a loveknot at the front, anchoring it with the pearl-and-diamond pin. He passed the remaining ribbon through the two slits at either side, popped the confection on his head, and tied the ribbons in a large bow.

Chastity was astonished by his nimble expertise. "Dress like this frequently, do you?"

He turned and smiled, disconcertingly female. "No, but I've dressed, and undressed, a number of females in my time." He fluttered his outrageous lashes. "Don't worry, young Charles. Your turn will come."

Chastity's body responded to a meaning he could not possibly intend. For a moment a vision of his long brown fingers slipping off her clothes swamped her reason.

He touched her arm and she flinched. He appeared not to notice and just pushed her gently ahead of him out of the door. "Let's see what Verity thinks of this transformation."

When they entered the parlor Verity looked up and stared. "My goodness! If I didn't know, I'd never guess."

"Let's hope that is true for everyone." Cyn looked over Verity in turn.

She was the picture of a rather slatternly maid. She still wore the plain, sleeved chemise, a skirt of cheap striped cloth, and a sleeveless laced bodice in a practical and ugly mud color. She'd added an apron, and a neckerchief, knotted in front. A cap covered almost all her hair. Cap, neckerchief, and apron looked suspiciously kin to the ones he wore. Unpleasant suspicions stirred in his head.

"I fear," he said, probing gently, "that people will think me a harsh mistress to dress my maid in the cast-off clothes from the local foundling home."

Verity's revealing face told him he was close to the truth. But what truth?

"It's the best we can do," said Charles sharply. "Do you think her looks are changed enough?"

Verity's hair had been darkened by grease rather than dye, and it straggled out of the front of her cap. The change was remarkable.

"It will do, I think," he said. "If we come face-to-face with someone who knows Verity well, it won't work, but the main danger surely is that bills have been posted, and the authorities alerted. They'll be looking for a young blonde lady with a child. I'm darker, and must look considerably older as a woman than my true twenty-four. What? Thirty-odd?"

Verity nodded and smiled. "We'll do it, won't we?"

He smiled back at her as if she were one of his raw recruits needing encouragement before the first battle. "Assuredly we will."

Spontaneously she held out her hands. When he took them she kissed him lightly on the lips. "Thank you. I'm so glad we found you."

"Captured him," corrected Charles sharply.

Cyn turned to his glowering damsel. He grasped her by the shoulders, and before she could react, kissed her as Verity had kissed him. She jerked back and scrubbed at her lips.

"My dear sir," said Cyn, tremulously, which was easy since he was fighting laughter, "a thousand apologies. I became carried away by my part!"

"Get carried away like that again," snapped his damsel, "and I'll gut you." She picked up a portmanteau and stalked off toward the coach.

By noon, Cyn had decided this adventure was a dead bore. Where was the challenge? Where were the dangers? Where were the dragons for him to fight?

All he was experiencing was the familiar swaying motion of the coach, the chill of a sharp November day, and the discomfort of his disguise. His legs felt smothered in skirts, the wool stuffing itched, and the coarse strings of the cap were fretting his skin. He'd thought a stiff stock around his neck was bad enough, but this was undoubtedly worse.

He'd removed the hat as soon as they were in the coach, but felt he had to keep the cap on in case a passing traveler looked inside the carriage. They'd already decided that to pull the curtains would make them look suspicious. Now he untied the strings of the cap and let them hang.

"Why the deuce," he asked, "would anyone make a cap out of such coarse calico?" Despite his irritation he spoke softly for the baby slept.

"For durability," said Charles unsympathetically. "After a score or so washings it will soften up."

"It would be better, surely, to buy the cloth already softened."

"But more expensive."

Curiosity stirred in Cyn again. "Where did these caps come from?"

"We just had them lying around," she said evasively, then smiled without warmth. "I'm sorry we had nothing more suitable for your delicate skin, milord."

"Why not?"

She flashed a sharp look at him. "Why should we have expensive folderols?"

Cyn glanced at Verity, who looked anxious. "Because you and your sister are gently bred. Your clothes, sir, though somewhat old-fashioned, have come from a modish tailor. So, if there are female garments, I would expect them to be of high quality."

Charles' color betrayed agitation, but she answered calmly. "Verity fled in disguise, and I certainly don't wear caps."

Cyn persisted. "Then where did these come from?"

Her jaw tightened. "Nana and I were making them for the Magdalene in Shaftesbury."

It was a plausible explanation, though Cyn doubted it. He relaxed back and fanned himself with his bonnet. "How charitable," he murmured. "Especially on your part, sir."

She bit her lip.

It was Verity who stepped into the breach. "He's claiming more credit than he's due. I'm sure all he did was to cut out the cloth."

The coach swung into an inn yard, and the conversation was abandoned with Cyn little the wiser.

The change was slow since Hoskins had no one to blow for a new team or help the ostlers. Though they were still on Cyn's prearranged route, he had decided not to use the teams of Rothgar's horses which awaited, and he'd told Hoskins to avoid the inns where he would be known.

As far as Cyn knew, Rothgar was in London, not at the Abbey, but once he learned of his brother's disappearance, Cyn suspected he would institute a search. No need to leave a blazing trail. He had no desire to be 'rescued' by the marquess a second time.

Now, however, they had to hire post horses at each stage, with postilions to care for them. Hoskins grumbled that the teams were mere cart horses.

In short, nobody was happy with the state of affairs.

Cyn casually scrutinized the inn yard for posters, or overattentive observers. Nothing. Perhaps there was no hunt at all. Chances seemed excellent of them reaching Maidenhead in two days without incident.

How dull.

Then he saw Verity's pallid face. At every stop, and whenever a horseman passed them on the road, she tensed with fear. The sooner she reached her Nathaniel, the better.

As they pulled out, the baby woke and began to cry. Within moments the complaint grew from a whimper to a howl—an amazingly piercing sound for one so small. Verity's face turned rosy as she put him to her breast under a shawl. Cyn politely looked away, though there was nothing to see. He found the mental image of a baby at the breast fascinating, however, and the effect was heightened by the soft slurping noises the baby made.

He wondered what it would be like to watch the mother of his child feed the babe, what it would be like to suck on nipples which produced milk. He slid a look at Charles.

He blinked, amazed at himself. Children? Marriage? Such things had no part in his life. Married life and soldiering didn't mesh. As the veterans said, 'When a soldier puts his cap on, he should know his family's covered.'

Anyway, if he had any thoughts of marriage, he'd be mad to consider his damsel-in-distress. She showed few womanly attributes. But Lord, it would be fine to have a wife with her kind of courage'...

The slurping stopped and the baby again set up a

screech. Verity hushed and gabbled and patted the child on the back. He kicked and screamed, red-faced and furious. Verity was almost as red. Cyn stared out the window, as if unaware of the racket, but wishing he could put his hands over his ears.

The screams lowered slightly in volume, and he glanced back. Charles had the baby now and was holding William with more confidence than anyone would expect of a young man. The baby had quieted to an occasional whine which might even be a prelude to sleep. They all sighed with relief.

William had obviously just needed a moment to catch his breath. He suddenly thrust his legs out and screamed even louder, as if in terrible pain. Cyn couldn't imagine what the problem was, but began to worry that the babe would expire in front of him. Children died from minor problems all the time.

Verity, however, looked embarrassed rather than terrified.

The noise went on and on. Charles jiggled the babe and looked every bit as alarmed as Cyn. Verity took the babe back and tried to put him to the breast again, but little William rejected it furiously. She sat him up, lay him down, put him to her shoulder.

Cyn decided that being confined in a coach with a screaming baby was a very effective form of torture. He'd give away national secrets to stop the racket.

Verity looked close to tears. "Oh, I'm sorry. It must be gas, but I can't seem to do anything ..."

Though he knew nothing about babies, Cyn knew a lot about horses, dogs, and raw recruits, and he thought that at the moment Verity was doing more harm than good. "Oh, give him to me," he said, rather more sharply than he intended.

She hesitated, but he took the howling babe anyway. He was surprised by the squirming strength of the tiny mite, and because he'd taken hold of more blanket than babe, he almost dropped him. Quite by accident, William ended up face-down on Cyn's knee with a thump. The child gave a burp, spit up on Cyn's skirt, and was quiet.

All three of them looked at the baby, expecting the ear-splitting noise to start again. Quiet reigned and William didn't even seem to object to his position. Cyn turned him cautiously. The child was a perfect little cherub, and even seemed to smile with gratitude as he drifted off to sleep.

Verity leaned forward to dab at Cyn's skirt with a rag, apologizing again. "I was fretting him," she said. "I'm sure that's why he had the gripe. He's normally such a good baby." She sat up again. "I'm so scared . . ."

Charles covered her hand. "Don't be, love. See, here we are close to Salisbury already, and no sign of pursuit. We have wound ourselves up into a stew over nothing."

"Oh, I do hope so."

"We'll stop soon for a luncheon." Charles looked a challenge at Cyn, but when he made no objection she asked more moderately, "Do you think we'll make Basingstoke tonight, my lord?"

"Not without a great push," Cyn said. "The road is none too good and I see no reason to hurry."

The sisters exchanged glances. "Where then?"

"The road between Andover and Basingstoke is very bleak, not to be traveled after dark. There's a White Hart at Worting and another at Whitchurch. Both good places. I suggest we see how far we can reasonably go."

"How is it you know this road so well?" Charles asked suspiciously.

"I traveled it not many days ago. There's not a great deal for a lonely traveler to do but follow the map." He pulled one out of a pocket by his seat and handed it to her.

She studied it, finding Salisbury. "Did you travel from Rothgar Abbey?"

"Yes."

"Where exactly is it?"

"Not far from Farnham."

"So at Basingstoke we'll be off your route?"

"Yes."

"Will we reach Maidenhead tomorrow?" Verity asked.

"That depends on the roads. I suggest we go north at Basingstoke to join the Bath road at Reading, then we'll be on a toll road. It should be better than this."

They seemed disinclined to argue, which surprised him. Was Charles mellowing at last?

Peace after Bedlam would mellow anyone.

He looked down at the baby, surprised by how pleasant it felt to hold the sleeping mite. He'd seen plenty of Hilda's daughter but never, as a mere male, been entrusted with her. The soft, pliant weight, the steady rise and fall of breathing, the dreaming sucking motions of the full lips all charmed him.

And this wasn't a perfect child. He had a rash on his cheek, perhaps from his tear-dampened blanket. Verity had changed him once today, but a sour smell rose from him. Cyn didn't know who the father was, but he suspected the child would never make his fortune with his face.

All the same, sweetly, trustingly asleep, the baby caught his heart and made him think again of children of his own ...

"Halt!"

The summons caught them all unawares. Charles put a hand toward the pistol-holster. Verity reached for her child.

Cyn held on to the babe. "Look innocent, damn you." This clearly was no attempt at robbery, and could only be a military patrol. The door was sharply opened. Cyn turned toward it with a look of astonishment. "Please!" he said in a whisper. "The babe is sleeping."

The young officer looked abashed, and then his eyes sharpened. Cyn had no doubt he was on the lookout for a mother and child.

An added complication was that Cyn knew Lieutenant Toby Berrisford very well indeed.

Chapter 6

"**M**y apologies, ma'am," said Toby quietly, going red. It was an affliction that went with his pale skin and red hair, but Cyn knew he never let it interfere with his duty. "I am ordered to keep an eye out for a young mother with a two-month-old child. I must ask your identity."

"I'm Sarah Inchcliff," said Cyn amenably. "Mrs. Richard Inchcliff of Goole, Yorkshire. I confess, sir, that it is true my babe is only a little over two months old, but I'm flattered you think me young." He gave Toby a teasing smile. "I'll not see thirty again and this is my sixth. Why do you seek such a pair?"

Toby frowned at Cyn but more in puzzlement than suspicion. "The young woman's wits have been turned by the death of her husband, and she has run away with her child. It is feared she will do him some harm."

Verity made a little sound. "Yes," said Cyn quickly, "horrible, isn't it? But if she is so deranged, would she be traveling in a private coach?"

"She might be befriended by some misguided person, ma'am, and that person could then be in danger. Who knows what a madwoman might do?" He was still frowning. "Forgive me, ma'am, but are we acquainted?"

Cyn faced Toby blandly. "I don't think so, Lieutenant,

79

but I am told I bear a strong resemblance to my cousins. My maiden name was Malloren."

His face cleared. "That's it! You have quite the look of Lord Cyn, you know."

"I'm flattered," said Cyn, adding naughtily, "He's quite excessively handsome."

"Isn't he just?" said Toby with a grin. "And a devil with the ladies. There's not a one can resist him. Well, Mrs. Inchcliff, apologies for interrupting your journey. If you should come across the poor wretch, put her in the care of the local magistrate. The child's guardian and the woman's father are both in the area, and will care for them."

Lieutenant Berrisford then slammed the door and William set up a squawk. Cyn saw his friend turn red as he made quickly for his horse. Cyn gave the baby to Verity, and as the carriage rolled by he waved his fingers coyly at the soldiers.

Verity put the baby to the breast again, her eyes wide with fear. "Father and Henry both hereabouts! Dear heaven."

"Those soldiers suspected nothing," Charles reassured her.

"But what if we meet with Father or Henry at an inn? We mustn't stop anywhere!"

"We have to stop," said Cyn with deliberate, authoritative calm. "For one thing, Hoskins cannot drive all day without a halt. For another, we all need food and rest. I will look after you. Besides, if you fret, you'll upset William again." He held her eyes until she relaxed a little, then smiled at her. She smiled tremulously back and returned her attention to the child.

Cyn considered Charles, who looked distinctly strange. It must be because of Toby's words about Lord Cyn's effect on women. He wondered if they were doing his cause with his damsel good or harm. "I wish I'd been able to ask Toby where your pursuers have made their headquarters."

"You do know him, then?" Charles asked.

"Very well, but we haven't met for three years. Don't worry. He won't twig it. I really do have a cousin called Sarah Inchcliff who lives near Goole."

She nodded, and resumed her frowning contemplation of the passing scenery.

By great good fortune the exhausted baby dropped off to sleep again. Cyn looked around for something to do, and saw the neat pile of news-sheets. These were the ones Mrs. Crupley had wrapped around their purchases. Nana had frugally saved them and sent them along in case they came in use.

He picked them up and smoothed them out. "A wondrous miscellany. Three sheets of the *Gazette,* two of the *Morning Post*—all different dates—and a sheet of the *Grub Street Journal.* I doubt there's any news of interest, but have you heard of the latest amusement? One reads the lines across the page to see what nonsense can be made. Just occasionally it throws up a treasure. Let's take a sheet each."

He became aware as he passed over the papers that Charles was strung as tight as a bow. What could be alarming her now? She took her paper, one of the *Morning Post* sheets, and looked first at the date. Then she relaxed. "Lud," she said, "these are ancient. This is from '59."

So, thought Cyn, there could be something revealing in a more recent news-sheet. Something about Verity, or about his damsel herself?

Cyn scanned his paper. "Here's one. It goes across from the obituaries to the news from Gloucestershire. 'She was a virtuous lady well known as . . . the best milker the shire has ever seen.' "

Charles said, "I don't believe it!" When shown the line she gave him the victory and set about a careful study of her own sheet.

"I have one," said Verity. "Look at this. It goes across three columns. 'Wentworth the highwayman . . . having conceived a strong affection . . . has increased the population.' "

"More than likely," said Cyn with a grin. "That Wentworth had a procession of weeping women following him to the gallows."

"I have one," said Charles. " 'An infant of three years . . . has piratically seized a merchant vessel' . . . If I cheat and go down two lines I can add . . . 'by judicious use of *sal volatile!*' "

"The navy should learn that trick," said Cyn, enjoying her relaxed amusement. He could make a life's work out of making his damsel smile . . .

'Struth, but a wiser man would leave the coach at the next stop and take to the woods before total insanity overwhelmed him.

Soon they entered Salisbury with its famous tall spire. "We should stop here if it's safe," Cyn said. "I confess, however, that if I were to make my headquarters in this area, I would choose Salisbury. It's admirably central, and anyone traveling from the Shaftesbury area to London or Maidenhead would be bound to pass through. We had best make inquiries first."

Hoskins had pulled into the Black Horse, a busy posting inn, but not the one where the Malloren horses were waiting. Cyn called up that they might be stopping, then leaned out to attract the attention of an ostler. A shilling caught the wiry man's eye. "Yes, your ladyship?"

"The Black Horse seems very busy today," Cyn said. "Will we be able to have a private parlor?"

"This ain't busy for the Horse, milady," he said boastfully. "There'll be private rooms to be had, never fear." He reached for the coin, but Cyn withheld it.

"And is this the kind of inn where the best people stay?"

"We have many important regulars, milady," he said proudly. "The Duke of Queensbury racks up here, and the Earl of Portsmouth. Why, the great Earl of Walgrave—him they call the Incorruptible—stayed here only last night, and left not three hours past." He fixed a suitably sober look on his face. "Looking for his poor daughter, he is. The young lady's gone mad, and is running around the country stark naked with her babe dead in her arms."

"She should surely be easy to find then," Cyn said dryly, and gave up the coin. As soon as the man left he looked at his apprehensive companions.

So their father was the Earl of Walgrave, one of the great lords of the land, known to all for his wealth, power, and almost Puritan rectitude. Hardly surprising that he had named a daughter Verity. Perhaps Charles was not Charlotte but Constance.

So why were the sisters not seeking this paragon's help?

This new element, however, certainly made their enterprise a great deal more interesting. The Earl of Walgrave could easily mobilize the authorities, including the army, to search for his daughter. Cyn couldn't help but doubt that Verity marrying her major would put an end to the problem. An officer could be broken for less. Cyn's own career might be in jeopardy if his part came out.

There was something else too—some other detail to do with Walgrave—but it tickled at the edge of Cyn's memory and refused to be pinned down.

He shrugged. The dice were cast, and he had never yet turned from an enterprise because of danger. He smiled at his companions. "He is, at least, long gone. *En avant, mes enfants.*"

The ostler had been correct. Though the inn seemed busy, there were still good private rooms to be had. Cyn took a bedchamber as well as a parlor.

As soon as they were alone, Verity said, "We should have told you. I'm sorry."

"It would have made no difference. But you have a formidable opponent, if opponent he is."

"Yes, and I fear Father is now on his way to Nana's, and will soon know some of the truth. I just pray Nana will be able to keep your part in this secret, my lord. I would not like you to find my father your enemy."

Cyn glanced at Charles. She looked pinched and haunted, and he no longer needed to wonder whom she feared. He wished he understood more. Certainly the earl would not be pleased with a daughter who chose to play the man, but was that the sum of her sins?

Cyn put a blunt question to Verity. "The Earl of Walgrave could keep both you and William safe from Horrible Henry. Why are you fleeing him?"

Verity bit her lip. "It's true. Perhaps I should go to him . . . I *can't* risk William . . ."

"Nonsense," said Charles crisply. "Father's off in the wrong direction, and when he turns around he still won't know whom or what he's looking for. Henry V . . . Horrible Henry knows even less. We'll get you to Nathaniel before Father can interfere." She turned to Cyn. "Father stopped Verity from marrying Nathaniel once, and would do so again."

"Ah. And instead he arranged your marriage to whom?" When they hesitated, he said, "Knowledge is power, and I think we need all the power we can get."

"Sir William Vernham," Verity said. "His brother is Henry Vernham."

"Never heard of 'em," dismissed Cyn with the arrogance of the high nobility, and considerable surprise. "How was Sir William more eligible than your major?"

The sisters shared a glance. "We don't know," said Verity.

"Rich?" Cyn asked.

"Fairly, but I can't imagine that weighing with Father. His own wealth is enormous. It is political influence he craves. He seeks high power. He believes he alone has the qualities to steer the nation to glory."

"And Sir William had this political influence?"

"No." For once Verity lost patience. "There's no point in badgering me, my lord. I'm not being difficult. My marriage had importance for my father, but it never made any sense to me. No more than . . ."

Cyn caught the conscious look between the sisters and knew they were concealing something, something to do with his damsel. He let the matter drop, though he had more questions about this fascinating conundrum.

He turned his most reassuring smile on Verity, and said, "Don't worry about your father. As Charles says, he's haring off in the wrong direction. You're of age, and entitled to marry whom you will. We appear safe now, so why don't you go and tend to young Sir William."

Verity went into the bedroom, comforted by his brisk confidence. Cyn removed his bonnet and poured a glass of wine. "For you, sir?" he asked Charles.

She was standing by the window watching the street, but at his words she turned. "No, thank you."

He poured a little wine into her glass anyway. When she questioned it with a look, he said, "I intend to demolish at least half this bottle, if not all of it. It will have to appear that you have done your part."

"You think of everything, don't you?"

"You find that unadmirable? My dear Charles, in normal times, I'm an officer in charge of the lives of a great many men. Carelessness is not a failing I permit myself."

Her chin rose under this rebuke before she looked away. "You think me a child."

"No," he said gently. "I think you very brave, given your circumstances. I just wish you would trust me and consider me your friend."

She met his eyes again, and he saw the faintest hint of softening. "You know nothing of my circumstances."

He wasn't sure how to handle this, but it was an important moment. "I gather you and your father are not close."

She laughed sharply. "No, we are not close."

Cyn sat and deliberately relaxed. "I wasn't close to mine either, but I admired him. How do you feel about the earl?"

He saw the tension leap into her. "That's none of your business!"

It was fear. He could smell it. He was well acquainted with the many flavors of fear. What had Walgrave done to her?

Before he could continue his questioning, servants brought in the meal and set it on the table. Once they had left, Verity rejoined them. The time for stripping the layers of his damsel's soul had passed. They all ate, though Verity needed some encouragement to consume enough.

"Father only needs one glimpse to know us," she fretted, pushing bits of steak pie around her plate.

Cyn covered her restless hand with his own. "People generally see what they think to see. Let your face go slack and stupid, and in your present outfit you could walk by your father in the street and he'd not recognize you."

Verity was only slightly reassured. "Perhaps we should hide here and write a letter to Nathaniel."

"I don't think so," said Cyn. "There will be some kind of regular check on the inns, and from what Toby said, I suspect your father and Horrible Henry have spun a pretty tale. Since the earl knows all about Major Frazer, he'll doubtless have told him the story too. He might believe it."

"He wouldn't!" Verity exclaimed.

"We can't take the risk. As soon as your major sees you, he'll know the truth."

"But," said Charles, "Father will have people watching Maidenhead and Nathaniel like a hawk."

"Yes, but we can deal with that. In that," said Cyn with a smile, "I'm your ace of trumps. The earl will be watching for Verity trying to sneak into the major's rooms, but Captain Lord Cynric Malloran can stroll up to Major Nathaniel Frazer on the street and talk to him without raising any suspicions at all. I will merely transform back into my real self. I even have my uniform in my baggage to lend an air of business."

They both seemed dumbstruck by this obvious solution. He looked at Verity. "Why don't you lie down and rest for an hour? It would be foolish to push on to Basingstoke today, so we have plenty of time."

With a wan smile, she went off to the other room.

Cyn regarded Charles, aware he'd deliberately arranged matters so they were alone. Noble intentions warred in him with carnal ones. He wanted to find out the truth of her so he could help her. He also wanted to explore her, body and soul, break down her reserves, and make love to her until there were no barriers left between them. At times like these he wished she were in skirts, and safe behind a barrier of propriety.

Faith! It suddenly hit him that the object of his lustful imaginings was the daughter of one of the highest men in the land. What the deuce was the Earl of Walgrave's daughter doing living in a cottage, dressed in breeches?

He topped up her wineglass, hoping it would loosen her tongue. "And how shall we pass the time, Charles?" he asked. "Cards? War adventures? Bordello stories?"

She handled it well. "As you know, I can share none of those with you."

"Not even the cards?"

"I have never gamed for more than pennies."

"Then we have something in common. I rarely play for high stakes."

That caught her attention. "Truly? Everyone does."

"It doesn't amuse me. I have no taste for giving other people my money, and find no pleasure in taking theirs, particularly if they can ill afford it."

She relaxed and drank from her glass. It was a gesture of truce, but before he could press his advantage, she said, "Tell me of your adventures then. In the army," she added pointedly. "Where have you served?"

"Mostly in the Americas. What is generally called the French and Indian War."

Her eyes brightened. "Did you know General Wolfe?"

"Yes." He eyed her humorously. "Are you a worshiper? He was a hard man to get along with, but a brilliant soldier."

"He labored under ill-health, I believe," she defended.

"True."

"Were you at Quebec?"

"Yes, and at Louisbourg, which is, I assure you, one of the most God-forsaken spots on earth. I think the French soldiers were pleased enough to lose it to us."

"Which was the worst battle?"

"Neither," he said with a grin. "We won both."

"But so many men were wounded and killed."

" 'Blood is the god of war's rich livery,' " he quoted, and when she looked a question, he said, "Marlowe."

"You enjoy soldiering," she said with surprise.

"I wouldn't do it if I didn't."

"Being a man, and a Malloren . . ."

He swirled his wine. "You are not lowborn, and soon will be a man. Perhaps you should join the army too."

It struck Chastity how peculiar it was to be having this conversation with a seemingly authentic lady who was knocking back an alarming amount of wine. Lord Cynric Malloren had a rare ability to tangle her mind. She had to admit, however, that the bizarre situation would tie anyone in knots.

"I don't think I have a taste for blood," she said.

"It's remarkable what we are capable of when tested."

"I find it difficult to imagine you as dangerous."

He looked up from under those ridiculous lashes and smiled. "Try me sometime."

The wine was affecting him; she could see it in his eyes, and the message there alarmed her. All the danger she had sensed this morning, both from him and in herself, rushed back. She leaped to her feet. "I think I'll take a turn around the town."

She was gone before Cyn could stop her. He cursed his drink-slowed wits. She shouldn't be out there. She hadn't even taken her wig and hat, and going about with a shorn head would attract attention in itself. It was all his fault. The conversation had been innocent enough, but wanton thoughts had stirred in him as they always seemed to when they were together. She had read him aright and fled.

It would only make matters worse if he pursued her precipitously. It would draw attention to them both. He put on his dratted cap and hat, and checked on Verity. She and the babe were asleep. He then picked up Charles' wig and tricorn, stuffed them in his muff, and went out. He remembered to take small steps and keep his head demurely lowered. At first, pretending to be a woman had been novel and amusing. It was rapidly becoming a dead bore.

In the entrance hall of the inn, one portly gentleman tipped his hat and leered at Cyn's bosom. Cyn wanted to plant the man a facer.

Salisbury's main street was wide and open, and there was no sign of the girl. Cyn stopped to speak to a woman selling chestnuts. "Did you see a young man, bare-headed, pass this way?"

The woman hooked an eloquent thumb. "Went down the river, luv."

Cyn turned down the alley indicated. He found himself in a tangle of winding lanes lined with cottages, gardens, and stables. Over three shoulder-high garden walls he glimpsed Charles, and beyond her, the river Avon.

He set off in her direction, but this warren was a veritable maze, and the lanes soon forced him away from his quarry. He plunged on, intent on getting Charles back to their parlor before she bumped into someone she knew. Then he caught the amazement on the face of a laborer in a corn factor's barn. He realized he was striding along. With a muttered curse, he started mincing again.

A few moments later his path turned alongside some gardens, and he had a clear view of Charles standing by the riverbank, tossing dead leaves into the water. A sadness, a loneliness in her pose caught at him, and he wanted nothing so much as to comfort and protect her. She wandered further along and out of his sight. If only she would tell him her problems . . .

He was snapped out of his thoughts by voices approaching.

"I tell you, I saw the trollop," drawled a well-bred voice. Cyn quickly slipped through a garden gate, and out of sight.

" 'Tis not the sister we're after, sir." This speaker was of a lower order, and Cyn guessed, a Londoner.

"Zounds, man, there's no reason for the one to be here without the other! She's as good as a prisoner since she made such a disgrace of herself." Cyn thought the speaker might be Henry Vernham.

What disgrace?

The two men appeared to have stopped nearby.

"But we checked that cottage a few days back, sir, and there weren't sight nor sound of Lady Verity."

"They were lying, or my sister-in-law turned up later." Definitely Henry Vernham. "That's neither here nor there. I glimpsed the chit heading toward the river. You go that way and I'll go this. With luck we can trap her quietly. I don't want any fuss. Once we have her, we have Lady Verity."

Cyn riffled through options with all the clearheadedness that came on him in battle—lightning-fast, rapier-sharp. He monitored the conversation at the same time.

"How'll I know her, sir?" the henchman whined. "Is she like Lady Verity's picture?"

"Not at all. She's a bold piece of goods. High and mighty, or was." Henry Vernham sniggered. "But you can't miss her. She has no hair."

"No *hair*, sir?"

"That's what I said. Her father shaved it when he caught her *in flagrante delicto.*"

Cyn's attention fractured.

Shaved!

In flagrante delicto?

With whom had she been caught? And why, in God's name, had the man not stood by her? His hand went for the rapier that wasn't there. That wrenched him back to his disguise, and his purpose.

". . . only saw her from the chest up," Vernham was saying. "She's wearing something mannish—a habit or such. But you can't mistake that hair. She looks a regular freak. Walgrave thought it'd trap her where he wanted her every bit as well as iron bars. That and the only clothes he allowed her. No true woman would poke her head out of the door looking like that."

Cyn realized his hands were fists, and he wanted nothing so much as to vault the wall and thrash Horrible Henry to a bloody pulp for the smug satisfaction in his voice.

Instead, as soon as the men moved away, he gathered his damned skirts together and worked his way across the turned earth of the garden toward the next wall.

This had no gate and he discovered that climbing a wall in heavy skirts presented problems. He heard something rip but made it over. As he hoped, the next garden did have a gate giving onto the meadow by the river. He was almost through it when a women shouted, "Oy!"

Cyn turned and saw a brawny housewife glaring at him, fists on hips. He feigned fear. "Oh, please, ma'am! My brothers . . ."

The woman gaped at him. Cyn quickly pressed a six-pence into her hand. "Bless you, dear lady," he murmured, then ran through the gate. A quick glance showed no sign of the hunters. He picked up his skirts and sprinted toward Charles. There was a rustic bench nearby.

He grabbed the girl and gasped, "Horrible Henry!"

He dragged her to the bench, flung himself down on it, and jerked her on top.

Then he kissed her.

It was just a pressing of his lips to hers, but she went stiff as a board. At least she did not fight. Cyn took the time to cram on her wig and hat. No one would be surprised to see them crooked in this situation. Over her shoulder he watched for their pursuers.

A sinewy, sallow-faced man came out of one alley as a handsome man-of-fashion came through the other. They looked around, then over toward Cyn.

Cyn turned his attention to his damsel. He put his large muff on her back so it covered part of her head, then made a thorough business of the kiss. His conscience sounded an alarm, but he easily muffled it. After all, this could well be the only chance he ever had.

She tried to keep her lips hard, but as he played his own against them they turned soft and sweet. So sweet. He tried to be gentle, though the taste of her leaped through him like an aphrodisiac.

He saw her eyes drift shut, and felt her response—the subtle movements of her body against the length of his, the clutching of her hands against his shoulders. He held her close, drowning in the pleasure of pleasuring her.

He longed to explore her mouth, but he knew he'd have a fight there, not least because she thought he thought her a man. Perhaps she remembered. She whimpered and tensed. Cyn's pleasure fled, and he felt a cad for taking such advantage. When someone cleared his throat, he was pleased enough to break the kiss.

Horrible Henry was looming over them.

Cyn gave a shriek and clutched Charles face-down to his bosom. "Adrian! We are discovered! No, dear boy, stay safe in my arms. They shall not hurt you." He fixed Henry Vernham with what he hoped were tragically intense eyes, and declared, "Only death shall part us, sir!"

"Zounds, woman. We have no interest in you and your paramour. Did a young woman pass by here? A young woman with very short hair?"

Cyn assessed his enemy. He was tall and dark, and handsome in a shallow kind of way. His eyes were narrow but not stupid. Cyn was tempted to mislead him, but merely simpered and said, "I'm sure the king could have passed by these last few minutes, sir, and I'd never have seen. Do you speak truly? You are not sent to tear Adrian from my arms?"

Herny Vernham's only reply was a sneer of disgust. He turned and stalked off back toward the town. The other man leered at the 'lovers' and trailed after. Cyn held onto his damsel until they were gone.

He allowed the feel of her to wrap around him, to weave into him. He knew with his nerve endings and his soul that he could make beautiful love with this woman. It was in the shape of her against him and beneath his hands, and the memory of the taste of her on his lips. It was in the faint aroma from her body, an aroma more potent than the finest French perfume.

He thought he could detect the slight swell of her bound breasts against his chest as she breathed. Her thigh had come to rest between his, a source of delightful torture. Driven by need, he slid a hand up between her wig and her head to feel the silky smoothness of her hair.

A shudder rippled through her.

He remembered what Henry had said. Walgrave had shaved her and forced her to wear the coarse penitent's garments, because he'd caught her in some man's bed. No wonder she preferred men's clothing. But that meant she was no virgin.

It didn't please him. Despite his lust for her, he didn't want her to be a wanton . . .

"Are they gone?" she asked quietly.

Cyn realized he was softly stroking the back of her head, offering comfort, not lust. His instincts at least had found her innocent of the worst. She must have been caught in her first misdemeanor, doubtless swept away by love.

What, then, had happened to her lover?

Reluctantly, very reluctantly, he let her go. She scrambled to her feet rather dazedly, not looking at him at all, and straightened her wig and hat.

"What was all that about?" she asked.

"I heard them planning to trap you. Vernham had seen you. I decided you'd have a chance in the guise of young Adrian. It appears to have worked." Not least because they were looking for a female, he thought, but he didn't say it. Really, he thought, it was becoming necessary to put an end to the masquerade before it endangered them all.

"We had better collect Verity and leave," she said.

"Yes, but carefully. How well does Henry know you?" Her face became pinched. "Very well."

Cyn almost asked, *Has he been in your bed?* "If he gets a good look at you, he won't be fooled then." Cyn pulled up her modest collar as high as it would go and pulled the hat down a little. The tricorn, however, offered little concealment for the face.

"Arm in arm, I think," said Cyn, "and talking. It will hide your features a little."

She was skittish but complied. They walked as quickly as they dared back to the inn, plastered against one another, heads bowed as if they were sharing secrets. Cyn saw Henry's henchman prowling the high street, but no sign of Henry himself. That wasn't altogether good news. The man could already be searching the inn.

His heart was beating fast, but not with fear. With excitement. This was what he had missed through these dreary months of convalescence. The edge of danger, the imperative of action.

They arrived safely back in their parlor, and he laughed for the joy of it.

"Stop it!" said Charles. "This isn't a game, you oaf. This is my sister and my nephew's life!"

He tried, but he knew he couldn't sober entirely. "Am I not preserving them? And we wouldn't be in this pickle," he pointed out, "if you hadn't stormed out for no reason."

She raised her chin. "Very well. I accept the responsibility. Now we must leave."

"Perhaps." Cyn went to look out the window, but the view of the high street wasn't particularly enlightening. A view of the coach yard would be more useful. "It might be better to wait until Henry leaves."

"He may be making Salisbury his headquarters," she countered. "And when he doesn't find me, he'll go through the inn with a fine-toothed comb."

Cyn looked at her with new respect. "I love a clear-headed partner. Rouse Verity. We'll continue our Adrian-and-his-lover act and pretend to be fleeing in guilt."

She colored at that but went toward the bedchamber door. She halted with her hand on the knob. "How could you do it . . .?" she asked stiffly, not looking at him at all. "A man kissing a man . . ."

"It was only a kiss, my dear boy," said Cyn lightly. "On the Continent men kiss more freely than we British. Besides, haven't you found there is always a certain amount of experimentation in a boys' school? Don't worry. I long since decided sodomy isn't a vice I favor."

Her pink cheeks turned red, and she hurried into the bedroom.

Chapter 7

$\mathcal{C}$hastity closed the door softly and leaned against it. Verity and the baby were both asleep and she hesitated to waken them. Or perhaps it was just that she needed a moment to think.

She went to the dressing table, took off her wig and hat, and looked in the cheval mirror. She was not in the habit of looking at herself these days, for it reminded her of the past, and what her father had done to her.

At first, with her hair a mere stubble, she had shunned mirrors and willingly worn the ugly caps. As it had grown a little, she had taught herself to accept the sight. It had become easier once she had thought of wearing her brother Victor's old clothes. She did make quite a handsome boy.

Her father had cleared Walgrave Towers of all Verity's and Chastity's garments so she would have no opportunity to use them, but he had not thought of Victor's and Fort's. Fort's clothes were far too large, for her elder brother, Lord Thornhill, was twenty-eight and a big man. Victor, however, was a slim sixteen. His old clothes had needed only the slightest alteration.

But she hated dressing this way.

She longed to wear silk gowns again, and hoops, and impractical, pretty satin slippers. She wanted to have long, lustrous curls brushing her shoulders, a kissing patch by her lips, and a fan. She picked up Verity's comb and imag-

ined it a fan. She extended it shut. *Do you love me?* She
pretended to open and shut it. *You are cruel.* She touched
it to her lips. *You may kiss me.* She drew it slowly across
her cheek. *I love you, Lord Cyn.*

She dropped the comb. No, not that! How had she come
to feel that way about Cyn Malloren when she'd thought
she would never trust a man again? Perhaps it had been
the look on his face when he held William. Or his kindness to Verity. Or his kindness to prickly Charles.

Perhaps it was his joyous spirit, the sheer zest with
which he faced life, his delight in challenge . . .

She turned away from the mirror, fighting the madness.
There was no place for fantasy at such a time of danger,
and anyway, it would only be the path to heartbreak. If she
revealed herself to be a woman, she would be a freak with
cropped hair. She would probably have to tell him she was
that whore, Chastity Ware. Even if he was interested in
her, it would only be for a quick roll in the nearest bed.

Lud, but she must be a whore at heart, for that impossible notion sent a tingle of longing through her.

It was all the fault of that fake kiss.

She had never much cared for kisses. When Henry
Vernham had forced a kiss on her, she'd felt like gagging.
She'd told her father, expecting to have Vernham punished
for it, but Walgrave had told her not to be missish with her
future husband. The next time Vernham had tried it, Chastity had jabbed him with her embroidery scissors.

That memory brought a grim smile of satisfaction to her
face. As punishment, she'd had to endure one of her father's chilling rages, but Vernham hadn't tried such an assault again.

Chastity had to confess, however, that while kissing Cyn
Malloren, she'd felt no urge to fight. The very opposite.
His kiss had made her feel warm and soft, and she'd
wanted to deepen it, to explore him more fully.

She pressed her hands over her face. And even if by
some miracle he cared, and still cared when he knew the

truth, she could not let anything come of it, for it would destroy him. They would never find happiness among sneers and scandal, and, worse than that, he would not tolerate any insult to her. Sooner or later it would come to a duel. She would be his death.

Chastity made her grim resolve. She must put all sentiment aside and concentrate on their purpose, getting Verity and William safe to Maidenhead. Then she would send Cyn Malloren on his merry way unencumbered.

She gently woke her sister and explained the problem. She soothed Verity's fears and helped her to prepare the baby. She smiled encouragement. "Ready? Don't worry. We'll be out of here in a twitch of a cat's whisker, and Henry will decide he was mistaken in thinking he saw me."

Verity made a gallant attempt to smile back, and they went out to join Lord Cyn.

"Ready?" he asked. When they nodded he said, "The coach is waiting and I've primed a gossipy maid with the story of my romantic flight with my young lover." He fluttered his lashes. "I think she rather envied me—an old hen with such a tender rooster. So, heads down and straight to the coach!"

They hurried down the stairs. As they crossed the hall toward the coach yard, Cyn said, "Go ahead. I'll follow in a moment."

Chastity wondered frantically what he was up to, but now wasn't the moment to debate the matter. She steered Verity out to the waiting coach. From within, she watched anxiously for Cyn's appearance.

She ducked back when she saw Henry Vernham stalking toward the inn. Through the edge of the window, she saw Cyn emerge and wanted to scream a warning. He stopped. Vernham stopped.

Cyn did a perfect play of a terrified, guilty female. He shrank back, half-covered his face with the paper in his hands, then scuttled past Vernham and into the coach. Vernham sneered after him and continued into the inn.

Cyn took his seat, an ostler slammed the door, Hoskins cracked his whip, and the coach pulled out into the high street.

Verity was pressed into the corner, clutching William far too tightly. "Did he see me?"

"Of course not," said Cyn, tossing the crumpled paper onto Chastity's seat. "'And we're away now."

"But he'll pursue us!"

"Why? He thinks he saw Charles, and that makes him think you're in the area. He'll inquire of every inn in Salisbury and find no Charles, and no one to fit your description."

"But," said Chastity, "what if he thinks to inquire about babies?"

"Good point," said Cyn with a sharply appreciative look. "With that tack he'll soon find that the naughty lady of the meadows had a babe the right age. He just might put the pieces together." He looked at Verity. "How clever is this man?"

She bit her lip. "He's no fool. He's a self-centered wastrel, but he has a shrewd brain when he cares to use it."

Cyn opened the hatch. "Spring 'em, Hoskins." The carriage bumped and rolled as the team went into a gallop.

Verity was white as a sheet. "We can't possibly escape! If they catch us, Lord Cyn, *promise* you'll do all in your power to get William away."

"Of course we can escape," he said firmly, "but I promise nothing will happen to your child." He put a hand over Verity's and looked into her eyes. "Trust me."

Chastity felt a pain in her chest, a real physical pain. If only Cyn would look at her as directly and promise to keep her safe. Oh, she was in a sorry state.

She remembered him describing his trade as an officer responsible for the lives of many men; she saw he would be good at it. He would be lighthearted in season, keeping spirits high, but underneath there would always be the steel of courage and efficiency.

She reminded herself of her resolve, but the awareness of her love was too new, and she found herself staring at him, drinking in every detail . . .

She wrenched her eyes away. They focused on the paper he'd tossed on the seat beside her. Her heart thudded. He had stopped to purchase an up-to-date copy of the *Gazette*. The front page was crushed back and she could see the headline of an item. BARONET'S WIDOW AND HEIR MISSING.

Oh, sweet heavens.

The names would be disguised in the usual way, . . . *widow of Sir W***m V****m, of Gloucestershire* . . . , but everyone who was anyone would know. Would the paper hint at past scandals in the family? More than likely, she thought with a shudder. What news-sheet could resist such a juicy *on dit*?

Cyn hadn't linked the Earl of Walgrave with Chastity Ware, she reasoned. He had been sick when the full torrent of Chastity's scandal had burst. He must have heard something, however, during his months in England. Let the name Ware enter into things and he must surely make the connection.

The gossipmongers and the caricaturists had quickly made the link between Chastity Ware and Haymarket ware, or whores. And what fun they had had with her Christian name! As soon as Cyn read the paper, he would know all. He would despise her—or, even worse, he would consider her fair game.

The newspaper assumed the nature of a cocked pistol, ready to be triggered by the next bump in the road. She tried desperately to think of a plausible excuse to throw it out the window . . .

"Charles!"

She jumped at Cyn's sharp voice and guessed he had been trying to gain her attention.

"Yes?"

"Pull yourself together. It's understandable for Verity to be a little overset, but I expect you to be made of sterner stuff. We are making plans."

At least that meant he wasn't reading the paper. Chastity assumed her apparent maleness like armor. "Good," she said crisply. "What are we to do?"

Cyn eyed her keenly for a moment, then nodded. "It is my assessment that even if Vernham does pursue us, he won't catch us till late afternoon. He'll have to stop and check each inn in case we've halted, and that will slow him. We can relax and make plans."

"But what if he alerts others, such as the military?"

"That is a danger, though even that sort of pursuit should be considerably delayed. I'm sure we have a good head start, but if Vernham does become suspicious we cannot possibly make Maidenhead without being caught. If we try to stop for the night on this road, he will come up with us, and these moonless nights are too dark for traveling."

"So what are we to do?" asked Verity with a calm which spoke volumes for Cyn Malloren's ability to inspire trust.

"I suggest we leave the London road and go to Winchester."

The sisters shared a look of astonishment.

"Winchester?" echoed Verity. "Why?"

He settled back. "Because no one will expect you to head in that direction, and I have a friend there who will shelter you. Inns are too chancy with the hunt so widespread."

"True," said Verity, "but if Henry guesses we are his quarry, he'll still be able to track us, stage by stage."

A little smile played on Cyn's lips. "Yes, but he'll be looking for an older lady, a youth, and a maid with a baby. He may suspect that Charles is Adrian, but it's less likely he'll realize I am male. Therefore, I propose that we transform ourselves into a new party."

Chastity's imagination was caught. Faith, but he was a cunning rogue. "What kind of party?"

"A military gentleman traveling with his wife."

"I am to be your wife?" asked Chastity, a traitorous thrill in her heart at the thought.

Cyn raised his brows. "You, sir? Why complicate matters like that?"

Chastity remembered the deception with a bump.

"Verity can play that role," he continued. "We are not, after all, trying to hide her from those who know her, just obscure the trail. We will also get rid of the baby."

"What?" Chastity and Verity cried in unison.

"Not really," he said with a grin. "But if Sir William will cooperate, we'll put him in my portmanteau when we're in public. If not, I'm sure it will surprise no one that a military man and his wife should have a child."

"And what of me?" asked Chastity, ridiculously hurt at the image of this happy family which excluded her.

"I suppose you should once more be the groom. The flat-brimmed hat is very concealing."

"I am to ride on the box?"

Cyn frowned. "No. Not just because of Hoskins' hostility, but because you would be very visible up there."

Verity frowned. "But I don't see how this will get me to Nathaniel. I won't give up my purpose, my lord."

"Of course not, but it's clear now that the London roads and Maidenhead are the center of the search. If the search is as thorough as it appears, I'm not at all sure we could get you close to your major in any disguise. I'll visit Frazer and tell him the tale, then he will join you in Winchester."

Verity laughed. "It's wonderful. I really think it will work!"

"Of course it will," he said with superb self-confidence. "So, I will assume my uniform—with great relief, I assure you. You will don my other female outfit and be my wife, and Charles will become the groom. We will leave unexplained your presence inside the coach, Charles."

Chastity had been thinking over this ingenious plan and had spotted a flaw. "But how are we to effect this change with no one the wiser? If one party enters an inn and another emerges, someone will be bound to notice."

Cyn's eyebrows rose. "My dear Charles, with such a head for detail you should consider a career as a quartermaster. And we can't stop the coach," he mused, "and change by the roadside, for the postilions would see all . . ."

"We'll have to do it in the coach," said Chastity slowly, her mind working out the details. "At the next stage we'll pull out the necessary boxes from the boot. That will arouse no suspicion. We will pull down the blinds and all contrive somehow to transform ourselves over the next ten miles. We'll keep the blinds down when we change horses, while Hoskins gives the new postilions to understand that his passengers are a military man with his family. Soon the blinds will go up and there we'll be!"

Cyn laughed. "Brilliant! The naughty lady and her Adrian, along with their suspect maid and baby, will have fallen off the edge of the earth. With the amount of traffic on this road I doubt Horrible Henry will ever sort it out, but with luck he'll spend days trying. I salute you, young Charles, indeed I do. If you have any interest in a military career, I'll find a place for you in my command any day."

It was ridiculous, thought Chastity, to feel so warm a glow at such a singularly pointless offer. It only slowly dawned on her that there was a flaw in her plan. It would require her to change clothes in front of Cyn in the intimate confines of the coach.

She shrugged. She would simply put the groom's clothes on over her brother's. It would have the added advantage of making her appear bulkier.

Now that the planning was over, her attention focused again on the *Gazette*. The newspaper lay on the empty seat beside her, and she was tempted to slide over and sit on it, but that would draw Cyn's attention. For the moment, he seemed to have forgotten it.

They drew into the inn at Norton and put their plan into operation. Cyn explained it to Hoskins, but it had to be Chastity who helped the man pull the bags out of the boot.

The coachman glared at her. "I don't know what your game is, young fellow-me-lad," Hoskins muttered, "but if you get Master Cyn into 'ot water, I'll wring your bloody neck."

"What makes you think I'm in charge?" Chastity retorted. "He's in command now."

"But if you 'adn't embroiled him in your tricks, he'd be safe at the Abbey now."

"He's not a baby."

"No, but he near cocked up his toes this summer, and if he has a relapse, you'll have all the Mallorens on your back. Not to say the marquess won't already've raised the 'unt up for him."

They found Cyn's portmanteau, and the box containing other clothing, and tossed them into the carriage. Hoskins gave her a final malignant warning look before climbing back up onto his box.

Chastity settled back in the coach, unsure what to worry about first—Cyn's health, the paper, or the fact that the formidable Marquess of Rothgar had likely joined the hunt. It was only as they rolled away from the inn that she realized she'd forgotten to get rid of the dratted *Gazette*.

"Hoskins says Rothgar will be on your trail," she said.

Cyn flashed her an unreadable look and took off his bonnet and cap. "He may not even know I've flown the coop."

"You make it sound as if he keeps you in chains."

"Bonds of affection can be as strong as bars."

Chastity sensed she was stepping on delicate ground, but she persisted. "I would have thought it would be no bad thing to be caught by the marquess. His power could be an asset."

"If one could be sure which side he'd be on."

That gave Chastity pause. To have Rothgar against them would be truly disastrous.

"We had best get on with it," Verity interrupted firmly. "Draw down the shades, Chas, and take William."

Chastity obeyed, then in the shadowy coach her sister helped Cyn with the infamous laces. Chastity smiled at the memory of their earlier adventure with the gown—a memory she would treasure . . .

She hastily concentrated on the babe. He was awake and happy to play. She gave him the newspaper, hoping he would gum it to a pulp, or shred it, but he despised such dull stuff. His eye was caught instead by Cyn's scabbarded sword in the corner. Chastity picked it up and let him play with the bright ribbons and gilded hilt.

Cyn glanced over. "Don't let him touch the blade." The fact that William was gumming the ribbons didn't seem to bother him at all. Truly, his very carelessness entranced her. He'd be a wonderful father . . .

Stop it, Chastity.

Cyn soon shed his dress, shift, and stockings—which items raised a giggle from Verity—right down to his drawers. Chastity hadn't considered this additional hazard to the changing arrangements—that it would have *him* changing in front of *her.*

Chastity found herself studying Cyn's legs and torso, and hastily averted her eyes. He pulled out his uniform and began to struggle into his white breeches. It necessitated thrusting first one bare leg then the other right by Chastity; there was no other way. She hastily passed William back to Verity before he was kicked.

She then wriggled to the side—almost incidentally ending up on top of the newspaper—but she couldn't get far from his legs. The sight of the hard muscles dusted with golden hair dried her mouth.

He bent his knee a little to reach the cuff and pull it over his heel. Verity squeaked as his elbow jabbed her.

"Hell, I'm sorry. This is a lot harder than I thought. Charles, work the thing over my heel, will you?"

Chastity gulped but obeyed. It necessitated grasping first his calf and then his warm, naked foot, which didn't do her thundering heart any good at all. She had always ignored feet, but now here was a fine specimen in her hands. She was assailed by the strangest desire to kiss his instep.

Now his other foot appeared for her attention. She pushed his breeches over that heel, too, sighing with relief to have the task done.

He half rose and wriggled the garment up to his waist. "Thank you. Perhaps you could help with the stockings, too."

Chastity looked up sharply to see him holding out white silk stockings. Red-faced with embarrassment, she eased the hose onto his long elegant toes, over his arched instep, and up his hard calf.

"Smooth them out a bit," he said rather gruffly.

Chastity flashed him a look, but he appeared fully involved with his shirt. She threw caution to the winds. How many more opportunities would she have to touch his body as she wished to? She kept her eyes lowered as she ran her hands up his calves, smoothing out every wrinkle, slowly and meticulously. Then she repeated the act on his other leg.

Her heartbeat was not fast anymore. It pounded in a deep way which made her dizzy. A heavy warmth pressed on her lower abdomen . . .

After a moment she realized it was coming from his right foot which rested low on her stomach as she attended to his left. His heel nestled snugly at the juncture of her thighs. A part of her very close to that heel throbbed like a wound, and she had an almost overwhelming urge to spread her thighs and push against him.

She tightened instead and moved his foot away. "There," she said.

"Thank you," he drawled, and tied his own garters. "I assure you, dear Charles, I'll happily do as much for you one day." He tucked in his shirt. "Ah, that feels better. Feel as if I've regained the use of my legs." He shrugged into the long, white waistcoat, fastened the eight silver buttons, then tied the scarlet sash.

Next he pulled out his regimental coat. It was a fine sight—scarlet with buff facings, glittering with gold braid on cuffs, pockets, and buttonholes down both sides. It took a fair amount of contortions, and a few muttered curses, but eventually he had the trim-fitting garment on. Now he looked a soldier in truth.

He tied a black stock around his collar and hung the silver gorget of rank around his neck. He smiled. "I must say, I feel more myself than I have in an age. I think I'll leave off the boots, however, until we stop. I'll probably kick one of you in the face if I attempt to put them on now." He opened his dressing-case and used a small container of water to scrub off his rouge. Then he took out a comb, mirror, and ribbon.

He passed the mirror to Chastity. "Hold that, dear boy, while I struggle with my hair."

Chastity watched as he combed his tawny curls and tied them neatly enough at his nape. She had always scoffed at young ladies who were *aux anges* at the sight of a scarlet coat, but now she felt the affliction. Captain Cyn Malloren looked magnificent in his regimentals. But then, to her he would look magnificent in anything.

Now, however, he had lost that illusion of softness. He looked authoritative, capable of handling any emergency, and ready for dangerous heroics. Chastity was reminded all too keenly that he was a soldier, and that dangerous heroics were his business. With the emphasis on dangerous. What had he said? "Blood is the god of war's rich livery . . ."

They would part in a day or two. He would soon forget a prickly youth called Charles, would never even know she was a woman, a woman who ... who felt warmly toward him.

She, on the other hand, would never forget him. For the rest of her life she would study the army news, hoping for word of him. She would scrutinize casualty lists in fear that his name would one day appear, a bleak acknowledgment that the laughter had been cruelly stilled ...

His voice jerked her out of her brown study. "Now," he said, "let's transform Verity."

"You are having nothing to do with it," said Chastity. " 'Twould be indecent."

His lips twitched. "I don't think your sister is as sensitive in these matters as you, sir."

"I—"

"Pax!" called Verity in amusement. "I will be stripping no further than my shift, and though that is rather risqué, I am quite able to handle the matter. However, I think Lord Cyn should hold William." She passed over the baby, who was immediately entranced by the gold braid. "I don't think he's likely to leak all over your magnificence, my lord, but I make no guarantee."

Cyn did not appear dismayed. "I've always held there's something suspicious about a pristine uniform. Rothgar thought my war-weary gear beneath the dignity of a Malloren—particularly as it had been chopped-about in the cause of practicality in the backwoods. He insisted on ordering this for me just weeks ago. It needs breaking in or I'll be taken for a Johnny Newcome."

Without apparent embarrassment, Verity worked her way out of her coarse servant's garments, and into Cyn's other outfit—the gray petticoat, the blue-and-black stomacher, and the Prussian-blue sacque. She knelt so Chastity could tie the stomacher laces, but managed the loose gown by herself.

Verity's ample bosom filled this bodice without assistance. Cyn stuffed the wool into his portmanteau.

Nothing could be done with Verity's greasy hair other than to comb it into a tight knot. With the cap and bonnet she looked genteel, but severe. That very severity disguised her, but it would not fool a relative.

"Keep out of sight," Cyn advised, "and when in public, keep your head lowered. Remember, people are looking for a fugitive, not a respectable matron, and people generally see what they expect to see." He looked at Chastity. "Now you, young Charles."

Chastity shrugged out of her velvet coat and pulled on the breeches and shirt over her brother's clothes. She took off her cravat and knotted the spotted kerchief around her neck in its stead. She pulled the flat-brimmed hat firmly down over her wig. "There," she said.

His smile was wry. "One of these days your modesty is going to land you in trouble, Charles my lad."

Chastity engaged herself in stuffing all the discarded clothes into the box.

Silence fell, and the shadowy coach became disconcertingly intimate. The babe grew sleepy in Cyn's arms. Both of them seemed remarkably at ease with the situation.

Chastity leaned back in her seat, pretending to be resting, but really studying Cyn Malloren through her lashes. Her relatively short lashes. She resented his lush lashes, but lusted after them for her children.

Stop it, Chastity.

It was no good. Her eyes insisted on drinking in the sight of Cyn and storing it away for the bleak future. His head was turned slightly away, so she could safely run her gaze along the firm line of his profile. To her surprise, she detected a resemblance to Rothgar. In ten or more years would Cyn be as intimidating? She doubted it. She didn't think Rothgar had ever had the reckless devil-may-care side to him which was Cyn's most marked feature, and one she loved.

His hands were beautiful, made more so by the gentle way they cradled the babe. How had she not noticed their quality before? They were long-fingered, and capable of strength or gentleness. She remembered them stroking her head and neck in that strange kiss, and wanted to be touched by them again. Even at the thought, a shiver of desire passed through her.

Cyn could feel Chastity's eyes on him like a heated touch. A few stolen glances had shown her studying him like an artist working on a portrait. He wished he had the same indulgence, but there would be other times, and he was pleased enough to have her so intent on him.

At least, part of him was pleased—his wicked part. It gleefully anticipated the time when they would have opportunity to explore each other fully.

His noble side bellowed that he must tell her he knew her to be female, so she would recover her maidenly modesty.

Except, of course, she wasn't a maiden.

He'd suspected from the first that she was not cold, or barred off from sensuality. Now he knew it to be true. A few moments ago her touch on his legs had been a lover's touch, and he'd been hard-pressed to maintain control. If it hadn't been for Verity he feared he'd have pulled his damsel into his arms for a ravishing kiss, and very likely more.

The coach passed through the next change without a problem, and Cyn and Verity stepped down for a moment to give everyone a clear sight of the captain and his lady. No one questioned them, but Chastity detected one lounging man whose eyes seemed markedly sharp. He did not look suspicious, however.

When they rolled on, she said, "Did you see . . . ?"

"Yes," said Cyn soberly. "It could be nothing, and I'd thought we'd lose the hunt by turning south. One thing's clear. We can't risk stopping on the road. We'd never conceal the presence of a baby at an inn."

"But the light's already fading," said Verity, pallid with fear and exhaustion.

"We'll manage with the coach-lights," said Cyn. "It's not far now. We have to press on. In Winchester we will be a few among thousands, and we have a private place to stay. On the road we'll stick out wherever we stop."

He was remarkably sober for Cyn Malloren. Chastity knew he shared her concern at the tightness of the net thrown over the south of England. It was not so much a search for a missing person, as a hunt for a fugitive. Her father's work, she was sure.

The baby woke and had to be fed, which distracted Verity from her fears. Chastity wished there was something reassuring she could say to her sister, who was afraid her child's life was in jeopardy. Nothing came to mind except that they were doing their best, and had a fighting chance. Largely thanks to Cyn. Without him, they would doubtless have been caught hours ago.

Cyn pondered the intense search and knew there was more to this escapade than appeared on the surface. He studied the sisters, wondering which was lying, and about what, and why.

After a loud, squishy rumble, it became obvious William needed his cloth changed. Very obvious. They had previously stopped to allow Verity to do this in the open air. Now, however, time was pressing and they did not want the postilions to know they had a baby here, so she accomplished the messy business in the coach with the windows open. The smell was surprisingly cheesy, but very strong. Unfortunately, Verity had only one small bottle of water with which to clean the child.

All in all, Cyn thought, trying hard not to pull a face like an affronted dowager, babies were not a romantic business. A man would have to be mad even to consider having a family while following the drum.

When she'd finished, Verity looked at the soiled rags. "The coach is going to stink of this," she said apologetically.

"Throw them out the window," Cyn suggested. "The post-boys will never notice."

When he saw the tentative way she prepared to do it, he sighed. "Give it to me." Why was it, he wondered, that nothing he'd encountered in war seemed quite as revolting as this squishy, pungent bundle? He took aim and hurled it over the passing hedge, and into the field beyond. Then he wished he had the means of washing his hands.

"If we want him to sleep later," Verity said, "we had best play with him now."

She sang songs and clapped William's hands in time to the tune. She bounced him gently on her knee. She laid him on his back and played 'This Little Piggy' with his goes. William chuckled and gurgled in the most obliging way. Cyn's enthusiasm for the continuation of the species revived. He glanced at his damsel. She watched the play with a totally feminine, maternal smile. She'd be a good mother.

Something tightened inside him.

He emphatically did not want her to have children with any man except himself. Plague take it. How had he fallen into this mess?

He tried out a few phrases in his mind. *My dear Lady* . . . what? Charlotte? If her name was Charlotte he'd forbid her ever to use it again. *My dear Lady Charles, I am deeply, wantonly attracted to the notion of marrying you and carrying you off to the war. I'm afraid a lot of your time will be spent away from me in billets in a foreign land—I do hope you are quick to learn foreign languages and customs—but I will come to you as often as the fighting allows. Of course you could stay with the regiment if you don't mind fleas, and mud, and the never-ending duty of tending wounds and sickness* . . .

He sighed. Her enthusiasm would be overwhelming.

He could sell out. Rothgar was pushing for it because of those stupid doctors, but Cyn had no desire to settle to a peaceful life. He would miss the camaraderie, the purpose, the challenge, the excitement, and the foreign lands. Lazing around London or growing turnips in the country would bore him to death, and doubtless lead him into mischief.

After all, boredom had embroiled him in this adventure.

His damsel laughed at the babe, her face reflecting the child's glowing delight. There was nothing cold or hard in her at all.

Plague take it.

Cyn sought distraction and saw the crumpled paper. The light was going, and so he made a flame and lit one of the candle-sconces. Then he reached over and picked up the *Gazette,* turning to the news of the war.

The Americans remained quiet and it seemed French power there was crushed. There appeared to be unrest in the colonies about new taxes designed to pay for their recent defense. That would soon fade. Most of the news concerned the scandalous Czarina Catherine of Russia, and the Prussian advance against Austria. Perhaps he would end up posted to Hanover or some such place. After the unpredictable wilderness of the New World, he feared it would be tame.

Having finished the military news, he looked up at the women. "Would you like me to read some items to you?"

"Yes, please," said Verity.

"No!" exclaimed Charles.

Interesting, thought Cyn. Again, she jibbed at a newssheet. What on earth could she have done to attract the interest of the press? He began to read aloud. He read a piece about the turmoil in Russia, and another about improvements in iron-casting, but all the time he scanned the pages for anything related to his damsel.

He found it.

He skipped over the crucial item to read about a fire in

Dover, and the trial of a sensational murderer who had apparently poisoned half his family before being caught. But he read slowly and managed to glean the other story at the same time.

It concerned Verity's disappearance, not Charles, and did not conflict with the story they had told. What then was the problem?

According to the paper, there was widespread concern as to the fate of the widow and child of Sir W****m V****m. It was feared that Lady V****y V****m had lost her wits because of the death of her husband and her recent confinement, which had by great good fortune produced an heir for the deceased nobleman. Both her father and her husband's family were offering a handsome reward for information which would return the afflicted lady to their loving care.

The rest of the item was genealogical.

Lady V*****y had been, before her marriage, Lady V***** W***, daughter of the Earl of W****e, and sister to Lady C*****y W*** . . .

Cyn stopped reading. Finally his memory had been triggered, and he could fill in all the missing letters.

His damsel's name was Chastity Ware.

The Notorious Chastity Ware.

Chapter 8

Cyn quickly began to read again—picking an item at random and landing on a dry essay about Weiman's translation of Shakespeare into German. He doubted he was making sense of it, for the greater part of his mind struggled to absorb his discovery. The piece ended, and he offered the paper to the sisters. They both declined, and so he laid it aside. He noted relief on his damsel's face.

On Chastity Ware's face.

It would take time for him to be at ease with that name instead of Charles, but despite her reputation, it suited her. What, though, should he make of her reputation?

He remembered Henry Vernham saying Walgrave had shaved her head after he had found her in a man's bed. It all fit, but only after a fashion. It did not fit with what he knew of her. He could not believe his damsel to be a shameless hussy who went from bed to bed.

And yet that was what the world believed.

When he'd been ill his brother Brand had come down from London with a selection of amusements, including the latest cartoons. There had been a number which addressed the gossip about Lord Bute and the new king's mother. There'd been related ones about greedy Scots sucking England dry while still flirting with the Stuarts. There had been a very funny bawdy one about the deposed

Tsar of Russia and his wife, Catherine, whom rumor said he had never bedded, though everyone else had.

And there had been one about the grand scandal of the summer, Lady Chastity Ware.

He supposed the Earl of Walgrave, the Incorruptible, had enemies who had been pleased to strike at him through his daughter. He had been shown—ugly and bloated—staggering back from a bed in which his buxom daughter lay cheerfully naked under a salivating lover, saying, *"No, Father, I won't wed him, I just want to f**k him."*

He flicked a look at the pristine features of the young woman opposite. They bore no resemblance to the blowsy female of the caricature. Probably the illustrator had never seen her, and cared nothing about her as an individual. It was just a bit of titillation for the masses, and a low blow at the powerful earl.

He knew there would have been any number of caricatures on the subject, posted in the windows for all to see, available for a penny plain, twopence colored, and passed from hand to grubby hand as a source of amusement.

Had she ever seen any? He hoped to God not.

Cyn had heard the story in lascivious detail from Brand. Apparently she'd been forbidden to attend Walgrave's rout because of some misdemeanor—gossip said some earlier bawdiness. Tenderhearted Lady Trelyn, Society's darling, had pleaded her case so well that Lord Walgrave and a group of guests had gone up to his daughter's room to liberate her.

There they had found her, as Vernham had said, *in flagrante delicto*. With so many people as witnesses, there had been no question of hushing it up, though her father had tried. The scandal could have been passed off if she had agreed to a hasty marriage, for most there would have kept the story to themselves, and there would only ever have been rumors. Lady Chastity, however, had absolutely refused to marry the man. She had, of course, been immediately ostracized, not so much for sinning as for not following the rules when caught.

Lord and Lady Trelyn—known for their irreproachable character—had supported her the longest, and refused to confirm the story, but in the end they too had done so, expressing great commiseration for the anguished father.

Another fragment of recollection. The lover had been her brother-in-law, Henry Vernham! His damsel had thrown away all caution for a man like *that*? The only explanation was the kind of fevered, unreasoning lust that rode some women, but he'd seen no sign of that in Chastity Ware.

Cyn glanced at her again. He wouldn't have thought her wanton. He certainly wouldn't have thought her stupid. If she'd played that game and been caught, the only sensible thing was to marry the man. Such a female would not find marriage too rigid a confinement.

And yet he could not think her such a female. His head throbbed with contradictions and suspicions.

Another memory. Rothgar had been displeased with the caricature, and it had disappeared, probably into the nearest fire. Rothgar and Chastity Ware would have met before the debacle. Perhaps Rothgar realized how little the cartoon related to the reality.

Had Rothgar too been in her bed? Cyn almost groaned aloud. He didn't want these thoughts, but they invaded his brain like maggots.

He could not deny that she'd been involved in something scandalous. In addition to the witness of the Trelyns, Cyn had the evidence of his own eyes and ears that the enraged earl had shaved off his erring daughter's hair and confined her to her old nurse's cottage with only the clothes of a penitent whore to wear.

'Struth, and she'd found a bold way to get around the restrictions! Her brother's clothes, and the appearance of a male. Damned clever, but damningly bold.

He had to admit to some sympathy for the beleaguered

father of Chastity Ware. But only if she was the hussy she as made out to be.

Chastity watched Cyn toss the *Gazette* aside and almost wept with relief. It had been like waiting for an ax to fall waiting for him to read that item. She had steeled herself for the sneer, for the disgust, and it would have been even more unbearable from this officer than from Mrs. Inchcliff.

How strange clothing was. Though it made no sense, she felt that Mrs. Inchcliff might have understood, might have given her the benefit of the doubt, whereas she knew Captain Lord Cynric Malloren would condemn her on the spot.

And, quite simply, her heart would break.

Cyn suddenly leaned forward and rapped on the roof of the carriage. Hoskins pulled up.

"I'm going to sit on the box for a while now that I'm male again," he said to the sisters. "I'll spell Hoskins and explain some of our plan. Anyone seeing us go by will be bound to notice my scarlet coat, which should throw off the hunt." He pulled on his boots, leaped down, and slammed the door.

"Goodness," said Verity, as the coach moved off again. "Isn't it strange? He's become quite a different person since he put on his regimentals."

Chastity too had detected something brusque in his manner. "I'm sure he's a very good officer," she defended.

Already she felt his absence like a gaping void. She had better get used to it. He would soon be out of her life forever. She picked up the paper. "I'm going to hide this before he comes back. I was in agonies, Verity. Look!"

Verity read the piece and bit her lip. "Oh, lud. All England must be on the lookout by now, so I mustn't be seen by anyone who knows me. And of course, they *had* to bring your name into it." She touched Chastity's hand. "I did think it would all blow over."

"It will never blow over." Chastity sighed. "One thing is sure—after all this I will never again accept gossip without question."

Verity shifted the baby in her arms. "It isn't just gossip, dearest, you must accept that. You were seen in bed with Henry, and by a number of people who are beyond reproach. How unfortunate that the Trelyns be there. Their word is unquestionable."

"But I didn't invite Vernham to my bed. I was fast asleep!"

"In the eyes of the world that hardly matters."

Chastity stared at her sister. "Are you saying I *should* have married Vernham?"

Verity sighed. "I really don't know, dearest. I suspect I would have, but then I've always been weaker than you. It's just that I'm beginning to realize how bad your situation is." She cast a glance at her sister. "Partly because of Lord Cyn."

Chastity stiffened. "What, pray, does he have to do with it?"

"Don't deny there's something between you. I can sense it. It's doubtless confusing him since he thinks you male, but as soon as he discovers you are female I think he will be interested. It's a shame nothing can ever come of it."

"There's nothing for anything to come of," said Chastity firmly. "And I have no intention of him ever knowing I am female. I think your wits *are* wandering, Verity."

It was nearly five o'clock and dark when they passed through the north pike into the ancient city of Winchester. The road was quiet since most travelers had already arrived at their destination, but there were still plenty of people about on foot.

Both Verity and Chastity kept out of sight. Cyn raised the hatch and called down, "We're avoiding the fashionable inns and going to the Three Balls. Hoskins assures me that even if Vernham or your father are here, they'd never stay at such a small place, but it's decent enough. Don't grow complacent, though. Remember your parts, and see if you can conceal the baby in the bag."

Chastity held open the portmanteau. Verity put a folded blanket over the unspun wool, then slipped the sleeping babe onto it. He sighed, then settled.

They laid a thin cotton cloth over him and partly closed the bag.

The coach swung sharply. Greetings were called. They peeped out to see they were in the lantern-lit yard of a small inn. It was an ancient place, with a shortage of right angles, and low-hanging eaves. It was charming, but definitely not the kind of establishment to attract the patronage of the high aristocracy.

The coach door swung open and Cyn indicated that they should climb down. Chastity saw that it would be wise to show themselves, to fix the illusion in the minds of the postilions. They left the portmanteau on the floor of the carriage and stepped down. Cyn courteously assisted Verity and ignored Chastity entirely. Chastity wondered wryly if she should go and help with the horses, but feared she'd expose the deception if she tried.

As the postilions unhitched their horses, the plump innkeeper bustled out to attend his patrons. While Cyn chatted to the man, Verity kept her head demurely lowered and stood quietly by his side. Cyn occasionally addressed a remark to her, calling her 'dear,' and touching her with gentle familiarity. Leaning against a wheel, hat down over her eyes, Chastity thought bleakly that they made a lovely couple.

She saw a bored-looked young man pop his head out of the inn door and come to the same conclusion. Did her father have a watcher at every inn in the south? Why? Concern for a missing daughter was one thing, but this was extraordinary. She prayed the baby would not wake.

Cyn paid off the postilions and the men clattered off. Then he arranged to store his carriage for a few days at the inn and to hire a riding horse so he could explore the area. He gave it out that he was in search of a house to lease. He took rooms for himself and his coachman, letting it drop that his wife would be staying with a friend.

It all went off without a hitch.

In no time they were strolling out of the inn yard, Cyn carrying the valise in which the baby still slept soundly.

"All clear. I don't think we'll have any trouble with Mary Garnet," said Cyn cheerfully. "She's always been a game one. Never wanted to leave the Canadas, but when the second child came, Roger insisted she return to England. She and the children are living with her father, a scholarly sort. We'll have to hope he puts up no objection."

It turned out as Cyn had predicted. When they reached the pleasant brick house on a quiet lane, Mary Garnet professed herself only too delighted to have a female guest, and her father seemed equally hospitable. Soon they were all in a snug parlour taking tea.

Mary was a sturdy young woman with apple cheeks and a ready smile. Her two children—an equally sturdy girl of five, and an elfin boy still in skirts—hovered shyly for a while. But then the girl was drawn toward the baby, and the boy toward Cyn's uniform.

"Da's a soldier," he gravely told Cyn.

"I know. I know your father very well. We have great fun together trouncing the king's enemies."

"With swords?"

"Swords and guns. Lots of lovely, noisy things."

The child leaned against his knee, wide-eyed. "You have a big horse?"

"I do indeed." Cyn smiled down. "Do you want to play horsy?"

The boy nodded, and so Cyn hoisted him onto his knees and began the chant.

"This is the way the ladies ride,
Nimble, nimble, nimble;

This is the way the gentlemen ride,
A gallop, a trot, a gallop, a trot;
This is the way the farmers ride,
Jiggety jog, jiggety jog;
And when they come to a hedge .... They jump
over!"

He lifted the squealing lad into the air.

"And when they come to a slippery place ..." The little boy held tight, brimming with expectation. *". . . tumble down Dick!"* Cyn opened his legs and dropped the shrieking child almost to the floor.

"Again! Again!"

Cyn obligingly began the performance all over again.

Chastity watched, an ache in her heart. He liked children as well as babies. He really would make a wonderful father—firm when necessary, but tremendous fun.

Stop it, Chastity.

She saw the little girl, Caroline, eyeing the horseplay enviously, clearly torn between the attractions of the baby in Verity's arms, and the sheer excitement of the game. When Cyn called a pause to catch his breath—more likely to let the little boy calm down before he fizzed over like shaken champagne—Caroline demanded his attention. "We're to have a new baby here too," she said.

Cyn's eyes sparkled as he looked at Mary Garnet. "I do hope that means Roger's had furlough."

The woman shook her head at him. "Of course it does, you rogue. He brought you home, as you well know."

"Brought me home?" asked Cyn blankly.

"Do you not remember? He wondered, though at times you were perfectly coherent, he said."

Cyn shook his head. "I hardly remember the voyage. I have him to thank for saving my life, then."

"Oh, I don't know about that, but he'll be pleased when I write that you are fully recovered. He wanted to visit before he sailed, but was told you were not up to it."

All good humor disappeared from Cyn's face. "The devil you say! I wonder how many other friends my solicitous brother barred the door to."

"Come now, Cyn," Mary said. "You were very ill. Roger said they'd lost hope until Rothgar appeared to take over."

Cyn frowned. "Appeared where? You make him sound like a damn apparition!"

Chastity couldn't believe how curtly he spoke to the wife of the man who had saved his life, but Mary took it in her stride. "Don't you remember that either? That shows how ill you must have been. He appeared at the dock when you arrived. Roger said it was positively eerie him standing there, as if he'd had prior notice."

Cyn's lips twisted slightly, but if it was a smile it lacked humor. "I assure you my brother does not use a crystal ball. Doubtless just accurate and speedy information. So he turned up and pulled me back from the jaws of death, did he? I suppose I should be grovelingly grateful to him. I must remember when next we meet."

Then he flashed a smile, like someone putting spark to tinder, and began to play with the little boy again. In a moment Caroline moved to his side. "It's my turn next," she said firmly.

Cyn finished a round with the boy and looked at the girl. "Are you sure this is suitable for a young lady?"

She nodded. "Papa plays it with me."

Cyn set the boy on his feet. "Perhaps, then. If we leave out 'Tumble down Dick.' "

Caroline frowned. "But that's the best bit, sir! Why should the boys have all the fun?"

Cyn flashed a querying look at Mary, but before she could comment, Caroline said, "It won't be naughty, sir. Look!" and hoisted her muslin skirts to show frilly drawers.

Mary groaned with horror, but Cyn laughed. He

scooped up the girl to begin the game, executing it with even more verve than he had used with her little brother. Soon her pretty beribboned underwear was revealed in all its glory.

Eventually he set the rosy girl on her feet. "There, love. That's all for now. I have business to take care of. But we'll stop by again soon, and you can ride again. I certainly don't see why the boys should have all the fun."

He was leaving. This was the end. Suddenly, Chastity could not bear it. Her noble resolve protested that she must let him go. Her love hungered for every minute they could have together. She'd maintained her disguise thus far. Surely it would be secure for a few more days?

He was heading for the door. Chastity followed him into the hall. "I think I should come with you."

He looked at her strangely. "Why?"

"I can't stay here. This house is too small. I might be recognized. You might need help finding Nathaniel. After all, you don't know him. Besides, you need someone with you. I don't think you realize how ruthless Father can be."

Chastity knew with despair that this was mainly a farrago of nonsense, but the last point was valid. She didn't think Cyn took the Earl of Walgrave seriously enough.

"I admire the thoroughness of your father's search," he said. His tone was pensively unreadable. "But are you sure coming with me would be wise, young Charles?"

Chastity took a deep breath. "Yes."

He nodded. "So be it. Tell Verity."

Chastity gave Verity the same reasons for her to go off alone with Cyn Malloren. Verity's face clouded with concern and she too said, "Are you sure this is wise, dearest?"

"No," said Chastity faintly, "but I can't let him go alone. He doesn't know. He still takes it lightly."

Verity sighed, but she pulled Chastity's hat low down on her head and kissed her. "Godspeed, dearest. Take care." There were tears in her eyes.

Chastity hugged her sister fiercely. "We'll be back soon with Nathaniel, I promise."

Within moments, Chastity was walking with Cyn down the dark street, feeling that she had finally broken with her former life, and was embarked upon a mysterious, and rather frightening, future. But the mystery and fear were centered much more on the man at her side than on their journey.

She glanced at him. "You like children, don't you?"

"Don't you?"

She'd forgotten again that he thought her male; lads weren't expected to be fond of children. One day she would destroy the illusion with a silly mistake, and the terrible thing was that she wanted to. She wanted to be able to face him honestly, woman to man, even if it meant he would find out that she was Chastity Ware.

"I don't know much about children," she said, which was true enough. She'd encountered few, and due to her disgrace, she'd not even met Verity's baby until this hectic visit.

"Nor do I," he said. "I'm the youngest of my family. Perhaps if I had a horde of them underfoot I wouldn't like them so much, but I find them refreshing."

"Yes," Chastity said thoughtfully. "Like a summer breeze, or a fountain on a hot day. You must feel the lack of children on the fields of war."

"I wish I did. The place often seems to be overrun by half-starved imps from hell. I feel sorry for them, but I confess I don't often find them refreshing. And yet they are no different in the essentials from Mary's darlings, or that boy there sweeping the crossing."

Chastity looked at the urchin. He had a post by a flambeau. If anyone approached, he nipped out to sweep the dust and droppings before his customers crossed, then deftly caught the pennies they tossed. She didn't usually notice such children, hardly thought of them as children at all. The boy was probably about eight—sturdy, grubby, but with a quick, sly look in his eye.

"Is your heart torn?" Cyn asked dryly.

She saw the boy inspect a coin tossed by a prosperous cleric and make a rude gesture at his back. "No. But I don't much care for that parson either."

"The word's full of children," said Cyn, and led the way to cross where the boy worked.

"Doing well?" he asked the boy as they went by.

The urchin joined them at the roadside, waiting for his fee. "Fair to middlin', Captain."

Cyn tossed him a coin. "That for knowing your insignia, or being a lucky guesser."

The boy grinned at the sixpence. "God bless you, milord!"

Cyn laughed and threw him another. "Right on both counts."

He and Chastity left the boy calling out ecstatic thanks.

"It's so tempting to do that kind of thing," Cyn said. "And so easy. But is it noble generosity, or just an economical way of feeling like God?"

Chastity shrugged. "I don't suppose it matters to the child. He'll eat well tonight."

"He didn't look particularly malnourished to me. He'll likely spend it on gin."

Chastity wondered if he jested, but feared he didn't.

She thought they were going straight back to the inn, but he stopped and knocked on a door. The sign said the establishment was Darby's Bank.

"What are you doing?" she asked.

"Knocking," he said, rapping again.

"It's closed."

"There are people within." He knocked a third time.

Lud, thought Chastity, does he think the nobility can get away with anything?

An angry clerk swung open the door, and began to tell

him to begone. Cyn merely said, "Lord Cynric Malloren. Is Darby about?"

In seconds they were inside, with everyone in sight groveling. An eminent person, tall and silver-haired, came to bow and scrape Cyn into an inner sanctum. Doubtless Mr. Darby himself. Obviously the nobility *could* get away with anything, the male nobility at least.

Chastity propped up a wall, and enjoyed the dirty looks she got from the clerks for this behavior. They soon bowed down over columns of figures again, however, doubtless anxious to finish and be off home for the day.

In a little while Cyn was bowed and scraped out again. He collected Chastity and headed on to the Three Balls. He radiated ill humor.

"What's the matter?" asked Chastity mischievously. "Wouldn't they give you any money?"

"They'd have given me the bloody keys to the vault," he said curtly. "Sometimes I hate being a Malloren."

"But you used it to get in there."

He looked at her coldly. "In your cause."

Chastity felt abashed. "Yes, of course. I'm sorry."

He sighed. "I shouldn't take my ill humor out on you."

"How is it they know your name?"

"Know my name! Hell, old Darby dandled me on his knee. The Abbey's not twenty miles from here and my damned brother's on the board."

Chastity had a number of questions but knew from his tone that silence would be wiser. The questions plagued her all the same.

Why was it that every time his brother's name came up Cyn Malloren lost his lightheartedness? If the Abbey was so close, wouldn't it have been simpler to take refuge there? Even the Earl of Walgrave wouldn't try to ride roughshod over Rothgar. Did Cyn really think his brother would hand them over to their father?

They arrived back at the inn with these questions un-asked and unanswered, but Chastity resolved to seek some answers before they parted. This rift with his brother seemed to be the only cloud in Cyn Malloren's life, and being in love, she would do what she could to lift it.

The innkeeper was dealing with the young man who had scrutinized their arrival. Mine host smiled and bowed, but as soon as the man left he spat into the hall fireplace. "Bloodhounds. Nothing but trouble."

"On the hunt?" queried Cyn. "What villain is loose?"

"Oh, no villain, milord. Just some poor young woman lost her wits and wandering. But that one's been hanging about all day. Don't they think I'd tell 'em if she came here? Apart from the reward, it'd be a kindness, wouldn't it? Now, sir, your room is ready and a tasty dinner will be on the table shortly. I assure you my wife is a fine cook."

He led the way toward the stairs.

"I have decided to keep my groom with me," said Cyn. "You have a room for him?"

The innkeeper nodded. "There's space above the stables with your coachman, milord."

Cyn flashed Chastity a guarded look, "I prefer that he sleeps close to me. He also serves as my valet when I need one."

"Oh, right, sir. There's a truckle under the bed."

Again a meaningful look. Chastity kept her face as blank as her mind. She hadn't considered this possibility.

"I would prefer separate rooms," said Cyn. "He snores."

"Lord, sir," said the innkeeper in some distress, "I don't have another room. This ain't a big place, and I just have the three, all taken. It'll have to be the truckle or the stables."

Cyn looked at Chastity as if giving her an opportunity to choose. Her brain had gone numb, however. She knew she should do anything to avoid sleeping in the same room as a man, especially this man . . .

Cyn turned back to the innkeeper and said, "No, I'll take the lesser of the evils. He can use the truckle. And provide an extra plate. Charles may as well eat with me."

Within moments they were in a small room made smaller by the sloping of the roof. "Do try not to snore, young Charles," drawled Cyn, "for if you wake me I promise to wake you in turn."

Chastity looked around the cramped room and knew a wiser woman would have avoided this, but she couldn't regret her folly. For all its limited space, it was a lovely chamber warmed by a well-built fire. The solid bed was made up with crisp, clean sheets. No speck of dust marred the mellow furniture, or the polished oak floor. A vase of dried flowers sat on a small table before the window, and potpourri scented the air. A washstand was set behind a screen in one corner, and a table was ready for the meal.

Once the truckle bed was pulled out the floor space would be almost gone, but otherwise it was charming. Chastity found herself imagining what it would be like if this were her wedding night, this her bridal chamber. It would be lovely. Perfect.

But if Lady Chastity Ware had just married Lord Cynric Malloren, they would be somewhere much grander. Here they were just master and groom, and she must keep it that way.

The innkeeper and a maid came in with the meal. Cyn said that they would serve themselves, and soon he and Chastity were settled before a princely repast. They had soup, sole, a pork pie, and a chicken. To complete the meal, there was cheese and apple tarts. Chastity ate for something to do, and found she was genuinely hungry.

After an interval Cyn said, "The innkeeper is correct. His wife is an excellent cook."

"Yes, indeed. And the whole inn seems well kept."

"A gem, in fact. Perhaps I should mention it to Rothgar. He can bring it into fashion."

Chastity chewed a mouthful of tender chicken. "Why does your voice have such an edge when you speak of Rothgar? Rumor says he is a devoted brother."

She thought he would give her a sharp set-down, but he merely said flatly, "He is an extremely devoted brother."

"Then why do you speak as if you hate him?"

His look was as piercing as a blade. "You're an impudent stripling. I do not hate my brother."

Chastity gathered another piece of meat onto her fork. "But you are angry with him."

He dropped his knife and fork on his plate, and for a moment she thought he would lay hands on her. He grasped his wineglass instead and took a deep draft of the burgundy. "I am at odds with him because he does not want me to return to my regiment. It's typical of his bloody interference, but I am no longer a child. It is merely a matter of persuading him that I am healthy."

Chastity also abandoned eating in favor of wine. Her nerves were on edge, but she felt it important to continue the conversation in order to help him. "I can understand that he might be anxious if you were as sick as Mrs. Garnet says."

He shrugged. "I suppose I was. I have very little recollection. But I am perfectly well now. Soldiering is my life, and he will not keep me from it."

Chastity felt a great deal of sympathy for the Marquess of Rothgar. She too would keep Cyn safe at home if she could, but she knew he was not a tame spirit able to settle to farming, preaching, or the law. "Surely he has no power to keep you from the army if you are determined."

He gave a sharp laugh. "You don't know Rothgar. With his combination of wealth, charm, and ruthlessness there are few in England willing to cross him. As long as he tells the Horseguards I am unfit, all I can hope for is an ornamental position well away from action. I'll not settle for that."

"If he's as concerned as you say, he'll be after you."

He refilled their glasses. "I'm hoping the fact Hoskins is with me will allay his fears, but you're doubtless right, damn him."

"Horrible Henry, his henchmen, Father, and Rothgar. I'm amazed we're still on the loose."

He suddenly grinned and raised his glass. "But we are, and I intend to keep it that way. Don't worry, young Charles. We will succeed."

They clinked glasses and drank, then fell to eating again. Chastity, however, was thoughtful. A good part of Cyn's motivation for helping them was wrapped up in his tangled feelings for his brother. What would happen if Rothgar caught up with them?

Cyn began to talk again, this time of military life—the lighter side of military life. His stories filled out her picture of him, but in no way lessened it. He wasn't boastful, but his courage, compassion, and resourcefulness rang through. He made her laugh, and once almost made her cry.

Then he switched to stories of the wonders of the New World, and carried her off to deep forests and magnificent rivers; described strange Indians, and abundant wildlife.

It was dangerous, this intimacy, and Chastity knew it, but she could not resist it. It was deliciously as if they were married and at ease with one another, as if this were in fact their wedding night.

She slid a wanton look at the inviting bed . . .

Stop it, Chastity.

She couldn't. She was entranced by his hands on cutlery and glass, and grew light-headed on their slender, tanned strength. She noticed for the first time a dimple which appeared in his right cheek when he smiled, and the way his eyes changed from green to gold according to his mood.

Her body grew hypersensitive, even to the movement of her own clothes. Everything played on her senses: the tang of apple wood on the fire; the clatter of wheels in the street; raucous singing in the tap-room; Cyn's voice rich and pleasant across the table . . .

He broke off what he was saying. "You're not eating, Charles. Are you finished?"

Chastity looked down at the cutlery in her limp hands, and set it down. "I think so."

"What, no dessert?" he teased, and picked up a tart. "You can't pass on these. They're superb."

He held it in front of her. "Open up."

Chastity looked at the apple tart. It was covered with a glistening, golden glaze, and edged with a frill of rich, yellow cream. She licked her lips, then slowly opened them. He put the tart between her teeth and said, "Bite."

His eyes captured hers over the pastry. She remembered a biscuit in Shaftesbury . . .

She sank her teeth through soft sweet fruit and crisp, crumbly pastry, absorbed the burst of flavor. As she chewed, she licked her lips, and felt the gloss of cream on them. She chewed on dizzily, still captured by his approving gaze. Man to woman, this would be flirtation . . .

No, man to woman, this would be seduction.

Was he trying to seduce *Charles?*

"It's very good," she said nervously.

"Is it?" he asked softly, and turned the tart to bite from the spot where she had bitten. He savored, and swallowed. "Mmm," he murmured. "A work of art." He slowly licked some golden crumbs from his lips. He took another bite, then extended the tart to her with a questioning look.

Chastity thought of Adam and Eve, and apples, and Paradise . . .

She hastily shook her head. She pushed to her feet, turned her back on temptation, and sought the cool of the window. "That was an excellent meal," she said gruffly, "but I'm full."

"There are occasions for sheer wanton indulgence, my dear Charles. This may be one of them." A concerto of meaning attended the simple words.

"That would be wicked."

"And are you never wicked?"

His power over her was not diminished by lack of sight

of him. Her heart pounded. Her nerve endings shivered for a touch. "I try not to be," she said huskily.

Cyn watched her, almost dizzy with desire. When she'd insisted on accompanying him, and blithely agreed to share his room, he'd been sure she was a wanton. He was more than willing to play that game if she wished. Perhaps a brief, lusty episode would rid him of his besotted affliction.

He'd amused himself wondering just when and how she would confess her femininity, and decided to leave the progress in her experienced hands. He'd relaxed too much, however, under the influence of good food and wine and her attentive gaze. The next thing he knew he was baring his soul, then flirting with her in the most blatant way.

And she'd confused him.

He feared his first impressions had been correct. She was an innocent who had made just one disastrous error. Though in that case, what had possessed her to come here with him tonight? Perhaps innocence of truly cataclysmic proportions.

Knowledge of her innocence created a desire in him that was brutal in its need, at the same time as it commanded him not to touch. His hand shook as he reached for his wine.

He studied her over the rim of his glass. He could see through her bulky layers of clothes as if she were naked. He ran his eyes down the pure line of her straight back, the rounded firmness of her buttocks, the shapely length of her legs. He ached to disrobe her slowly, to gently explore every inch of her silky skin, to taste the salt of it and drink in the musky perfume of her most intimate places. He longed to watch that bewildered naivete turn to wonder.

He stood abruptly. "We had best get to bed if we're to be on our way early in the morning. There's a necessary in the yard. I'm off to use it."

Chastity turned to see the door close behind him. She blinked with surprise, but let out a long sigh. She knew they had both just had a narrow escape for which she should be very grateful. She wasn't grateful. She felt raw with need.

She sighed. Perhaps a name was predestination. Verity, after all, could not tell a lie. Perhaps being called Chastity meant she could never be wanton.

She straightened her spine. They had escaped that moment of danger, and she must make sure there would be no more. If she didn't think she could accompany him without shattering her disguise, then she must go to Mary Garnet's now.

She assured herself it would be all right. This would be the last night on the road, for they would make Maidenhead tomorrow.

She hurried behind the screen and used the chamber pot. She quickly shed her outer clothes, keeping on her good-quality shirt and breeches. Then she pulled out the narrow truckle bed and snuggled under the covers, pretending to be fast asleep.

It was a long time before he returned. She began to grow concerned about his safety, but there seemed nothing untoward when he finally appeared. Chastity watched him prepare for bed through slit lids, knowing it to be an intrusion but unrepentant. To her disappointment, he changed and washed behind the screen, emerging in a nightshirt to climb into the bed. She lay listening to his quiet breathing.

She had often slept with Verity, and knew the comfort of a warm body close in the night. She imagined what it would be like to have Cyn's body beside her, brushing against hers, his particular aroma all around her. She tried to block such thoughts. They did no good, and certainly didn't promote sleep . . .

Cyn's sixth sense had told him she was still awake and made him cautious in his preparations for bed. Now, he listened for any sound that would confirm it. He half hoped for, half dreaded, an invitation of some kind. Still keyed up despite the long walk he'd taken, he knew that the slightest encouragement would be enough to overcome all his scruples . . .

Chastity felt the atmosphere of the room press heavily upon her. She was aware of his breathing, his presence so close. She had to stop this before she did something foolish. She imagined herself back in Nana's cottage, helping with the housework, feeding the hens, reading one of the books with which she passed the time. She had discovered accounts of travelers and delighted in them, finding escape in going with them to distant lands . . .

Cyn accepted that there would be no coy gesture, and on the whole was glad of it. He didn't know what would come of this situation, but he wanted more from his damsel than a burst of lust.

Doubtless she was sleeping after all, and so should he. He put his mind to it. During years of campaigning, which often provided unsatisfactory sleeping quarters, he'd developed the ability to bring on sleep regardless.

The room settled into somnolent tranquility.

Chapter 9

❧

Chastity woke to the gray light of an early morning, and the distant clatter of the inn. For a moment she wondered where she was and why she was sleeping in her clothes. Then it all came back.

Verity, Winchester, Cyn . . .

She opened her eyes a crack and looked up at the bed, but from the low pallet she could not see the occupant. She gingerly slid from under her blankets, anxious to be done with her toilet before he awoke. She eased to her stockinged feet . . .

. . . To see Cyn sitting by the window, feet up on the sill, watching her. "I was about to wake you, lad," he said easily. "I've ordered breakfast. We must be on our way."

"Right," said Chastity, and scuttled behind the screen. Did a woman pissing sound different? She hoped not.

She put on her second layer of clothes, her wig, and her hat, and emerged fortified. He looked her over as if he would make a comment, but before he could speak, the innkeeper and a maid bustled in with a hearty breakfast. He shrugged and gestured her to the table.

Adventure must sharpen the appetite. Chastity found she could do a hungry youth's justice to the ham, eggs, kidneys, and fried bread.

"We should reach Maidenhead today, shouldn't we?"

she asked as they both mopped up the last of the food on their plates.

"If all goes well and the weather holds. Let's be on our way."

Within the half hour they were trotting out of Winchester. The hired horses were hardly prime bits of blood, but they were sound enough, and seemed built for endurance. This was as well, for they would have to carry their riders more than thirty miles this day.

The air was sodden and Chastity gave thanks for her double layers of clothing and heavy riding cloak. The sun lurked behind sullen clouds, making no attempt to brighten leafless trees and skeleton hedges that stood stark against dark plowed earth. She hoped the gloomy day was no predictor of their luck.

Cyn, however, was bright-eyed. Did nothing ever cast the man into the blue-devils? "Cheer up," he said. "The day'll be better yet. We'll find Frazer and put an end to Verity's problems. Then we can look to yours."

Chastity jerked on the reins so that the horse jibbed. "What?"

"Have a care. His mouth's doubtless like iron, but that's no reason to rasp it. I can hardly send you back to your cottage-prison without making a push to help. I'm a devoted knight-errant, don't you remember?"

"I'm hardly a damsel in distress."

He looked at her almost seriously. "Still, I'd like to help. What crime caused you to be sent into exile?"

"Disobedience," said Chastity bleakly.

"You have a deuced strict father."

"True enough."

"And how long is your punishment to last?"

Chastity could not bear this. The temptation to pour out her woes to him was too great. She looked at him coolly. "My petty problems are none of your concern, my lord. Let us but settle Verity and I will return to Nana's, and you'll be free of us both."

He accepted it, but she didn't much like the intent look he flashed her before speeding the pace.

A good canter drove the chill from her bones, but did little for the chill in her heart. They were racing toward the end of their association.

She resolutely put past and future out of mind, and set to enjoying these brief hours of Cyn. Laughter bubbled at the sound of that, and she let it out. He grinned at her and she grinned back. The day rapidly improved.

Again he showed his gift for geography. They frequently left the busy road for country bridle paths, heading always northeast toward London, but cutting across the main routes, for Maidenhead lay to the west of the city.

He didn't push the pace, but Chastity gave thanks for the many hours of riding astride she'd put in during her exile, for otherwise she'd never have been able to keep up. As it was, when they halted at midday to feed themselves and the horses, she could swagger into the inn with just the right air.

They ate in the common room, sharing a table with a carter, an elderly medical man, and a pasty-faced clerk. Chastity wondered why Cyn risked eating in public when they could have hired a private room, but she enjoyed the experience. She'd never eaten in such company before. She soon discovered why Cyn had chosen a public room. Gossip.

"Lot of military men about," said the rotund carter, eyeing Cyn's uniform. "French trouble, is it?"

"Not as far as I know," said Cyn. "There's some concern that the current war might encourage the French and Jacobites to try again, but hardly here on the south coast. Ireland more like."

"Troublemakers," said the carter, and spat, though whether he referred to Jacobites or Irish wasn't clear. "Still and all, I've been looked over by patrols all along the London road. Sommat's up."

"I can tell you what," said the pinch-faced doctor, dabbing at his lips with his napkin. "A poor lady is wandering witless. Widow of a gentleman, and that man's heir along with her."

The carter frowned as he masticated a huge mouthful of beef. "A hell of a lot of red-coats for one mort. I've never seen so many, not even during the '45."

"You exaggerate," said the doctor. "We could scarce move without being questioned at that black time. Not that I objected. If I had my way, every Stuart sympathizer in the land would be done to death. It offends me deeply to know that there are still those going free who would have flocked to the banner of Charles Edward Stuart. But now we even have a Scot as the king's right-hand man!"

The clerk interjected at this point to state that his mother was Scots, and that not all Scots were traitors. Soon heated politics became spice for the meal, with the doctor continuing his tirade against Jacobites and Lord Bute.

When the doctor left, the carter spat again. "That man's the sort who'd hand his granny to the hangman and call himself a good man. Especially if there was a farthing in it."

"But it is our duty to oppose treason," remarked Cyn.

The carter eyed his uniform uneasily, but said his piece. "Aye, but opposing treason always brings out those with an ax to grind, and those who like to see others brought low. Many a fortune changes hands in hard times."

"That's true enough," said the clerk sourly. "And some of the gainers no doubt as treasonous as the losers if the truth were told. Take the Campbells, for example." He too rose to his feet and dusted himself off. "You should keep your eye out for the missing lady, though, Captain. I intend to. There's a handsome reward offered, and that wouldn't be blood money, for she'll be the better for being found."

"Aye, that's true enough," said the carter. "But with the hunt so thick up near London, she'd need to be a fairy-woman to be north of here. 'Tis a pity to say, but she'll likely be fished out of a river one day soon, baby and all." He rolled out to assemble his eight-horse rig and continue his long, slow journey into Somerset.

Cyn and Chastity too went to order their mounts. As they waited for their horses, Cyn said, "Did I detect some sympathy in you for the Jacobites? Is your heart touched by Bonnie Prince Charlie and his gallant highlanders? If so, we are on opposite sides."

"No, I'm no Jacobite. But from what I hear the highlanders were brave and true to what they believed. The reprisals were too harsh. So many families ruined, and whenever I drive under Temple Bar and see the heads still rotting there . . ." She shuddered. "As our friend the carter said, there are doubtless many traitors who've avoided detection—the sneaky ones who waited to see which way the wind would blow, while the brave men paid the price."

Cyn mounted. "You're too rosy-eyed, lad. A good many Jacobites just hoped to be on the winning side. The sorry truth is that most men are out to gain from what they do."

As she checked the girth and swung into her saddle, Chastity said, "Even knights-errant?"

Cyn gave her a hooded look. "Even them."

As they cut north over the Exeter road the sky clouded over again in a way that threatened a downpour. Dusk came early in November, but it looked as if it would be earlier still today.

"Doesn't look good," said Cyn with a glance at the sky. He urged his mount faster and Chastity followed suit.

Not long after, his horse cast a shoe.

Cyn let loose a string of vivid, multilingual oaths. "I'll have to lead him to the next village," he said, "and hope there's a smithy. There's a spire over there that looks promising. Come on."

A drizzly rain began to fall, and they both pulled up the hoods of their cloaks.

"I doubt we'll make Maidenhead tonight," he said with irritation. "With a storm threatening, we'd be better not to try." Then he shrugged. "In fact, it's no great loss. If we stop for the night in some out-of-the-way village, we'll be less noticeable than if we turn up late and bedraggled in Maidenhead, where doubtless the net is tightest."

He looked up, as if wondering at her silence.

"Yes, you're right," said Chastity. Another night on the road. Oh, Lord.

By the time they came into the village of East Green, Chastity's head was throbbing with tension. They stopped at the Angel, a plain square building on the main street, with a small coaching yard beside it. The door opened to spill warm light and pleasant chatter into the yard. The hearty innkeeper assured them there were rooms to be had, and a smithy just down the road. His ostler would take the horse down and have it seen to.

There was no obvious watcher here, but the first thing Chastity saw inside the Angel was a notice nailed to a post.

MISSING. REWARD. And below it a creditable line drawing of Verity. It had been done from the portrait painted just after her marriage. It was a good likeness, but very much of a great lady, with high-piled hair, low-cut bodice, and diamonds around her neck. Chastity suspected that Verity in her present guise, even as the proper matron rather than the sluttish servant, could stand by the poster and not be recognized.

Cyn caught Chastity's eye and winked. She winked back, relieved to know the search was so handicapped.

And the innkeeper had said *rooms*. She wouldn't be tempted to foolishness.

It was going to be all right.

They were discussing the rooms and dinner with mine host when a voice boomed. "Cyn Malloren! It *is* you! By the Lord Harry, you're a sight for sore eyes. I thought you'd snuffed it!"

They turned to see another officer emerging from the taproom. He had a jolly look to him, with round cheeks and big blue eyes, but he was also well over six feet and built like a stone monument. When he grabbed Cyn, Chastity half expected the smaller man to break.

"Gresham!" declared Cyn with every evidence of delight, despite the embrace. "What are you doing in the back of beyond?"

"Ah ha!" declared Gresham. "This is your lucky day, boyo. No need of rooms," he said to the innkeeper. "Captain Malloren'll be up to Rood House with me."

"Rood House?" queried Cyn. "Your place?"

"No, Heather's." He wrapped an arm around Cyn's shoulders and steered him toward the taproom, throwing back over his shoulder, "More of that punch, landlord, and quick about it!"

Chastity rolled her eyes and followed. Was Cyn Malloren known and loved the length of England? The two officers sat at a table by the fire, draining the last of a bowl of hot punch. Chastity sat on a bench close by. Apart from one quick glance to check her location, Cyn appeared to ignore her as he and his friend caught up on the news.

A handful of local residents sat in the tap, addressing the Angel's home-brewed. They eyed the young officers with mild, good-humored interest, then resumed their gossip and dominoes. The click of the tiles soothed Chastity's nerves.

The landlord bustled in with a new brimming, steaming bowl. Chastity regarded it with some alarm. Had this giant already drained one of those? If she was any judge, it contained mostly rum and brandy. In no time at all they'd both be under the table.

Gresham showed no sign of wear as he filled two glasses with the stuff. Nor was he unobservant. "He yours?" he queried with a nod at Chastity. "He want some?"

"Yes on both counts," said Cyn, sprawled at ease in his

chair. "But don't feed him too much. It's a tender sprig not long from its mother."

Chastity grimaced at this description but enjoyed the delicious, spicy drink. She felt the hot spirits weave into her blood and relax her. She leaned her head against the wall and refused to worry about anything for the moment.

Lord, to have peace, and friends, and ordinary days . . .

She listened with half an ear to the conversation, but heard only war news and anecdotes about people she didn't know. The two men laughed uproariously at things that didn't seem the least bit funny to her.

She began to feel left out, cut off from Cyn's real world. She even sniffed back a tear. At that she sat up with a jerk and stared suspiciously at the drink in her glass. 'Struth, was she becoming a maudlin drunk?

At that moment two more men erupted into the taproom. "Fear not," one declared dramatically. "We are arrived to carry you from this dull spot unto Elysium!" This dark-haired gallant was not in uniform but in a magnificent, if disordered, suit of green satin, richly trimmed. It became clear this was Heather—Lord Heatherington—owner of Rood House. His companion was Lieutenant Toby Berrisford.

It was Toby who said, "Cyn! I'd heard you were recovered, but I'm glad of the evidence of my own eyes!"

Lord Heatherington, who was visibly drunk, focused his gaze with difficulty. "It is, by gad, the mad Malloren himself. What blessed day! Our festivities have yet another cause!"

The scene degenerated into pandemonium. The locals grinned at the young men, but Chastity scowled. Could Cyn Malloren not keep a serious task in mind once revelry was available? Perhaps there had been good reason for her to accompany him after all.

When everything was sorted out, it appeared Cyn was going to spend the night at Rood House, to help Lord Heatherington celebrate the death of his grandfather, which long-anticipated event had finally put the viscount, an ex-captain, in possession of a fortune.

Cyn took Chastity aside. "It would cause more talk if I refuse. You had best stay here."

"No!" said Chastity. Lord knows when he'd emerge, and in what state.

"You'll be safe enough. This place is off any main route."

"You need someone along who'll keep a sober head."

"If I know Heather, it'll be wild up there," said Cyn with crisp authority. "You stay here."

Before Chastity could react to the order, they were interrupted.

"Odso! What have we here?" Lord Heatherington asked with drunken bonhomie. "Your man? Where's Jerome?"

"Resting," said Cyn. "His leg's bothering him. This is just a local lad acting as groom. He may as well stay here."

"Not at all! Room for all, and my staff are having the devil of a party as well. Come along, lad. We'll put hairs on your chest, and starch where you need it most!"

Chastity found herself swept toward Lord Heatherington's coach. She threw an alarmed glance at Cyn, but he merely shrugged, though she thought he looked vexed. It was as he said, however—to make a fuss would just raise questions. Toby Berrisford, for example, might recognize the young man who had been with Mrs. Inchcliff, and thus start thinking about Mrs. Inchcliff and a baby.

They were cramped with five in the coach, especially as both Gresham and Heatherington were large men.

"Should have left Charles to ride on the box," said Cyn, and pushed Chastity down on the floor in such a position that her face was hidden against her knees. "Stay down there, lad, and keep out of everyone's way."

Chastity grimaced to herself but knew she had to be careful. Berrisford was no fool and didn't appear to be drunk. At least, she thought stoically, the carriage had a thick, luxurious carpet on the floor, not lousy straw as would be the case with a hired one.

As the carriage picked up speed, Heatherington burst into song and the others soon joined in.

"Oh, here is a ditty, in praise of a titty,
That's pretty as pretty can be. Tra-la!
Come give me a titty, my sweet little pretty,
And you'll have your jollies of me. Tra-la!"

Chastity glanced up between knee and hat-brim, wanting to share her amusement at this silly song with Cyn. He wasn't looking at her at all but taking a healthy swig from a bottle between verses. He seemed thoroughly in tune with his company, rot him.

The men seemed to have an unlimited store of similar songs. The tunes were monotonous, the words lacked any claims to poetry, and the subjects were all lewd. Chastity would have received a first-rate education in bawdy matters if she understood any of it.

She frowned over it. "Nether hole" she feared she did understand, though the song which involved it made no sense. But what did drinking from the nether cup refer to? The obvious interpretation was too ridiculous.

It all sounded ridiculous anyway.

The men roared their approval of being tied up, tied down, eaten—*eaten!*—and having five women in a row. Chastity was distracted by the logistics of this. Did that mean actually lined up, she wondered, or one after the other?

They roared their approval of smooth shoulders, round buttocks, and enormous breasts. Chastity thought sadly of her own modest ones. They'd hardly spill out of anyone's hands.

They sang of the glory of a great bushy thatch between

a wench's legs. Chastity lacked that too. Just a modest amount of brown curls.

In Society men paid pretty compliments to soft cherry lips and shining cornflower eyes. Was this what they really wanted? If so, what had she to offer? No breasts like melons, no bulging buttocks, no thicket between her thighs.

Now they were on about kissing a rosy bum. That sounded as if someone had had a spanking.

Ah, now they were singing of more normal matters— cherry lips. Cherry *nether* lips . . . ?

She was hauled up and shoved out of the door to find they had arrived at their destination. Her hauler was Cyn and he looked vexed again. In fact, he looked in a rage.

"I'm sorry," she muttered. "I couldn't think of a way not to come."

"Nor could I," he admitted. He dragged her close. "Listen carefully. I'm going to find you a safe spot, and when I do you're to stay there at all costs, or I promise you, you'll have the rosiest bum around."

She stared at him. "Is that what that meant?"

He looked briefly heavenward. "Just keep your eyes and ears shut." His hand shackled her arm as they went into the house.

Rood House was a handsome Jacobean construction, with leaded windows and steep gables. It was made for elegance and madrigals, but behind the carved doors, Bedlam reigned.

The gracious oak hall with its wide staircase was lit by only a couple of flaring, smoky lamps, but it was full of people. Some were felled on floor or stairs by drink and lust. Others wove before Chastity's eyes en route to other chambers. If the shrieks, raucous singing, and discordant music were any indication, this house was the scene of a bacchanalian revel. The air was sickly-sweet with smoke, spirit fumes, and sweaty perfumes.

The noise deafened Chastity, but it was the smell that

made her head spin. She swayed against Cyn, and his hold became less controlling and more supportive.

Berrisford and Gresham disappeared immediately into the throng. Heatherington smiled benignly on his revelers.

"Quite a party, eh? Your lad can go and join the festivities below."

"No," said Cyn. "I'd rather keep him with me."

Heatherington gave them a distinctly strange look, but shrugged. "Come on, then. Come see our theater."

Cyn held back. "You didn't say this was an orgy, Heather."

"What good party isn't?" Their host frowned blearily at them. "Getting prissy in your old age, Cyn?"

"Merely giving thought to my uniform," said Cyn. "It's new. Have you a room where I can change?"

"Must have . . ." said Heatherington vaguely. A voluptuous redhead had attached herself to his arm and was rubbing against him. Her breasts were as good as naked, but her face was covered to just above the lush red lips by a silver mask. Her attentions enthralled their host. "Big place, this . . ." he muttered. "Must have room . . ."

It was no wonder the man couldn't string four words together in view of the way the redhead was distracting him. Chastity swallowed a nervous giggle. If anyone groped her like that, she'd be in trouble! Strangely, the woman was vaguely familiar. Chastity looked around. About half the women were masked. This suggested they might be ladies of Society out for amorous adventure, as was said to happen at the Hell-Fire Club.

"Whoa, puss," said their host to his tormentor, slapping her invasive hand. "Steady on there a minute." He turned to Cyn. "Just go upstairs and help yourself. Any room you fancy. Help yourself . . . Help yourself to anything . . ." He turned to his disobedient companion, and was lost to them.

Chastity edged closer, trying to identify the woman, but Cyn hauled her away. "Into voyeurism, are you? I've certainly brought you to the right place then, haven't I?"

He steered a steady course through the shifting, drunken throng despite being propositioned three times before they reached the stairs. He paused to give each female mild, postponed encouragement.

"My, you *are* going to be busy," said Chastity through her teeth.

His grip on her arm tightened to the bruising point. "All in a good cause. Don't want anyone asking awkward questions, do we?"

They stepped over a couple who had passed out in one another's arms, and climbed the stairs.

A young, unmasked woman was coming down. Heavy paint and many patches couldn't hide the pockmarks on her face, but her figure was admirably curvaceous. She eased her bodice lower, which hardly seemed possible, and swayed her hips. "My, what do we have here? Two handsome lovers for Sal. Lucky me . . ." She licked her lips and eyed them with professional expertise. She sidled up to press against Chastity. Sour sweat and heavy perfume washed out from her body. "I love 'em young," she whispered. "My specialty, young ones is. Let Sally show you how, sweet." Her hand reached out. Chastity twisted away and pressed against Cyn.

He put an arm around her.

The whore shook her head. "That way, is it? Bloody waste. Your sort are in the library, luvs." She wandered down the stairs in search of other partners.

Cyn dragged Chastity up the stairs. "You do realize you're ruining my reputation," he snarled. "I'll have to roll every woman in the house just to prove I'm not a flaming sodomite."

Chastity glared at him. "It's your fault we're in this stew. You're the one with the disreputable friends!"

He looked as if he wanted to murder her.

It was quieter above stairs, but no more decorous.

The noise from below faded and blended with bumps, groans, and shrieks from the nearby rooms. Perhaps some people hadn't made it to the rooms, for items of clothing were scattered about. Two odd shoes littered the floor; a pair of striped stockings festooned a picture frame; a lace-trimmed cravat hung from a sconce. A goblet had been knocked over on an oak chest, and the pooled wine had dried to a sticky stain.

"How long has this been going on?" Chastity asked.

Cyn ran his hand through his hair and looked around distractedly. "God knows, but they're on their second wind ..." A noise and a blast of cold air made them both look down into the hall. A new batch of people was pushing in. "Or they just keep getting new blood," Cyn added. "Word of this revel has probably traveled the Home Counties. One thing," he said with a wry glance at Chastity. "It's doubtless crippling the search. Toby's hardly keeping his mind on it ..."

Chastity could not pay attention. She was frozen with horror. One of the new arrivals was her brother, Fortitude Harleigh Ware, Lord Thornhill. She had no doubt he would recognize her in a moment, even in her disguise. Her face after all was unchanged, and he'd seen her shorn.

"What is it?" asked Cyn sharply.

At that moment they had to press together to avoid being run down by a couple—a bedraggled, masked wench fleeing a red-faced man. The wench laughed as she screamed, and did not run very fast. She ducked into a room just opposite Chastity. Her pursuer lunged after.

"Got you, you saucy tease!"

The woman, who certainly had the required breasts like melons, and was showing the fact to the whole world, fluttered her hands and batted her darkened lashes. "Oh, sir, I fear you have ..."

The man unfastened his breeches and leaped at her.

Cyn slammed the door, muttering, his question clearly driven from his mind.

Chastity was dazed by the scenes around her, but it was Fort's arrival that had her sick with fear. What in God's

name would her brother do if he found her here? Beat her?
He'd more likely murder her. He'd believed that she'd invited Vernham to her bed, and raged at her for not stopping the scandal by marrying the man. If he found her in
this place, and in men's clothes . . .

And she had Cyn to worry about. It would come to a
fight and Cyn could be no match for Fort, who was a
huge, strong man, skilled with pistol and sword.

"Come on!" Cyn snapped. "Let's find a room for you."

Chastity didn't need to be dragged, but he dragged her
anyway. Without a qualm, he opened every unlocked door.
Every room was occupied. In most she saw just a heaving
quilt—though Chastity could swear there were more than
four feet at the end of one bed—but in one room she
glimpsed a pair of pale pumping buttocks.

She giggled. It looked so silly.

Cyn was back to muttering.

At last he opened a door on an unoccupied room. Cyn
flung her into it and shut and locked the door. He leaned
against it. "Plague take the lot of 'em," he muttered.

Humor or hysteria bubbled up in Chastity and she collapsed, giggling, on the big, rumpled bed. When she
gained control he was leaning on a corner-post smiling at
her, but strangely.

"I'm sorry," she said, "but it's all so ridiculous."

"It is, isn't it?" He turned away to look around. "If I'm
not mistaken, this is Heather's own room. He said we
should suit ourselves, so we have." He flung down his
portmanteau and pulled out his blue suit, brushing it off
ruefully. "Jerome would have a fit to see me in such a rag,
but in this company no one will care."

"No," said Chastity, proud of her careless tone. "It'll
doubtless be ripped off you in minutes."

He flashed her a look but merely said, "More than
likely. The harpies will be after fresh blood. They'd just
love to get at you. Are you sure you don't want to take
this occasion to expand your education, lad?"

Chastity put her hands behind her head. "Hardly. It's fertile ground for the pox."

"Not so naive, after all," he remarked. "The whores will at least have been guaranteed clean before they came here, though whether they'll be that way when they leave . . ."

He shrugged and stripped out of his uniform, down to shirt and drawers.

"And what about the ladies?" Chastity asked, determined not to let his body distract her from her resolve.

"What about them?"

"The masked women aren't whores, are they?"

"Depends on your definition of a whore." He fastened the velvet breeches and put on the brocade waistcoat, smoothing it down to his thighs.

Chastity found herself distracted after all by the lithe length of him. Tears pricked at her eyes; she couldn't for the life of her think why she was so miserable. There was Fort, of course, a complication she'd not looked for. But he frightened her; he didn't make her heart ache.

It was Cyn who was doing that. He slipped into his coat and checked himself in the long mirror to see whether he'd please one of those whores below. Chastity supposed she could stand up and reveal that she was a woman too, but much good that would do her. In this house there were beauties to suit any taste, highborn and low, all willing and available. Chastity Ware was nothing but a freak.

Cyn knotted a soft, lacy cravat around his neck and fixed it with his sapphire pin. He nodded at his reflection. " 'Twill do, I think."

He went to the dressing table and tidied his hair, borrowing a wide blue ribbon for his bow. He smoothed out the lace at wrists and throat, then inspected Heatherington's pots and boxes.

He brushed on pale powder to give his face a fashionable pallor. He flicked open a patch-box and quirked a brow at Chastity. "Do you think?"

He was turning into a new creature—not hey-go-mad adventurer, not soldier, but Society creature.

"Not without powder in your hair," said Chastity coldly.

He sighed. "Doubtless you're right, and powdering's so messy. Besides being the very devil to get out." He sniffed Heatherington's perfumes, and shook one that pleased him onto an embroidered, lace-edged handkerchief, then tucked it through a buttonhole. He put on his black shoes with high red heels and bowed to her with a flourish. "Will I do?"

Chastity swallowed. He was gorgeous. "Will anyone look before they tear your clothes off?"

He smiled slightly. "Probably not, but one has one's standards."

He checked the adjoining door and turned the key in the lock. "In fact, I don't intend to become embroiled. For one thing, we both need our sleep before tomorrow's adventure. For another, I've no intention of risking the pox. But I'll have to be seen for a while. I'll try to have a word with Toby and discover how the hunt is going. I'll return as soon as I can." He halted at the door to the corridor. "Lock the door and keep it locked to all except me." He looked sharply at her. "Yes?"

Chastity raised her chin. "Yes. I assure you I have no desire to share this bed."

"And yet there is only one, my dear Charles. I fear you'll have to share it with me."

Chastity had overlooked this obvious point. "I'll sleep on the floor then."

He smiled lazily. "I'd be offended, stripling. It's a large bed and I don't have lice."

"It is a foible of mine, Lord Cyn. I sleep alone."

"We'll see." With that he was gone.

Chastity flew to the door and locked it. Perhaps she wouldn't even open it to him.

Reaction set in and she pressed her hands to her face. How the devil had she come to such a pass?

* * *

Cyn waited until he heard the lock click. At least she'd obeyed him thus far, but he placed little reliance on her doing so forever. He smiled and shook his head. Lord, she had courage, but it was being severely tried. Would she break before he could end this charade and protect her properly?

A roar from below stairs spoke of some mighty achievement. He didn't care to speculate what. If he'd had any idea what kind of affair this was, he would have made an excuse to stay at the Angel.

Still, he felt he could relax now he had his damsel tucked safely away. He could relax too in the knowledge that no matter what had happened in the spring, she was an innocent in any way that mattered. Her reaction to this place told him that.

He wished he didn't have to leave her. Any woman here, no matter how beautiful, held no appeal beside the fascination of his damsel. He just wanted to be done with this adventure so he could force the truth from her and plan their future. He made his way downstairs to mingle, anticipating the moment when he could return to Chastity and sanity.

Chastity wandered the bedroom restlessly. She could just imagine Cyn in the arms of one of those harpies— being groped, slobbered over, and stripped to satisfy a whore's lust. She found her hands were fists. It wasn't fair! Once she'd been beautiful and he wouldn't have left her so easily.

She pulled off her wig and stood in front of the mirror. A freak. A hard-faced, bitter freak in breeches. Frantically she stripped off her male clothing and unwound the bindings around her breasts. Soon she was naked.

She gave a shuddering sigh.

She ran her hands down her body. It wasn't a bad body. She knew she wasn't a crowning beauty like Nerissa

Trelyn, but her body wasn't at all bad. Nerissa Trelyn, though, had glossy pale-blonde curls. She had big cow-eyes with lashes thicker than Cyn's. She had breasts like melons, though Polite Society described them as a hand-some bosom . . .

Chastity's hands stilled. Nerissa Trelyn: daughter of the Bishop of Peterborough; wife of Lord Trelyn, image of propriety; Toast of London and social arbiter; one of the people who had seen Chastity in bed with Henry Vernham and condemned her.

Nerissa Trelyn was Heatherington's seducer!

Chastity looked vaguely around. She picked up a brown satin dressing-gown and slipped it on. She curled up in a big chair by the fire and poured herself a glass of wine from a decanter there.

Could she be mistaken? she wondered as she sipped. It scarcely seemed believable and yet she was sure, mainly because of the distinctive, mellow voice. She wore a red wig over her blonde hair, but it was she. The great Lady Trelyn was here playing the whore.

Could she have recognized Chastity?

No, she'd definitely had her eyes and mind on other matters.

On the whole, Chastity wasn't surprised that Nerissa Trelyn had lovers; the world knew she'd married Lord Trelyn for his money, and he appeared to be a cold, dry man.

But for her to be in such a place . . .

And she'd had the gall to condemn Chastity Ware!

How many more were here? How many more hypo-crites?

Chastity drained the glass and stood. She had to find out. She began to drag on her clothes again but paused. Her brother Fort. If she bumped into him, he'd know her.

She needed to be masked. But only the women were masked. If she dressed as a woman, with wig and mask, surely no one would recognize her. Chastity had recognized Nerissa Trelyn by her voice and so would be careful to disguise her own.

She hovered uncertainly. She wanted, quite desperately, to stay safe in his room. But she wanted, just as desperately, to confirm the unbelievable—that Nerissa Trelyn was reveling below stairs—because if it were so, there might be some way to use the information to help her own situation.

She'd do it. Just a brief and cautious foray.

Chastity flung open the doors of Lord Heatherington's armoire, but found it contained only men's clothing. She beat her hands together in frustration. She could doubtless assemble a female costume from the bits of clothing lying around this house, but she didn't dare go searching.

The adjoining room. She'd go odds it belonged to a woman.

In a moment she'd turned the lock and was in. Yes! Clearly a woman's room. Now, would the clothes fit? A glance in the armoire told her they would—not perfectly, but well enough.

She couldn't suppress a laugh of delight at the selection of pretty gowns before her. It had been so long since she'd seen such delicious confections. She threw off the dressing-gown and pulled on a sheer white silk chemise with elbow-length sleeves edged with a double layer of foaming lace. She shivered with pleasure as it slithered over her skin, a mere veil over her body, not substantial at all.

Next she chose a padded petticoat of white satin trimmed with yellow ribbon. She stepped into it and tied the laces at her waist. A brocade stomacher went on top, its V front coming down over the waistband of the petticoat. She had some trouble tying the laces in the back, but there was no question of summoning a servant and so she did the best she could, smiling at the memory of dressing Cyn, sighing at the thought of what it would be like to be dressed, or undressed, by him.

She pushed such thoughts aside.

She looked at herself in the mirror. The stomacher barely covered her nipples and pushed up the fullness of her breasts. Their swelling was only covered by the filmy chemise. She'd never worn such a bold bodice before, but she liked it. After her long, arid masquerade it felt so wonderful to be a woman again.

She took down an open gown of yellow-and-brown-striped silk and put it on, hooking it to the stomacher at the sides of the waist. Above and below it spread open to show both petticoat and stomacher. The elbow-length sleeves showed the lacy frill of the chemise.

She twirled, laughing for the pleasure of fine things, for the rustling, slithering feel of silk. The skirts hung rather limp and would be better for hoops, but if the lady who owned all this had hoops she was wearing them. The padding of the petticoat gave some fullness, and Chastity was clearly a little taller than the true owner, for the skirts did not trail.

It occurred to her that this could be Nerissa Trelyn's room. She sought for clues but found nothing to confirm her suspicions. Suppressing her conscience, she searched thoroughly. Nothing in any of the drawers.

Then she found a small ivory box. In it were two letters, two heated love letters. She sighed with frustration. They were probably from Lord Heatherington but were addressed to Desirée. The name meant nothing, for fashion dictated that a man address his beloved by a fanciful name. Chastity had been Bella to one suitor and Clorinda to another.

But then she wondered whether Heatherington kept *his* love letters.

She hurried to search his room. After unsuccessfully checking boxes and drawers—the sort of places where a lady would carefully store her *billets doux*—she at last found one stuffed carelessly into a jacket pocket.

The lady's style was more flowery, but no less outrageous. It made Chastity blush to read such a lustful communication. The note was addressed to Hercules and signed Desirée, but must surely be in the writer's own hand. It was hardly the kind of letter one would dictate to a secretary. Would the writing prove to be that of Lady Trelyn?

Chastity placed the letter carefully in the waistcoat pocket of her suit. She was more anxious than ever to continue her investigation, to seek a firm identification of Nerissa, and detect any other hypocrites cavorting below.

But she needed a wig, and there was none. For a moment she thought she would have to abandon her adventure, and was aware of guilty relief, but then she remembered the black wig Cyn had bought from Mrs. Crupley. Was it still in his portmanteau?

She found it was. It was a poor specimen of coarse black horsehair, but she thought it would do for this occasion. She dragged a comb through it to tame it, then dusted the curls with the powder in the lady's room—a rather unpleasant pink, perfumed with roses. Chastity coughed as the stuff billowed around her.

It worked, however. When she put the mass of curls on her head, the powder softened the unlikely dense black, and made the effect quite pleasing.

Chastity made free with the lady's dressing table. A rabbit's foot dipped in rouge gave extra color to her cheeks, and a finger in a pot produced cream rouge for the lips. She dusted her face with white powder, and affixed a black velvet heart by her mouth—an invitation to a kiss.

Chastity assessed herself in the mirror with satisfaction. A fine lady stood there, ready for a ball or for court, though perhaps a little over-painted for the latter. She looked older and bolder than herself. For sure, Toby Berrisford wouldn't recognize a certain youth, and Fort wouldn't recognize his sister. Chastity Ware had always dressed demurely, as befitted a well-brought-up young lady in search of a husband.

And she looked well. Her waist was trim, her shoulders smooth and white, and if her breasts lacked the mass of cantaloupes, they were still shown to advantage by the low bodice.

She reminded herself that she did not seek to be admired. In fact this costume might garner her more *admiration* than she could handle. On the other hand, discretion in dress would stand out here like a cherry in a bowl of peas. She twitched the stomacher just a little higher, assuring herself she would only go out among the revelers for a little while, and would be very careful.

She couldn't help wonder what would happen if she met Cyn like this. Would he recognize her? Surely not. Would he admire her? She pushed such speculations out of mind. He'd be more likely to put her over his knee. For tonight, she'd keep well out of Cyn Malloren's way.

As for other admirers, all the men appeared to be drunk and she should be able to dodge and outwit them. It was not as if there was a shortage of willing females.

Finally, the mask. She tied on a black velvet half-mask, which had the added advantage of securing the wig. She nodded at her reflection. She wouldn't know herself.

There was only one pair of shoes and they were too small. Nerissa Trelyn made much of her tiny feet.

Chastity shrugged. She doubted anyone would be surprised to see someone in bare feet in this house. As a last gesture, she picked up a vial of perfume, but when she smelt it, she grimaced at the heavy, sickly rose odor.

She remembered the perfume Cyn had bought. What had he done with it?

She returned to Heatherington's bedroom, locking the adjoining door, and rummaged in Cyn's bag. She found the crystal vial. She unstoppered it and sniffed with delight at the complex blend of spice and flowers, underlaid with elements that spoke of lust. She hesitated, wondering if wearing it might not be dangerous in this place, then told herself that such a discreet invitation to intimacy would be swamped by all the other odors. She wanted to wear it for herself, because it was wonderful, and made her feel powerful in her womanhood. She dabbed some at her elbows and between her breasts.

The aroma drifted up warm from her body to dizzy her mind. Cyn Malloren had exquisite taste. What a shame, she thought, that their fates would keep them apart.

Chastity admitted the truth. Part of her desperation to find out who was here tonight was a forlorn hope that she could glean some information with which to help repair her reputation. Then she could meet Cyn on honest ground.

She swallowed tears at such a hopeless task, but would not give in to them. She had learned to be a fighter and this was the only chance of a weapon to come her way.

Chapter 10

ⲟⲟⲟ

Still, Chastity needed a full goblet of the rich hock before she had enough courage to venture out. Then, with a last reassuring glance at the stranger in the mirror, she cautiously opened the door. The corridor was deserted, though it was only too clear that most of the rooms were still in use. She locked the bedroom door and slipped the key down her bodice, shivering slightly at the chill.

Or perhaps it was nerves.

She needed to mingle with the throng below, but didn't fancy descending the wide main stairs in clear view of anyone who cared to look up. She guessed there would be a lesser staircase at the end of the building and went that way. She found the secondary stairs and encountered only a couple of bosky servants before attaining the ground floor. A short passageway brought her to the edge of the hall.

It was quieter than it had been when she arrived, and only a half-dozen sleepy or drunk people were sprawled about. She cautiously drifted by them. Five were male. The sixth was an unmasked woman snoring in a man's arms, but no one she recognized.

Chastity guessed the other revelers were in the various rooms. Laughter, chatter, and music seemed to swirl from all quarters, but above all echoed singing from the back of the house. It was accompanied by clapping and stamping feet, and occasional roars of approval.

Chastity had experienced the terpsichorean style of Heatherington and his friends, and had no desire for more. She headed in the other direction, the side of the hall closest to where she stood.

If this house remained as it was built in the days of King James, the rooms would run from one to the other around three sides of the hall. She started at the front.

She entered a small dining room where two couples were rolling together on the floor. Chastity couldn't tell who they were, and her nerve wasn't up to going close enough to find out. She hurried into the next room, a much better populated one.

This was a gaming room with all the knife-edged intensity to be expected of people who chose cards and dice over bodies. Men and women, masked and unmasked, moved fortunes over the tables, watching cards and dice with feverish, glittering eyes. Chastity shuddered. She'd always seen something evil in gaming.

Still, she took a deep breath and began to work her way around the room, scrutinizing the players. Heavens, there was old Lady Fanshaw. There was no weapon in that, however. The world knew she was mad for cards and would go to hell itself for a game. In fact, thought Chastity, she would find nothing here. If she revealed that the queen herself was here at play, everyone would yawn.

As she headed for the next room a hand snared her wrist. "Alone, *cara?*" She was jerked down onto a middle-aged man's lap. "Come, bring me luck." He paddled his plump fingers over her breasts.

Chastity suppressed an urge to struggle. Nothing was more likely to cause speculation. Instead she collapsed against his chest and draped her hands around his neck. He chuckled and turned his attention back to the game. Chastity watched through the slits of her mask, and when she saw from his avid expression that the hand was approaching a crucial point, she wriggled provocatively and kissed his cheek.

As she'd planned, he pushed her away. "The devil, woman. I can't see me cards!"

She gave a pout and escaped. That had been easy. She had to confess she was beginning to enjoy herself. Behind the anonymity of her disguise, she felt safer than ever in her life. She wasn't Lady Chastity Ware. She wasn't a disgraced woman. She wasn't even Charles. She was newborn.

Alerted by a shout of laughter, she stopped to look at the play at another table. Here, the stakes were not money at all.

A black woman was dicing against all comers. Men rolled the dice, but quite a few women watched the game. If a man threw eight or less, the negress added his guineas to the pile before her. If he threw more he kept his gold, and she lowered her bodice a fraction and raised her skirt a good inch. Her pink silk bodice hung on her nipples, exposing most of a magnificent chocolate-colored chest. Her skirt was halfway up her thighs.

The dicing grew feverish. Chastity too was caught in the fascination of waiting for that bodice to fall. Three men rolled and lost. The negress laughed with a flash of fine white teeth. "Who now, gentlemen? It lacks but ten to the hour. When the clock strikes, I rearrange my clothing and we start all over again."

Two more men rushed forward to roll the dice. Again they failed.

A long white hand adorned with a ruby signet scooped up the ivories. "Your fate has arrived, Sable."

Chastity stifled a gasp.

It was the Marquess of Rothgar.

He must surely have just arrived, for he was impeccable in crimson brocade trimmed with black. Snowy lace foamed at his neck and wrists. His black hair was unpowdered. His fine, handsome features seemed carved in marble in the flickering candlelight.

The negress, Sable, grinned. "I win anyway, milord, for if I lose, you win me."

Rothgar shook the dice in the box. "How charming. Perhaps I need a house-slave . . ."

The woman's grin became predatory. "Not if you value your neck, milord."

Rothgar smiled coolly and threw. Two sixes gave him the definitive victory. A roar of approval shook the room.

Sable scooped all her winnings into a pouch at her belt, then stood. She twitched sinuously and the pink silk of her loose bodice slithered to her waist, evoking a collective groan from the men. Dusky melons in truth, thought Chastity. Rothgar, she noted, looked politely unimpressed.

Sable slowly inched up her skirt until she was naked to the waist, and tucked it into her waistband. She twirled before all the watchers, revealing a dark, curly thatch between her legs. Then she swayed over to Rothgar and walked her fingers up his chest to his jaw. "Well, milord, would you waste this on scrubbing floors? Did I mention that you only win me for the night?"

"Alas," he said, and flicked open a gold snuffbox, "and these floors are not even mine. Your foot, slave."

Sable stepped back, and with perfect balance stretched up one leg before him. He placed a pinch of the brown powder on her instep and cupped her heel. He inhaled the snuff, first into one nostril then the other.

When he straightened his head he retained her heel, keeping her leg stretched up. Sable showed neither physical nor mental discomfort. In fact, perhaps at a signal from him, she swayed over backward, went into a slow handstand, and from there back to her feet facing him. The maneuver gave all the watchers a fine view of her private parts, which were naturally or unnaturally a scarlet red. Cherry nether lips!

Chastity realized she was gaping and shut her mouth with a snap.

Rothgar applauded gently. He held out a hand, and as if she had been the finest lady, correctly dressed, led Sable from the room.

Chastity sucked in a breath. She'd never even imagined anything like that, and it had leeched away her feelings of confidence. She was badly out of her depth in this company. She longed to flee back to her room to hide under the covers and wait for morning.

But she still had her mission to accomplish and something else to worry about. She didn't think Rothgar would recognize her, though he had a devilish reputation for omniscience, but she knew Cyn wouldn't want to bump into his brother here.

The problem was she couldn't warn Cyn without destroying her disguise, all of it.

Sable's entertainment being over, the watchers were milling around reviewing it. They seemed sated for the moment. Chastity only had to talk her way past two invitations to dalliance as she made her way to a desk in a corner.

It wasn't locked and she found paper, pens, and ink. The pen needed trimming and the ink was syrupy, but she managed to scribble *Rothgar is here*. She folded the note and pushed it down behind her stomacher. If she had the opportunity she'd slip it to Cyn.

She hurried into the next room, which turned out to be a gallery running across the back of the house. It was being used as a ballroom, if such rompings could be called a ball. A trio scraped away to produce music, but they were deep in their cups and wild in their rhythms. The dancers were equally wild in their moves.

Here Chastity at last began to gather names for her mental list. Lady Jane Treese, by the stars—the most malicious gossip in England. Meg Cordingly, Susan Fellows, and Letty Proud. The plump redhead would not be so proud if word escaped that she'd been tossed from hand to hand the length of the room, her skirts flying every which way.

In London, Chastity had heard sly speculation as to whether Letty's hair grew the same flaming red all over. Now the world knew. Instead of triumphant, Chastity felt sad. It would be impossible to use any names gathered here without causing great hurt.

Moreover, she envied the revelers. Their behavior might be lewd and wrong, but for this brief moment they were happy. She could hardly remember what happiness was.

A man grabbed her and swung her into a merry dance. With horror, she realized it was Fort.

"Hey, my pretty, don't look so shocked. Tell me your name."

He really was quite handsome with his blue eyes, curly brown hair, and even teeth. He smiled beguilingly. How long was it since he'd smiled that way at her? Not so long ago, though it seemed a lifetime.

"Are you incognito?" he asked. "Give me a false name, pretty one. I'll not care."

"Chloe," she said, thinking of a starchy aunt, her father's eldest sister.

He laughed. "Not my favorite name but never mind." He dragged her close and kissed her.

Chastity froze. This was a terrible sin, wasn't it?

He pushed her away angrily. "What's the matter, doxy? Am I not to your taste?"

"I'm sorry, sir," she gasped, in a breathy, twittery voice. "I . . . I don't feel well. I need a place to throw up!"

" 'Struth," he said with a laugh, and steered her over to the door. "Go down that corridor and you'll be outside. Good luck to you."

With that he returned to the dancing. Chastity smiled sadly. That was the careless kindness she remembered from the past. Fort was a hard man and easily angered, but not unkind. She considered everything from his point of view. He'd been one of the ones to catch Vernham in her bed, but he hadn't been really angry until she'd refused to marry. Only then had he joined with her father in berating her.

Chastity hovered in the corridor, watching her brother. Was he here just for the party, or as part of the hunt? He must be concerned about Verity, but it would be typical of him to enjoy himself too when occasion presented. He found another partner, and after a while left the room with her. Chastity gathered her courage and returned to the dancing, seeking yet more evidence.

Heatherington passed through the room, applauding his guests, his paramour by his side. Chastity worked her way closer. It was surely Nerissa. That teetering walk, and a habit she had of stroking her neck as if checking for wrinkles . . .

A man moved in front of Chastity, blocking her way. "Alone? Surely not. Not anymore, at least." He held out his hand in an invitation to the dance. It was the large Captain Gresham. He hadn't changed from his uniform and it was disarranged, his white waistcoat hanging open, his cravat gone, and his shirt open at the neck. He'd lost his wig too, and revealed dark hair shorn to a stubble.

Chastity went to him. Alone, she would be constantly accosted, and why shouldn't she have a moment of pleasure too?

For a while they danced moderately, but then he picked her up to twirl her in the air. Chastity squealed, fearing she was showing her all, and that her wig would fly off. She was also terrified by his size and strength which made her like a child in his arms. She realized she'd never before been out in the world unprotected by father, brother, or Cyn, but here she had no one to save her from this giant.

He lowered her slowly against his body. She sighed with relief to have her feet on the ground again, until she realized his maneuver had rucked up her petticoat at the front so a good part of her legs was bare.

He gave a mock growl and kissed her.

Chastity was totally helpless. One mighty arm clamped her in place. His other hand held her head, and her skull seemed to fit that hand as neatly as an orange would fit her own. His hot mouth assaulted her and when she resisted, his thumb slid forward to force open her mouth. His heavy tongue invaded. This had never happened to her before.

She felt swamped, engulfed and overpowered, but her senses were swimming, and she knew her mouth had softened under his skillful pressure. That frightened her more than anything.

He drew back, slowly. "That's better, my pretty. What's the matter? You have someone else here?"

Grasping the escape, Chastity said, "Yes."

"Too bad." His hand moved up to press and circle over her breast.

Too hard. It hurt. The trace of pleasure had gone, replaced by terror. She was going to be ravished, here in this room. She'd *never* been pawed like this, even by Henry Vernham.

She strained back against Gresham's rock-hard arm, desperately seeking an escape, but he took the opportunity to bite her neck. "Too bad, indeed," she gasped. "But I slipped away from him because he wouldn't feed me. Truly, sir, I'm famished. I . . . er . . . can't give my mind to other matters until my stomach stops aching."

He laughed and nibbled at the upper curve of her breast. "In truth, I'm starved myself now you mention it, and I don't suppose I should really eat you, delicious though you are." *Eating,* thought Chastity hysterically. *This is what they meant!* "Heather must have food here somewhere," he said, "and we'll both need to keep our strength up, won't we?"

Dizzy with relief, Chastity smiled at him. "Especially me, sir," she said coyly. "You being so big."

"You won't believe it, my pretty, I promise you." He grabbed her hand and clutched it to his bulging penis.

Chastity froze in disbelief. It would tear a woman apart!

He chuckled. "Are you sure you want to stop for belly-food? You can eat me all you want, and I promise to fill you up."

At his words, Chastity's stomach almost did rebel. "Oh, yes," she said quickly. "More sure than ever!" All she wanted was to be free of him, and then she'd be off to her room and safety. She had a few names and her nerve had utterly gone.

He steered her into another room, his arm protection from the crowd, but also imprisonment. It would be almost impossible to break free, and if she did, he'd catch her in a moment. Would a scream for help achieve anything? If it did, it would probably expose her identity.

She felt almost faint with horror at that thought.

She'd rather be ravished.

She would have to convince him she was as eager as he and hope he'd leave her side for a moment, perhaps to serve her with food.

She wasn't paying much attention to her surroundings except to note that the room was crowded, until those around let out a roar. She jumped. "What is it?" she gasped.

"Haven't you seen the theater yet, sweetheart?" Gresham asked. As if she were a child, he hoisted her on his shoulder.

Chastity realized they were in Heatherington's 'theater.' A plinth had been built at one end of the room and chairs set out for the audience. The entertainment was so popular that the chairs were all full and people were standing all around the room. Presumably this was where the singing had taken place earlier, but now the performance was not music but copulation.

The couple were both naked except for full-face masks. They grunted and contorted in a most extraordinary position that Chastity would not have believed to be physically possible.

She fought her way down.

"Not to your liking?" Gresham asked in surprise.

"Er . . . too stimulating!" Chastity gasped. "I really must control myself until I eat."

He chuckled and moved his back against the wall. He pulled her to him. "Hot, are you?" he asked. "Pity to waste it . . ." He pulled up her skirt at the back and fondled her thighs.

Chastity wriggled desperately, but this only seemed to encourage him. Someone bumped into her from behind, knocking the breath out of her, but also knocking Gresham's hand away.

"Beg pardon," the person murmured. Chastity stiffened as she recognized Cyn's voice. Part of her wanted to hide; part of her wanted to scream for help.

"Gresham," he said casually. "I see you've found yourself a pleasant armful."

"Indeed," said Gresham, and turned Chastity in his arms. "Meet Lord Cyn, my pretty." He placed his hands possessively over her breasts.

Chastity prayed for the earth to swallow her. Cyn looked remarkably untussled for someone who'd been in this mayhem for over an hour. He clearly had no suspicion as to her identity. He smiled at her with careless good humor and gave a slight bow. "Charmed, my dear."

Chastity didn't want him to recognize her, but nor did she want him to leave her here in the clutch of this giant. If necessary she'd reveal all. "The same, I'm sure," she said in her false voice. "I'm not averse to entertaining two, handsome."

Gresham's hands tightened. "Hey, none of that."

Cyn smiled. "I'm afraid that isn't my game either, pretty one. If you want to seek me out privately later . . ."

And how many assignations is that you've made? thought Chastity. And how many have you kept?

Gresham chuckled. "She'll be worn to a frazzle by later, my friend. I'd seek another partner if I were you."

Chastity forced a smile. "Oh, very well, but can't we at least get to the food?"

"All right, all right," said Gresham, "we'll find it." As an aside he said to Cyn, "A wench of truly ferocious appetites."

"She'll need to be," said Cyn. "As it happens, I know where the food is. Come on, and I'll show you."

The next room after the theater was almost empty and the people there appeared to be simply talking. Unfortunately one of the people present was Rothgar, offering snuff to no less a person than the Earl of Bute, confidant and mentor of the young king, supposed lover of the king's mother! Was this place, then, the true face of Society? Could the king himself be present?

Chastity glanced at Cyn, but he didn't seem to have noticed his brother, and Rothgar had his back to them. Where, Chastity wondered, was the luscious Sable?

Then they entered the next room where two tables were laden with food and drink. Unusually, there were no small tables, and so people had to eat standing up. A dozen or so guests were doing so, with strange hilarity.

Strange until Chastity and her escort arrived at the tables. Even food, apparently, was not beyond the lewd ingenuity of Lord Heatherington.

Down the center of each table, food had been formed into the shape of a body—a woman's on one, a man's on the other. Most of the interest centered on the female figure. Parsley nestled at the juncture of her blancmange thighs, and glacé cherries formed the nipples on the half-melons of her breasts. The men were leaning over to nibble off those cherries, which they then replaced from a bowl by the side.

Chastity looked to the other table, where the cherry was predictably on the end of a cucumber. She grabbed some innocuous bread and cheese, thinking she'd never be able to eat cucumber again. Gresham moved over to take a turn at the cherries. This was her chance, but Cyn had stayed with her.

She wondered what he would do if she slipped away—it was none of his business after all. On the other hand, this would be the only moment to warn him of his brother's presence.

She hesitated. She had to escape, but she could warn him first. He turned to the table to pick up a chicken leg and she plucked the note out of her bosom. She leaned over beside him, pressing against him as she reached across for some grapes. She slipped the note into his pocket.

He turned quickly, frowning at her.

"Why, what is it, my lord?" she asked, nervously.

"Nothing," he said, but with an intent look, as if he was seeing her for the first time.

Chastity glanced at Gresham, who grinned at her and leaned down to seize a cherry in his teeth. He'd be back in a moment. "I must go," she said. "I need to relieve myself!"

He too glanced at Gresham, then grasped her wrist. "Come, then. I'll show you where."

He dragged her from the room. Gresham let out an enraged bellow. Cyn pulled her down a short corridor and out into the chilly night.

"What are you doing?" cried Chastity, gasping from the cold wind.

"Finding you a place to piss, my lovely. That is what you want, isn't it? Or was Gresham more than you could swallow?" He wasn't like Cyn at all. He sounded hard and angry.

"But it's so cold!"

He whipped off his coat and wrapped it around her. It formed a prison and he used it to drag her close.

"My lord . . . !"

His lips silenced her. They were hard and allowed no refusal, but Chastity melted. She'd hungered for this for so long. Did it matter that he didn't know who she was? She'd take this moment and treasure it.

Once she surrendered, she was lost. Her arms slid around his body. She molded herself to every inch of him. She took his tongue inside her, sweet and spicy . . .

He suddenly broke free and dragged her further along the building behind some bushes, hushing her. He seemed breathless. Chastity was in a daze.

Then she heard Gresham. "Where the devil is he? Ho! Malloren, you rogue! Come out and return my wench!"

After a few more curses he went back into the house and slammed the door.

Cyn rose and pulled her with him. "Do you want to rejoin him?"

Chastity shook her head. She wanted to stay here with Cyn forever, safe and warm in his coat, and let the world go hang.

He raised her chin with his knuckles. "What then do you want?" Still there was that hardness, but one thing was clear. This moment came from heaven. It was a chance to love Cyn without endangering him.

"I want you," she whispered.

He caught his breath. "I wonder why . . ."

There was no answer to that and so Chastity waited. He let his hand travel down her neck and shoulder and slid his fingers behind the stiff stomacher to touch her nipple. This evening had been too much for her, and her senses were disordered. She collapsed back against the rough brick wall and let him do as he willed.

He rolled her nipple gently, and Chastity shivered in response. He pressed his hips against her, and she couldn't help but thrust back at him.

"You do want me, don't you?" he said softly. "Well, my sweet little wanton, so too do I want you." He pulled his fingers free and led her further along the house.

"Where are we going?" asked Chastity, feeling raw in the cold night.

"Via the kitchens. I don't really want to have to duel my friend over you. You're hardly worth that, are you?"

Again that hardness gave Chastity a frisson of unease. She reminded herself that he didn't know who she was; he thought her a whore, or a lady of very easy virtue. Did she really want to be treated as one?

But, imperfect as it was, this would be their only chance. She went with him.

Chapter 11

They entered the kitchen and Chastity staggered at the heat and noise, amazed the house wasn't on fire. The servants were roaring drunk, but trying to manage the spits and keep food and drink moving above stairs. Some had given up. A leg of mutton smoldered, and one drunken woman snored, slack-lipped, in a corner.

No one noticed as Cyn appropriated a basket and put in some sliced meat, fruit pies, and a pot of whipped cream before leading Chastity onward. She looked back and saw a cook turn around and search blearily for his cream.

They passed the butler's pantry which conveniently had a half-dozen bottles of wine open. One bottle and a couple of glasses went into the basket. Chastity ventured a protest.

Cyn glanced at her. "You did complain of hunger, sweeting. I intend to satisfy you in all respects."

He was smiling and yet still she sensed a chill behind it. In a way she welcomed the coolness. She didn't want him to feel warmly toward this chance-met doxy.

Yet again, she acknowledged, they were living a lie.

He led the way to a set of narrow servants' stairs. There were candles standing in a row, and a lamp to light them by. Cyn lit one and gave it to Chastity to carry as they climbed the stairs.

Cyn would have been hard put to express what he felt

at this development. She was a wanton, after all. He'd left her safe in her room then found her, painted in her true colors, playing the whore. She had no reason to join this company except to seek a man.

He could have wept.

On the other hand, he was going to have her. If she thought to trick him as she'd tricked Gresham, she'd catch cold at it. She'd expressed willingness; she had come without protest; soon he'd be able to assuage the lust that had been tormenting him for days. That kiss alone had been enough to set his body throbbing.

And by God, he'd make sure she remembered him. Perhaps she had rolled in bed with half the men in England, but she wouldn't forget Cyn Malloren.

He led the way up two flights of stairs and opened the baize-covered door into a quiet, dusty passageway. "I thought so. Nursery wing. And long unused."

In this quiet corner the orgy below might as well not exist. It was cold, though, and even within his coat, Chastity shivered. He checked the four rooms, then indicated one. This had probably been the nurse's room, for it had a narrow bed with a blanket and quilt still on it.

He placed the basket on the floor and checked the fireplace. "There's kindling still here and a few coals in the scuttle. Perhaps we can have a fire."

Chastity put the candle on the floor, its light meager even in the small room. She hugged herself in his coat, drowning in the faint aroma that was Cyn, but beginning to have doubts. What was Lady Chastity Ware doing in this dusty room with this man? How had her life led to this moment?

There were some mouse-nibbled books on a shelf, and he tore them up to start the blaze, then applied the candle. Flames leaped up, then the dry twigs crackled. Chastity moved instinctively closer to the fire.

He looked up. "I think it will catch, and the chimney

seems clear. It will be a while, though, before it gives much warmth."

"At least there's light." The room already seemed cozier for the fire.

He pulled the mattress, blanket, and quilt off the bed and laid the mattress on the floor. He spread the blanket over it and bowed with courtly elegance. "Your couch, my lady."

Chastity acknowledged that once she sat on the mattress her fate was sealed. She subsided onto it in a swirl of silken, perfumed skirts. And a certain amount of dust.

He brought the basket to put on the floor before sitting beside her and spreading the quilt over their legs.

She pulled his coat close around her shoulders. "Aren't you cold in shirtsleeves?"

He gave her a slanting look. "Not in the slightest."

Chastity looked away. His expression had just raised her temperature a good few degrees.

He poured wine and passed her a glass. She sipped it, feeling it spread warmth throughout her, feeling it immediately weave up into her brain. She expected him to leap on her at any moment and wished he would, before her nerve failed. "I really do need to eat," she said quickly.

"Or you'll be drunk?" he murmured. "Perhaps I want you drunk, sweeting."

She glanced at him through the slits of her mask and put down the glass. "Do you think you need to get me sozzled to have your way, milord?"

His lips twisted. "No. That would be ridiculous, wouldn't it?" He reached out and traced her lips, a touch that burned. His voice was seductive as he said, "Did your nurse ever tell you not to play with your food?" He took a slice of beef and slowly rolled it. "Now, what does this remind you of?"

Chastity frowned over it. "A roll of beef?"

He considered it. "Too small? You're doubtless right."

He rolled two more slices around it and showed it to her. "Is that more to your taste?"

He put the meat into her left hand, grasped her right and guided it to his crotch. "What do you think?"

Chastity froze. *Eating, again.* But she was supposed to be a wanton and had to behave like one. She smiled as best she could. "It seems about right," she said in a strangled voice. In fact, it still seemed too small. Were all men enormous down there?

"Eat then," he said softly.

Chastity would as willingly have eaten a snake, but she had no choice. She licked her lips, brought the meat to her mouth, and bit. The bulge under her hand leaped as if she'd bitten into it. She concentrated ferociously on chewing the tender meat. What would a whore do now?

She tried to move her right hand, but he held her there. "I would like some wine," she said.

He used his free hand to pick up her glass and raise it to her lips. When she had drunk, he leaned over to taste the drops still lingering on her lips, the bulge moving like a live thing under her captive hand. Then he too drank from the glass.

"Eat," he said softly. "You'll need your strength."

Chastity was in a daze. She'd expected to be grabbed, kissed, fondled, and entered. She hadn't been sure she would like it, just that it was something she had to do. She certainly hadn't expected she would have to do anything other than submit.

He was clearly ready for her, so why the delay? She dropped the half-eaten meat. "I think I've had enough."

"But you're a lady of ferocious appetites. Perhaps you have a sweet tooth." He moved to reach for the pies and cream, which meant he had to release her hand. Chastity sidled a few inches away, and the key inside her stomacher pressed on her ribs. She suspected it would prove an embarrassment very soon, and quickly fished it out and popped it under the mattress.

Cyn was contemplating a pie thoughtfully and Chastity guessed what was to come. Seduction with food seemed to be his preferred technique. An effective one, too. Because of their previous encounters, she was already sensitized. All the confused longing created by a Shrewsbury biscuit and an apple tart returned to swell the tangled longing she felt now.

He bit into the pie, and crimson juice spurted onto his hand. "Cherry," he said with a grin. "How appropriate."

He moved the pie to his other hand and held the juicy one out to her. Obeying the silent command, Chastity licked the juice. It was sweet and tart, with the salt of his skin to add savor. The sleek flesh of his hand ran against her tongue. She placed her mouth over his flesh and sucked.

He gently disengaged his hand and held out the pie. "Eat."

Chastity took a bite. Juice ran again. He angled the pastry and the juice ran onto her breasts. She squeaked and raised her hands to protect the gown, but he captured them and tumbled her backward.

He used his tongue to clean off every trace.

She lay there entrapped by strange desires.

Clever fingers unhooked the gown, untied the laces of the stomacher, and cast it aside. Chastity lay beneath him in her filmy silk chemise and petticoat, her gown open. She wondered if he found her lacking.

A look at his face told her he did not. He was flushed and dark-eyed, entranced, as his fingers traced the swell of her breasts. Rapturous power swelled in her. "Do I please you, milord?" she murmured.

"You are beautiful, as you know." His voice was scarcely as loud as a whisper.

His hand went to her mask-strings, but she caught it. "No! I remain masked."

"Is your reputation so precious, then?"

"It is to me."

He ran a thumb over her cheek along the edge of the black velvet. "Am I to be trusted with a name?"

"No," she whispered, "but you may call me Chloe."

"Chloe, is it? Will you laugh at my pain?" Softly he quoted, " 'Kiss me, Dear, before my dying; Kiss me once, and ease my pain.' "

His lips came down hot on hers. Sweet heaven, she'd give anything to ease a pain of his. Tears swelled in her eyes and she thanked the mask that hid them.

Suddenly he left her. She sat up, afraid that in some way she had displeased him, but he had picked up the pot of whipped cream. With a smile and a twitch of his eyebrows, he took a dollop and dropped it in her cleavage.

Chastity looked down and gaped. He pushed her back and spread the cream over the upper swell of her breasts. Then she felt him ease away the chemise and knew she was bare, felt more cream land and be spread.

She waited, breathless, for his mouth. Instead a finger swept across her breasts and was presented before her eyes. "Eat. You are hungry."

Chastity didn't have to part her lips for her mouth was still open in shock. She flicked out her tongue and took a little of the cream. It was flavored with orange liquer. "It's very good," she whispered. "We really shouldn't waste it."

He smiled. "We're not going to waste it." He slowly sucked the rest of the cream off his finger, then gathered more and presented it to her again. "Take it all this time, sweet Chloe. All."

Trapped by his eyes, Chastity took his finger into her mouth, tasting the cream, slick, cool, and rich. She swallowed. When she would have let his finger go, he said, "No. Keep it. Suck on it. Nice and slow . . ."

His head lowered and he licked some cream from her breasts in a long sweep. Dreamlike, Chastity kept sucking on his finger.

She felt his tongue swirl around first one nipple, then the other, and caught her breath at the sweetness of that sensation. His tongue tickled the tip of each one. "Ah, my beauties," he murmured, "you envy my finger, don't you?"

Chastity abruptly stilled her mouth.

He leaned down and took one nipple into his mouth and abraded it with his tongue. A thrill shot through Chastity and she did the same to his finger.

"That's right, sweeting," he said softly. "Show me what you want."

Chastity waited for what he would do next. He did nothing. Then she understood him. Tentatively, she sucked his finger. He sucked her nipple. She sucked harder. He matched it. It became strangely as if she pleasured herself. She sucked deep and slow, feeling a fever grow and burn in her.

A throbbing started between her legs and she stirred restlessly. She heard whimpering sounds and realized they were coming from herself. And faith, neither of them was truly undressed yet!

He moved on top of her and rubbed against her. It helped a little, but not a great deal. Desperate, she drew his finger deep into her mouth, but he laughed and dragged it free.

"Sweet heaven, Chloe. One of us will draw blood at that rate. Here, undress me."

To Chastity's amazement he stood and seemed to expect her to do exactly that. She lay for a moment, fevered with lust, thinking he'd have to change his mind. Wasn't he as desperate with need as she? Apparently not. Dizzy, and throbbing, she struggled to her feet. She looked down at herself. Her open gown hung from her shoulders and from the waist up she was all stained milk, cream, and bare skin. She hitched the chemise up again over her breasts.

She worked at the buttons on his long waistcoat, her fingers unsteady and clumsy, her nerves burningly aware of his body. She gave up halfway and splayed her hands over his chest, looking for help to his shadowed, intent face.

Thinking to urge him, she reached up to kiss him.

His lips played against hers, but then he drew back. "The sooner you're done, sweeting, the sooner we can progress."

The fever lessened a little, though Chastity could have wept to see it go. What crazy game was this? She began to be afraid that he was intent on torturing her, and that they never would make love.

She finished the buttons with great speed. As she unfastened the lowest one, she felt the rigid hardness of him. That reassured her a little. He needed a woman—needed her. She remembered how it had been when she'd been unknotting those laces. Hesitantly she pressed and stroked.

He caught his breath. "Depends whether you want this fast or slow, Chloe."

Chastity had no way of knowing. She took her hand away.

"Ah," he said on a long out-breath. *"Une connaisseuse. I expected nothing less."*

His tone jarred, but this was all turning out to be other than Chastity had expected, so why should his attitude surprise her? She pulled his shirt out from his waistband and eased it up over his chest. She found she loved running her hands up the silky muscles. She paused to circle them there, almost in a trance.

He pulled out of the sleeves himself and worked it over his head.

Chastity ran a finger down the livid scar that slashed across him. "How did you get this?" A woman would be bound to ask.

"A saber. At Quebec."

"It must have bled a lot."

"Like a slashed wineskin. Ruined my best uniform."

Chastity was swamped by memories, bittersweet. She knew it wasn't supposed to be like this between them, but this was the best they could hope for.

She looked down at her breasts, her bare breasts, still streaked with cream. She gathered the last of the cream and spread it gently down his scar. Then she licked it away. She could see and feel the depth of his breathing, though he stood quite still.

The bulge in his breeches pushed against her belly.

"Come on, Chloe," he said sharply. "Slow is one thing, but if you drag this out much longer you'll waste my attributes."

Chastity jerked under his tone and quickly unfastened the buttons in both his breeches and his drawers. Grasping her courage, she pushed them both down. His penis sprang free against her.

She grabbed it with both hands.

A moment later she didn't know why. Perhaps it was an attempt to control the thing, but now she had it throbbing in her hands, and no idea what to do with it.

With unsteady lightness, he said, "Kiss it and it'll be very nice to you."

She looked at the moist tip then up at him, wide-eyed. He shook his head and peeled her fingers away. She was glad to let go. He quickly stripped out of his nether-wear and stockings until he stood magnificently naked.

Chastity stared her fill. There was only the slightest glossing of softness to Cyn Malloren. He was all taut, beautiful muscle. Reality faded. Her disguise, her masquerading as a whore, her past and future, all became shadows. There was only herself, and Cyn, and this moment.

She gasped when he caught her chin and forced her eyes to meet his. "I need facts, sweet Chloe. You're not as experienced in all this as you try to pretend, are you?"

Chastity wanted to lie, for fear that he'd throw her out, and go seek one such as Sable, but he demanded truth. "No," she said.

He nodded and took a steadying breath. "Now this is important, and if you lie to me, I swear I'll beat you. Are you a virgin?"

Chastity hesitated. She guessed that if she said yes this

would all end here and her ferocious hunger would be unassuaged. On the other hand, she wasn't physically a virgin, so he'd never know.

After the fiasco with Vernham, Chastity had summoned her doctor to examine her and certify her purity. Her father had found out and brought in some woman—she claimed to be a midwife, but Chastity suspected she was keeper of a brothel. Her father's loathsome henchman, Lindle, had held her down while the woman broke her hymen and took away her feeble proof of virtue.

When Dr. Marsden had called, she'd tried to send him away, but her father had forced her to accept the examination by the saddened physician. Chastity had been warned that if she ever tried to tell her story, Dr. Marsden would give evidence of her wickedness.

"Well?" Cyn asked sharply. "It's not so hard a question."

"No," said Chastity. "Of course I'm not a virgin."

He searched her eyes. "Is that the truth? I meant what I said. I'll beat you if you've lied about this, and I'll know."

Chastity swallowed, but met his eyes. "You won't make me bleed, I assure you, milord. I've had a man in my bed before." Both statements were completely true.

He released her chin. "So be it." He pushed her open gown off her shoulders and it fell to the floor, then turned her to undo her petticoat laces.

His fingers against her spine sent little shivers through her, and when the petticoat fell he ran his knuckles up and down the cleft of her spine; bone, silk, and flesh. She swayed back against him, and he nibbled gently at her nape.

Then sneezed.

"Damn. Why the hell did you have to wear powder?" But his tone was amused as he turned her.

"I'm sorry. As you have guessed, I am not very experienced at these matters."

His hands cradled her breasts. "I don't think experience affects that. I've known some women wise in wickedness who don't seem to realize how creams and hair-dressings can interfere with delight."

His thumbs lightly brushed her nipples through the silk. The feverish longing built in Chastity again, more strongly for having been denied before. She moved to pull off the chemise. He stopped her.

"No, sweeting, leave it. I'm not sure I'm ready for the full glory of you yet."

He picked her up and laid her again on the mattress.

"I'm ready for you," said Chastity.

"Are you? Let's see."

He knelt between her legs. He put his hands on her ankles and slid them slowly up her legs, his calloused fingers rubbing deliciously against her smooth skin. Chastity twisted restlessly, opening her legs willingly to his invasion, but his hands stopped at her thighs. He flexed his thumbs there against the satiny inner skin.

Chastity pressed her head back. "Oh, sweet heaven, what are you doing to me?"

She felt his head there, between her legs, his lips where his thumbs had been. She jerked up onto her elbows. "What . . .?"

He nipped her. "Don't ask so many questions. Does it feel good?"

Chastity was shaking. "I don't know. I feel . . . desperate."

She felt fingers in the hair between her thighs, sliding in the fluid there. "You are, aren't you? It's as if I rubbed more of that cream here."

His fingers slid into her. Chastity collapsed back with a guttural moan that shocked her with its primitive sound. She pushed against his hand and he met her hard, rubbing against her. He slid up to take her nipple in his mouth and sucked in rhythm with his hand.

Chastity was lost. A part of her brain was still sane, and

knew she was probably shouting her desperate need of release. She would rather be quiet and ladylike but found it impossible. She tried to apologize, but instead she stretched herself wide and thrust up at him.

Then he moved. His mouth and hand left her and she felt him hard against her.

"Yes," she breathed.

He slid into her slowly, almost tentatively. Chastity whimpered and thrust up to engulf him. He was big, she was tight, but the stretching fullness was delicious.

She thought she heard a strange sigh as he settled in her. Then he eased out.

She wriggled after him, terrified he would leave her. He slid in again and she shuddered with relief.

"Never fear, Chloe," he said gently, running a tender hand across her cheek, "I won't leave you aching. Come, let us find our end."

Thrust met thrust, slowly at first as they learned each other, gentle and caring. But then need took over and they raced to an explosion that tore Chastity's mind asunder.

She floated up from that darkness and sucked air into her empty lungs, knowing she would never be the same again. She was scoured clean, both full and empty, dazed and yet alive as never before.

He sprawled on top of her, breathing deeply, hot and sweaty. When he stirred, they were stuck together by sweat, juice, and cream, and had to peel themselves apart. Cooler air brushed over her damp skin and she laughed with delight.

He leaned over her, eyes dark and mysterious, but smiling at her pleasure. "One thing's for sure, my Chloe, you've had oafs in your bed before. Why waste all this glory on them?"

She wanted to tell him the truth, but it would shatter a golden moment. And she wasn't at all sure he wouldn't beat her for the lie she'd told, even though it had been the truth. "I was an ignorant fool," she said.

He shielded his eyes and ran a hand down her arm. "And now?"

"And now I know better."

"And what will you do with that knowledge?"

She knew then what she must do. He didn't think he was the first, but he knew—heaven knew how—that he'd been the first to show her that ecstasy. Now he felt responsible, as if he had taken her maidenhead. Knight-errantry again. Did he try to help every wounded stray in his path? He already had Verity, William, and Charles on his hands; he didn't need a lascivious Chloe to fret over.

She must cut him free.

She eased to a sitting position. "I'll know my worth from now on," she said frankly. "I'll not give my favors lightly in the future."

His hand rested on her thigh. "Is that a promise?"

She nodded. She wished, quite desperately, that she could speak the thoughts of her heart—that she loved him and could never imagine these intimacies with any other man, no matter how skillful. She longed for a moment of honesty between them, just once.

But this night was all they would ever have and honesty would ruin it.

And this night wasn't over yet.

She looked thoughtfully at his penis, limp against his thigh. He chuckled and said, "Soon, I have no doubt."

He sat up and pulled off her soiled and creased chemise, wrapping them both in the quilt. To snuggle with him like this was an unexpected bliss, perhaps more than she could handle. Certainly more than she could willingly forgo . . .

He poured them more wine. "Tell me about yourself."

Chastity hadn't bargained on conversation. "Would you pluck out the heart of my mysteries, then?"

"Yes, indeed. I'd strip you to your very soul."

She shivered. "Why don't you tell me your secrets first, milord."

"My secrets . . ." He stared into the glowing fire. "Is it

a secret that I'm often afraid before battle? It's not one to my fellow soldiers because we all share the weakness. Only a fool lacks fear. I don't fear death. I fear maiming."

Chastity clenched her hands on her glass. Death was the last thing she wanted to talk of. "Do you not have any less *military* secrets?"

He slid her a glance. "Do you want a list of my lovers?"

She certainly did not. "Is that the total of your interests? Love and war?"

"Perhaps. How long does it take, I wonder, to know someone? To fall in love."

Chastity gazed into the secret world of the fire. "A moment, or forever."

"True enough. Now, you owe me a secret."

She shook her head. "I am made entirely of secrets and mysteries, and if I give away one, I will fall apart."

Like an explosion, he pulled her to her feet, dragged her over to a small speckled mirror on the wall, and held her there. She saw them both, naked, made strange by rippled glass and flickering light. He was Cyn, his hair rippling to his naked shoulders; she was a mystery, even to herself. This woman with her dusty dark hair, mask, and swollen lips was no one she knew.

"Watch," he said, "and I will show you mysteries."

He began to touch her with skillful thoroughness, all the time watching her watch this strange wanton woman in the mirror melt into desire. Her head fell back against his shoulder. Her lips parted. Her bosom rose and fell with deep, hungry breaths. She looked at him in the glass. He was not swamped by desire, but watchful.

"I don't like this," she said.

"Liar."

"I don't like leaving you behind. Come with me."

He nipped her shoulder. "I can discover all the secrets of your body and use them to shatter you into pieces, but you will not fall apart. You will be stronger for it."

She tried to resist his skillful touch. "That's not the same."

He increased the pressure of his hand between her thighs, and a shudder overwhelmed her will. "It's the same," he said. "Tell me your secrets."

Another wave of aching desire rippled through her. She closed her eyes. "What do you *want?*"

"All of you. *Trust me.*"

She spread her legs. "I trust you."

His hand stopped. "Not for that. Trust me with yourself."

She shook her head. "I have nothing for you, Cyn Malloren." She broke free and ran, swooping down to catch up her clothing. He brought her down on the mattress, weighing down her body with his own, her wrists in his grasp.

His eyes were dark. "This is not the end."

"I told you, I have nothing more."

"Yes, you have. I want all of you. I want your secrets."

Chastity struggled. "You're mad!"

"Indeed I am. Can't you feel it, what's in this room, damn you? After this, can you go to another man?"

"I won't go to another man!"

"Trust me!" He kissed her with passion. Chastity kissed him back as she wept. This time the tears leaked out of the mask and he drank them from her cheeks. "Cry, cry for us, Chloe. Whatever else, you'll never forget this."

He made love to her again, with mouth and hands, and every nerve in his body. At first she struggled against the passion, fearing the wildness of it, the violence of his intent, but then she surrendered.

He would not let it be easy. Twice he brought her high, then stopped despite her pleas, cooling her with wine and cream until reality returned, a reality full of longing.

She swore at him, hit out at him.

He turned her gently and massaged her back, using the cream for lubrication, until she turned languid and floating, and found a kind of peace. Then he pushed her up on her knees and touched her from behind until she gasped with need once more.

"Devil take you, Cyn Malloren," she whispered, "if you let me down again."

He laughed and slid to lie under her, looking up at her. "Fly for yourself then, Chloe. Ride me."

She straddled him and engulfed him with hungry urgency, sliding up and down him with the sweetest friction in the world. She watched him dissolve, but she'd learned her lessons well. With supreme willpower, she stopped, hovering over him.

His eyes flew open. His fists clenched. "Oh, sweet wanton harpy from hell . . . Do I have to beg?"

"Yes," she said.

His eyes were nothing but darkness. "Please," he whispered.

Chastity settled again and sent them soaring.

They slept. Chastity woke half over Cyn with the quilt dragged roughly on top of them. The fire was dead, and the light through the dusty window suggested the first touches of dawn. She eased up cautiously, shivering in the chill air, but he didn't stir.

She could hardly see him in the gray light and wanted to desperately. She reached to touch him but pulled her hand back. Tears choked her at the knowledge that this was the end. After this night, she'd have to flee.

Hardly breathing, she slipped into the chemise, petticoat, and gown. She carried the stomacher for it would be too difficult to struggle into here. She doubted she would meet anyone at this dead hour of the night, but if so, in the gloom, the clothes she had on should do.

She retrieved her key from under the mattress and eased open the door, wincing as it creaked. He still didn't stir. She slipped out, down the narrow stairs, and fled back to Lord Heatherington's room.

* * *

Cyn opened his eyes as soon as she left. This was certainly a cold, bleak aftermath to the most heated night of his life. He closed his eyes and relived it, not proud of all of it, but aware that in the end it had been good.

One thing was certain—he could not now live without her; he could not let her live without him.

The pain had been physical when he'd recognized the perfume worn by Gresham's whore. He'd felt as if all the pleasures of life had turned to dross because his damsel was a wanton, not a misjudged angel. He'd stolen her from his friend more with a mind to vengeance than pleasure.

He'd been prepared to be disgusted by a whore's tricks, and had been seduced by gallant ignorance. He'd truly expected to have her confess to being a virgin, and been prepared, at great cost to his sanity, to leave her one. Even as he'd entered her he'd expected to find that she'd lied.

And been disappointed to find her truthful.

But it didn't take much to steal virginity, after all, and it was clear as day she was no practiced trollop. Perhaps there'd just been Vernham . . .

He shook his head and smiled. She was doubtless sneaking back to her identity as Charles. It would be hard, but he'd leave her in it until he'd worked out what best to do. The future would not be easy. The world would stare at a Malloren marrying a ruined woman, and Rothgar would do his damndest to stop him.

But despite the world, despite Rothgar, despite everything, he'd have her, and keep her, and make her sing with delight night and day. There'd be difficulties, but difficulties kept away boredom.

He stood up and stretched, feeling king of the world. He whistled as he dressed and tidied their unlikely love-nest.

Chapter 12

⁀

Chastity knew only two routes back to Heatherington's room. One would take her outside, the other through the front hall. When she opened the door to the outside, a mist as thick as drizzle chilled her. She shivered, closed the door, and headed for the hall. She looked down at her almost-bare chest and wondered if she should try to put on the stomacher, but the house was silent. She just pulled the front edges of her gown close together and hurried along.

She froze when she heard faint voices—she thought from the gaming room—but decided those addicts were no hazard and slipped into the hall.

Only one smoky lamp still burned, and rank odors of sweat and drink hung heavy in the air, but the hall was deserted. A few items of clothing lay straggled about, and a large dark stain on the polished oak spoke of a spill. She assumed it wasn't blood. If anyone had lost that much blood, there would have been a commotion.

Then again, if wholesale slaughter had taken place this past night, would she and Cyn have noticed?

Despite the bleakness of her situation, she couldn't help but smile at the memories. She had never imagined love-making to be like that; passion had fused them, like iron in a forge. They had no future, but this one night had been worth all the pain it would bring.

But only if Cyn never knew Chloe's identity. She must

be gone before he stirred. She picked up her skirts and ran for the stairs. Her foot knocked against an empty flagon which spun off to clatter against the newel post.

"What have we here?"

Chastity whipped around to see the Marquess of Rothgar standing in a doorway in the halo of light from a branch of fresh candles. He placed them on a table and came over to her.

Chastity turned to run up the stairs, but he moved with surprising speed and caught her arm, not harshly, but with enough strength to prevent escape.

"Please, sir," she said, putting on a country burr and keeping her face averted, "let me go."

He turned her face toward him. "Unwise to try to pass as a country girl, my dear. Only the highborn ladies here are masked."

Chastity clutched her gown together, feeling as half-naked as she was. "Perhaps I want to be thought a highborn lady, sir."

"I wonder why? They aren't being paid."

Somehow he'd turned them both so that he now stood between her and the stairs, a formidable barrier. Chastity's heart started to pound with fear.

He considered her with a slight smile on his fine lips, though his eyes were shadowed and she couldn't be sure the humor reached them. Her legs were trembling. What in heaven's name did he want?

He looked as opulent and unsullied as he had hours earlier, and in no need of sleep. Was he human? Had he come to Rood House by accident, or tracked Cyn here? It was impossible that he connected her to his brother, even if he knew Cyn had arrived here with a young man . . .

He pulled a pouch from his pocket, opened it, and poured a stream of guineas into one hand. "I've been passing the time at the tables," he said. "This pouch for the rest of your night."

Chastity clutched her gown even tighter. "It's . . . it's almost dawn."

"True."

Chastity swallowed and shook her head. "I'm too tired, sir."

He raised a brow. "Another mistake. A whore is never too tired. What are you then—a lady or a whore?"

Desperate, Chastity tried to push past him, but he simply moved to block her, and stood like a wall in her way.

"I'll scream."

"Do you really think that would do any good?"

He had moved to the first step, which made his impressive height even more overwhelming. It hurt Chastity's neck to look up at him. "What do you want, sir?"

"Milord," he corrected gently. "I wonder where you spent the night."

Chastity met his eyes. "With a lover."

"So I supposed, and one who has left you too tired. Is that an achievement, I wonder?"

Chastity again tried to step around him, and again was blocked. She couldn't cope with this. At any moment she would burst into tears.

He pulled a pin out of his lacy cravat—a black baroque pearl set in gold—and twirled it before her. "This pin for a kiss."

Chastity looked at it and the twirling made her dizzy.

"And then you'll let me go?"

"You're not very flattering, child. But yes, and then I'll let you go. If you still wish to escape."

Chastity knew rather more of kisses than she had the last time Rothgar had kissed her, and the prospect frightened her. But it was, after all, only a kiss, and at any moment Cyn could wake and pursue her. "Very well, milord."

He put his hands on her waist and lifted her effortlessly to a higher step than his so that she stood only half a head shorter than he. The action dislodged her hands and her gown flew open. She grabbed for it. He was there first. He pulled the two halves together and fastened them with the pin.

Then he looked at her.

Chastity stood calmly, determined to pay her forfeit with dignity.

"You should have defined *kiss* before you agreed to the bargain," he said softly.

She felt her eyes widen. "A kiss is a kiss."

"What then is a kiss?" His hands moved to her shoulders and his thumbs brushed her collarbone. It was not unpleasant, but she was mainly thinking that Cyn could appear at any moment. Apart from the fact that he'd reveal himself to his brother, and probably get into a fight over this embrace, she would have lost her chance to escape.

"Just your mouth and mine," she said briskly.

He laughed. "What poor measure you give, my dear. Very well, just your mouth and mine."

He took his hands away and leaned down to let his lips play on hers. They teased and tugged until she found her mouth softening. She had the strangest need to clutch at him before she fell, but clutched her stomacher to her chest instead. She should have put a time limit on the kiss.

His tongue swept out across her inner lips and she softened further. She closed her eyes and recognized his skill, even as she wished he'd get it over with. Her ears stretched for the sound of Cyn's footsteps. Or would he take the outside route?

He could already be in Heatherington's room!

Rothgar's tongue thrust into her relaxed mouth. Instinctively, Chastity spat it out. Her eyes flew open, fearing retribution.

He was smiling, if a little ruefully. "Poor measure indeed." He stepped back. "Go on your way, little bird."

Chastity moved to return the pin, but he stayed her hand. "Keep it. I have found our encounter most instructive. You could answer me one question, however, if you feel you haven't earned the bauble."

Chastity moved a few wary steps higher. "Yes?"

"Did the kisses you received during the night please you more than mine?"

"Oh, yes," said Chastity, and only then realized she was smiling, probably blushing.

He gave her an elegant, flourishing bow. "Then may you have more from the same source."

Bemused, Chastity turned and fled.

She hesitated at the door to Heatherington's room. Cyn could already be here. Even if he were not, it would hardly be surprising if their host had decided to use his bed, and found a spare key. She turned the lock and opened the door slowly. The room felt empty.

She crept over to the bed. It was definitely empty. She fumbled for the flint-box by the bed and made a flame to put to the candle there. There was no sign that anyone had been here since she had left.

She collapsed onto the bed, shaking and perilously close to being overwhelmed. She wanted a hole to hide in, and a long time to gather the splintered pieces of herself together again, to gain the courage to go on. She had no time. She must change back into Charles and leave.

She began to work the pin out of her gown. It wasn't easy. Rothgar had woven it deep through the thickest part of the silk. She looked up and caught sight of herself in the mirror. Stars in heaven, but she looked the veriest drab!

Her wig was askew and her lips looked thoroughly kissed. The pink powder had dusted over the black velvet mask and the shoulders of her gown. Her gown was barely decent, and without a stomacher her breasts seemed all too lush.

The fastidious Rothgar had been attracted by this?
Never.

So what had he wanted? As she stripped off her woman's clothing, Chastity worried at it. Oh, if she'd taken him up on his offer to purchase her body for a few hours, she had no doubt he'd have gone through with it, but the offer had not really been serious. Yet he had not been willing to let her go, and his offer for a kiss had cost him dearly.

It frightened her that she didn't understand his purpose. When she'd been Lady Chastity Ware in London, Rothgar hadn't frightened her; he'd just thrilled her. Now, a fugitive entangled with his brother—of which entanglement he would never approve—she quaked. His actions added urgency to her flight.

Cold water stood waiting in the jug and she poured it into the bowl to wash away the sweat, cream, and cosmetics. Blushing, she cleansed the traces of lovemaking from between her legs. Her hands stilled. What if she was pregnant?

Lud, what would she do then? She must have been mad! Her father would surely kill her. She placed her hands over her abdomen, as if there could already be changes, then pulled them away. She'd handle that disaster when she had to. Even so, she could feel a soft core of longing at the thought of bearing Cyn's child, but it gave her another reason to flee.

He had unwittingly made love to a young, unmarried lady, and even though he didn't believe she had been a virgin, she knew Cyn Malloren would feel he had to marry her; a child would seal his fate. She couldn't trap him with that cheap trick, trap him into a marriage that would ruin his career, and alienate him from his family forever.

She hastily cleared away all evidence of her masquerade. She stuffed the wig back in the portmanteau, then realized that would tell Cyn instantly who she had been. She pulled it out and flung it into the back of Heatherington's armoire. She hoped Cyn would forget its very existence. She tossed the clothes and mask in with it.

She picked up the pearl pin and wondered what to do with it. She was tempted to leave it, and yet she sensed it was a gift honestly given. What had Rothgar meant by that last question, about the kisses she had received during the night? From another man it might have reflected pique that he didn't please her, but not from Rothgar.

Again she had that frightening lack of understanding. She pushed the pin through the facing of her jacket. If the worse came to the worst, it might buy her a few meals one day.

She put her own tie-wig on her head and her slouch hat on top. Once more Charles looked out of the mirror. Her face of the night before, soft with passion, blurred over the real image. She could almost imagine Cyn behind her, his hands on her body . . .

She dragged herself out of this maundering and forced herself to hurry. She turned through Cyn's uniform pockets and found his money. She took half.

In a moment of weakness, she clung to his red coat and drank in the aroma there. Sweet heaven, how could she leave him?

Sweet heaven, how could she stay?

It would be impossible to maintain her masquerade after last night, and now more than ever she could not let him know. It would be to trap him by deceit.

Perhaps more than that; perhaps he had come to care for the mysterious woman he had made love to. She remembered the fierce intensity with which he'd demanded her secrets.

Perhaps today he would be looking for Chloe.

Well, both Chloe and Charles were going to disappear . . .

Chastity froze.

If they both disappeared, would he make the connection? Surely it would not take much to trigger a link in his mind. She covered her face with shaking hands.

Was it more dangerous for him if she stayed, or if she fled?

She paced the room, but suddenly she knew. She had to stay. For Cyn's sake, she had to preserve the charade.

Chastity replaced the money. She studied herself again

in the full-length mirror to be sure she'd removed all trace of Chloe. Her lips looked fuller and redder today, but that was all.

She put her hand to her crotch. The past night had shown her that maleness tended to be visible. She was lucky not to have been caught out before, though of course no one had suspected anything and the double layer of breeches helped. If Cyn developed any suspicions, they must be countered.

She went back to the portmanteau and took out the wool that had formed Cyn's bosom. She rolled a tube of it, thinking of Cyn both limp and hard as she estimated size. Limp would do fine. She had no desire to have anyone think her aroused.

She found she was standing there, hands still, remembering . . . It wasn't fair. Why couldn't there be a chance for them? She remembered the names she had gathered, and the letter. Perhaps there would be a way to use them. Perhaps she could find the woman who'd broken her hymen. Perhaps Henry Vernham would confess.

Perhaps, perhaps, perhaps.

They were all faint chances, and a good part of the world would never believe her honest, but she would try. She would fight.

She looked at the roll of gray wool and stuffed it down her breeches and added another ball at the juncture of her thighs. Then she studied herself in the mirror again and nodded. The illusion was subtle, but if anyone questioned her gender and looked, or even touched, they would lose their doubts. She hoped that applied to Cyn as well as the others.

She checked rigorously that no evidence remained of Chloe. Then she disordered the bed as if she had slept there, and sat down to wait.

Not long after, there was a tap at the door. Chastity opened it a crack and let Cyn in. Did he look at her intently, or was it just her tense nerves, and her desire to fling herself into his arms?

"I hope you had a peaceful night, young Charles."

"Tolerable," Chastity said primly. "You, I gather, did not."

He looked at her from under lids made heavy by love-making and lack of sleep. "Why do you assume that?"

"From the fact that you did not return here. I can only assume you found another bed, but not to sleep."

He began stripping off his suit and putting on his uniform. "Oh, I caught some sleep, but if I doze off on the road, I trust the virtuous half of our party can steer me to Maidenhead."

The word Maidenhead made Chastity blush, which was a great piece of foolishness. She hid it by packing his suit into the bag. She felt a crackling in the pocket. Had the man not even found her note? What to do now? Rothgar worried her. He could hardly take them prisoner, but if they bumped into him, he would surely delay them.

"Do you want this paper?" she asked, holding it out.

He took it with surprise and read it. " 'Struth."

"What is it?"

He gave her a look. "Rothgar's here."

"That note's from him?"

"Hardly. Someone thought to warn me. I wonder who."

"Will he stop us?"

"No," he said absolutely. "But the only reason he would be at an affair such as this would be in search of me. I fear we have him hot on our trail."

"Why would he be pursuing you like this?"

"Simple, bloody interference." He straightened his uniform, checked the room; and buckled the bag. Once again, any mention of his brother had his temper on edge. "Ready?"

Chastity was surprised at how easy it was to slip back into the Charles and Cyn roles. She even felt a twitch of jealously toward the wanton Chloe who had occupied his night. She shook her head at this folly and followed him out of the door.

He headed for the main stairs, and she caught his sleeve, thinking of Rothgar. "There's . . . There will be a secondary stair at the end of the building."

He raised a brow. "We're not fugitives. We're here by invitation."

"What about your brother?"

His jaw tightened. "I am not reduced to skulking down the servants' stairs to avoid Rothgar."

"Very well," she snapped. "Go to hell your own way."

He hesitated, then set off away from the main stairs. At the bottom of the smaller staircase, he took a passage which led them into the servants' quarters.

The house seemed dead in the gray morning light. The kitchen was cold and deserted. Except, they discovered, for three weary servants who'd rolled up in blankets near the fire.

Cyn shook his head, but with a hint of a smile. "When Heather celebrates, the world has a headache. This event will go down in the history books." He found the larder and helped himself to half a cold meat pie, a cottage loaf, a hunk of cheese, and some apples. He drew two tankards of ale from a keg and passed one to Chastity.

She drank it. "Will we not breakfast at the inn?"

"We're not going to the inn. If Rothgar's here, he doubtless knows we left the horses at the Angel. He'll have it watched. We'll see if we can borrow some of Heather's horses without a fuss."

Chastity couldn't resist. "I thought you weren't going to skulk around for fear of your brother."

He flashed her a very unpleasant look. "I'll simply avoid a confrontation if I can. Come on."

Outside, the heavy drizzle seeped into them, chill and damp. Chastity shivered and pulled her cloak closer.

It took time for them to find the stables in this gray world, but at last they were inside, looking at the rows of horses. This place, however, was not completely unattended. An old man hobbled forward. "Need your horses, sir?" He peered at them with habitual suspicion. "Didn't reckon there'd be any up this early today."

"I don't suppose there'll be many others," said Cyn easily. "I'm Lord Cynric Malloren, on government business. Lord Heatherington promised me the use of two horses."

The man looked dubious, but was clearly unwilling to contest such crisp authority. He went to saddle two thoroughbreds. Cyn gave Chastity the portmanteau and helped.

As they mounted, Cyn posed a question in an offhand manner. "I think my brother is here. The Marquess of Rothgar. I don't suppose he's stirring yet?"

"None but you's up yet, milord."

"Ah well, if you should see him, tell him I'm sorry to have missed him."

With that they urged the horses out of the yard and down the lane to the road.

Chastity edged up beside him. "Wouldn't it have been wiser to bribe the man to silence?"

"Rothgar would just pay him more to speak."

"So you leave what amounts to a challenge."

His teeth flashed in a grin. "By the time he's risen and breakfasted, we'll be in Maidenhead, and he can catch us if he wants."

He pushed ahead and Chastity muttered a few choice epithets at his back. His ill-feeling toward his brother could prove disastrous, but she couldn't warn him that Rothgar was already up and on the prowl without revealing her secret.

They cantered along until they found a milestone giving some hint of where they were.

"The devil of it is," said Cyn, "that I lost track of our location during that coach ride."

"Distracted by the lovely songs, I've no doubt."

"You know what, young Charles, you're going to turn into a prosy bore if you don't learn to enjoy yourself."

"I assure you I can enjoy myself when the circumstances are right."

"Can you? I live to see the day."

Chastity hid a secret smile.

Cyn too hid a secret smile. Her spirit as was strong as ever.

He scanned the dense gray sky, which was brighter where the sun was struggling to make itself felt. "One thing's sure, we need to go north. We'll be bound to cross a London road at some point."

They rode for an hour, and by that time the drizzle had ceased and some of the mist had faded. They stopped and shared the pie. Cyn yawned. Chastity had to fight not to yawn with him. How much sleep had they had last night? Three or four hours, no more.

"Tired, my lord?" she asked sweetly.

"A little. What of you? You seem a little stiff. Perhaps you're not accustomed to so much . . . riding."

Chastity kept her pink face lowered. He didn't know the half of it. Her muscles were somewhat stiff from the riding yesterday, but it was the lovemaking that had left her so sensitive between her legs.

"Never mind," he said with a hearty slap on the back. "We can have no more than six miles to go."

They soon hit the Oxford road, and at a posting inn called the Five Rings they discovered Maidenhead lay but two miles east. They cantered along the busy road, passing carters, and drovers, and people on foot. Stagecoaches and private carriages bowled past.

Chastity suddenly gasped and reined in.

"What is it?" Cyn asked.

"My father's carriage just passed."

"Going which way?"

"East. Toward Maidenhead."

"Hold up, then. We'll let him get well ahead." He laid a hand over hers briefly. "Don't worry. We knew he'd be about. Henry Vernham too, no doubt, unless he's still combing southward for Mrs. Inchcliff. They're not looking for us, at least not for me."

The sight of her father's carriage had brought all Chastity's terror of her father to the fore, but she knew what she must do. "Cyn," she said.

"Yes?"

"The important thing is to deliver the message to Major Frazer. If by any chance my father spots me, you must cut free and continue with our mission."

He frowned slightly. "And leave you to face his anger for being on the loose?"

Chastity's stomach knotted at the thought of her father's anger if he caught her roaming the country dressed as a boy, but she summoned up a cocky tone. "I'll get a jawing for leaving Nana's, but that's hardly a dire fate."

"Yet Verity seems to fear your father. Why is she not willing to seek the earl's help?"

"Only because he'll stop her marrying Nathaniel."

"But otherwise, she'd feel safe with him?"

Chastity knew he needed reassuring. "Yes. Why not?"

"I just wondered."

"He is a stern man, and believes he has every right to direct his daughters' lives. That's all."

"And his son's," he added pointedly.

Cyn the Protector. Chastity needed all his concentration on Verity's problems. "I'm still a schoolboy," she pointed out, "and should be doing as I'm told."

"I think he'll beat you."

She shrugged. "Quite likely. I'll not die of it."

Cyn nodded and they rode on.

Chastity didn't know what the earl would do if he caught her. She'd never been involved in anything so outrageous in her life. After all, her father knew she hadn't really invited Vernham to her bed. The whippings then had been to force her to agree to the marriage, and the earl had obviously expected her to break under quite mild pain.

She had discovered him to be skilled at the terrifying application of quite mild pain.

There had rarely been any question of her father doing her permanent damage, or leaving scars—though on one occasion her defiance had driven him into an almost murderous rage. That had been when she'd begun to wonder about his sanity, and truly fear for her life. He had controlled himself, however, before doing his worst.

Her brother, Fort, had been the one more likely to break her neck. He had a scarce-manageable temper, and he'd believed she'd smirched the honor of the family. Now, however, she felt she could face Fort, even if he had his hands round her throat. The thought of facing her father turned her knees to jelly.

"We're almost there," said Cyn. "Keep your eyes peeled and your head down."

"That sounds a trifle difficult."

He quirked a smile. "I never said this would be easy."

"Yes, you did."

He laughed.

They arrived at the first cottages of Maidenhead as the church clock stuck eleven. They had seen no sign of the earl, but he would be lodged at one of the many inns. Maidenhead sat on the busy Bath road and boasted any number of posting inns. Stages and carriages crowded the busy high street, and people bustled in and out of shops.

Cyn swung off his horse and indicated that Chastity do the same. "You'll be less noticeable down here. The thing is to find you a safe spot, then I can search out Frazer. There's no barracks here, so he's doubtless billeted on someone, but there must be a command post."

Chastity wanted to stay with him, but knew it would be foolish. She was the hazard. "If only we knew which inn Father was at . . ."

Cyn halted before the Fleece Inn, where an ostler hovered, alert for approaching business. "Good day," he said.

"Would you know if the Earl of Walgrave is staying here?"

"Nay, Captain," said the man. "He be up at the Bear."

Cyn tossed him a penny and moved on. "So, we avoid the Bear. He'll doubtless have all the inns watched, but he's not looking for me or you."

They stopped at the Saracen's Head. Chastity tugged down the brim of her hat before leading her horse into the yard. Grooms came forward to take the mounts, and Cyn and Chastity were soon in the inn. Cyn bespoke a private bedroom and parlor, and engaged mine host in idle chat which encompassed the eminent people presently in Maidenhead, the presence of the military, and the strange case of the lost Lady Vernham, whose poster seemed to be everywhere.

By the time they reached their rooms, they knew that the Earl of Walgrave had been back and forth along the Bath road in search of his daughter; that a company of infantry readying for departure to the Continent was billeted on the town under Major Nathaniel Frazer; that the major's headquarters were at Cross House down by the river; and that the poor lady was feared dead. The word was out along the river to find her body, and that of her babe.

Cyn established Chastity in the rooms with everything she needed. "You are to stay here."

"Very well." She couldn't resist the plea: "Try not to be gone too long."

"It shouldn't take long. You might give some thought to our course if Frazer won't have anything to do with our plan. It could put his career on the line."

Chastity raised her chin. "He won't fail Verity. Are you saying you'd put your career before your true love?"

"Who says I have one? But no," he admitted softly, "I wouldn't. I have some income beyond my pay, however, and a powerful family to back me. What of Frazer?"

"He has a small estate, but his family are not the like of yours."

"Well, we'll see what he says." He seemed reluctant to leave. "Stay here," he repeated. "Don't grow restless and wander off. And lock the door. There's no reason for anyone to disturb you."

"Fine," she said impatiently. "I'm not a fool. Get on with it and it'll be the sooner done."

When he'd gone, she turned the key in the lock. The action was strangely reminiscent of last night, but this time she had no intention of sneaking out of the room in any guise. She took a seat by a window that gave onto the bustling high street. She watched the busy scene, but was largely involved in seeking paths for her future.

If she found the woman who had stolen her virginity, perhaps she could force her to confess. She could threaten to expose Nerissa Trelyn if she didn't change her story, and call upon other women at the orgy to support her. It all seemed rather hollow. If the women called her bluff, who would believe her? And in order to tell her tale she'd have to admit to being at the orgy herself.

Her only hard evidence lay in the letter. She took it out and studied it. It was certainly scandalous enough, and after a night of love Chastity understood it rather better.

> . . . I dream of you, my Hercules, my Atlas, when I lie in my cold bed of duty. I think of your mighty rod in my satin pocket and Weak T. thinks I moan for him. When we met last week at the theater, I was wearing your handkerchief between my legs. Does it make you swell to think of it? I vow, your monogrammed silk was soon wet with my desire. I will do the same again, so think of it when next we meet.
>
> Will you do as much for me? I have enclosed the ribbon from my chemise—the pink one you will remember. Tie it on when next we meet, but not too tight, my noble stallion, or I fear you would die of it.

*Oh, I pant for you even writing this. I cannot bear
it. I will come. I promise. I will risk all for you . . .*

When Chastity had first read this she had been disgusted
at the libidinous tone, and scandalized that a Society matron could be so lost to discretion. Now she largely felt en-
vious. It doubtless was in Lady Trelyn's handwriting, and
could ruin her, but Chastity doubted she could bring on another the sufferings she herself had endured.

What had Nerissa Trelyn done, after all, but to tell the
truth—that she had discovered Chastity Ware in bed with
a man? Chastity would be asking her to lie.

She rested her head on her hand. She'd be better off
thinking of a place to seek refuge from her father. Her favorite governess had married a vicar in Westmorland. That
seemed suitably out-of-the-way . . .

She jerked back. Across the street she'd seen a man
staring at her, and now he'd slipped away. She could
hardly believe he'd recognized her, and yet there had been
something so rat-like in his movements . . .

How stupid to have been sitting here in the window!

She leaped to her feet. What should she do?

She'd promised Cyn she wouldn't leave, but she
couldn't stay in this room like a rabbit in a hole, waiting
for the terrier. She grabbed some money from his bags and
ran out, down the stairs.

No one unusual lurked in the entry hall. Perhaps someone kept watch on the place, but no one showed any interest in her. She slipped down a passageway toward the
kitchen. She opened a door to see the innkeeper sitting at
a table eating his dinner.

He rose to his feet, not best pleased. "You wanted
something, young sir? You should have rung your bell."

Chastity knew she had to keep out of her father's hands,
but also avoid any connection of Cyn with herself. She'd
thought of a story. It wasn't very believable; it all de-
pended on whether the innkeeper could be bought.

She flashed the man a guileless smile. "I'm afraid I have a confession to make, sir. I have run away from home, you see. I have a mind to join the army, but my father won't have it. He says I am too young. Captain Malloren was kind enough to help me when I was in difficulties, and he's going to fix it for me to join his regiment. But now I've seen my father in the street, and I'm afraid he might not understand the captain's part in this affair. He's an important man and could make trouble. So I'm going to hide until the captain returns. If you please, could you not tell my father I've been here?" She slid three guineas onto the table.

The innkeeper looked at the coins a moment, then they disappeared into his pocket. "Well, stap me, young sir. Not in favor of his son joining His Majesty's army! What is the world coming to? Why don't you slide out and hang about with the horses? You'll be safe enough there, and I'll tell the captain when he comes back."

Chastity gave him a wide smile and ran out the door. A coach stood in the yard, about to pull out, but presented no sign of trouble for her. She sauntered over to the stables.

As soon as she entered, she was grabbed from behind. A hand covered her mouth, and another grabbed her crotch. It jerked away as if stung and she was released. She wanted to run but knew her only chance was to face them.

"What the hell . . . ?" she shouted, whirling around.

The two skinny men looked uneasily at one another. They were both complete strangers, thank heavens.

"Sorry, lad. We're on the lookout for a young lady, run away from home. Thought you was her."

Chastity took a wide-legged stance, hands on hips, trying to look like a cocky stable lad. "A young *lady?* Plague take it, do I look like a young lady?"

"No, lad. And keep your voice down. You'll scare the young miss off."

Chastity looked them over. "I'm not sure you're up to

any good." She picked a horse at random and tried to look purposeful by topping up its hay and water bucket. Her heart raced with fear. Thank God she'd padded her breeches. Yesterday, they would have had her. It was so hard not to hurry. Eventually, she strolled back and passed the two men with a sullen, suspicious look, then continued into the busy inn yard. She had no idea what to do now, but knew she had to stay clear of Cyn. She headed for the street.

It was a little quieter than it had been earlier, for many people were at their dinner. She felt more exposed. Where could she go? The church. She headed toward the spire, trying to match the pace of the other people on the pavement, stopping occasionally to glance in a shop window and check for pursuit. She was looking blankly at a selection of china when a hand grabbed her neckcloth.

"God damn you to hell. I didn't believe it when Father told me!"

Reflected in the window, Chastity saw her brother, Fort.

Chapter 13

Her cravat was pulled so tight that Chastity could hardly breathe, but then Fort clearly decided not to cause a scene and released his hold. She had no chance to escape, for he grabbed her arm in a brutal grip. "Come on."

Chastity thought of resisting, of seeking help from the curious onlookers, but knew it was pointless. Fort would tell any intervener that it was a case of a runaway schoolboy or servant, and they'd believe him.

She glanced around for Cyn, but then forced herself to put the idea out of her head. For Verity's sake she must keep her family in ignorance of the plan and Cyn's involvement. Even though she felt sick at the thought of facing her father, she allowed her brother to tow her along Maidenhead's high street.

She glanced at Fort, wondering if it would be possible to turn him to their side. He was furious at the moment, but she had to admit that any right-minded brother would be furious to find his sister wandering England dressed as a groom. Was there any chance of convincing him that their father's plans for Verity were wrong?

She remembered the Fort of the night before when he'd been kind after his fashion; and the elder brother who'd generally been indulgent. She stopped dragging against his hold and he relaxed it a little.

When they turned into a side street, she asked, "Where are you taking me?"

"Father's hired a house here."

That made her pull away, and she almost broke free. He cursed and seized her.

"Fort, please let me go!"

"Why the devil would I do that? To let you play the harlot with some man? I can think of no other reason for you to be traipsing around the country in such a guise."

Chastity almost protested that it was a lie; she was accustomed to knowing that the accusations against her were false. But last night she *had* played the harlot for a man.

"I'll go straight back to Nana's," she promised desperately.

"You certainly will. Father will see to it, unless he has a stricter confinement in mind." He dragged her onward and she had to go.

"Fort, I'm ruined! What purpose is there in keeping me close? Let me go to perdition my own way!"

He grabbed her shoulders and shook her. "You've already made our name a byword! Am I to let you loose to do your worst? I'll see you dead first!"

He hauled her down another street and through an arch into a little close. Four quiet houses opened onto the tiny square, with something deserted about all of them. In fact, this enclave seemed set apart from the world. Anything could happen here undetected.

Chastity shuddered and pulled back. "Fort, no. You don't know what Father can be like!"

"Don't I, by gad? I hope to hell he does whip you, and thoroughly too!"

Fort forced her to a black-lacquered door and rapped. Chastity gave up hope when it was opened by George Lindle.

This man was officially her father's secretary, but a quiet clerk did the actual paperwork. Lindle was more of a henchman, a bully-boy, though a suave and elegant one.

His round, shining face broke into a wide smile. "Praise be," he declared. "We have one lamb safe." Chastity noted that, as always, his eyes remained flat and cold. Her legs were turning weak at the sight of him.

Lindle had held her down or tied her up for her beatings, and for her deflowering, and he'd never stopped smiling. She'd begun to think there was something wrong with his mouth, and that he *couldn't* stop smiling.

But perhaps he just enjoyed seeing people suffer.

"Yes, Lindle," said Fort. "We have one lamb safe, which gives me hope we'll soon have the other. I'll take her upstairs. Send word to my father."

"The earl has gone to discuss the search with the colonel of militia at Slough, my lord. I will send a message immediately, but it will be some hours before he can return."

Chastity offered a fervent prayer of thanks.

Lindle turned away, but then turned back, a picture of the unassuming, willing servant. "Should we not take steps on our own to secure Lady Verity and her son, my lord? It would not do for them to come to harm . . ."

"True," said Fort. "Well," he asked Chastity, "where are they?"

"Why ask me?" She had a flash of inspiration. "Why do you think I'm here? I'm looking for them."

"Why here?"

"For the same reason as you—Nathaniel." She feigned alarm. "Do you mean no one has found any trace of her yet? Oh, lud! Perhaps she *has* thrown herself in the river. But why? Why? I tell you true, no one will convince me she is in despair because of the death of Sir William!"

She had them fooled, or at least off-balance. She hid her satisfaction as the two men exchanged worried frowns.

"I'll put her upstairs," said Fort at last. "You send that message."

He took Chastity to an empty room. As soon as she saw it, her hopes of escape leaked away. The room had been prepared to hold a prisoner, and her father and Lindle did not make mistakes in such matters.

It had doubtless been a bedchamber, but now it was a shell, stripped of anything an ingenious soul could use for escape. There was nothing on the walls except marks where pictures had hung, nothing on the floor but a trace of dust. The one moderate window had no curtains, and she knew without checking that the frame would be nailed shut.

Glass could be broken, though.

There was a fireplace but no fire. Unfortunate, that, for she would not have hesitated to set fire to the house. The grate had been swept clean of even the smallest cinders. Could the chimney be climbed? She doubted it, but she'd give it some thought. She'd do anything to be out of this house before her father returned.

Her only hope was to enlist Fort, or at least keep him with her. The earl would not unleash his full range of cruelty before his son, and certainly would be sure not to fall into one of his rages. After all, the Earl of Walgrave was a model of dignity, nobility, and fair-mindedness. The Incorruptible.

Chastity had never been fond of him, but she had believed his public image until she had fallen afoul of him.

Fort looked at Chastity and sighed. "I don't know how you've come to this pass, Chastity. Is it true that you don't know Verity's whereabouts?"

In the face of his genuine concern, Chastity found it hard to lie to him, but she managed it. "Yes. I hoped she'd be in Maidenhead, safe with Nathaniel."

"She was safe in her home," said Fort tersely. "I can't understand why she would flee like that. And to run to a man. Do you know what the world will say?"

Chastity was all too familiar with the world's way with a reputation. "She must have been desperate, Fort. She must have thought she was in danger."

"In which case she would have come to her family. She and her child would have been safe with Father."

This was tricky ground. "One would think so. Of course, she always loved Nathaniel, so he might have been first in her mind . . ."

Fort stared at her. "To run away virtually in her petticoat, in November, with a babe, and to run to a man she flirted with years ago? Nay, I fear she's gone mad as well. I don't know what the world's coming to."

"Don't you see, Fort," said Chastity earnestly, "she *must* have had a reason. What about Henry Vernham? He won the guardianship of the child, didn't he? Perhaps he drove her to it."

His lip curled at the name. "I'd believe almost anything of that cur, but not that he'd harm a Ware. The Vernhams are a disgusting breed, but not that stupid."

"Disgusting!" Chastity echoed. "Then why didn't you oppose Verity's marriage to William?"

"Why the devil should I? He was Verity's choice."

"Verity's choice? Nonsense. He was *Father's* choice."

"Father's?" Fort scoffed. "Lord knows, it's been the devil of a job for me to find a woman high and mighty enough for his taste. Why would he promote an alliance with the likes of Sir William?"

"Why would Verity want to marry a man like that? Fort, you know she always wanted to marry Nathaniel."

He shrugged cynically. "She wouldn't be the first woman to decide a title, even a paltry one, and a fortune—no matter how gained—are worth more than a handsome face. Nathaniel Frazer has next to nothing."

Chastity wanted to hit him. Couldn't he *see* what nonsense that was? "I tell you, Fort, Verity didn't want to marry Sir William, and would cheerfully have gone to Nathaniel in her shift. You know her. Has she ever been interested in titles and fortune?"

Fort did look shaken, but said, "It makes even less sense for Father to have encouraged such a match."

"He encouraged one between me and Henry Vernham."

Fort laughed bitterly. "Only after the weasel had been found naked in your bed!"

Chastity gaped. Did he really believe that? He clearly did. The futility of trying to correct the error overwhelmed her. It was like trying to move a mountain with a spoon, especially as she would first have to convince him their august father was none so noble.

She abandoned the argument and pursued something Fort had said. Once she had believed what had happened to her had been a mere twist of fate, but recently it had become clear that there had to be a pattern. It was probably too late to salvage her own reputation, but if she could understand the events, perhaps she could save Verity's.

"What did you mean about Sir William's fortune?" she asked. "You said 'no matter how gained.' What did you mean?"

But Fort was looking at her clothes with a pained expression. "If we don't want Father to skin you, we'd better find you some decent garments." He went to the door and shouted for Lindle, but another voice called back that the man was out.

"Never mind, Fort," said Chastity. "It won't make that much difference. What about Vernham's fortune?"

He shook his head. "Just that it's common knowledge that he came into a lot of money after the '45. He was one of the special investigators sent to look into accusations of Jacobite sympathies, and everyone knows there were some Stuart sympathizers ready to pay to have their activities overlooked."

Chastity remembered that Verity had remarked on the same thing, but there didn't seem to be anything in it to explain events. She went to the window. It overlooked a small garden shielded from other houses by tall trees. Again, very private. A guard stood in the garden watching her. So much for that escape route. "How do you come to be here?" she asked her brother.

"Where do you expect me to be? Lounging in a coffee house? I'm here looking for Verity. When we found you'd disappeared, I thought she must be with you and reasonably safe. Now, I'm worried all the more. Do you swear you don't know her whereabouts, Chastity?"

Chastity reminded herself that she didn't know Verity's exact whereabouts. She could be in any room of Mrs. Garnet's house, or in the garden, or even out of doors if well-disguised. "I swear," she said firmly.

Fort accepted it. He paced restlessly. "And I'd go odds Frazer was telling the truth when we asked him."

"What was his reaction?"

"Great concern. He wanted to set off in search himself, but we persuaded him to stay here in case Verity tries to seek his help. Though why the devil she'd go to him, not us, I don't know." He turned and glared at Chastity. "I don't know why you couldn't stay where you were put, or why you'd want a worm like Henry Vernham in your bed—"

"I didn't!"

"Then why the devil was he there?" he bellowed.

"How the devil would I know?" she shouted back.

He slapped her. "Watch your tongue, you trollop."

Chastity covered her stinging cheek, tears in her eyes. During her masquerade she'd grown used to expressing herself as no young lady would.

"I'm sorry," she said. "I'm half out of my mind with worry, too, Fort." Then she said, with all the intensity she could, "I *didn't* invite Henry Vernham to my bed. I swear it. I *detest* the man. He tried to rape me!"

He was unimpressed. "So you claimed at the time, but it won't wash, sister dear. No one heard a scream out of you until you were caught."

"I was asleep until you all burst in!"

"You expect me to believe that a naked man climbed into your bed and half undressed you without you waking up?"

"Yes, I do. Others may not believe me, but you should, Fort. I've always slept sound. Don't you remember the time you carried me fast asleep into the corridor and put me under the dragon-stand, so I screamed the house down when I woke to find its jaws about to engulf me?"

A smile twitched his lips. "True, but you were only ten then."

"I'm still the same."

He frowned over it. "But Henry Vernham could hardly have known that. If you didn't invite him, he could only expect you to set up a screech, and he'd be a dead man. Look, Chastity," he said quite kindly, "you doubtless made an error of judgment. No one would condemn you utterly for that, and he is a handsome man if you like that style. But you should have married him. It was your only choice."

"Even if he sneaked into my bed with just that plan in mind?"

"How could he know he'd be interrupted, or that Father would take the kinder view and think of marriage?"

Because Father arranged it so, Chastity wanted to scream, but Fort would never believe it. "He had offered for me and been approved by Father."

"Because you wanted him. You can't play hot and cold, my girl."

"Who said I wanted him?"

"Father."

"Father was—" She bit back the word. "He was mistaken. Oh, Fort, believe me. *Why* would I want to marry Vernham? I don't find him handsome, and he didn't even have wealth and a title to sugar the dish."

He frowned, and she thought she had finally made an impression. "Are you saying you're still untouched?"

She opened her mouth to say yes, but then closed it and swallowed. She'd give up the past night to be able to say yes, but her innocence was gone. "No," she whispered.

She saw the pained disappointment set on his face. "But

not Vernham?" he commented bitingly. "How busy you've been. Who then had the honor of my sister's deflowering? Give me a name and I'll see him dead."

"I can't."

He grabbed her. "A name!"

She stayed mute. He shook her, then threw her onto the floor. "Did you roll in the hedgerow with a stranger, then? How many have there been since? God, you sicken me! Where did you come from, to be like this?"

He loomed over her, rage darkening his face, hands in big fists capable of smashing her bones. She thought he'd thrash her. Then he turned and slammed out of the room. She heard the key turn. She sank her head in her hands.

Unless her father condemned himself in his own words, neither Fort nor anyone else would believe the tale. It was just too incredible. She almost doubted it herself.

And now she had to worry about Cyn. If his part in this mess ever came out, Fort would tear him apart.

She had to get away. She doubted she could hold out against her father again, and she mustn't let Cyn's name pass her lips. She checked the chimney, but as she'd thought, it was too narrow. Only the smallest climbing boy could work his way up there.

Without much hope she considered the door. A squint down the keyhole showed the key was still in there, but she doubted it would do her much good. To test her hypothesis she knocked on the door.

"Yes, milady," said a man quite respectfully. As she'd thought, there was a guard at both window and door.

"I would like something to drink," she said, to explain her action.

"Right," the man said, but he didn't leave. She heard him call out. "Oy, Jackie, Lady Chastity wants a drink."

Within minutes, they brought Chastity a wooden beaker of water, and some biscuits. No plate. They were being careful not to give her anything that could be of use.

Alone again, Chastity regarded a Shrewsbury biscuit

sadly, and ate it slowly in tribute to Cyn Malloren. It wasn't as good as the fresh ones they had bought in Shaftesbury, but the memories were sweet.

Thinking of Cyn stirred her spirit. She wasn't the bewildered girl of months ago, when last she had been her father's prisoner. Her experiences had toughened her, but it was Cyn Malloren who had lit her spirit. She knew now she had a right to be strong, a right to be angry.

Unfortunately, that didn't stop her from being afraid. She knew her father was a man to be feared. When she had opposed him over her marriage, she had not realized the lengths he would go, the depths of his cruelty. She had survived by a kind of numb fatalism. Now, she trembled every time she thought of being once more in his power.

She hated to just wait, so she prowled the room again, but found no escape. She remembered Fort's comment about clothes and knew she would be forced to change, doubtless into some ugly, penitential clothing. That made her think of Lady Trelyn's letter. She certainly didn't want it to be found on her. Her heart almost stopped at the thought of those explanations.

Listening desperately for approaching footsteps, she looked for a hiding place in the stark room. There were no loose floor-boards, no nooks and crannies. She began to think of trying to eat the thing, but then she found that the wooden mantelpiece had pulled a little from the wall, leaving a gap. Shuddering with relief, she forced the letter into the space.

She would retrieve it if she could do so safely, but if not it could stay there, doubtless to titillate some householder in years to come.

She wondered sickly if there was any possibility of Fort recognizing her as his dancing partner of the night before. That would be her end for sure. How could she explain her presence at what was doubtless the most notorious orgy of the decade?

She checked all her pockets again, making sure they

held nothing to make matters worse. Satisfied at last, she sat and leaned her head against a wall. It was chill in the room and she was glad of the groom's clothes over Victor's. She wished she had the riding cloak too. It was very quiet. She wondered what time it was, and after a while, heard a distant clock chime two.

With luck, Cyn and Nathaniel were on their way, but in case they had been delayed, she must hold out as long as possible. She'd ridden hard the day before and missed sleep last night. Despite her fears, she dozed off. She dreamed of a shipwreck, of being thrown this way and that . . .

"Plague take you, Chastity. Wake up!"

She blinked her eyes open to find Fort shaking her, and more with concern than anger. When he saw she was awake, he let her go.

"You really do sleep sound, don't you?" He looked thoughtful. Perhaps he was beginning to believe part of her story. She had little thought for that now. Her father was here, Lindle at his shoulder. She scrambled to her feet.

The Earl of Walgrave had married late in life and was now over sixty, but he was a robust, impressive man with shrewd blue eyes, a noble nose, and fleshy jowls. He was dressed plainly for traveling in brown velvet, lightly laced with gold, and a gray bagwig, but simplicity did not diminish his presence. He filled the room. He carried an elaborate but light gold-headed bamboo cane. Chastity remembered that cane.

"Thank you, Thornhill," said the earl coolly. "You may leave."

Chastity flung Fort an appeal with her eyes.

Perhaps he noted it. He still looked thoughtful. "I'd like to stay, sir. If, as you think, she knows where Verity is, I'd like to be the first to learn it. Heaven knows what perils my poor sister may be risking."

"Heaven, and any man of experience," commented the earl in his mellow voice. He sounded calm, but Chastity could tell he was displeased by this development. She knew then that her instinct had been correct. Despite his violence, despite the fact that he now thought her wanton, Fort was her security in this situation.

The earl took two majestic steps forward until he stood before her, then rested his hands on the knob of his cane. "You sadden me, daughter. I confess, I am at a loss. To see you here in such shameless garments, running from the protection of your home . . . And I fear you have infected Verity with your wickedness. You have not come here in search of your sister. You have brought her here in a petty attempt to spite me."

Chastity was as terrified as she had expected to be, but she found she wasn't paralyzed by her father anymore. Her wits were still working. Her hope here was to make her father reveal something to Fort.

"Why would my bringing Verity here spite you, Father?"

A slight narrowing of his eyes and mouth acknowledged the change in her, but he lost none of his dignity. "For my dear daughter to go anywhere for help other than to me is a blow. I can believe that Vernham may have done something to make Verity flee her home, but surely she fled to Walgrave Towers to seek my aid. It was you, you unfortunate creature, who persuaded her to this mad enterprise. What did you hope to gain?"

Chastity almost fell into the clever trap and admitted the plan. "I came to Maidenhead," she parried, "because I knew if Verity went anywhere other than Walgrave Towers it would be here, to the man she has always loved. Perhaps she thought you would yet again prevent her from marrying him."

"Prevent?" queried the earl in astonishment. "She chose freely to marry Sir William."

"Freely?" Verity scoffed. "You bullied her into it, you hypocrite, just as you tried to bully me into marrying his brother!"

The earl shook his head sadly. "Come here and present your right hand, palm up."

Chastity felt a chill run through her. She'd played into his hands. Before her masquerade as a boy, before her freewheeling time with Cyn Malloren, she would never have spoken to her father thus in any circumstances. But she'd known it would come to the cane sooner or later.

"Father," said Fort in muted protest, though Chastity could see he was shocked by her words.

"My dear boy," said the earl sadly, "she is wild and growing wilder. I cannot permit it. It pains me to beat her, but you see for yourself that gentler means are useless." He looked at Chastity again. "Obey, or you will be forced."

She obeyed, but he was trying to pretend this was a new development and she wouldn't allow that, no matter what it cost her. "It's all right, Father," she said pertly, "You taught me the rules while you were trying to beat me into marrying your friend Henry Vernham. I haven't forgotten."

She walked forward and held out her hand, cursing the fact that it trembled. It hadn't shaken the first time. She hadn't known then how much it would hurt.

The cane slashed down and fire leaped across her palm. She clutched it to her chest, fighting tears.

"Let us hope there will be no more impudence," said the earl. "You are never to question my righteousness as a parent. Never. Now, you will tell me where Verity is."

"I don't know."

She saw him register her honesty, but he was a shrewd man. He put the knob of the cane under her chin to force her eyes to meet his. "You will tell me then where you saw her last."

She hesitated and knew it. "At Easter at Walgrave Towers."

The earl turned to his son. "She's lying."

"Yes," said Fort. "For God's sake, Chastity, why are

you doing this? Verity could be in terrible danger, and her child even more so. Tell us, so we can protect her."

Chastity gave up the pretense. "Only if Father promises to let her marry Nathaniel."

"What nonsense," the earl said. "There is no question of any marriage until her year of mourning is up."

She forced herself to look unflinchingly into his eyes. "Promise that you will permit it then."

Red touched his cheeks, a flare of warning. "I will promise *nothing*. Do you seek to bargain with me, you impudent hussy? You will tell me your sister's whereabouts simply out of filial obedience, and trust me to arrange her welfare."

"As when you married her to Vernham?" she sneered.

"Extend your right hand."

Chastity's lips trembled as she obeyed. The cane slashed down on the previous welt, and a cry escaped her.

The earl fell silent. Chastity waited, clutching her burning hand, tears running down her cheeks. She knew it could only get worse. This was nothing, but it didn't feel like nothing. How long could she hold out before telling all? How much of a start did Cyn and Nathaniel need? She glanced at Fort, wondering if he would help her, but she had lost him again when he realized she did know Verity's whereabouts.

Why, she wondered, was her father so desperate to find Verity? Simply from the need to control? It was possible, and yet her instinct said no. This desperate search had the same strangeness as Verity's marriage to Sir William, and Chastity's proposed one to Henry Vernham. Something underlay all of it.

Unlikely as it seemed, Vernham must have had a hold over the Earl of Walgrave.

What? What?

Fort came over and took her stinging hand in a gentle hold. He moved her a little way from their father, which was a good sign. "Hurts like the devil, doesn't it? Do you mean he did this to try to force you to marry Vernham?"

"And other things . . ." Chastity looked over to where the earl was talking quietly with Lindle. That boded no good. "Fort," she said quietly, "there's something wrong about this, something that doesn't make sense."

"Perhaps," he admitted. "But it doesn't affect the fact that we have to find Verity."

"She's safe," she assured him. "Honestly. Staying with a very pleasant and proper family."

Lindle left the room, and Walgrave came over to Chastity and Fort. "Has she told you?" he asked. "Often a little kindness after harshness works wonders."

"She says Verity is safe with a proper family."

Chastity flicked Fort a glance, but knew that this maneuver hadn't been planned, at least on his part.

"Indeed," said the earl. "That relieves my paternal anxiety considerably. It will only be assuaged, however, when I am able to clasp my eldest daughter and my only grandchild to my breast. The direction, please."

Chastity shook her head.

"And why are you intent on keeping Verity from me?"

Chastity knew it was impossible to answer that question without offending his righteousness as a parent. Though it took more courage than she knew she possessed, she extended her poor, abused hand.

The earl raised his cane, but only to put it under her trembling hand, rubbing gently against the knuckles. "You, I fear, are possessed of a devil, and it will take more time than we have here to drive it from you. Fear not, I will attend to it in time." He let that promise sink home. "But my sweet Verity? What has caused her to so distrust her father? Eh?"

Chastity was keyed up for pain, would almost welcome it to have it over with.

"Well?" asked the earl. "Tell me how you turned Verity against me."

"She needed no turning," said Chastity. "She did not flee to Walgrave Towers, but to the cottage. She had no desire to seek your help."

Still the blow did not come. She knew this trick too. This waiting, which was almost worse than the pain.

The earl had explained it to her once during those terrible days. When he'd given in to rage and beaten her severely, the effect had been strange. It had fed her numb strength and he knew it.

"Brutality drives some people beyond reach," he had said. "It also leaves evidence that can be inconvenient. On the other hand, quite small amounts of pain can break a strong man if properly applied."

Now the earl put the cane softly on her palm and rubbed with it. She gritted her teeth against the sting. "And why did Verity have no desire to seek my help?"

Verity had cut herself off from her father because of his treatment of Chastity, and only secondarily because he would oppose her marriage to Nathaniel. Chastity could tell him this, but an intensity in the earl's manner caught her. What made this question so important? Would he say something revealing?

He tapped the cane on her hand, demanding an answer.

At the third tap, Chastity's nerve broke. "Because of how you treated me."

He studied her searchingly, then used the cane to push her hand down and walked away. Chastity's knees almost gave way, but she remained standing, knowing it wasn't over.

There were no sounds from outside this isolated house, and it felt as if everyone in the room held their breath. Chastity began to count. She had found it the only way to avoid being driven to desperation by her father's calculated use of silence.

She had reached sixty-five when the earl turned. "A petty reason for risking her life and that of her child. Very unlike Verity. I fear you must have spun her a tissue of lies. Ah, well, it will become clear when we find her." The door opened. "And here is Lindle with some more appropriate clothing. We will leave you to change, daughter, and resume our conversation when you have a more fitting appearance."

Chastity was beyond reasoning what Fort made of this, but she noted his reluctance to leave her. He was firmly shepherded out. The key turned in the lock and she was alone. She collapsed to sit on the floor and blow on her stinging hand.

The punishment had been nothing. It hadn't even been an attempt to force the truth out of her but, as he said, a reaction to her lack of filial respect. But it had also been a way of priming her for what was to come, of reminding her how it had been the last time, when her palms had blistered, and Lindle had held her hands up because she could no longer force herself to do it. When her back, and buttocks, and legs had been a mass of weals.

And this time it would be worse. It would be worse because he was more ruthless, and more desperate. This time he wouldn't care if he scarred her, or did her permanent harm. She didn't know why he was so desperate, but she could sense it. And he would soon be back.

Chapter 14

⌒~⟝∽∽∽⟞~⌒

Chastity pushed herself to her feet. This was what her father wanted. He wanted her to be alone in the fading light, growing more fearful by the moment. She needed to do something. She might as well change her clothes. She had no objection to being female again.

As she began to undress she wondered where Cyn was now. For a traitorous moment she prayed that he was nearby, planning her rescue. Then she thrust that thought away. She had to want him to be on his way to Winchester and Verity. She'd told him, if she should be caught, to cut free and get Verity to a new place.

She stripped naked and hurried into the women's clothing—silky chemise, taffeta petticoat, and sleeved bodice. It surprised her that the garments were of such fine quality, but she supposed even Lindle had not been able to find any pauper's clothes at short notice. Heaven knows where he'd found these, for the colors were clearly not intended to go together. The chemise was pink, the petticoat colquelicot scarlet, the bodice green and yellow stripes.

She had to struggle with the hooks at the front of the bodice. Not only was it too small, but it was indecently low. No matter how she tried to adjust it, it barely skimmed her nipples, and at the slightest movement they popped free, leaving only the pink chemise to cover them, and that was so fine as to be transparent.

She stuffed them back in and looked down at herself in horror. The colors were tasteless, the bodice indecent, and the petticoat stopped inches above her ankles. This was not by accident. Her father was dressing her like a whore.

She wanted to change back into her male garments, but that would only result in her being stripped by the odious Lindle. She had no doubt that her father and his toady would not return until they had found a way to get rid of Fort.

How strange that her brother, whom she had thought of as the enemy, had now become her bastion.

As no footwear had been provided, she put on her male stockings and boots. They looked ridiculous, but were warm and more decent. Also, for warmth and decency, she draped her coat about her shoulders. Something pricked her fingers.

Rothgar's pin! Lud, another piece of evidence against her, and it would not fit in the crack behind the mantel. After a moment she fixed it to the inside of her petticoats. It should go undetected there even if they stripped her. If they found it, she could claim it came with the garments. They were not long off another body. She could smell that.

There was still no sound of approach.

Don't stand here waiting and worrying, she told herself. Do something. She walked the room thinking about everything that had happened.

Months ago, when Fort had berated her for her behavior, she had seen him as one of the conspiracy bent on her ruin, but now she saw that he too was her father's victim, though he did not know it. Could she open his eyes?

He'd had reason to believe her unchaste, and now she'd confirmed it, which didn't help her cause. He doubtless wouldn't protest if she were whipped. But she didn't think he'd stand by for Walgrave's calculated cruelty. The trouble was that the earl would find a way to get rid of him before starting on that tack.

Chastity kept track of time only by the chiming of the

distant clock and the fading of the light. Four times she tensed when footsteps come to the door, but no one entered. It was just part of the torment. She tried not to let it weaken her.

Then the key turned. She faced the door, summoning her strength. It turned back. Another trick. She cried then, but forced herself to stop before anyone heard. She applied her mind to seeking solutions instead of straining for footsteps.

Her father could be pushed into losing control. Perhaps he would reveal something in that state, but Chastity shuddered at what he might do to her at the same time. She prayed that Fort refuse to be sent away, but knew it was futile. Fort didn't realize yet that the earl was the enemy.

It was full dark and the clock had just struck eight when the key turned again. This time the door opened. Her father entered, followed by Lindle bearing a candle-stand which he placed in a corner. Fort was not with them. Chastity braced herself.

"Your brother has gone to check on Major Frazer," said the earl blandly. "He will be back in a little while." He looked her over. "That jacket hardly matches the outfit. Take it off."

It was pointless to fight these minor skirmishes, and so Chastity obeyed.

The earl nodded. "You may keep the boots. I wouldn't want you to catch a chill." His eyes traveled over her, every touch making her feel unclean. "A most becoming outfit for you, my dear. Lindle, you are to be congratulated."

"Thank you, my lord."

"You may now take away those improper clothes, Lindle, and dispose of them."

Chastity watched in despair as the male garments were removed from the room. She tried again to adjust the striped bodice, then forced herself to stop. Such actions would only give her father satisfaction.

The earl watched her coolly. "You know me by now, daughter. I am not to be denied."

"And yet I did deny you."

His eyes narrowed, betraying that her words had hit home. "So, do you think you won?"

"No. But neither did you."

He raised his cane and she flinched, but he only touched her head. "Your hair is almost becoming bearable, isn't it? I fear it will have to go before we part."

Chastity closed her eyes and forced herself not to beg. She couldn't help remembering what it had been like when it was just a dark stubble, how ugly it had been.

"But you mustn't think too badly of me, my dear," purred the earl, which terrified Chastity. "See?"

She opened her eyes. Lindle had returned with a wig, a charming honey-brown wig. It was very like her natural color. She looked sharply at her father.

"Indeed. It is made from your own hair." The earl hooked it onto the gold knob of his cane and presented it to her. "Tell me where Verity is and you may have it. Come, try it. Lindle, a mirror."

The earl fitted it tenderly onto her head. Chastity shuddered at his touch. Lindle appeared with a long mirror which he propped against the wall. The earl steered Chastity in front of it and for the first time in months she saw herself as she should be. Thick glossy waves framed her face in an exact reproduction of her natural style, as if the horror had never been ...

The wig was snatched away and she cried out. She was a freak again. She saw the full effect of her costume. A freak, and an indecent one! She covered her chest with her hands and turned away.

Her father snared her hands and held them tight behind her, forcing her to face the mirror. She closed her eyes. He arched her so her nipples sprang free of the bodice. "The rouge, Lindle."

Chastity writhed but was helpless as her chemise was pulled down and something rubbed on each areola.

"Look," said her father.

When she refused, he twisted her arms until she obeyed. The crests of her breasts were a virulent scarlet. She might as well have been naked, despite the chemise.

"How can you do this?" she cried to her father. "How can you let that . . . that *creature* touch me!"

He showed no remorse, but he released her aching arms. "You bring it all on yourself," he said as he strolled away. "I have given you everything that a daughter could desire. I would have ensured your welfare, but you have no trust, no sense of duty to your family, to me your father. Now you see the cost. That rouge, by the way, is a staining one. You will not be able to wash it off. But you may well find it appropriate."

Chastity turned slowly to face him, recognizing the approach of some new device.

He took out his gold pocket-watch and flicked it open. "It is now a quarter past eight. Tell me Verity's location by nine and you may go free. Remain obstinate, and you will be delivered to a bordello down by the river. The abbess is eagerly awaiting such a tasty morsel, and assures me she will choose for you only the most *interesting* customers. Do you know what that means? A few months ago, I would have thought not, but now I wonder. What adventures have you been enjoying, daughter, since I unwisely left you at liberty . . . ?"

"You can't!" she gasped.

"Indeed I can. You are no longer of any use to me."

The reptilian coldness of it struck Chastity dumb, but on the whole she was relieved. Her father would keep his word—he always kept his word—and would let her go if she told him where Verity was. She would do it, just before nine o'clock. She would be free, and by the time Walgrave or his minions arrived at Winchester, Verity would be gone. Thank heavens the earl didn't know there was a third person in all this.

The earl pointed at the wig on the floor. "As a further inducement, if you oblige me, you may have that as a *douceur*." He turned toward the door.

Chastity fought hard not to show her relief.

He turned the knob.

She eased out a long breath.

He stopped. "What have I forgotten, Lindle?"

The servant made no reply to this rhetorical question. The earl turned back. "Ah, yes. There is the question of my daughter's punishment, isn't there?"

Fear shot through Chastity as a real pain. She'd let him fool her again.

The earl saw it and smiled. "Let me see." He began to count on his strong, spatulate fingers. "One, you left your home without permission. Two, you dressed in indecent clothing. Three, you wandered about England and even gathered some money." He raised his brows at Chastity. "Would you care to tell me how? No? No matter. Four, you have led your sister astray and put her and her child in danger. Five, you have been impudent and obstructive to me. Six, you are unrepentant. Kneel on the ground."

"No, damn you!" Chastity cast around for any kind of weapon, but there was nothing. *Nothing.*

"Seven, you use foul language. Lindle."

The secretary moved forward, amiably implacable. This time, no matter how hopeless, Chastity would not submit. There was no trace anymore of the paternal in this. It was driven solely by revenge and spite.

She fought, even managing to bite Lindle, but he overpowered her, wrenching her hands painfully behind her back. He tucked her head backward under his arm. His armlock on her almost choked her, but she kicked. Nothing was in reach of her boots.

He hauled her skirts up and she felt the chill air on her legs and buttocks. She let out a piercing shriek that was mostly rage. They couldn't do this to her again. They couldn't!

Lindle tightened his arm, choking her silent. The cane whistled and fire leaped across her thighs.

"You must learn, you she-devil!" snarled her father, and lashed her again. "You must learn! No one defies me! No one!"

A third blow bit into her thighs and she let out a strangled cry.

"Good God, Father. What are you doing?" Fort cried, bursting into the room.

Chastity was released. She crumpled to the ground, fighting for breath.

"Discipline," snapped the earl. "Do you too deny my right?"

Fort was white with shock. "No, of course not. But this is hardly proper, or appropriate."

The earl's color rose high, and he was close to losing control. Chastity prayed that Fort would finally see him for what he was. But Walgrave won the struggle with himself. "You may be right, my boy," he said ruefully. "Yet the girl stretches my tolerance with her defiance and her selfishness. She still will not assist us to find her sister."

Fort came over and gently raised Chastity. "You must," he said. "Frazer has left his command. He gave some story of a family emergency, but I doubt it."

"I knew it," snarled the earl. "Damn you . . . !"

Chastity saw Fort's eye's widen at the sight of her clothes, and she didn't try to hide the indecency of them. "If he's gone to Verity, Fort," she said, "she'll be safe."

Fort turned to the furious earl. "I suppose that's true, Father. Frazer will see to her welfare."

The earl's color deepened to purple. "Has my whole family run *mad?* Am I to stand by while my elder daughter elopes with an officer within weeks of her widowing, and do *nothing?* Why, after this trollop—" He jabbed Chastity sharply in the breast with his cane so that she cried out. "—has dragged our name in the dirt, who knows what will be said? Doubtless that Verity killed her first husband to be free to wed her lover. Even the child's paternity will be in doubt." He was spitting by the end.

A horrified Fort had pulled Chastity to his side for protection, but now she broke free. Her father hovered on the brink of revealing his true nature, and she would push him over. "No," she shouted. "You may have ruined me, you loathsome hypocrite, but I won't let you destroy Verity!"

The earl slashed at her face with his cane, but she blocked it with her arm. A scarlet weal sprang up.

"Stop it!" Fort shouted, and seized the cane. He snapped it and hurled the pieces aside.

"Lindle!" howled the earl. "Knock the traitor out!"

Still smiling, the burly secretary closed on Fort. The earl, now spitting with rage, urged him on. Chastity, for the moment, was ignored. She could do nothing for Fort, and she doubted his danger was as great as hers. She took her chance and fled, grabbing the wig as she went.

"Stop her!" bellowed the earl. But Chastity, wings on her heels, was already down the stairs and out into the close. One of the earl's men stood there, but he wasn't a big man. She caught him by surprise and knocked him over.

She sprinted down the narrow deserted street, her short skirts now an advantage. It was dark, though, and she went flying over a cask someone had left by their doorstep.

She picked herself up, gasping and trembling, and forced herself to slow a little. Behind her, voices called, but the pursuit was not yet well-organized. She thought of trying for help at some house but dismissed the idea. In her present garb, no respectable person would let her through the door and besides, almost anyone in England would turn his errant daughter over to the Earl of Walgrave.

She pushed her red nipples back into her bodice and plunged down a dark alley, then turned swiftly into another, then another, her only intent to lose any pursuer. She had no idea where to go, or where to seek help.

Would Fort be in any condition to assist her?

If only Cyn were around. She caught back a sob. It seemed another life, those few sweet days in his company.

Down a narrow street she flew, grazing her elbow on a wall. Past a gaping night-soil-man. Into another dark alley, gasping for every breath. Was she running in circles?

Suddenly, the alley disgorged her by the side of the Thames, on the docks. Small vessels bobbed at anchor, and nearby a song drifted out from a tavern. For a moment that cheerful sound comforted her, but then she remembered about a brothel down near the river. She shuddered and shrank into the shadow of a bend in a wall, knowing this was no place for her to be.

She took a moment to catch her breath and tried to throw off the panic that tangled her mind. It was no good; it had all been too much. She hurt. She was terrified of worse to come. She was a hunted thing now, seeking only a hole to hide in. She stretched her senses for any sound of pursuit.

What should she do? She'd been desperate to escape her father, but now she was alone at night, penniless and close to naked in a strange town. In the roughest quarter of a strange town and looking as she did, she had no hope of help.

She realized she was clutching the wig and pulled it on. It would make her look a little less peculiar.

It was tempting to stay here, cowering in the shadows, but she had to move. She'd be safer in a better part of town. Perhaps she could hide in a garden or a shed until daylight. What then, she did not know.

Voices approached and she froze, pressing back against the wooden wall behind her. Four men strolled by, complaining in a thick burr of the price of tobacco. When they went into the tavern, the volume of the singing abruptly

rose, then fell. When they were gone she sagged with relief and tentatively crept out of the shadows.

A flickering lantern outside the tavern shed a little light,
and she could see that the area was deserted—of people,
at least. Two fat rats scurried past that feeble light.

Chastity fought back a whimper and sidled down the
building until she came to another alley, a mere dark gap,
leading into shadows. She entered its maw. Her boots slid
on the slimy ground and the stink made her want to vomit.
Doubtless the other alleys had been the same, but she'd
been too panicked to notice.

She thanked heaven she couldn't see what this narrow
passageway was like, but feared what she would step into
next. She remembered the alley in Shaftesbury and the
dead cat. This alley smelt as if it held any number of them.

It held a live one. She stepped on it and it scratched her
knee and fled, yowling.

Dear heaven, she thought with a whimper, was there an
inch of her that was not cut or bruised?

She put a hand out to touch the chill stone of a wall at
her right, doubtless the wall to a back yard. She ran her
hand along it as she staggered forward, for it gave assur-
ance of reality in the dark. In front of her all was pitch-
black. Only above, if she looked up, was a narrow band of
gray—the cloudy sky.

She began to think she would never see light again. She
heard a strange noise and realized it was her own gasping
whimpers. She gulped them down.

Then she glimpsed light ahead. It was only a faint
golden glimmer, but she stumbled toward it as if it were
the gate of heaven. The alley broke into a slightly wider
lane, leaned over by old narrow houses, mostly dark. One
had a guttering flambeau by the door and it was that she
had seen.

It was as if sanity had returned to an insane world.

There was nowhere to hide here, though. No breaks between the houses, no steps. She raced toward a wider

street, desperate to get away from the river and into concealment.

Voices ahead!

She froze, looking right and left, but it was hopeless.
She shrank back against a wall, praying that this not be her
pursuers, that these men not come her way . . .

But then they appeared, a linkboy lighting the way for
two scarlet-coated officers—one rotund, one slender. The
officers were jovially drunk, but steady on their feet.

Chastity edged toward a door, hoping it would look as
if it were her home, and that they would pass her by. Faint
hope. They stopped. The thin one raised a quizzing-glass
and smiled. With a shared leer, they sauntered toward her.

"Well, good evening, my pretty," the fat one said cheerfully.

Chastity could only do what a lady would do if rudely
accosted. She stared past his shoulder. Her chin was
gripped by hard fingers which forced her to face the thin
man. He was not ill-looking, but his expression was hateful. "Lost your manners, hussy?" he sneered.

Chastity's strength was gone. She hurt. She swayed with
exhaustion. Tears spilled out. "Please, gentlemen, I am not
what you think!" She saw her highborn accent have some
effect and scoured her mind for a story. Why not a bit of
the truth? "I am a gentle lady kidnapped from my home
and sold into a brothel! Help me, please."

The men shared a glance, then studied her again. They
were listening, but she didn't think her words were having
the right effect. The thin one's expression had become
even more disgusting. She covered her breasts with her
hand.

The fat one turned to the linkboy. "What do you think,
eh? Lady or whore?"

The boy seemed to regard this as a sideshow designed
for his enjoyment. "Looks a right whore to me, Captain."

"My thought entirely." The man turned to Chastity.
"Your story may be true, my pretty, but it's clear you've

been at your trade a while. Why balk at a few more guineas? Let's taste your wares, and then we'll send you home to Mama, eh?" He guffawed at his joke, and the thin one sniggered.

"I'm untouched!" Chastity pleaded. "Oh, believe me, sirs! I'd only just been delivered to the place when I escaped."

"Well then," drawled the thin man, bright-eyed, "we are the lucky ones, aren't we? Mrs. Kelly charges ten guineas for a virgin. Hold her, Pog, and I'll toss you for it."

"You're on, Stu." The big man wrapped Chastity in beefy arms. Chastity yelled, but only got one cry out before his fat hand clamped over her mouth, stinking of snuff and onions. She kicked, but he just laughed.

The thin captain took out a crown and spun it, gleaming, in the dim light. He covered it on the back of his hand and quirked a brow at his friend.

"Heads," said her captor.

The thin man peered at the coin. "Damme, you win. Never mind, you'll have her well-greased for me."

Chastity's captor spun her around. "Come here, me darling!" He plastered his hot, slimy mouth over hers. It was the end. Chastity bit his tongue and kicked again. He cursed and let her go. She went for his eyes.

He knocked her down with a savage blow to her head. She lay stunned for a moment, then scrambled to her feet. He tried to grab her, but his friend had the same idea. The two men tangled and fell. The linkboy laughed.

Chastity spat at him and ran, but a flailing hand grabbed her skirt and brought her crashing to the cobbles. The hand dragged her back to the men. She kicked and pummeled wildly at everything about her. She almost won free, but a new assailant grabbed her from behind. She thrust back with her elbow and heard a gasp.

"It's all right," said an amused, if pained, voice. "I won't hurt you."

Chastity froze, then twisted. "Cyn . . ." she whispered.

His eyes widened in disbelief. Chastity flung herself into his arms.

Cyn was frozen with shock. This beautiful, bruised, bedraggled doxy was his damsel? What in Hades had been going on? He'd been scouring the town for her for hours.

"I say, get in line. She's ours." The two officers were on their feet and belligerent.

"A spicy one, ain't she?" said the thin man. "Plenty there for three, but we've tossed and Pog won."

She tensed and whimpered. Cyn wanted to kill them, but he couldn't risk such drama. Her name might come out. "Alas," said Cyn, smiling without humor, "Pog has now lost."

"Damme, you can't do that!"

"Indeed I can. Come, my dear."

He had half-turned when the whine of a sword leaving a scabbard alerted him. He spun back, thrusting Chastity behind him, and slid out his own rapier. There was no time for niceties. He barely had time to deflect the thin man's point from his heart.

Then he was balanced and engaging him, testing him. He found no contest. The man had only moderate skill and was in his cups. Cyn could skewer him any time he chose, but dared not. Already curtains and doors were chinking open as people peeped out to see the excitement. Soon the Watch would be on the scene. He set to persuading his opponent to retreat without bloodshed.

At first, Chastity stood in a daze, watching as Cyn's blade flickered in the dim light, as the slender weapons hissed and snapped of death. Then she saw a movement and glanced to the side. The other man, Pog, was sidling toward her, his wet-lipped leer telling of his intent.

Chastity grabbed the linkboy's torch and thrust it at the man. "Keep away!" He staggered back, cursing.

"Don't set him on fire," said Cyn, and danced back a few steps until he was close to her again. He flashed her an encouraging, even humorous look. He was even finding enjoyment in the situation, damn him!

"Look," he said to his opponent, not at all out of breath, "I'm better and faster than you, and sober to boot. I have no desire to draw blood, but I'm in something of a hurry. How about it?" As if to prove his point, he severed a silver button from the thin man's uniform and sent it flashing into the gutter.

"Damme!" the man sputtered, knocking the sword away.

Cyn returned in a flash to remove another button.

"Oh, let it be, Stu," growled Pog. "The skinny trollop's not worth the candle."

Stu snarled, but he lowered his rapier and put on an air. "Damme, but you're right, Pog. Doubtless a well-worn bag." He slid his sword home and put on a swagger. "Let's go find a better. But don't cross me again, sir," he said to Cyn. "I'll remember this night."

They strolled off, the linkboy with them, and within moments Chastity found herself alone with Cyn. It hit her like a fist that he'd not been surprised to discover she was a woman. "You know!"

He pushed his sword into its scabbard and flashed her a rueful smile. "Yes, but now's neither the time nor the place. Let's get out of here." He placed an arm around her and hurried her along the lane toward the High Street.

Chastity had a thousand things she wanted to say, but could understand there might be a need for haste.

How long had he known?

She was no longer alone.

He must know she was Chastity Ware.

The worst was perhaps over.

Had he known last night? Had she trapped him after all?

This drained the last of her strength. Her legs turned to rubber and her head began to swim. Only his strong arm enabled her to continue on.

Chapter 15

Cyn was half-carrying her by the time they reached a crude stable, not the one belonging to the Saracen's Head. He carried her in and set her on some straw. There were just a half-dozen horses there, all of them draught horses except theirs. There was only one dim lantern and it hung outside the door. Cyn carried it in and hung it on a hook.

"I moved the horses to this place in case the Saracen's Head was under watch." He turned to her and saw her clearly for the first time. All humor left his face and he knelt before her. "Dear Lord, what has happened to you?"

Chastity tried to stuff her bright-red nipples back into her bodice. Her hands were shaking and it was impossible anyway. She started to cry. She was enveloped in his coat—warm from his body—then in his arms. "Hush, love, hush. It's all right now. I won't let anyone hurt you."

She laughed at that, somewhat wildly. He muttered a curse, then put a flask to her lips and tipped it. Neat brandy burned down her throat and shocked back her wits, but she couldn't stop crying. He kept holding and soothing her until the tears stopped.

After a while he moved her so he could see her face, and tenderly wiped the tears away. She expected questions and had a list of them herself, but he said, "We need to be away from here. Can you ride?"

241

Chastity wanted to rest, perhaps to die, but she gathered her resources. Her father and brother mustn't catch him. "I suppose so . . ." She looked helplessly down at her clothes.

His eyes followed hers. "What . . . ? Never mind." He picked up the portmanteau. "Put on my spare clothes. They'll be too big, but anything's better than what you have on."

She went behind a partition and stripped off the hateful garments. She wished she could burn them, but she stuffed them in the bag so there would be no evidence that she and Cyn had been there.

She pulled on a pair of Cyn's drawers, a shirt, his blue breeches, waistcoat, and coat. The shirt had been worn and his smell lingered on it, strangely sweet to her senses. The breeches were loose in the waist but were held up by a belt; the legs ended down on her calves, but her boots would cover that. The coat was far too wide at the shoulders.

She knotted a soft cravat around her throat and realized she was still wearing the wig. Reluctantly, she took it off and put it in the bag. She'd thought she'd grown used to her cap of hair, but after having been herself for a little while, it once again seemed freakishly short. She squared her shoulders and walked out.

He smiled. "Welcome back, Charles." At his tenderness she closed her eyes in despair, realizing clearly for the first time that all her good intentions had come to naught.

He'd saddled their horses as she changed and now he led hers over. He reached up and touched her hair. She flinched, but he wouldn't let her move away. He stroked the back of her head. "I've wanted to do that for so long . . ." He let the horse's reins fall. "The wig is pretty, but your short hair is beautiful too."

"You can't mean that."

His touch was gentle and loving, the warmth of it trickling down her spine. "I do. You have a face that needs no ornament, no distraction. I've also wanted to do this for so long . . ."

His lips were soft at first, and gentle, but in no way hesitant. Chastity knew she should fight, but this was their first honest kiss, and she could not reject it. She kissed him back. He deepened it, opening his mouth warmly, using his hands, his whole body to sweep her beyond reason into a world ruled only by the senses.

She tasted him, honey-sweet, brandy-rich, then her mouth too was demanding, her hands seeking.

He pulled back with a shaky laugh. "Dear heaven, love, I wish this were the time and place . . ." He touched her cheek. "Don't look so appalled. Everything will be all right. Trust me."

"I'm Chastity Ware. It can never be all right."

"I'm Cyn Malloren. Trust me."

The feeling of exasperation was familiar. "Even a Malloren can't change the world."

He smiled that lazy smile that could make her toes curl. "Try me sometime. Come on." He cupped his hands to help her mount.

Chastity abandoned the fruitless argument for the moment. He'd learn there were some things beyond repair, and if she didn't let him make commitments, or let him learn she was Chloe, he'd soon tire of this game.

It was only as she raised her foot to put it in his hands that she realized riding was going to hurt. She gritted her teeth and didn't make a sound as she landed on the saddle, but tears sprang to her eyes. Thank heavens her father hadn't progressed to whipping her buttocks. The pain from her stinging thighs was bad enough.

Cyn was mounting his own horse so she had a moment to overcome the worst of it. How far could she ride, though?

She had no choice. If she told Cyn of her injuries, they would both stay here and be trapped. Her father made a bad enemy at the best of times, and now she wasn't even sure he was sane. If he could turn on his son and heir, what would he do to a stranger?

She took the reins in her left hand and hoped Cyn wouldn't notice. They rode out into the dark lane side by side and Cyn headed away from the town.

"I scouted here earlier," he said. "This lane leads out of Maidenhead to the village of Woodlands Green. I doubt it will be watched. It's smooth and simple and lined with hedges. It should present no difficulty even in the dark if we take it slowly."

Chastity gave a prayer of thanks for the slow pace. Each swaying motion of the horse gave her a twinge of pain, but she could bear it at a walk.

"Tell me what's been happening," she said.

"I could ask the same of you," he said, but complied. "I found Frazer without any trouble. He was completely on our side. Seemed to have a dim opinion of your father, which I suppose is natural as the earl had refused his suit. Anyway, he made an excuse to go home, but of course he's on his way to Winchester. If he can travel in the dark, he could reach there by midnight. I wish there was more than a quarter moon."

"Then what will he do?"

"He's to take Verity to a place called Long Knotwell, where his brother, Tom, is the parson. By great good fortune, Frazer has just spent a couple of months based there, recovering from a minor wound and taking furlough. It establishes his residency so they can be wed there without difficulty."

"Where is Long Knotwell?"

"Not far from Fleet. Frazer made a rather bad joke about Fleet weddings, but of course such hasty ceremonies are illegal these days. As we don't have time for banns, they'll need a Public License."

"Lord. How does one get one of those?"

"From a bishop. In this case, the Bishop of London, as Long Knotwell is in his diocese. It's usually necessary for one of the parties to present themselves and swear oaths about the legality of the union, but we decided I would try for the license with Frazer's sworn statement in hand, while he gets Verity to Long Knotwell. At a pinch, the Reverend Frazer will marry them anyway. Such marriages are usually upheld if there is no legal impediment. Anyway," he added dryly, "I'm hoping the fact that the bishop is my mother's uncle may ease things."

"The power of the Mallorens again. But then shouldn't you be in London now?"

He turned to her. "I had to see you safe."

"Why?" she demanded in exasperation. "Time is of the essence. My father seems desperate to get his hands on Verity. I told you to forget about me if I was caught!"

"You never do what you're told," he said lightly. "Why should I?"

She hissed at him. "Don't you dare make a joke of this!"

She saw him smile—the pale of his teeth in the dark. " 'He that is of a merry heart hath a continual feast,' " he quoted. " 'Tis my nature, sweeting . . . But I'll try to be serious if that's what you want." His voice turned coolly authoritative as he added, "Why don't we start by you telling me your story, beginning with why you left the safety of the inn?"

There was a hoot and a whir as a hunting owl floated close overhead. Something rustled nervously in a nearby hedgerow, but otherwise the countryside was silent. Cyn too was silent, with a silence that demanded answers.

"I was spotted at the window," Chastity said reluctantly. "I didn't want the searcher to trap me in that room, for it would link me to you. So I left. I bribed the innkeeper not to tell anyone I'd been with you. I told him I was running away to enlist, and he became full of patriotic fervor— three guineas' worth, to be precise."

"So I gathered. As far as I can tell, he at least gave three guineas' worth of silence. Then what?"

"I tried to wait in the stables for you, but some of Father's men were already there. I only narrowly escaped them, but I had to go into the street. Fort caught me."

"Your brother? He's on your father's side, is he?"

"Not any longer. It was because of him I escaped."

It was uncomfortable to be having this conversation in the dark. She couldn't see his expression and his voice gave nothing away, but she sensed an emanation of power from her right-hand side. This was the officer questioning her.

"Escaped from where?" he asked.

Chastity hastily edited her tale. "My father had hired a house and Fort took me there. They locked me in a room. I convinced Fort that I didn't know where Verity was, that I'd come to Maidenhead in search of her. When Father arrived, however, he wasn't fooled. He forced me to change out of my male clothing." Chastity sought evasion, but found none. "He threatened to sell me to a brothel if I didn't tell all."

Cyn turned sharply. "He *what?*"

"He didn't," she added quickly. "Do it, I mean. He doubtless knew I'd give in before it came to that." Chastity wasn't defending her father so much as protecting Cyn. If she told the whole truth, he might insist on riding back to have it out with the earl.

He'd die.

Leashed anger underlaid his voice when he spoke again. "How did you escape?"

"Fort objected."

"Good of him," said Cyn with an edge like a blade.

Chastity did feel genuinely inclined to defend her brother. "He found it hard to believe that Father could be so evil. Anyway, they quarreled and that gave me my chance to escape, but I had nowhere to go."

"And looked like a dockside whore. Dear Jesus. Thank heavens I found you when I did."

"Amen," said Chastity softly. "But you still should have

cut free earlier in the day and gone to London to get the license. Is that where we're going now?"

"I'm not sure you're up to it."

Nor was Chastity, but she knew he'd never abandon her. She couldn't be responsible for a delay. "I'm fine," she said cheerfully. "I even had a nap this afternoon."

They rode on steadily. Chastity gathered all her strength. She thought of martyrs, of Horatio at the bridge, of Pheidippides at Marathon. Her task was slight by comparison, her injuries minor.

All the same, it must be all of twenty miles to London and nearly as far again to Long Knotwell. She didn't know if she could make it. She'd learned that human beings had tremendous reserves when tested, but hers seemed to have been drained. She could bear this walking pace, but when morning came and they speeded to a canter, she feared she'd fail.

Even this snail's pace made the cloth of the drawers rub against the weals on her legs. Despite her resolutions she kept shifting, seeking a more comfortable position. She must stop it. The slightest evidence of distress would alert Cyn, and that would be the end.

They came into Woodlands Green as a clock struck ten, and passed quietly through the sleeping hamlet.

"Where are we going now?"

"South, I hope." The devil-may-care humor was back in his voice. It exasperated her even as she cherished it. It seemed impossible that anything terrible could happen to her with Cyn Malloren by her side.

"Why south? I thought we were going to London."

"But any watch will be on the Bath road that passes through Maidenhead. If we go south we should meet with the Southampton road and make good speed from there. Tired?"

"A little," she confessed, knowing a denial wouldn't be accepted. She wondered how many more miles this detour would add to their journey.

"I'm not sure that I shouldn't leave you somewhere . . . but whenever I do that, you end in a pickle."

Chastity stared at his shadowy shape. Was that an admission that he'd recognized her as Chloe? Surely he would have to say something . . . "What exactly do you mean by that?" she asked carefully.

"I left you at the Saracen today and found you half-naked in a man's arms."

She sagged with relief. "You needn't make it sound as if I planned it so, and it hardly establishes a pattern."

"But perhaps it's fate," he said lightly. "If you're destined for a man's arms, I'd rather it be mine."

Chastity lacked the resolution to pursue the matter. What would she do if it became clear that he recognized Chloe? She melted at the thought of being in his arms again, but squashed the selfish longing.

Cyn glanced at the shadowy shape of her in the dark. There were a great many things wrong and he didn't know all of them. She seemed as fragile as cracked crystal, ready to break at the slightest shock. What had they done to her? She hadn't told the whole truth.

Had she, in fact, escaped the brothel?

Had she been raped?

He longed with an aching intensity to consign Verity and her major to the devil, and sweep Chastity off to a place where he could mend all her hurts. He wasn't sure he could feel easy leaving her anywhere, even inside a friendly armed fortress. He had an insane desire to drag her in front of him and ride with her in his arms. It was impractical. She'd think him crazed. Why did he feel she was crying? Curse this darkness. "Are you all right?" he asked again.

"Of course I am," she snapped.

He forced his worries down. He could do nothing about them here. "This lane's rough, and I feel as if we're going to ride into the Slough of Despond at any moment. I'm going to lead my horse." He swung off.

Gritting her teeth, Chastity followed suit.

"You don't need to."

"I'd rather," she said with great honesty. Walking wasn't entirely painless, especially now her weals had been rubbed by the cloth, but it was preferable to riding.

They had to place each foot carefully, for the lane was badly rutted and had deep puddles in places. They didn't avoid all of them. Chastity gave thanks they were both in boots.

They passed through two silent hamlets. At each one Chastity almost begged that they stop and seek shelter. She fought the weakness and trudged on. She could go another mile, just one more mile ...

She had set herself—long ago, it seemed, and in another world—to ensuring Verity and William's safety. This was the last stage and she would not fail them.

She stumbled and Cyn grabbed her hand. She gasped.

"What is it?" His finger gently touched and found a weal. "Are you hurt?"

"It's nothing."

"What happened?"

She pulled her hand away. "I hurt it. I scraped it on something."

She pushed on and he followed. Chastity had tears in her eyes, as much from weariness as pain. She blessed the darkness that concealed them. She prayed that he wouldn't make her talk.

He stopped. "I think, though I'm damned if I'm sure, that there's a barn over to our right, far enough from a farm to be unlikely to have cattle in it. We need a rest."

It was too tempting. Would she ever get moving again if they stopped? "I'm fine. We're in a hurry."

"At this pace? I wanted to be well away from Maidenhead, but we're certainly that. It makes as much sense to rest ourselves and the horses, and make good speed later, as it would to push on and exhaust ourselves. We're even risking injury. Come on. There's a gap in the hedge here."

Chastity had to follow, and in truth a large part of her was already succumbing to the allure of rest.

The dark shape turned out to be a barn, though a ramshackle one. It contained some hay, though, and Cyn settled the horses with it, then piled the rest and covered it with his cloak. "Come on, trooper. Time to bivouac."

Chastity eased down, feeling every ache and pain, but relishing the sublime relief of rest. He sat down beside her in a shifting rustle. She could scarcely see him, but he was a beloved warm presence. He tucked her cloak over them.

He lay back and touched her shoulder gently. "Lean on me. You'll be more comfortable."

"What about you?"

"I can imagine nothing more delightful."

Chastity wanted to, but feared he wanted to make love. She was too tired. He'd probably find her hurts. She had resolved not to allow that kind of commitment.

"I'm not trying to seduce you," he said calmly. "You have my word on that. We both need our rest."

She couldn't distrust anything he said in that steady voice. Chastity lay back gingerly and found the hollow of his shoulder. It seemed designed to cradle her head. His arm came around her like a shield and the warmth of his body soothed her chill. Exhaustion washed over her, weighting her lids, fogging her brain. "Won't it be dangerous for us both to sleep?"

"Why? If your father finds us here, he'll be using witchcraft. Go to sleep, Lady Chastity."

"Don't you mind?" she mumbled.

"What?"

"That I'm Chastity Ware."

"I mind very much for your sake, love."

She tried to make a movement of protest, but was too exhausted. "You can't love me."

"Don't be bossy. I can do what the hell I like. Go to sleep."

* * *

The next thing Chastity knew was his hand touching her face.

She opened her eyes to see a pale early light trickling into the barn through gaps in the boards. Her eyes felt gritty, her head ached. Everything ached. The few hours' rest hadn't helped.

"That bastard bruised you," he said soberly. "I should have killed him."

"It wasn't him you were fighting."

"I should have killed them both."

She smiled wanly. "Start defending me, Cyn Malloren, and you'll have to take on the world."

"Why not?" he asked lightly. "All I ask of life is challenge."

She closed her eyes in despair, but then forced them open. She'd be asleep again otherwise.

He kissed her gently on the lips. "The first time I've kissed you in the morning. May it be the first of many."

Her heart trembled, but she said, "Unlikely."

He touched her chin gently. "Why is that?"

"Once we have the license and see Verity married, you can carry on with your own life."

"Mmm," he said, looking at her with lazy eyes. She thought she recognized that look. She began to ease away.

He put out a hand to stop her. "I promised not to seduce you, Chastity."

"Yes."

"I always keep my word. Do you believe me?"

She couldn't deny that. "Yes."

"Then believe that this kiss is just a kiss, not a prelude to more." His hand moved tenderly, subtly against her cheek. "Forget the past. Forget everything. You are a highborn young lady who finds herself taking shelter with a rascal, a rascal who is smitten with her charms into stealing a kiss, but who can be trusted not to try to steal more. You can relax and enjoy it. Even if you feel obliged to slap him for it later . . ."

He sank down on top of her and kissed her gently. At first his lips were as soft as her own breath, but then they took possession of her with slow, drugging skill which sent warm delight flowing through her. It dizzied her mind away from the chill of reality.

When he drew back she couldn't help but smile at him. "Kiss many young ladies like that, my lord, and you'll not escape the wedding knot."

"Perhaps I don't want to." He raised her hand to kiss the palm. And froze. "What the devil . . . ?" He looked sharply at her. "Those aren't scrapes."

She tried to pull her hand away, but he held on to it. "Who caned you? Your father?" Before she could answer, he grabbed her other hand to inspect it, then released it. "Why?" he asked. She'd never imagined his eyes could be so dangerous.

She hastened to diffuse his anger. "I was impertinent. He was doubtless within his rights." She smiled wryly at the memory. "Among other things, I called him a foul hypocrite."

He relaxed a bit, shook his head, and soothed her hurts with a feathery kiss. "A strict patriarch indeed. How old are you?"

It seemed strange that he did not know. "Nineteen."

"You're too brave and bold for nineteen, but I wouldn't beat you for it. Doesn't he know he has a treasure?"

She realized Cyn didn't understand about her father. Chastity herself didn't understand how her father had come to be as he was, but she felt she might if she once had a chance to ponder the pieces of the puzzle.

She told Cyn, "He doesn't regard a bold female as a treasure. He wants me meek and sweet like Verity. We should be on our way."

She said it reluctantly, and he responded the same way. Neither of them wanted to leave this little heaven they had found, but duty called. He pulled her up by her left hand.

By superhuman effort, Chastity didn't cry out as her stiff-ened legs shrieked with pain. But he noticed.

"What is it?" he asked.

"Just stiffness," she said quickly. "I bruised myself all over when I fell on those cobbles. I'm starved, though. I don't think I've eaten since yesterday breakfast."

"Lord, haven't you? I shared a fine dinner with Frazer. Right then, on our way, and the first order of business is to feed you."

Chapter 16

Chastity didn't think she could make it onto the horse, but he accepted her story of stiffness and bruises, and helped her up. As bruises, abraded skin, and tender scabs shrieked, she told herself it would get better as she loosened up. She didn't believe it.

They rode slowly into a village called Wickford and halted at the Brown Cow. It was a simple, low-thatched inn, and not a posting house, but the innkeeper professed himself able to serve them breakfast in the taproom. This proved to be empty so early in the day, but already warm with a blazing fire. Chastity eased with relief onto a settle there and held out her hands to the warmth.

Cyn stood at the other side of the fireplace and studied her thoughtfully. "You really are at the end of your tether, aren't you?"

"I'll be all right when I've eaten," she lied. What else could she say? He wouldn't leave her behind. He said nothing, but she knew he didn't believe her, and with reason. She forced herself to sit straighter. "We can't give up now."

"No, I don't suppose we can." He was unwontedly sober for Cyn Malloren, frowning as if over an unpleasant prospect.

A maid came in and laid a table for them. In a moment

she returned with a loaf of hot bread, butter, and a pot of coffee. Chastity's stomach growled.

Cyn laughed. "Come on, then. Get started on this as we wait for the rest."

He seated her and cut a thick slice from the loaf, layering it well with butter. As she sank her teeth into it, he poured her coffee. "Cream? Sugar?"

She nodded, her mouth full of buttery bread. As soon as she'd swallowed, she drank some coffee. It flowed into her like liquid comfort and spirit, and was much more to her taste than brandy. She could feel herself come back to life. She grinned at him.

He grinned back.

How primitive one could become. At this moment, a gift of food spoke more eloquently of love than jewels or flowers.

At the thought of love, she sobered. She took another thoughtful bite from the bread in her hand. She feared she knew what unpleasant duty he was contemplating—that of marrying this young lady he had unwittingly compromised by spending three nights in her company. And that was without knowing she was also Chloe. She was touched that his honour would drive him to offer marriage even to the Notorious Chastity Ware, but she would not allow the sacrifice.

"That's my girl."

She flicked a glance at him. He sat studying her, chin on hands. His eyes were shielded, yet she sensed something deep behind the lashes.

She looked down again, more confused than she could ever remember. She wished, quite desperately, that they were safely back in the days of Cyn and Charles.

Again, it was as if he picked up on her thoughts. "I like the fact that we can acknowledge the truth at last," he said softly.

She kept her eyes on the bread. "How long have you known?"

There was a pause, then he said, "From the beginning."
Her eyes jerked up to his. *"What?"*

His expression was rueful, and not a little wary. "You
were very good at it, but I noticed the . . . er . . . lack of
attributes."

Chastity felt her cheeks heat, but at that moment the
maid and the innkeeper bustled in with platters of eggs,
sausages, ham, and beef. They were offered ale or cider,
but refused. By the time the servants had left, Chastity did
not know what to say.

She helped herself to food, then just looked at it, despite
her hunger. "Why did you say nothing?" she asked. She
wanted to ask, *Do you know about Chloe?* but that would
be to give away, perhaps, more than she need.

He cut into a slice of ham, then put his knife and fork
down, no more able to eat than she. "I could sense that
you needed the disguise, love, long before I knew of your
problems. I didn't know what would happen if I forced
you to acknowledge the truth, but I suspected it wouldn't
be good. At least from my point of view."

She looked up sharply. "What do you mean by that?"

A slight smile twitched his lips, but his eyes were very
watchful. "I wanted—I needed—to know you better. What
would you have done if I'd challenged you the first day?"

Chastity thought back. "I don't know. Probably left you
behind, tied to the bed."

He let the smile free. "I knew my instinct for self-
preservation was sound. And you'd have been caught before the day's end."

"Yes." Hunger became insistent and Chastity began to
eat, but her mind reviewed their association. Dear heaven,
had it only been five days? She admitted he'd had a problem. But then she remembered his teasing—the garters, the
Shrewsbury biscuit, his taunts at poor naive Charles.
Those dratted laces. She stared at him.

He winced, but his lips were twitching.

"You devil," she said with soft intensity. "You . . .

you . . ." The twitch became a grin. He was laughing at her, damn him!

Chastity picked up the dish of soft butter and hurled it at him. It landed squishily on his gold-braided uniform, then slid down. While he sat stunned, she followed it with the loaf of bread, and the contents of the jug of milk.

He leaped to his feet, dripping. "Plague take you, woman!" When she looked for more ammunition, he pushed her away from the table.

"You low creeping swine!" she yelled at him.

"Snake."

Chastity gaped. *"What?"*

"Swine don't creep. Snakes do." He was back to laughing at her.

"I don't believe this! You've lied to me, tormented me, led me into the most terrible situations." She emphasized each point with a poke at his squishy waistcoat. "And now you're going to correct my *English!"*

He let her poke him back against the table, but he wasn't at all repentant. "You kidnapped me, stole my goods, bound me, threatened me. And when it comes to tormenting, my sweet, wanton harpy from hell, you could give lessons."

Chastity felt the blood drain from her head, but the only words that came out were an inadequate "Oh, dear."

He stepped forward and now it was her turn to retreat. "I choose to take that as an endearment." He grabbed her by the shoulders. "We're two of a kind, Chastity Ware. If I hadn't known Chloe with my brain, I'd have know her with my body."

She tried to jerk away, but he wrapped her in his arms. "I'm sorry if I've hurt you." He gently tilted her chin up. "But deuce take it," he said, the grin breaking out again, "it's been worth every entangled moment."

She tried to glare, but the merriment in his eyes brought a gurgle of laughter from her. "Are you *never* serious?"

"Not if I can help it." He dropped a kiss on the end of

her nose. Then, disconcertingly, he turned truly serious. "But I'm not an idiot, or a flibbertigibbet, Chastity. I'm a man, and a soldier. I've seen things I hope you never see."

He hesitated, frowning. Chastity didn't know what was wrong, but she wanted to soothe him. She held him a little tighter and hoped he read it aright. He hugged her back, so perhaps he did.

"I remember a battle," he said soberly. "It was the most damnable weather. Icy sleet. It wasn't too bad during action, but when night fell we were stuck in the open with no shelter." He looked down at her, watching her. "We built a shelter of corpses, ours and theirs, and slept very snug . . ."

Chastity swallowed and tried not to show the horror she felt.

His eyes met hers. "That's my life. Could you share it?"

"Sleep among corpses?" It came out rather squeakily.

He laughed shortly. "They're actually more peaceful than rats or fleas . . . But no, I don't suppose it would come to that. But I make no promises." He put his knuckles under her chin, preventing her from looking down. "I'm asking you to marry me."

"You can't marry Chastity Ware."

"We've had this conversation before. There's no one to stop me from doing whatever I want."

"What about Rothgar?"

"Not even him. I'm of age and my income, limited though it is, is beyond his control."

"Are you warning me you're poor?"

Humor twinkled in his eyes. "An impoverished Malloren. Heaven forfend! We'll have enough for a life of genteel comfort, when war allows us to enjoy it. Marry me, love."

"You don't have to do this," she protested. "I was a ruined woman before I met you. I look a freak—"

His lips silenced her, gently at first, then heatedly, hungrily. Her response was powerful, and frighteningly beyond her control.

His clever lips released her, and his breathing was as unsteady as hers. "You are not a freak, Chastity Ware, unless that's to mean you are unique. Your hair, if that's what bothers you, will grow. I like it as it is, but if you want, you have the wig." His hand traced her face. "I am not offering you marriage out of duty. You are beautiful. You are more beautiful to me than any other woman, even unadorned. You are brave. You have quick wits and a lively tongue. You are the only woman I have ever met who can match me in spirit." He grasped her hand and pressed it against him. "You rouse my desire in a way that is both frightening and wonderful. Do you remember that first day?"

The feel of him hard under her fingers flooded Chastity with a multitude of memories, making her hot and aching, but she remembered him spread-eagled on the bed. She nodded.

"Even then," he said, "my body knew." Absentmindedly she stroked him. He shuddered. She snatched her hand away and pulled out of his arms.

"It's just lust," she said. "It will pass."

"There's no such thing as just lust. Lust is a dirty word for desire. I suppose in time all things will pass, but my desire of you will not soon fade."

"Do you know how little time we've known each other?" she demanded, fighting both herself and him.

"All my life," he declared.

"Five days," she pointed out grimly.

He waggled his eyebrows. "I was new-born the day I met you."

"Will you be *serious!*"

"No," he said with a flippant gesture of his hands. "I tried serious. It's clear I'll have to tease you into marrying me."

She found the strength. "I'm not going to marry you."

He just shrugged. "We'll see."

She wanted to throw things again.

He saw her glance at the jam-pot and moved to block her, laughing. "Are we going to conduct our fights as well as our love with food? I can think of any number of variations on the theme. Honey, for example, would be better than butter. So sticky. It would take a long time to lick away . . ."

Part of Chastity wanted to hit him over the head with the poker. Most of her wanted to surrender to this blissful insanity for the rest of her life.

"You're messy too," he pointed out.

Chastity looked down and saw that her clothes were now smeared with butter. "But not *wet,*" she countered.

He felt his soggy coat. "True. I'd better change back into the clothes you are wearing, then. It's time you became a woman again."

"I won't wear those indecent clothes."

"Of course not, though they'll perhaps do as undergarments. I'm sure we can buy you a gown."

He was shifting the ground under her unsteady feet. "But I'm supposed to be a man."

"There's no reason for that anymore." He smiled with startling sweetness. "I want to travel with you as a woman, love. If you're really going to give me my *congé,* it's the least you can do, to give me a few brief hours of truth before we part."

A few brief hours of truth before we part. It was a concept of such sweetness, Chastity surrendered. "How do I ride?"

"Astride if you want, like a country woman. Or we can see if there's a side-saddle to be had."

Chastity wondered whether skirts would make matters more comfortable. Then she saw his face, and saw that he had read her again.

He took her right hand and studied it. The mark had

faded a little but was still red and tender. "Time for you to tell me everything that happened to you, Chastity."

She pulled away, but he wouldn't let go. "It's not important," she said. "We should be on our way. Verity and Nathaniel could be waiting."

"It's important. It's hurting you to ride, isn't it?"

"I'm just not used to so much riding."

"Or . . . lovemaking. Is that it?"

Her color was rising again. She twisted against his hold. "Why are you tormenting me like this?" she protested. "I can ride." Then she was free. She headed to the door.

He blocked her. "You're lying to me."

Chastity cursed the fact that she seemed never able to deceive him. "If I want to lie to you, Cyn Malloren, I will."

"Not about this."

Now he was as serious as anyone could wish, and formidable too. Chastity turned away, refusing to speak. She hated the memory of Lindle's hands on her, of being whipped like a child. She wouldn't speak of it.

Cyn's hands came to rest on her shoulders, gently, cherishingly. How could still hands express so many wonderful things? "You must tell me," he said softly. "It will be all right, Chastity. I promise you. Trust me."

She could not resist that plea. "He caned me . . . On my thighs. It wasn't much, but it hurts . . . It should be a little better by now . . . "

His hands tightened, then slackened. He turned her and searched her face. "Is that the truth?"

"I don't seem to be good at lying to you." He laughed, and she could hear the relief. "What did you think?" she asked.

He shook his head. "It doesn't matter."

He moved away and it was her turn to block him. "Oh, no, you don't. You bullied the truth out of me, Cyn Malloren, and now you'll pay for it. What did you think?"

He met her eyes. "I thought perhaps you hadn't escaped the brothel."

She stared at him. "But . . ."

"But what?"

She didn't want to complete her sentence, but she knew he'd be back to bullying in a moment. "But I wasn't that sore yesterday. So why would you think . . . ?"

He shook his head, but tenderly. "You're an innocent, my darling. I rejoice, and prefer to leave you thus."

He would have returned to the table, but she held on to his coat. "Oh, no, you don't. Educate me."

A light flashed in his green-gold eyes. "Ah, I intend to. All in my own good time."

Chastity wouldn't be diverted. "Tell me."

He gave in. "If you'd been used in the brothel, or raped elsewhere, you'd be in pain, perhaps even torn."

"Torn," she said blankly.

"You see why I can't leave you unprotected in this cruel world, my love. You're too innocent." His kiss spoke of fear and the need to protect. The buttons of her waistcoat surrendered to his fingers. Her breasts felt their gentle worship . . .

A choked sound made her jerk away.

They turned to see the innkeeper at the door.

Chastity flashed Cyn a horrified glance, but he was grinning, not at all abashed. "Ah, we are discovered. It is as you suspect, my good man, we are runaway lovers. May I hope you look kindly on Cupid's victims?" This hope was accompanied by a guinea.

The guinea disappeared and the innkeeper nodded, still goggle-eyed.

Cyn smiled at Chastity. "My lady needs these outlandish clothes to escape from her tyrannical parent, but she would be more comfortable in a gown. Are there any about for sale?" He held up another guinea.

The innkeeper nodded. "Yes, milord. I'll see to it, milord."

"And a room in which we can change. As you see, I had a small accident.'

The man took in the butter and milk, and his eyes widened even more. "Of course, milord."

"And, in the unlikely event of anyone asking questions about us, either now or later, you and your people will never have seen us." This statement was not accompanied by money. The tone was enough. It was all Malloren, and said clearly that he'd be back like an avenging angel if the man caused trouble.

Soon they were in a bedchamber, with warm water to wash with, and a blue closed gown for Chastity. It was probably some servant's best, for it sported a few ruffles and some crude embroidery, but it had a tired, well-worn look.

Cyn held it against her. "It should fit. But one day soon, my love, I want to see you in finery of your own." He smiled slowly. "Then I want to strip it off you, layer by silken layer."

Chastity blushed, and couldn't stop a betraying glance at the bed.

"Yes," he said softly, and began to take off his clothes.

For a moment Chastity wondered if she'd misunderstood, but when his drawers came off, she knew she hadn't.

He stood before her, hands on hips. "Well?"

"Well what?" she asked, clutching the gown in front of her like a shield.

"I want to make love to you, honestly, openly, in the light of day. No masks, no disguises."

He was erect with desire, but made no move toward her. If she balked now, she knew he would let her.

But Chastity also knew this could be their only chance for an honest mating, and since he knew about Chloe . . .

It was weak, but she couldn't summon back the strength to resist. His plans for marriage were impossible, and she didn't think she could live with any man in sin. By tomorrow they would be parted forever, and now—ah, now, she wanted him with soul as well as body ...

With trembling hands, she struggled out of her clothes, but she held the last item, his drawers, as an inadequate shield. She couldn't seem to raise her eyes to his.

She heard his soft exhalation. "Do you know," he said reverently, "there is nothing the least boyish about you."

Chastity could feel the rosy heat creeping over her body. She didn't know what to do.

"Come to me, darling, of your own free will."

She looked at him then, and the tender love in his eyes broke through her fears. With a choke of embarrassment, she ran into his arms. He held her tight, and she could feel the shuddering emotion in him too.

"Dearest one," he murmured. "Sweetheart. Dear heart. Don't cry ... "

Chastity looked up at him. "This hurts too much!"

He laughed, but shakily. "We can handle part of the hurt, I think."

"Cyn!" she protested.

He silenced her with a kiss and carried her to the bed. But when he placed her there, it was face-down, and when she would have rolled, he held her.

She bit her lip at this silence, then his hand and lips brushed over her welts.

"What kind of man is your father?" he asked quietly.

"A dangerous one. Don't cross him, Cyn."

"I will kill him if I get the chance."

This time he let her roll over and she stared at him. "You won't get the chance." But she wasn't sure. She had never seen him like this. Even with those boors who'd been fighting over her, he'd not been like this.

"I'll make the chance."

She grabbed his rigid arm. "No. Leave it be. He has the right to chastise me."

"He has no right to terrify you."

Chastity took a deep breath. "Cyn, I want your word

that you'll not go after my father in any way." She saw no flicker of weakening on his face, and pushed harder. "Or I'll leave this bed and get dressed."

He moved back slightly. "Go then."

Chastity felt chilled, abandoned.

He stood. Left her. "I can control my need of you. Your father deserves to die, and not just for that beating, and the clothes he gave you, and the threat to put you in a brothel. There's more to it than that, isn't there?"

The sharp question took her unawares, and she knew she'd answered without words. His resolve frightened her, and she dreaded what would happen if he tangled with her father, but his leaving hurt the most. His need of her could not, after all, be as great as hers of him.

He read her again. He had picked up his drawers. He let them drop and came back to the bed, leaned down, and kissed her. "I ache for you." Then he was gone.

She leaped up and grabbed him around the waist. "Then love me. Please."

He turned slowly and looked at her, shuddered as he let his control slide. His kiss was so drowningly deep that when she found herself on the bed, she didn't quite know how she came to be there.

It was a tumult this time, but a gentle one, as he soothed every hurt, eased into every movement with perfect care.

"It's all right," she whispered. "It's all right. You won't hurt me. Come to me. Come to me."

She adored his body with her own, twining around him as supple as a vine, hardly able to tell his touch from her own. His hands and mouth were everywhere, as were hers. Their joining had the sweetness of the right key in a fine lock, and it opened the gates to a heaven beyond scandal, beyond duty, beyond pain . . .

But then, inevitably, Chastity was dropped back into bleak reality, and the knowledge that this was one moment in a life that would be without him. She flung an arm over her eyes and fought a silent battle against tears.

His right hand continued to cherish her. "Chastity."

She had to move her arm and meet his eyes—his darkly serious eyes.

"I need to know," he said. "You were not a virgin the other night. Who was it? Where? How?"

"How many?" she asked bitterly.

His hand soothed her. "No, Chastity. This isn't an accusation. I just need to know. I need to know everything about you."

"Am I to be allowed no secrets?"

His expression softened. "We've had this conversation before too, haven't we? I don't want us to have secrets. I'll tell you all my lovers, if you'll tell me yours."

Chastity fought a rear-guard action against his insistence. "I'm surprised you can remember all yours."

He kissed her. "Don't leap to conclusions. I've never made love to a woman lightly, and I don't use camp followers. Anyway, I suspect your story is important if we are to unravel this mystery. Tell me what happened to you."

Chastity didn't want to, quite desperately. It would make him even angrier with her father, and she had to wonder what his reaction would be to discovering Chloe had been a virgin. In all seriousness, he'd promised to beat her.

He frowned at her silence. "Don't you trust me? I give you my word, nothing you can tell me will make me love you less. If you were taken by a regiment, I wouldn't hold you in less honor. Trust me, Chastity. Please."

"It's an unfair weapon, that," she muttered, but she told him—about Henry Vernham's proposal, the pressure put on her to marry the man, the bed incident, the beatings, and the forced breaking of her hymen.

Her voice faltered at the growing fury in his face.

"He will die," he said. "Vernham too."

"No!" She grabbed at him. "Leave it, Cyn. Nothing can mend it."

"I will find a way to mend it, and avenge it." But then he leashed his fury and gently ruffled her dampened hair. "But for you, Chastity, not for myself. I love you and my love is greater for knowing what you've endured."

At this tenderness, tears finally escaped her.

He held her close. "Don't cry, love, please. It's over. You'll never have to be afraid, or alone, again. I promise you that, and I always keep my word."

She wished she could believe him, but she had learned her cruel lessons well. She pushed away from him. "How?" she demanded. "You're a wonderful man, but you are just one man. You can't change the world, and my father will crush you."

Humor flickered in his eyes and spread to a grin. "My dear, have you forgotten I'm a Malloren?"

She stared at him. He leaped off the bed and pulled her to her feet. "Dress, wench," he said, and landed a light but stinging slap on her behind. When she spun to glare at him, he said, "That's for lying about being a virgin. And," he added tenderly, "to show that I always keep my word."

He began to pull on his own clothes and so, in a daze, she followed his example. She slipped into the grubby pink chemise, the gaudy petticoat, and then put the blue dress over all. Without her asking, he came to help her with the back fastenings. Sweet, casual intimacy.

Chastity went to the small mirror and put on her wig. The dress was plainer than any she'd worn as Lady Chastity Ware, but it was decent, and in its simple way, not unbecoming. Her wig made of her hair, her own wavy, honey-brown curls, seemed to wipe away the past months. She smiled wryly. As if anything could.

Cyn moved behind her and put his hands at her waist, stroking her sides. "No whalebone," he said approvingly.

"I don't have stays or I'd wear them."

"Shall I promise to strip you if I ever find you in any?"

She turned. The incorrigible teaser had returned. "Idiot.

How could I wear a fashionable gown without stays or stomacher?"

"Ah," he said triumphantly. "So you are coming around to the idea of fashionable life again."

"No. It's impossible!"

"Nothing is impossible."

Chastity gave up the argument. He'd realize soon enough. Let them once come up with anyone from Society, or let Rothgar get wind of this attachment, and it would be crystal-clear that Chastity Ware would never be accepted in Society again. "We must go," she said. "We've let too much time slip by as it is."

He pulled out his watch. "By my reckoning, twenty minutes."

Chastity stared at him. "So little?"

"How long do you think these things take?" he teased. "Of course we'll have many nights of long, languorous loving, but think of all the merry twenty minutes ahead of us. Or even less." She saw the change in his expression and her nerves fired a warning.

He flicked open his watch again, then pulled her over to the bed. He pushed her back. Before she had time to react, he undid his breeches, lifted her skirts, and entered her.

Her body leaped with shock and pleasure. "Cyn!"

"Delicious sin," he said, eyes alight with mischief. He worked slowly in her, his thumbs rubbing her nipples. Then one hand moved low between their bodies to circle. Chastity gasped and closed her eyes as the fever took her. Dimly, she heard her own cries, and his gasp.

Then he set her on her unsteady feet again and flipped open his watch. "Four minutes. You see, the opportunities are endless."

She put a hand on his arm to steady herself. "You're mad."

"Mad for you, O, cream-pot of my life." He draped her riding cloak around her shoulders. *"En avant."*

Chastity was on her way downstairs before she had properly collected her wits.

He commanded their horses and paid the reckoning. Chastity tried to ignore the curious stares of the inn servants, a great many of whom seemed to find an excuse to pass through the hall.

She saw a few more guineas disappear into the innkeeper's pocket. "For your cooperation," said Cyn, adding pleasantly, "Remember that I look coldly on those who displease me." He turned to offer Chastity his hand, then turned back. "By the way, my name is Malloren." It was delivered with an air worthy of Rothgar himself, and Chastity saw the innkeeper's eyes widen.

As they walked out she asked, "Does the name Malloren engender fear the length and breadth of the country?"

"I doubt it, but here it does."

"Why?"

"We're within ten miles of Rothgar Abbey." He looked at the horse and standard saddle. "Are you sure you can manage?"

It was a time for honesty and she had nothing left to hide. "I can ride, but I'm not sure how far." She used the mounting block to ease into the saddle, then arranged her skirts.

"You don't have far to go. I'm taking you to Rothgar."

"What? We don't have time for detours, Cyn, and why go to Rothgar? You've been avoiding him for days."

"I must confess," he said as he mounted, "I hope he's not there. I meant Rothgar Abbey. You'll be safe there. I don't need you to get the license, and you'll slow me down."

Put like that, how could she object? All the same, she shivered at the thought of being plunged into his family, not just as the Notorious Chastity Ware, but now, as Cyn's mistress. It would surely be as obvious as if she wore a brand.

Her anxiety was increased when she realized that Cyn too was unhappy about the plan. As they walked the horses down the village street, tension positively radiated from him. "You don't have to take me to your home. You could leave me here."

"No. You'll be safe at Rothgar." He had that air of a man who has made up his mind. Chastity sighed and concentrated on steering through a flock of geese.

When they had clear road again, she remarked, "If you are willing to take me to Rothgar, you could have taken Verity there."

"And probably should have."

"Why didn't you?"

He flashed her a guarded look. She saw a muscle in his jaw twitch. "Because it would have spoiled my fun, damn it!"

Chastity bit her lip to keep from smiling. The admission had cost him a great deal. "Why spoil the fun now?" she said lightly. "Leave me here."

He stopped his horse and took her hand. "No, Chastity. The time for foolishness is over."

"I've come to like foolishness." That teasing tone didn't lighten his attitude at all. "Please, Cyn," she said seriously. "I don't think I can bear any more reality just now."

"What do you mean?"

Was the man stupid? "I'm Chastity Ware, and your whore. I can't go to your family."

He pulled her head around to face him. "You are Chastity Ware, and my future wife. If my family doesn't accept you with open arms, I'll cut myself off from them forever."

"Cyn, no!"

"Ride," he snapped, and slapped her mount's rump to get it on its way. Chastity muttered a few choice opinions of men, but he ignored her.

She found she could ride at this steady pace. The bulk of her skirts and a time of healing had erased most of the pain. Nothing could erase her dread of what was to come, however. She searched for ways to prevent this new disaster—that she cause Cyn to break with his family.

All too soon, he turned toward a gate in a hedge and opened it. Chastity followed him through with foreboding, though it led only into a field.

"Home ground," he said, confirming her fears. "But there's a few miles yet to go. How are you?"

"I'm fine. But Cyn," she said before he could speed up again, "couldn't you leave me in a cottage, or such?"

"No," he said abruptly, then rode off at a canter.

Chastity held her horse in and waited. He reined in and wheeled back, mouth set, tight as a bow. "If necessary, I'll truss you up and carry you, Chastity. That will be a pretty picture."

In this mood, he'd do it too.

"Cyn, I'll come, but only on one condition."

"What?"

"That you promise not to blame your family for what happens."

"Why are you so sure they'll reject you? By the devil, we're none of us of unspotted purity—except possibly my sister."

"I'm sure your sister is virtuous. If she's at home, she'll have to turn her back on me. To do otherwise would be to sink herself as low."

"Devil take it, will you stop talking like that!"

"It's the truth, and you can't change it!"

"I can do what I damn well please! If I present you to my family as a virtuous lady, they had better treat you as such."

"Virtuous! I'm your mistress!"

He closed his eyes briefly. "I should never have touched you, should I? I shouldn't have used you as I did this morning, even in fun. I've eroded your self-respect."

"Cyn, no!"

He looked down at his hands on the reins, his mouth

bitter. "Before that night in Rood House, no matter what the world said, you knew you were pure. That gave you the strength I admired from the first. I've taken it from you."

"Are you saying I'm weak now?" She made it a challenge, hoping to jerk him out of his bitterness, but she knew in a way his words were true.

He met her eyes. "Weaker."

"Thank you," she said flatly.

"It's the truth. I've taken your honor."

"You didn't take anything. I gave it, freely and with joy."

"But I should have waited until we were wed."

"That would be to wait forever."

"Not at all," he said calmly. "I intend to bring back a license for us as well as Verity."

"You can't," Chastity pointed out, not without relish. "I'm under age, and Father will never, ever consent."

His horse shifted under a sudden movement. "Plague take it, I'd forgotten that. We'll find a way." He shrugged. "If not, we'll wait until you're of age. When will that be?"

"A year next April."

"A wait," he remarked, "but not forever. You'll spend the time with my family."

"Oh, Cyn!" she protested. "Now, I'm not just to be presented to them, I'm to make my home with them?"

"Yes." He touched her hand. "Chastity, I know your experiences make it hard, but I'd like you to trust me, just this once."

"I trust you, but . . ."

"My family will not reject you. I am sure of it."

"Not even your sister?"

"Not even Elf. She'll be startled, and suspect you're not good enough for me. But she'd suspect that of any woman in the land."

"And Rothgar?"

"The same."

Chastity didn't believe a word of it. "Then why are you geared for battle?"

His eyes widened in surprise, but then he laughed. "I told you a secret once—that all soldiers are afraid before battle. I'm not wound up for a fight, love, I'm just afraid."

"Of what?" she asked in surprise.

He shrugged uneasily. "Perhaps afraid isn't quite the right word . . . It's a natural disinclination to back down. I once told Rothgar to his face that I'd never accept anything from him, that I'd make my way in life on my own merits. Now I'm going to have to back down."

It was said simply, but she knew from the way he had always been on edge about his brother that this wasn't easy for him. That it was a great sign of love. "To ask him to receive me?" she asked gently.

"No," he said in surprise. "I take that for granted. But the world of Society is not my world. If we're to disentangle your situation, we'll need his help."

"*What?* Cyn, even Rothgar can't whiten my sepulcher."

A familiar grin lit his face. "But he's a Malloren. Like me, he loves nothing so much as a challenge. Come on."

Still she held back. "You didn't promise. If your family won't accept me, you must not blame them."

He shook his head. "Very well, I promise, but it won't be necessary. Trust me."

Chapter 17

They came at the house from the side and rode directly to the stables. Rothgar Abbey was a solid Elizabethan house from this angle, but Chastity could see it had a more modern Palladian facade. The grounds too were a mix, with formal knot-gardens and topiary close to the house, and rolling parkland beyond. Peacocks stalked among the formal gardens, while deer grazed the meadows, discreetly kept from the gardens by a sunken ha-ha.

An air of order and prosperity glowed about the Abbey, making it very like her own home. It was not what she had expected of the home of the rakish marquess.

They left the horses with a startled groom, and Cyn led her toward a side door. He was visibly tense, and Chastity was in a fine state of nerves. She wished she didn't have to do this, but if she did, she wished desperately that she had something better to wear than a mixture of whore's and servant's garments.

He seemed to sense her unhappiness and stopped to kiss her. "Trust me, Chastity."

What could she say to that? She bolstered her fragile self-confidence with the thought that at least she had hair.

The side door led into a plain corridor between storage rooms, and they progressed some way before meeting anyone. Then a maid swung around a corner, jerking to a startled halt. She bobbed a curtsy. "Welcome home, milord,"

274

she said, and flattened out of their way. Even in this unexpected situation, she showed her training and allowed only the slightest flicker of her eyes toward Chastity.

"Thank you," said Cyn. "Who's here?"

"All the family, milord."

At his nod, the maid hurried off.

That meant his sister, Chastity thought, who would be horrified to be in the presence of Chastity Ware. That meant Rothgar, who—heaven help her—might recognize the whore at Rood House. Chastity's nerve broke.

"Oh, Cyn," she whispered. "You don't have to do this. It will put them in an impossible situation." She seized her courage. "You don't need Rothgar's help. I'll be your mistress, and my reputation won't matter a fig."

He turned sharply. "Your reputation matters to you, and you will not be my mistress." He looked steadily into her eyes. "In fact, I give you my word now, Chastity. I will not bed you again until you are my wife." Before she could think what to say, he grasped her wrist. "Come."

It was walk or be dragged.

They emerged suddenly into a magnificent gild-and-marble hall. Two liveried footman stood there, and even these well-trained individuals stared at their sudden appearance.

"The marquess?" Cyn asked.

"In the Tapestry Room, milord," said one footman, and hurried forward to open a door.

Two people were in the small, tapestry-hung room—a red-haired woman in filmy white silk sat on a chaise, and Rothgar in a dark suit stood by the fireplace. They both turned at the opening of the door.

"Cyn!" the woman cried, and rose to run forward. "What a wretch you are to give us such a fright!"

Cyn released Chastity to swing his sister into a hug. Anyone in the world could tell they were sister and brother, and now Chastity remembered they were twins. The resemblance was not very close, however, for Lady

Elf—surely not her real name, thought Chastity—had red hair and blue eyes.

Cyn let go of his sister and took Chastity's hand. "Elf, this is Lady Chastity Ware. I've brought her to stay for a while. Chastity, this is my sister, Lady Elfled. In the family we call her Elf. I never explained our strange names, did I? Our father had a positive passion for things Anglo-Saxon. He managed to prove to his satisfaction, at least, that our bloodline contains little Norman contamination. So he named us all after Anglo-Saxon heroes and heroines."

An unkind critic would have said Cyn was babbling, and putting off the moment of truth.

Chastity had seen his sister's eyes widen at her name and flick to her oldest brother, but Lady Elf made a good recover. "Elfled was the Lady of the Mercians," she said. "A mighty character, and virtual ruler of England for many years. Cynric was merely a tolerable minor king. Rothgar has the burden of being called Beowulf. He, of course, was a mythic hero."

With this, she avoided actually welcoming Chastity and neatly turned all their attention to Rothgar, who had not come forward, but stood waiting by the fire. Chastity swallowed. Was this a preliminary to rejection? And what would Cyn do then?

Chastity's eyes met Rothgar's across the room. He was studying her, his expression completely unreadable.

They were all moving toward Rothgar. Beowulf. She'd never considered what his Christian name might be. She wasn't sure it suited him, though Wolf would. She realized that, mentally at least, she too was babbling.

He was in a plain brown country coat and buckskin beeches, but not one whit less impressive than he had been in brocade and lace.

"Rothgar," said Cyn quite steadily, "I believe you have met Lady Chastity. I have brought her to stay, since she is to be my wife."

Lady Elfled gasped. Chastity forced herself to keep her chin up and meet Rothgar's cool gray eyes as she waited for the explosion. It did not come. He bowed. "Then we are honored to have you here, Lady Chastity. Won't you be seated? Unless you would prefer that Elf show you directly to your room?"

Was that a hint that she should leave him and Cyn alone to fight? Chastity sat firmly on a chaise.

"Perhaps you would like some tea, Lady Chastity," said Elfled nervously. "Or some other kind of refreshment."

"No, thank you." Chastity knew she should pay more attention to Cyn's sister, but all her faculties were fixed on Rothgar and Cyn.

"We are pleased to see you home," the marquess said to his brother. "And well?"

"Perfectly well, thank you."

"And—forgive me for mentioning it—my coach? There was some talk of highwaymen . . . ?"

"A mere jape. The coach, and Hoskins, are in reasonable order in Winchester."

"Ah, you relieve my mind. Winchester," he mused. "A sudden interest in antiquities?"

"A sudden avoidance of villains," said Cyn bluntly. "I've been adventuring. In fact, the adventure isn't over and I must be on my way. I just need your word that you will treat Chastity with the respect due to my future wife, and that under no circumstances will you give her over to her father."

Rothgar glanced cryptically at Chastity. "Walgrave? You have it. There's no love lost between us."

"And the first part?" Cyn persisted.

"My dear boy," said Rothgar gently, "as a guest in my house, she is due all respect, regardless of her future."

It was a neat side-step, and Chastity saw Cyn's mouth tighten in recognition. It contained the necessary promise, however. Cyn turned to Chastity. "You'll be safe here. I'll be back as soon as I can, perhaps even today." He fixed her with a look. "Promise me you won't leave, for any reason."

She didn't want to be abandoned here, wished she could once again ask to go with him. "How can I promise not to leave? What if the house burns down?"

"Don't be facetious."

"That from you?" she exclaimed. "Am I allowed to walk in the gardens, even?"

"Only under escort."

"Cyn, really—"

He leaned forward, caging her on the chaise. "Promise me," he said.

She saw he was in deadly earnest. "Very well. Now, will you please go and get Verity's license."

She saw the flicker pass over Cyn's face and bit her lip. He'd not wanted to mention Verity.

"Ah," said Rothgar, "so you have a finger in that pie. I'm pleased to hear Lady Verity and her child are well. And, perhaps, in Winchester?"

"No," said Cyn coolly. "I hope that by now they are in Long Knotwell awaiting a marriage license."

Rothgar accepted it without a blink. "Do you need any help acquiring it?"

"No, thank you." But Cyn hesitated, bracing himself.

Chastity thought the atmosphere could be cut with a knife. This was no time to be asking Rothgar's help in her lost cause. She rose to her feet. "Cyn, go, please. Once Verity is safe, there will be time for other things."

He grasped her shoulders and pulled her to him for a quick, heated, and most improper kiss. Chastity was left flustered and quite unable to meet her host's eyes.

Cyn headed for the door. It swung open to admit another man, as tall as Rothgar, as gingery as Lady Elfled. Another Malloren. Bryght or Brand?

"Greetings, little brother! Safe in the nest at last."

"Not for long," said Cyn briskly, but not rudely.

The newcomer looked intrigued. Rothgar said, "I think

it would be wise for Brand to accompany you, Cyn." For Rothgar, the tone was remarkably tentative.

Cyn swung around. "Plague take it, I can find my way to London without a nursemaid!"

"So I would hope. But travel is always chancy, the roads are cluttered with undesirables, and your mission appears to be important. A companion could be useful and will not slow you down."

Silence hung heavily for long moments, then Cyn said, "Very well. If Brand is willing." It was delivered in the manner of one agreeing to an amputation.

"Nothing could please me more," said Brand dryly. "And here I am dressed for riding. I'll call for my cape and we're off."

He left the room. Cyn took a visible breath and walked back to his brother. "I'm going to the Bishop of London, with the bridgegroom's sworn statement. If you sent a note along, it might reassure Uncle Cuthbert about the matter."

It seemed a simple enough request, but Cyn had said he'd sworn not to take help from Rothgar, and it was clearly true. Lady Elfled's face, and even Rothgar's, told Chastity this moment held significance.

"There is no impediment to the marriage?" Rothgar asked calmly.

Cyn looked at Chastity. "Not to my knowledge."

Chastity said, "Absolutely none, except the opposition of my father. As Verity is of age, that presents no legal impediment."

Rothgar went to a desk, scrawled some words on a sheet of paper, sanded, and sealed it. He gave it to Cyn. "You will take the license directly to this Long Knotwell?"

"I had better."

"Perhaps we should meet you there, then. Lady Chastity will wish to see her sister wed, and it would be wise to have influential witnesses."

Cyn frowned at Chastity. "She's tired . . ."

"I'm well enough," Chastity said quickly. "I want to be there and make sure everything is all right."

"In a coach," said Cyn firmly to his brother.

"But of course. It will, unfortunately, have to be my second one."

Cyn let out a crack of laughter. "It will suffice. And as I intend to marry Chastity as soon as possible, I'd appreciate it if you'd consider how to restore her reputation and obtain her father's approval of the match."

Brand overheard the request as he returned and let out a muttered " 'Struth!"

Even Rothgar seemed lost for words, but then he said, " 'Twill be my pleasure." There seemed to be layers of meaning to the simple words.

Cyn merely nodded, then he and Brand departed.

Chastity was left with the marquess and Lady Elfled.

Rothgar looked at Chastity again. It was not a particularly unpleasant look, and yet it made her want to squirm. Cyn was right. This moment would be a great deal easier if she knew in her heart she was pure.

"We have work to do," he said at last. "But I suspect you have been hard-pressed, Lady Chastity. Why don't you allow Elf to pamper you a little, while I set some wheels in motion?"

"There is no need for this, my lord," said Chastity firmly. "I know the marriage is impossible, and Cyn will come to see that too."

Rothgar's brows shot up. "My dear! With a Malloren, all things are possible." With this bit of arrogant sacrilege, he left the room.

"Oh, dear," said Lady Elfled.

Chastity swallowed. "I'm sorry. I didn't want this."

In a moment, Lady Elfled was beside her on the chaise. "Please don't be upset, Lady Chastity. It's not you I'm oh-dearing about. It's us—the Mallorens. We seem unable to do anything in a simple way . . . But you have thawed the ice between Cyn and Rothgar. You are a blessing, not a curse."

That was laying it on a bit thick, thought Chastity. "I'm sure they could smooth any misunderstanding without my assistance."

"One would think so, but they haven't managed it for the past six years."

Chastity stared at her. "They've been at outs for six years?"

Lady Elfled sighed. "At outs is not quite it. Cyn has come home on furlough, for he certainly would not cut himself off from me, and there have rarely been harsh words. But there have been barriers. Cyn has never accepted any help. I wasn't present, but I understand that when Rothgar stopped Cyn from joining the army, he cast doubts upon his ability to survive unaided."

"How foolish," Chastity declared. "On behalf of the marquess, I mean. Cyn is remarkably capable."

"Yes, he is, isn't he?" said Lady Elfled with glowing pride. "But truly, one wouldn't have guessed when he was younger. It was one scrape after another for both of us. Rothgar has accepted the truth for years—he's very proud of him. But you know men. Once they take these positions, it's as if they are on either side of a gulf with no way to cross. You, my dear, are a much-needed bridge."

Lady Elfled Malloren was totally charming, and her welcome of Chastity seemed genuine. It occurred to Chastity to wonder why such a pretty, gentle woman had not married by twenty-four. It was doubtless true that Cyn was prettier—something in the bones—but with her red-gold hair and clear complexion, Lady Elfled was not lacking, and her manner was lively and kind.

Chastity decided to put the lady's mind at rest. "I'm pleased to be a bridge, my lady, and I will not create a new chasm. I meant what I said. I am not going to marry Cyn."

"Have you told him that?"

"Yes."

"And what did he say?"

"He didn't take it to heart, but he will when he realizes how impossible it is."

Lady Elfled laughed. "My dear, you have a great deal to learn about Mallorens. Rothgar does not know the meaning of the word impossible, and Cyn is never balked from his goals. That is why they came to such a crisis in the first place. Now, as we are to be sisters, you must call me Elf, if you do not find it too ridiculous. And I will call you Chastity."

There seemed no point in fighting over it, and so Chastity agreed.

"Good. I am going to enjoy having you here. You can have no idea how tedious it can be to be alone with just brothers. Men have no true sensibility."

Chastity's expression must have protested that, for Elf grinned and said, "Are you going to tell me Cyn is the heart of sensibility? It must be the power of love, for I've not noted it before. Now," she said briskly. "I am going to be very sisterly and suggest that what you would like above all things is a bath, and some more suitable clothes."

Chastity blushed to think of what she must look and smell like, but she could not take offense at such a delightful offer. "Yes, I would."

"Come, then."

Orders were given and Chastity was led upstairs to Lady Elfled's own room, cozy with a fire.

"I believe we are of a size," her hostess said, and waved a hand at a set of armoires. "Choose what you will." A maid came in and Elf said, "Ah, Chantal, assist Lady Chastity. Do you mind if I stay?" she asked Chastity.

Chastity thought of her weals, bruises, and scarlet nipples. "I would prefer to bathe in private."

It was a strange request from a woman who had been

raised with servants, and she saw Elf's eyes register it, but nothing was said.

Two more maids came in with a tea-tray, and plates of cold meat and cheese, breads, and cakes. The two ladies nibbled as Chantal presented clothes for their approval.

"If you're traveling to the wedding," Elf said, "you want something elegant but not too fragile. What colors do you favor?"

Despite her resolution to cut Cyn free, the sight of such masses of beautiful clothes made Chastity long to appear before him just once as her true self—the beautiful Chastity Ware. "A deep pink has always been my best color," she said, "but I don't think . . ."

Elf clapped her hands. "Chantal! *La langue de la reine!*" As the maid went to another armoire, Elf said to Chastity, "It was *absolutely* the color a year ago, but it turned out to be quite impossible with my hair."

Chantal spread a beautiful gown on the bed. It was a deep raspberry silk, sprigged in a lighter shade and ruched around the edges of the open skirt. From a drawer came a petticoat of cream, sprigged in the raspberry shade, and a stomacher of matching brocade and seed pearls.

"Lud," sighed Elf, "I'm falling in love with it all over again . . . But," she said quickly, "take it. You'll be doing me a kindness. Chantal will kiss your feet!"

"Indeed, milady," said the maid with a giggle. "Once or twice a month Milady Elfled orders the dress, and I die a thousand deaths until she decides against it."

It was only too clear that the color would be disastrous against Elf's pale skin and red hair, and so Chastity blissfully agreed.

Silk underwear was also laid out, and then they were told the bath was ready in the dressing room.

Chastity took the stockings and chemise and went to bathe herself, only too conscious of being remarkable.

Once stripped she looked at her body in a clear light. No wonder Cyn had been angry. She had scrapes and bruises she'd not even been aware of. The weals on her thighs were a dull red. She had dark finger-marks on her arms, and a nasty swelling on her temple where the odious Pog had felled her.

And there were the nipples. What had it cost Cyn not to even mention them during their lovemaking at the inn?

For a moment she felt like finding a hole to hide in, but then she reminded herself that Cyn had never seen her looking pretty. He would. Just this once.

She sank into the huge painted tin bathtub with a sigh of contentment. The water was just the right temperature, and a delicate perfumed oil had been added. On a stand beside the tub were cloths and fine soap. This was the life to which she had been raised.

She washed every inch, then she tossed off her wig and washed her hair. In this one respect, her disfiguring crop was useful. She dried it with a towel and relaxed in the tub.

She forced herself to face her bleak future. Even Nana was doubtless now barred to her. Her father would cast her off entirely, and she couldn't cling to Cyn. She'd have to take care of herself.

The thought terrified her.

Perhaps she could be an actress . . . But she had no particular talent in that direction, and most actresses were said to be whores. If she couldn't bring herself to be Cyn's whore, she certainly could be no other man's.

She thought back to Cyn's request of Rothgar—that her reputation be restored and her father's consent be obtained. If only . . . But the reaction of all present had emphasized just how impossible a dream it was.

She climbed out of the bath before she fell to weeping. She dried herself, combed out the wig, and put it on. She dropped the silk chemise over her head, and it slithered down to her calves. This was a more proper garment than the one her father had provided, or the one she'd found at Rood House. It was delicate but opaque, and hid most of her wounds. It was beautifully edged with white-on-white embroidery at the hem and neck, and included a foam of exquisite silk lace at the elbows.

It made Chastity feel beautiful just to wear it.

She eased on the white silk stockings clocked with rosebuds and tied the pink garters, smiling sadly at the memory of the garters Cyn had bought in Shaftesbury. Perhaps she could rescue those garters if Verity still had them, and treasure them into her lonely old age.

The tickling little fear came back to her. What if she were pregnant? But she wouldn't let that sway her. She must find a way to cut Cyn free. She would handle other problems when she had to.

When she returned to the bedroom, Lady Elfled smiled at her. "Do dress. I can't *wait* to see that gown on you. I'm sure it will be perfect."

Chantal assisted Chastity into the hoop frame which would hold the light skirts out without the bulk of heavy petticoats. The white silk petticoat that went on top hardly weighed a thing. The brocade stomacher felt comfortingly secure around her torso and over her breasts.

Chastity watched in the mirror as the layers performed a magical alchemy upon her appearance. Her spirits lifted. It was like armor—a fragile, gossamer armor, but armor all the same. Within it she felt all woman, and empowered.

"You have a lovely figure," said Elf frankly. "Your waist is trimmer than mine. To achieve that effect, I'd have to be gasping."

When Chantal had tied the stomacher laces, she held up the gown and Chastity slid her arms into the sleeves. The maid fastened it at the front and, with a slither of silk on silk, the outfit was complete.

"Parfait," breathed Chantal.

"Indeed," said Elf. "That certainly is your color."

Chastity smiled at the image in the mirror. The deep pink brought out roses in her cheeks and lips; the beautiful cut of the stomacher pushed up the swell of her breasts without the slightest hint of indecency; the opaque silk of the chemise covered that swell in a soft, tantalizing cloud.

She moved, feeling the light silken skirts sway and dance, held out to a six-foot span by the hoops. She twirled, and sank into a court-curtsy, laughing for the delight of being a woman.

Elf took her hands to raise her. "Oh," she said, "I wish I had what you have!"

"What is that?" asked Chastity.

"A power over men."

Chastity felt her face burn. "I don't ... If I do, it has served me ill."

"Has it?" asked Elf, rather sadly. "But you have Cyn ready to fight dragons for you."

Chastity didn't understand the wistfulness in the other woman's eyes. Surely Lady Elfled Malloren, with her rank, her dowry, her looks, and her sweet nature, had attracted the attention of many men. "I'm sure any man would be willing to fight dragons for you too, Elf."

"Perhaps," said Elf, but with a sigh. Then, "Come," she said briskly, before Chastity could comment. "let Chantal apply a little *maquillage* to conceal that bruise, and we will see what my august brother has planned."

Chastity sat obediently for the maid to work. "I don't care for heavy paint," she told the girl.

"Bien sûr que non," said the maid. "This is for country wear, after all, milady. Just a cream over the *meurtrissure,* and a little rouge on the cheeks and lips ..."

When the skillful maid finished, the bruise was scarcely noticeable, and Chastity's looks were subtly enhanced. Chastity smiled. "You are a genius, Chantal."

"Bien entendu," said the maid complacently. "I will select other garments for you, milady." She twinkled a mischievous, three-pointed smile. "Be assured that they are ones Milady Elf should never wear."

"Horrid monster," said Elf, without rancor. "She has the

right of it, though. You'll be doing a kindness by removing temptation. Chantal, dispose of those old clothes."

The maid gathered Chastity's garments, then gave a little cry of annoyance. "I have pricked myself!"

Before Chastity could say anything, she had pulled out the pearl pin. "Is this yours, milady?"

Chastity thought of denying it, but she could see a wide-eyed Elf had already recognized it. "Yes," she said, and took it, weary of deceptions and deceit. She fixed it in the front of her stomacher, then looked at Elf, who had become very pale. "Rothgar's not my lover," she said.

"Oh," Elf murmured. "Good. Really, I don't know what would happen if two of my brothers fought over the same lady . . . Are you ready to go down?"

Chastity looked in the mirror again, and despite her appearance, trembled at the thought of facing Rothgar. She needed a weapon. "I think . . . I really think I need a fan."

In a moment she had one, a painted cream parchment. She flipped it open, then let it riffle shut. She took a deep breath. "Now," she said, "I am ready."

They found Rothgar in the Tapestry Room. He was staring thoughtfully into the fire, but turned at their entrance. Chastity saw genuine admiration flicker over his features, and he gave her a deep bow.

"Lady Chastity, I am reminded why my brother is *ensorcelé*."

Chastity curtsied deeply. She flicked open her fan and regarded him from behind its protection. "Your brother, Lord Rothgar, has never seen me like this."

He raised her. "Then I rejoice for him even more." He saw the pearl pin. His lack of surprise told her he'd known she was the half-dressed woman he had met on the stairs of Rood House. But since when had he known?

Elf looked between them anxiously, but Rothgar smiled at his sister, a smile of genuine warmth which said much about his feelings for his family. "If that gown was in your wardrobe, my dear, I am deeply grateful to Lady Chastity for coming among us to relieve you of it."

"Horrid man. Some redheads can wear pink."

"Some, yes. But not you, and not that shade, I fear." He settled both ladies in chairs. "I think we should assume that Cyn can deliver the license to Long Knotwell today. I believe an hour and a half in the coach should take us there. Perhaps we should leave in one hour. If it is necessary to stay the night, there will, no doubt, be somewhere to accommodate us."

"I am to come too?" asked Elf.

"Assuredly. I must go, to escort Chastity. You must come with us as chaperone."

Elf's eyes flickered to the pin. Rothgar sighed. "What a low cast of mind you have to be sure, my dear. Lady Chastity did nothing unseemly for that bauble." His eyes were satirical as he added to Chastity, "You may want to consider, however, whether you wish to explain it to Cyn."

"I have done with subterfuge," she said coolly.

"Excellent." Chastity heard a wealth of meaning in that. "Elf, my dear, perhaps you could arrange for some items for Lady Chastity to take with her in case we need to stay the night. If Chastity's sister is also poorly clad, she would surely appreciate more sacrifices from your wardrobe, especially an outfit suitable for her wedding."

Generous Elf rose immediately. "Of course." At the door she hesitated and raised her brows. "I thought I was to be chaperone, brother dear."

Rothgar smiled at her. "I assure you, I never ravish my brothers' promised brides."

"None of your brothers has ever *had* a promised bride before," she pointed out.

"Even so."

With a shake of her head, Elf left.

Chastity pulled out the pin and offered it to Rothgar. "Here, my lord. You had best have it back. Not because of Cyn, but because I do not want it."

He made no move to take it. "But it looks very well there, and you earned it."

When he refused to take it, she let it fall to the carpet.

He ignored the valuable pin and considered Chastity. "I had quite made up my mind to marry you, you know," he said, startling her into unfurling her fan again. "I see my instincts were sound, as always."

Chastity's heart began to flutter. Dear Lord, not more complexities. She fanned in the rapid way that warned a gentleman that the topic was not to her taste. "Are you claiming to *love* me?"

"Oh, no," he said calmly, watching her with those cool gray eyes. "If I loved you, none of this would have happened, would it? But you interested me . . ."

Chastity felt as if she were fencing with him, and suspected she was outclassed. She flipped the fan shut and tried a crude, slashing move. "I was with Cyn at Rood House."

"But of course," he parried lazily.

She threw another wild blow. "I intend to marry him."

"But of course," he said again, a master swordsman toying with a novice.

"Why 'of course'?" she demanded.

"Because if you didn't," he remarked, "you'd be just the whore you are painted."

It was a thrust at the heart. She looked down at the fan in her hands. "Perhaps I am," she whispered.

"But I couldn't possibly permit my brother to marry such a woman."

Chastity felt hope leave her, hope of something she had determined to deny herself, and yet had clung to all the same. She raised her chin to face him. "You might not be able to stop him."

She expected him to sneer at such a challenge, but instead he abandoned the contest and stared pensively into the fire. "You are quite correct. And I would not dare try to balk Cyn again."

It appeared, incredibly enough, an admission of defeat. Chastity found that she was, quite unconsciously, drawing her open fan across her eyes in a message of sympathy. "Why not?" she asked.

"I have a somewhat autocratic tendency," he said levelly. As well say a wolf has sharp teeth, thought Chastity. "When Cyn wanted to go soldiering, it seemed inappropriate. He was not even eighteen and looked younger. If a serious thought had ever crossed his mind, I had been unaware of it. On the other hand, I had extricated him from any number of scrapes, the consequences of which could have been serious. The army has a harsh way of dealing with mischief, even from its officers . . ."

He looked directly at her, and her fan was no protection at all. "You would not, of course, have ever seen a flogging."

Chastity shook her head.

"Men are flogged even for mislaying their equipment. Fifty lashes, perhaps. For more serious offenses, the total rises into the hundreds. Officers are generally immune to such punishment. They can, of course, be shot. You must remember the execution of Admiral Byng, whose crime was not applying himself sufficiently to the relief of Minorca. He was shot, as Monsieur Voltaire so succinctly put it, *'pour encourager les autres.'* "

Chastity let the fan fall closed in her lap.

"I misjudged Cyn, of course," said Rothgar contemplatively. "It was boredom that led him into mischief. He has ordered and supervised any number of floggings, and at least two hangings." He looked at her. "I am not saying that is as difficult as enduring the punishment, but I am a magistrate, and I know it is not easy."

Chastity tried to imagine Cyn in such a situation and failed. Her winsome, lighthearted lover was capable of such harshness? Then she remembered the casual story of the shelter made of corpses. It had been a warning, deliberately given. Did she know him at all? How could she expect to from less than a week of mayhem?

"Why are you telling me this?" she asked, and it was a plea that he stop.

"To answer your question. You asked why I wouldn't try to balk Cyn again. When I refused to arrange his orderly entrance into military life, he ran away and took the shilling. I extricated him from that, of course, and brought him home, but it became clear nothing short of chains would stop him. I had to give in, but the lingering consequences of my misguided objections have been severe."

"What do you mean? He seems happy with his life."

"After a fashion. But I set up barriers between him and his family, and by my very interference I prevented him from taking the easy way. I have almost killed him."

"No. His illness was not your fault."

"Wasn't it? He would not give in to it." His lips twisted in a kind of self-derision. "I haven't given up my meddling, and I know what he does. Another man would have acknowledged that he was sick, and sought help. Cyn, however, feels he must constantly prove his self-sufficiency."

Chastity didn't know what to say. She rather feared Rothgar was right. She also knew it had cost the mighty marquess a great deal to be so honest with her; she could be no less.

"I don't intend to marry him," she said.

"Don't you? But I must insist."

Chastity stared at him. "I beg your pardon?"

"Quite apart from his wishes, which are important to me, I remember Rood House. If you do not marry him, you are no better than you have been painted. I refuse to believe my judgment to be so at fault."

Chastity erupted to her feet. "Damn your judgment! Do my wishes count for nothing?"

She half expected a slap, as Fort had slapped her, but

Rothgar merely raised a brow. "Are you saying you do not wish to marry him?"

"Yes."

"That the passion you have shared was just base lust?"

Chastity felt her face flame. She wanted to say yes, and deny him his victory, but the words wouldn't come. It was as good as a denial.

He grasped her shoulders. Chastity flinched, but he said, "Peace, my dear. My intentions for once are both honorable and benign. You can no more deny Cyn the right to wed you than I could deny his right to choose his way in life. If you try, you risk pushing him into disaster, as I nearly did."

"There can be no greater disaster for him than marriage to me."

A smile tugged at his lips. "There is bound to be, and I assure you he will find it."

Defeated, Chastity leaned forward against his shoulder. To her dismay she began to cry, weary tears of despair. Apart from Cyn, who was as much problem as support, this was the first strong shoulder to be offered her since before Henry Vernham had sneaked into her bed. Rothgar said nothing, but his arms were firm about her, and his very aloofness was a part of his reassuring power.

When she conquered her tears, he sat her on the chaise and gave her a handkerchief.

"Lord Rothgar," Chastity said, blowing her nose, "it cannot be. Even if he is able to weather being married to me, do you think I want to be forced to move in circles where every back will be turned on me?"

"Of course not," he said, as if they were discussing the weather. "We will just have to straighten out those unfortunate rumors."

"Unfortunate rumors!" She wondered if he was mad. "I am thoroughly ruined, my lord. There's not a wellborn lady in England will stay in the same room as me."

"Elf didn't flee. Are you questioning her birth?"

"Of course not. She accepted me out of love for her brother."

"Then we will have to hope he is widely loved."

"You are being ridiculous." She wondered at her temerity but faced him all the same. "I have no doubt Cyn would be drummed out of his regiment for marrying me."

He raised his elegant black brows. "Then I would buy him another one. He should be a colonel anyway."

Chastity was lost for words.

He sat down opposite her and stretched out his long legs. "Now, tell me why you were in bed with Henry Vernham."

Chapter 18

Chastity shook her head. She didn't want to go over it again, when he wouldn't believe her, and could do nothing about it if he did.

"Don't you want to resolve this?" he asked.

"It can't be done."

"Let us at least try."

The sheer power of his will shattered hers. Haltingly, she told the story, even including her father's part in it.

"Walgrave did this to force you into marriage with the likes of Vernham?" he asked.

"Yes."

"Why?"

"I don't know." They were back to fencing, but the fact that he was challenging her meant he took the matter seriously. It was more reassuring than daunting.

"Does it seem reasonable to you?" he asked. "What you would expect from your father?"

She looked away from those indomitable gray eyes. "Not at the time. Now, I don't know. I think he's mad."

"Why do you say that? What has he done since?"

Chastity didn't want to talk about it. "Lord Rothgar, this is pointless. There's nothing to be done."

"There's always something to be done, but I need all the facts." When she still hesitated, he said, "Don't you want to take your rightful place in Society again, to marry Cyn without a cloud over your name, to be happy?"

Tears swelled in her eyes. "It's *impossible* . . ."

"With a Malloren," he repeated, "nothing is impossible. Well?"

Chastity sighed. "As you say, there's the matter of Father trying to force me into marriage with Vernham, which made no sense. There's also the desperation with which Father has been pursuing Verity. He claimed it was paternal concern, but there is something more. I don't know what, though."

"He claimed? When was this?"

Chastity fiddled with the fan. "He caught me in Maidenhead. I thought he'd be furious to find me there in men's clothing . . ." She realized Rothgar wouldn't know of her disguise, and faced him defiantly, "I've been dressing as a man for months."

"That doubtless accounts for a certain refreshing briskness in your manner. Was there a reason?"

Chastity didn't want to talk about that either, but after a moment she took off her wig.

"Ah," he said softly. "Your father?"

She nodded and restored her appearance.

"A not-inappropriate punishment for an erring daughter, I suppose. Was that the sum of it?"

She told herself the whippings had been more to force her to the altar than to punish her. "Except for the clothes." At his look she said, "They came from the local house of correction."

"And you preferred something more suitable. I salute you, my dear. So, your father did not rage at your unseemly dress, but . . . what?"

"He believed I knew where Verity was, and he wanted her. His anger toward me seemed mainly because he thought I'd encouraged her to evade him. I know he regards his daughters as mere pawns for his playing, but his manner was not in keeping with the situation."

Rothgar leaned his head back and contemplated the painted ceiling. "And Lady Verity fled . . . why?"

"She didn't trust Henry Vernham. As soon as he turned up to take his position as guardian, she feared he would do little William some injury."

Rothgar studied the ceiling with rapt attention. A clock chimed the quarter, dimly echoed elsewhere in the house. A coal rolled, sparking in the grate. At last he spoke. "Why did your father marry Lady Verity to Sir William? He too was a nonentity."

Charity couldn't stand this. "I don't know. Don't you think we've struggled to understand it? Nothing makes any sense, but what's done is done. If Verity ends up safe and happy, I'll be content."

He lowered his eyes. "But that will not solve Cyn's problem, and I fear even your sister's happiness may be in jeopardy. Unhindered, your father could make the new couple's life extremely difficult."

That was all too true. "But what can I do?"

"Help me discover what is behind all this. There is something, something we can use. I can smell it. Tell me everything. Every little thing."

In her own cause, Chastity couldn't have done it, but for Verity she would do anything. She went over every confrontation with her father, recalling his words as best she could, detailing—eyes on the fan—his minor and major cruelties. She could be particularly clear about her time in Maidenhead, as that had been so recent.

If her story affected the marquess, it did not show in his face or voice. "So your father asked particularly about why Verity had not run to him."

"Yes, but he would be surprised. I think, despite all, he believes himself to be a good father."

"What reason for her actions could frighten him?"

"Frighten him?" Chastity echoed in surprise.

"Oh, yes, Chastity. You have been telling me about a very frightened man. He must have thought Verity was avoiding him because she knew something to his detriment."

"She knew he'd mistreated me."

"Would that matter with him?"

Chastity had to shake her head.

"I think," said Rothgar, "this matter hinges on the death of Sir William Vernham."

Chastity frowned. "But it can't. He died of a seizure and anyway, it happened after my problems."

"The same factors could be behind both. What connection existed between Sir William and your father, before Verity's marriage?"

"None."

"Think," he said sharply.

Chastity snapped back, "None, I tell you. Sir William was a nobody, a lowly squire, with more money than breeding."

"He was rich?"

"Not by your standards, or Father's, but richer than most of his sort. Fort said he made his money as a Special Investigator after the '45, stealing valuables or taking bribes to overlook evidence of treason. Loathsome man."

"Yet when this loathsome man asked for Verity's hand, he was given it," Rothgar mused. "He must have had a hold over your father. Can you imagine what?"

"No. Father is the Incorruptible, remember. He doesn't gamble, he is moderate in drink, I have never heard even a rumor of women . . ."

"What about treason?" The words dropped like a stone.

"What?"

"Would your father sacrifice his daughter, both his daughters, to save his head?"

"Treason! Father!"

He leaped to his feet and began to prowl, reminding Chastity of nothing so much as a hunting beast. "Treason," he repeated. "It smells. It smells right. The one thing that is certain about the Earl of Walgrave is his ambition. What if he lost his nerve back in the '45 and thought Bonnie Prince Charlie might be victorious?"

"But he's always been strong against the Jacobites!"

"Words cost little. His friendship with Prince Frederick tied him to Hanover, but with the Royal Family packing their bags as the Jacobites approached London, he might have seen everything slipping away. There is still a memory in the land of the way things were when the Stuarts returned in 1660, and Charles II rewarded his faithful friends. Little chance then for a servant of the Commonwealth, no matter how worthy. Not too surprising if your father made discreet contact with the Jacobites."

Chastity was numb with shock.

The marquess continued, almost lovingly, "And what if some evidence fell into the hands of Special Investigator Sir William Vernham, and the man had wits enough to conceal it in such a way that merely killing him would do the earl no good? You know, those investigators did not generally make a great deal of money out of their unpleasant work. Few of the guilty had much to offer, and few situations here in the south of England were ripe for that kind of plucking. But the Earl of Walgrave . . ." He smiled. "Vernham must have received his income from the earl for over fifteen years."

"And Verity?" Chastity asked.

"Perhaps Sir William wanted to tighten his hold on the earl. Possibly he genuinely desired your sister. There would be your dowry to consider as well. Perhaps it was simply an abuse of power, the taunting of a chained lion. A very dangerous thing to do. I wonder if that was not the blow that broke your father's mind. Money to men like us is of little account, but to be forced to link his blood with such a cur . . ." Rothgar's voice was almost a snarl at the thought.

"And it was demanded again with me . . . But then why did he try to force me to it so cruelly?"

"Because Sir William still had the whip hand." Rothgar stared at nothing. "Perhaps still has it, even in death."

"What do you mean?"

"If there is evidence, where is it? Your father must be desperate, no longer knowing from whom to expect attack."

"What of Henry Vernham?"

"I doubt he would have been seeking the child if he'd had a greater source of treasure in his hands."

Chastity sucked in a breath. "Unless he is seeking that source . . ."

Rothgar turned sharply to her.

"Perhaps he hasn't been seeking the child to murder him, but seeking what his brother had. He must think Verity holds the key . . . Lord Rothgar!" Chastity exclaimed. "Verity has been carrying around this document. Sir William impressed upon her that if he died, she must take it to the Lord Chief Justice in London. She supposed it affected the inheritance, so she took it when she fled . . ."

His eyes were bright. "Where is the document now?"

"She has it with her. But Lord Rothgar," Chastity said urgently, "even if your speculations are correct, we can't use it! It would not only destroy Father, but all of us. The property would be seized by the Crown . . . Fort . . ."

"It won't come to that," he assured her. "But if it is an incriminating document, it is a powerful weapon. It will certainly gain the earl's acceptance of your and Verity's marriages."

"And will prevent him from destroying Verity's Nathaniel. But then someone else will be Father's enemy. I fear it will be you."

"I am as able to guard myself as Sir William, I assure you." He smiled. "Fate is a sly harpy, isn't she? Sir William arranges to expose your father if the earl kills him, but never thinks to die so suddenly before his time. A seizure in the arms of his mistress, and the whole situation explodes. Your father, guessing Verity to be the key, has been running ragged after her. Then he finds you in his way. No wonder he raged."

As he said, it did all fit. "Lord Rothgar, I have to point out that this will not make my marriage to Cyn any easier. My father's opposition has always been the minor part. I meant what I said before. I will not ruin Cyn. I will kill myself first."

"Don't be melodramatic. Do you not think it would destroy him to cause your death?"

Chastity gasped under that attack. "I see no hope whichever way I turn!"

"Whereas I begin to see light." He rang a bell and a footman entered. Rothgar scribbled a note, sealed it, and gave it to the man. "A rider is to take this to Henry Vernham. He was last heard of in Salisbury, but has also been scouring the Southampton road for his sister-in-law and her baby."

The footman left with the note.

Chastity stared at Rothgar again. Did he think he was God? "He could be anywhere, and what does the note say?"

"My men are well-trained and enterprising. He'll be found sooner or later. The note informs him of his sister-in-law's wedding and invites him here for the celebration. I have already invited your brother—"

"Here?"

"Assuredly. Plans are in hand for a muted festivity— muted only because your sister is so recently widowed."

She was caught in a whirlwind. "But we can't be sure of Fort," she protested. "For all you know, he could tell Father."

"I hope so. But I have already sent a similar invitation to your father."

"What?" She leaped to her feet, instinct telling her to flee.

He grasped her hand to stay her. He turned it and studied the dull marks. "He will never hurt you again, my dear."

She pulled her hand away. "He will stop Verity's marriage," she snapped. "He'll doubtless arrive with Henry Vernham in train, ready to tear the baby from her arms. You and your Malloren arrogance are going to ruin everything!"

"Oh, I doubt it," he said, and smiled with a glint of excitement Chastity recognized all too well.

"Oh, God," she groaned. "It's as Cyn said. You love a challenge. You don't care about the *people* involved. I don't know which of you is the worst!"

"Oh, I am," said the marquess, and picked up the pin from the carpet. He refixed it in her stomacher. "The poor boy is a mere amateur."

Chastity looked down at the pin. "Something terrible is going to happen," she said with a shiver. "I know it."

"Terrible things have been happening, not least to you. We are going to put a stop to it." He raised her chin. "You are a fighter, Chastity Ware. Don't turn and run now."

She swallowed. "I'm scared."

"Most people are before a battle."

"That's what Cyn said."

"And Cyn assuredly knows."

They set off to Long Knotwell in a virtual parade. Chastity, Elf, and Chantal traveled in a coach. It doubtless was the marquess' second-best coach, but it was fine enough, and in this case the escutcheons blazed out in unblemished arrogance.

Rothgar rode, along with his other brother, Bryght.

"Arcenbryght," Elf whispered when Chastity was introduced to him. "With a name like that, it's a shame he's such a dismal creature these days."

Bryght Malloren was as tall and strong as his older brother, but as he wore a brown wig, Chastity could not tell his natural hair color. His eyes had a touch of Cyn's greenish-gold, but none of his warmth. He gave the distinct impression that he had better things to do.

"You mustn't mind Bryght," said Elf as soon as they were settled. "He's like that with everyone these days. Wounds of the heart. I'll explain some other time."

Including the two brothers, they had twelve outriders, all armed. This seemed more than a little excessive, and Chastity said so.

"Rothgar is ready for trouble," Elf remarked without great concern.

Chastity shuddered. "This could end up as war."

"Oh, I don't think so. The days of the feuding barons are well past. He's doubtless just making sure your father cannot try any mayhem."

They passed the journey in light conversation of social matters, and Chastity was pleased to have it so. It created an island of normalcy in a stormy sea. It was a temporary haven at best, but she welcomed it.

But then Elf said, "Here I am chatting about theatrical excitement, when you must have had such adventures in real life. How I envy you!"

"My adventures were not particularly enjoyable."

"I know they must have been horrid"—Elf sighed. "—but I still envy you. How will I ever meet a dragon-slayer, if I never come within breathing distance of a dragon?"

Chastity didn't know what to say and found herself sharing a speaking look with the maid. Despite Elf's extra years, she seemed in some ways an innocent child. "You have an older sister," Chastity said. "She must have found a man to her liking."

"Oh, yes, but Hilda's always been so placid. She just quietly fell in love with Lord Steen, and quietly married him. Now they're off in Somerset quietly producing quiet babies. I'm afraid I have a taste for stronger men, but my brothers chase them off on principle. They want me to marry another Lord Steen."

Chastity's lips twitched. "And you want to marry a Rothgar . . ."

Elf laughed. "Or a Brand, or a Bryght, or a Cyn. A man who'd face down the devil. Alas, I fear I am destined to be an old maid."

They rolled into Long Knotwell in mid-afternoon, causing considerable excitement. People came out of their houses to gape at the cavalcade. Children ran alongside, trying to peep into the coach. Chastity heard one girl call, "Is it the king, Jimmy?"

They drew up before the vicarage, and Rothgar came to open the carriage door and lead them into the house.

It was a modest place, and soon seemed full of Mallorens. The vicar, Reverend Thomas Frazer, came forward. "Ah, Lady Chastity, I'm pleased you are here." He cast a nervous glance at the two large Malloren men in his parlor. "Your sister and my brother are above stairs. We only await the license."

In a moment Verity was with them, hugging Chastity. "How well you look! I have been so afraid something terrible would happen to you while I stayed in comfort. Mary Garnet was all that was obliging, and then Nathaniel came and brought us here. No adventure to it at all!"

Verity sounded just a touch disappointed. Chastity decided to leave her sister in ignorance. "And little adventure to my story either," she said. "Cyn should be here shortly with your license. Come and be introduced to Lady Elfled Malloren, Cyn's twin. She is lending you some clothes. You must pick what you like for your wedding."

Verity smiled tearfully and thanked Elf. "In truth, it's silly even to think of such a thing when it's being married to Nathaniel that matters, but I did want to have something special for the ceremony."

Chastity turned to greet Nathaniel, an old friend and neighbor. In a room full of Mallorens, he appeared rather ordinary, but he was a fine figure of a man, with even features and shrewd eyes. Clearly in Verity's eyes, he outshone even the marquess.

"I must thank you for looking after Verity, Chastity," the major said. "I know you must have been the spine of the operation."

"Really, Nathaniel. Is that any way to speak of your bride?"

He colored. "You know I adore her, but no one would claim she has the nerve to hold up a coach."

Chastity smiled. "Perhaps that was crass stupidity, not cool nerves, though I hope it has worked out in the end." She drew him a little apart. "Nathaniel, I have to warn you, Rothgar intends that you and Verity return to the Abbey after the ceremony, but he has invited both my father and my brother there. He has even told them that the wedding is to take place here! With any luck they'll not arrive in time to do mischief, but . . ."

Nathaniel flashed an angry look at the marquess, arrogantly formidable in gray velvet. "The devil you say! What's he about?"

"Who can tell, though his intentions seem good. I just thought I'd warn you. But I don't think Verity should know. She'd have the vapors."

He raised a brow. "Is that any way to speak of your sister?"

Chastity had to give him that point.

Elf and Chastity then went upstairs with Verity to explore the boxes Chantal was unpacking. The maid eyed Verity, then nodded. "The blue," she said. "It also becomes Milady Elf, but it is for a wedding . . ."

Elf silenced Verity's objections with a negligent hand. "It must assuredly be the blue. I have a dozen more, I promise you."

Verity's wedding gown, therefore, was a sky-blue grosgrain, closed in the skirt, but open in the bodice to expose an echelle stomacher of white bows, going from tiny at the waist to wide at the cleavage. The neckline was wide and made the most of her beautiful chest and full breasts. There was also a matching choker collar of blue silk, embroidered with pearls and fastened at the front with a bow.

With her hair dressed high, she looked every inch the grand lady. The vicarage did not boast a full-length mirror and so she had to accept their assurances that Nathaniel would be delighted by her appearance.

A knock on the door brought the Reverend Frazer's middle-aged maid. "They said to tell you all's ready below, miladies."

A flutter of excitement unsettled Chastity. That meant Cyn was here. She nervously twitched at her pink skirts.

Verity took her hand and squeezed it. "You look beautiful too, dearest. More beautiful than you were before. In the spring you were a pretty girl. Now you are a ravishing woman."

Chastity started, wondering if it was so obvious that she and Cyn were lovers.

The vicarage parlor was bursting at the seams with the addition of two more Mallorens. Cyn looked up quickly as the door opened, and stared at Chastity almost as if she were a stranger. Instinctively, she flicked open her fan to shield her face from that heated gaze.

She heard Nathaniel say admiring, loving things to Verity.

She heard Rothgar arranging details with the vicar.

Her eyes were drawn to Cyn.

He came over to her. "If I had seen you like this," he said softly, "I don't think I would have dared aspire so high."

Chastity found her voice had abandoned her and used the fan, fluttering it in a way that expressed agitation and interest.

"When Rothgar sorts it all out," he said seriously, "I won't hold you to anything. You can do better than a rough soldier." He suddenly saw Rothgar's pearl pinned to her stomacher and his eyes widened. "Perhaps you already have."

Chastity stopped fluttering. "Cyn, really . . . !"

But then the reverend was chivying them to the church. Cyn escorted Chastity, but it was as if there were a wall between them. She should be glad, really she should, but she hated it. She needed to say something to breach the wall, but knew this wasn't a time for personal matters. She remembered Rothgar's strange invitations to her father, brother, and Henry Vernham, and told Cyn about them.

"Interesting," he said, still very cool. "He will have his reasons, and having asked his help, we mustn't quibble."

The ceremony went forward without disturbance. Chastity remembered Verity's first wedding, when she'd spoken her vows woodenly, staring straight ahead. This time she said them with love, looking into Nathaniel's intent eyes.

Chastity swallowed tears, and by great willpower she did not once look at Cyn during the ceremony.

Elf and Rothgar stood as witnesses, thereby putting the full weight of the Mallorens behind the match.

When it was done Rothgar said, "Now we must get you all back to the safety of the Abbey. We have a celebration planned, and there's light enough if we leave now."

With the reminder that Walgrave could turn up at any moment, no one needed encouragement. Even the Reverend Frazer was persuaded to accompany them. The excuse was that he too would want to celebrate his brother's wedding, but everyone knew it was to make sure he wasn't available to take the brunt of Walgrave's rage.

Verity and the baby joined the other ladies in the coach. The men all rode. Nathaniel kept his mount close to the coach, as if he could not bear to be further away.

Elf sighed. "Another dragon-slayer."

Verity gave Chastity a perplexed glance.

Cyn didn't ride by the coach, but seemed to be in conference with Rothgar, probably being filled in as to their suspicions. She wondered if she should tell Verity about it now, but she put the moment off. The idea that their father had dabbled in treason would tarnish this moment of happiness. When they arrived at the Abbey, and Verity's baggage was available, Chastity would ask for the document. Would it prove to be as important as they thought, or a disappointment? Would it make any difference to Chastity's future? Was there any chance on earth that her reputation could be salvaged, that she too could have a wedding day?

She couldn't allow herself to hope for anything so unlikely. As well hope to be a virgin again.

They arrived at Rothgar Abbey just as the sun set, and were soon within its elegant opulence. Rooms were already prepared for Chastity, and for Verity and Nathaniel. A nursery maid stood prepared to help with the baby. A celebratory dinner was about to be served.

When Chastity thought to ask Verity about the document, she found the newlyweds had already disappeared to the privacy of their room. She glanced at the marquess, but he exhibited no great impatience.

She caught Cyn staring at her, but he made no attempt to talk to her.

She should have been glad.

Her heart ached.

She sought the sanctuary of her own room, determined not to cry. After all, if he thought she was under Rothgar's protection, he would leave her be. She was pacing, bolstering her resolve to cut Cyn free, when Verity knocked and entered. A bright-eyed Verity, made radiant by happiness.

"I can hardly believe it, Chastity!" Verity exclaimed as they hugged. "We've done it! And the marquess says he can ensure Nathaniel does not suffer by it." She colored with the blush of love. "Nathaniel would not even listen to my concerns, dearest. He said if there was any problem with the marriage, he'd spirit me abroad to do it."

Chastity kissed her. "I'm so happy for you, Verity. Did the marquess say how he will keep you safe?"

"No," said Verity with a trace of anxiety. "Do you doubt him?"

"Oh, no, but . . ." Chastity set herself to explaining the incredible. "This is going to sound strange, Verity, but we think that everything that has happened could be explained if Sir William had a hold over Father—a hold that came because Father committed treason back in 1745. We think that Sir William must have had a document linking Father to the Stuarts."

"Treason? Father?" said Verity, exactly as Chastity had, but then nodded slowly. "I confess, it would have to be something of that magnitude to account for it."

"And we think," said Chastity carefully, "that the document you have carried around was not a legal one, but the incriminating evidence."

"Heavens!" gasped Verity.

"So will you give it to Rothgar so we can see what it is?"

"Of course," said Verity, then her eyes widened and she went pale. "Oh, lud!"

"What?"

"It was in the pocket of my servant's gown."

Chastity remembered bundling that up when they changed in the coach. "What happened to it? You didn't throw it away, did you?"

"No, I left it with Mary Garnet. In the excitement of seeing Nathaniel, I forgot all about the document." Verity clapped a hand to her mouth. "I said she could give those clothes to the poor!"

Chastity picked up her skirts and flew downstairs to find Rothgar. A footman told her he was in his study, and she rushed there.

Rothgar looked up. "Chastity. What is it?"

She explained about the evidence.

"Ah," he said alertly. "It is as well you asked her. There is no time to lose."

"What will you do?"

"Send for it immediately. I think Cyn had better go, as he is known to these people."

"He's been in the saddle for two days," she protested.

"He's a soldier, and assures me he's well."

This was taking nonprotectiveness to extremes, but Chastity was distracted by another thought. "I've remembered something else."

"Yes?"

She told him about the women at Rood House, only then realizing that he had been there, and doubtless knew the place had been full of supposedly respectable women. She carried on, determined to be thorough, and explained about Nerissa Trelyn's note. It had nothing to do with treason, but she had promised to tell him all.

His eyes glittered with interest. "Ah. You said the note was explicit. Can you remember any of it?"

Chastity blushed to think of it, but she dug in her memory. "She called him her Hercules ... There was something about his handkerchief between her legs at the theater, and a ribbon around his ..." She looked at him and shook her head, her cheeks burning. "I cannot recite such stuff ..."

"It's all right," he said gently. "I see the tone. I just wanted to be sure it was more explicit than the usual love note."

"Oh, it was certainly more than that."

"And you left this note behind the fireplace? Tell me again how to find the house."

She gave him directions as best she could, and he wrote them down. Within moments Bryght Malloren had been summoned and sent off to retrieve the evidence. He seemed pleased to be able to avoid the celebration.

"You think it is of use?" Chastity asked. "I have no desire to harm Lady Trelyn. She only told the truth when she confirmed my shame."

"You're too kindhearted. Nerissa Trelyn would ruin anyone in a moment if it served her purpose. But I doubt we'll have to harm her spotless reputation. Half the world knows she's a trollop, you know. It amuses them to pretend otherwise. Most of the world knew you were an innocent victim—such things can be sensed—but it amused them to vilify you. Every now and then we require a sacrificial victim on the altar of propriety. It reassures us that there are some standards left. It's not a pretty picture."

"You are part of it," she pointed out.

"A major part," he acknowledged amiably. "But I never hurt the innocents."

He came forward and raised her chin to kiss her lips. "I almost envy my brother . . ."

Chastity knew with a sixth sense that Cyn had entered the room. She twitched out of Rothgar's lax fingers and faced him.

"Is that how your name is to be restored?" Cyn asked with a chilly tone worthy of Rothgar himself. "True enough. No one would dare question the honor of Rothgar's bride."

"Not to my face, at least," said Rothgar calmly. "But we are concerned, I think, with what is said behind our backs."

Chastity felt like a lamb between two wolves.

Rothgar looked at his brother in a way that sent a shiver down Chastity's spine. "If you doubt Lady Chastity's honor for one second because of that kiss, Cyn, you are not worthy of her. I have a task for you, but it will wait a few minutes."

The door clicked shut behind him. Cyn and Chastity were left alone. "What the devil's between you two?" Cyn demanded.

Chastity knew that she could use this moment to cut Cyn free, but only at the price of destroying his relationship with his brother. "There is nothing between us," she said.

"Then why are you wearing that pin?"

She had forgotten it, and her hand fluttered up as if to conceal it. "He gave it to me at Rood House."

"Why?"

Chastity could not bear his icy tone. Wrong though it might be, she wanted, she needed, his tender care. "You can't really think anything of this, Cyn," she protested, and moved into his arms.

He held her off. "Why?" he demanded.

Bewildered, she touched his cheek.

He shook her hand off. "Chastity, why did Rothgar give you that pin?"

"For services rendered!" she snapped, backing away. "You are the stupidest man!"

"I'm sure I am, but I'm amazed you managed to fit him in."

"Cyn Malloren, you've run mad! He teased a kiss out of me."

He grabbed her arm and dragged her close. "And paid with that pearl," he scoffed. "What kind of fool do you think I am?"

She rapped his knuckles hard with the fan. "Release me, sir! I have nothing more to say to you until you are sane again."

He released her, but only to pull her into his arms again. "I'll never be sane again. Oh, Chastity, I don't know what to make of you as a fine lady. You terrify me. You'd make such a wonderful marchioness." His hand traced gently down her cheek. "Please don't let Rothgar kiss you again."

It was sweet to be in his arms, but bittersweet. "Do you really think I could be interested in him?"

"How can you not be? I meant what I said earlier. Once your reputation is restored, you will have no need of me. There will be many finer suitors for your hand, doubtless including Rothgar. He kisses no woman without a reason."

It was hard, so hard, but she left his embrace and forced the cool words out. "Very well. Perhaps I will marry Rothgar after all."

He flashed her a bereft look, but nodded. "Good. If your reputation is not restored, though, we must marry."

She faced him sharply. "I won't allow that sacrifice!"

"I took advantage of you . . ."

"I was completely willing . . ."

He groaned and pulled her back to him for a kiss. Then his lips explored the curve of first one breast, then the other, weakening all her resolve. "You look delicious, like raspberries and cream . . ."

"Cyn, food again . . . ?"

"Mmm."

Chastity tried to be cool, but longing swept over her, empowered by his skillful touch. She surrendered with a whimper of despair . . .

A brief rap at the door allowed just enough time for them to break apart before Rothgar entered. He coolly assessed them and said, "Excellent. Cyn, there is urgent business in Winchester. Are you up to it?"

A flickering glance told Chastity that Cyn didn't want to leave her, but he accepted the duty. "I can manage with a fresh horse."

"Good." Rothgar crisply explained the situation. "I'll send two grooms with you, but it will go easier if you are there to make the request of your friend's wife. And if she's already disposed of the garment, you'll have to track it down and retrieve the document."

" 'Struth. Am I to prowl the worthy poor, picking pockets?"

Rothgar's lips twitched. "Do what is necessary. Once you have it safe, you can rest as long as you are in a secure place and the grooms keep watch."

Chastity shivered at this sense of hovering danger. If anyone discovered Cyn had that document, he would be a target. Henry Vernham would kill to get it; the Earl of Walgrave would destroy half the world to have it gone. This was no time to hold back.

She took Cyn's hands and kissed him. "Take care. Please."

Chapter 19

The wedding dinner was a strange affair. Verity and Nathaniel had eyes only for each other. Elf looked wistful. Brand and Rothgar made desultory conversation about political matters. Chastity worried about Cyn.

Though she had known him for such a brief time, they had rarely been apart. She wasn't used to worrying about him *in absentia*. She realized Rothgar and Brand were discussing the war. That interested her, as Cyn's safety rested on it. "Do you really think the war will soon be over?" she asked.

"Almost certainly," said Rothgar. "Since the battle of Wandewash in India, and the surrender of the Canadas, French expansion is blocked. Now that King George has withdrawn support from King Frederick, Prussia will have to come to terms." He smiled in acknowledgment of her feelings. "You may not have to face the thought of Cyn in battle in the near future."

"Perhaps he may be posted at home for a while," said Elf hopefully. "I have seen so little of him in past years, and I have only just come to know you, my new sister."

Chastity knew she should protest, yet this acceptance of her future as Cyn's wife was too delicious a fantasy to abandon entirely. She sat in a silent dream as Elf wondered where Cyn would be stationed, and even progressed to speculating as to future nieces and nephews.

The meal ended with toasts to the married couple. Elf rose to lead the ladies away, but Nathaniel rose too. As pink as his bride, he indicated that they were ready for bed. With an admirably straight face, Rothgar wished them a good night.

Elf led Chastity up to her boudoir to take tea. "It will soon be your turn, too."

"I allow myself to dream," said Chastity. "But in all honesty, I don't see how it can be."

"Rothgar will manage something," said Elf confidently, "and Cyn will not be deterred by a mere matter of reputation. I hope it can be straightened out, though, for it will make everyone a great deal more comfortable. Speaking of comfort, I intend to escape this bodice immediately. I'm sure Chantal laced me especially tight to compete with your waistline. I feel as if I'm about to pop."

The maid soon had them both in charming negligees, loose gowns trimmed with lace and ribbons, and they settled in comfortable privacy for a chat and tea.

"Can you tell me more of your family, Elf?" Chastity asked.

Elf poured boiling water on the leaves in the pot. "Of course, since you are to join it. As you know, there are the six of us, all with strange names. Rothgar's mother made no objection, and so the pattern was set."

"You have different mothers?"

"Didn't you know? She died when Rothgar was five. Father married again soon after. I scarcely remember my own mother, for she and Father both died when I was but seven. Cyn is said to resemble her the most, wretched man."

"Lord Rothgar must have been young when he came into the title."

Elf passed the tea in a dish of Chinese porcelain. "Just turned nineteen, and with responsibility for five siblings, two of them hell-born twins. He took it seriously. He's been very good to us."

"It is clear he feels strongly about his family."

"Yes. He really should marry, and I think he's coming around to it, though that may change now."

Chastity sipped. "Why now?"

"He has been hoping one of the others would marry to carry on the line, but Bryght's plans fell through. Now Cyn is to be wed, I fear Rothgar will drop his intent to find a bride."

"I don't understand why the marquess should expect his brothers to do his duty."

"Ah," said Elf, and for the first time seemed hesitant. "Well, it's a family scandal and you are to be family. It's not something that need bother you in any case. It's his mother, you see."

"Rothgar's mother?"

"One gathers she was not a very pleasant person."

"But can he remember much of her?"

"He remembers something. Strong events trigger memories. She bore a second child, a daughter. She killed the babe."

Chastity inadvertently splashed a little of her tea. *"What?"*

"It's true. The child was but a few days old, and she strangled her. Rothgar was there when she did it, but was too little to stop her. He was only four years old, but he remembers. I think that is why he is so protective of us. He is still trying to save his baby sister."

Chastity put down her dish of tea before her trembling hands caused another spill. "But why would she do such a thing?"

Elf shook her head. "No one knows, but I've heard it said that some women are driven mad by childbirth. She was locked up afterward, of course, and not allowed near her son. She took some wasting disease and died."

"It's a terrible story, but why would the marquess not wish to marry?"

Elf was somber. "He is concerned that it could be in the

blood. He has always been very careful not to lose control."

"I think he should disregard it. Who knows how children will be?"

"But some qualities are passed on. The color of hair and eyes. A gift for music or art." Elf smiled reassuringly. "You certainly mustn't let it affect your plans, Chastity. Now, why don't you explain your family to me. Have you sisters other than Verity?"

"No, just two brothers. Fort—Fortitude, that is, and Victor. You see, you don't have a monopoly on strange names. Fort is the oldest, he's Lord Thornhill. Victor is just sixteen."

"What are they like?"

"Oh, Fort is a typical man. He loves riding, and shooting, and the new sport called boxing. They put on padded gloves and hit one another until one of them falls down. Can you imagine it? Despite such horrid tastes, he's quite kind really, but not very sensitive."

Elf laughed. "As you say, a typical man."

"As for Victor, we've been fighting since he was born, so I'm no judge. He'll doubtless improve with age." She stifled a yawn, then blushed to be so rude.

Elf immediately put down her tea. "How thoughtless of me. You must be exhausted."

"I confess, I am," said Chastity. "I had little sleep the last two nights."

Elf's color flared. Chastity almost hastened to correct Elf's obvious assumption that there had been two nights of lovemaking, but then realized that it was not entirely an error. With a strained smile, she said good night and went to her own room. Once there, she sighed.

She wasn't made for scandal. She hated this feeling of being less than virtuous. Cyn had been more right than he knew when he said their lovemaking had weakened her. If they couldn't marry, they must part, for much as her body longed for him, she would die in a life of shame.

* * *

In the morning, Chastity was woken with a cup of delicious chocolate, and the information that her brother had arrived and was anxious to speak to her.

She leaped out of bed, nerves a-tingle. She had a cowardly urge to summon Elf to accompany her, but she suppressed it. Despite the kindness of the Mallorens, she was alone in the world, and must behave so.

She discovered she now had a wide selection of clothes, most of which, as Chantal had said, would not suit Lady Elf. With the maid's assistance, she dressed in a demure India cotton morning gown of orange printed in brown. In this case, the orange was almost exactly the color of Elf's hair, and the effect would have been startling.

The lady was clearly in the habit of buying without truly considering the matter. The gown looked well on Chastity, however, and the modest, though expensively embroidered, ruffles at bodice-edge and elbows created the demure appearance she wanted.

Would Fort still be on her side?

She found her brother in the Tapestry Room, prowling.

"Good morning, Fort," she said, striving for dignity and composure.

He turned suddenly, and she saw he had a black eye and a bruised lip. "Oh, Fort! Did Father do that?"

"Lindle to be more precise." He grinned painfully. "I'm delighted to report that he's in worse shape. I broke his nose."

Chastity laughed. "Thank you, thank you, thank you!"

His eyes were warm as he looked at her. "You're vastly improved, Chastity."

"Thanks to you. I'm sorry for abandoning you . . ."

"Devil take it. I'm glad you had the sense. But once I'd knocked Lindle out, and escaped Father's clutches, I scoured the town for you. I had some lurid imaginings. I virtually took a couple of brothels apart."

Chastity went to him and kissed him gently. "Thank you. But Cyn was doing the same."

"Cyn?" he said with a puzzled frown that told her he'd heard *sin*.

With a choking sensation, Chastity realized he knew nothing of Cyn Malloren. But how else could she explain her presence here? If she'd thought of the necessity, she'd have come up with some kind of story . . .

"Sin?" he asked, cooling rapidly.

"Lord Cynric Malloren," Chastity said, licking her lips, wondering if she should summon protection after all. "He . . . er . . . escorted Verity and me to Winchester."

"A Malloren," Fort spat. "I wondered how you ended up here. And how did he come to be in Maidenhead?"

"He helped me find Nathaniel, of course," Chastity said brightly. "Surely you can see that."

"Alone?" His eyes lit with anger. "The two of you on the road overnight, alone?" His hand went to the hilt of his sword. "Where is he?"

"Not here," she said quickly. "And Fort, you are not to hurt him."

"Am I not, by gad!"

"He wants to marry me!"

"Hah! He wants to marry Chastity Ware? You're a bigger fool than I took you for!"

She thumped his chest. "I thought you believed in me!"

He swung a fist at her, but controlled it with a caught breath. "You told me you are not a virgin."

"Yes," she said, meeting his eyes, "but I was."

"Then he's a cur."

"No."

He took a deep breath. "Sister, you clearly do not understand these things."

"I understand them perfectly. I was not seduced, Fort. I went to him willingly, because I love him."

"He is a cur to take advantage of you."

"He didn't think me a virgin then, Fort. Promise me you won't fight him."

"I'll promise you nothing." He turned away and ran his hands through his disordered hair. "I'll have you and Verity out of this hellhole. *No one* trusts a Malloren, especially with a woman. They'll doubtless pass you around." He swung back to sneer at her. "If they haven't already."

"Fort, stop this!"

He stopped, but only to stare at her. "Cyn Malloren! I knew I remembered that name. He was at—" He broke off and then said, "At a certain place."

He was talking about Rood House.

"Have you breakfasted, Fort?" Chastity asked quickly.

"I heard Cyn Malloren was fighting over a wench," he sneered. "How do you like that, sister dear? But three nights since, your honorable seducer was squabbling over a whore."

Then he started counting nights. She could see it in his eyes.

"That was the night you spent on the road with him on your way to Maidenhead . . ." His puzzled frown turned to an expression of horror. "Dear Lord in heaven . . ." Chastity retreated strategically behind a sofa, wondering what her chances were of reaching the door.

"I thought that teasing Chloe was familiar!" His voice swelled to a roar. "You filthy little trollop!"

"You were at Rood House too!" she screamed at him.

He charged at her, and the sofa suddenly seemed no barrier at all. Chastity looked for a weapon and grabbed a large Chinese vase, the best defense to hand.

Fort stopped.

He stopped because a glittering rapier was at his throat, wielded by Rothgar, who had appeared as if by magic.

"Ah," said Fort. "Another Malloren. Is she whore to the whole family, then?"

"My dear Thornhill," said Rothgar softly, "she is to all

intents and purposes one of the family. If you offend against her, I will be forced to take it personally . . ."

Even Fort appeared to be sobered by the concentrated malice in the marquess' voice.

"She doesn't deny that your brother ruined her," Fort said. "I'll have satisfaction of him."

"That is between you and him. But it is your father who has ruined her. Whose side are you on?" The unwavering sword at his neck carried a lethal promise.

Fort ignored it and looked steadily at Chastity. She sent him a silent appeal. He sighed. "Hers."

Rothgal lowered the sword. Chastity only then realized that Brand and Elf were in the room too.

"Then we are all on the same side," said Rothgar smoothly, as if that violence had never been. "Let me tell you about your father . . ."

Time hung heavy at the Abbey as everyone waited for Rothgar's plans to bring results. No one was entirely sure what wheels Rothgar had set in motion except the marquess himself, and the only clear sign he gave was to casually order preparations for a grand masqued ball in five days.

"Five days," said Elf calmly. "And who is to attend?"

"Everyone I have invited," he said enigmatically.

It became clear that Rothgar had invited all the local gentry and a good part of the aristocracy.

"Won't they think it strange to be invited to a grand ball at such short notice?" Chastity asked.

"Oh, no," said Elf. "He always does things this way. A whim takes him and he holds an event. They are accustomed."

"Well, I suppose they are accustomed to a scrambling kind of affair then. It took weeks of planning for my father to hold a ball this spring."

"Scrambling," said Elf with Malloren hauteur. "Of course not."

Chastity found herself swept up into a whirlwind of efficient organization. Large numbers of extra staff were summoned from London. Messages went to Rothgar's other estates demanding provisions. Both staff and provisions, of course, all came by the fastest means, regardless of cost. A dozen crates of geese came by post chaise.

Fort stayed on at the Abbey. He appeared to accept the likelihood of his father's guilt, but he was not particularly mellowed toward the Mallorens. He kept to himself as they awaited Cyn's return. Cyn, who would bring the document that could ruin the whole Ware family. Cyn, who was his sister's seducer.

Fort looked like a man who lusted for someone to kill.

"What a horrible brother," said Elf as she directed the rearrangement of furniture. "He doesn't seem to care for you at all."

"Perhaps he cares too much," said Chastity. "What would Rothgar do if he found you in bed with a man?"

Elf went wide-eyed at the thought, but said, "He wouldn't turn against me."

Chastity didn't argue, but she thought Elf overoptimistic. She hoped her new friend's illusions were never shattered.

In the evening of the next day, Bryght returned from Maidenhead with the letter. Chastity and Elf were with Rothgar when Bryght walked into the Tapestry Room and gave it to his brother. "The house was deserted, and Walgrave is no longer in Maidenhead." Somewhat grimly, he added, "You didn't tell me who the letter was from."

"I didn't tell you to read it, either," remarked Rothgar with an unmistakable touch of humor. Rothgar's humor was generally cause for concern.

Chastity saw an angry muscle twitch in Bryght's jaw. He hadn't shaved that day, and looked more sullen and angry than usual. "Was I to ride my arse raw to get the damn thing, and not stop to check it wasn't a laundry list?"

Rothgar scanned the perfumed paper and his brows rose. "One glance would tell you it wasn't that."

"One glance told me who had written it. I recognized the writing, and the perfume."

"Ah," said Rothgar, with a smile that was positively beatific, yet the most chilling thing Chastity had ever seen.

Bryght's jaw was working in an alarming way and his hands were fists. "You sent me deliberately."

Rothgar didn't deny it. "You have never believed the woman to be less than perfect."

"I'm not sure what I believe now. Would she have come to this if she'd married me?"

Chastity realized with horror that Bryght's lost love was Nerissa Trelyn.

"She chose Trelyn of her own free will," Rothgar pointed out.

Bryght turned on his heel and slammed out of the room.

"As you see," said Rothgar to Chastity, "I have a score of my own to settle with Nerissa Trelyn. But even so, I will not destroy her unless she insists on it."

Chastity shared a horrified look with Elf, but that lady just shrugged as if such dramatics were an ordinary part of life. Lud, but living with the Mallorens was like living in a dragon's lair, with Fort as an invading eagle.

When a second day passed without Cyn's appearance, Chastity began to worry about his safety. Three times she was on the point of begging Rothgar to send out a search party, but Cyn would hate that if he were safe. Besides, Rothgar's confidence was so overwhelming she feared he'd be mortally offended at the suggestion of a problem in his plans.

She buried her worries under the work of helping Elf organize the ball. Elf seemed to have all the details in hand but one.

"We need a theme," she said. "A ball must have a theme."

"Flowers?" said Chastity.

"Not in November," said Elf with a grin. "Not even for a Malloren. Medieval?" she mused. "No, for people would wish to be in costume, and there is not time. Venetian? Terribly overdone . . . Ah," she suddenly said. "Chinese!"

"Chinese?" queried Chastity, following her hostess as she headed toward the subterranean depths of the house.

"Why did I not think of it before?" Elf burbled happily. "Come along. You'll see."

What Chastity saw was a pile of bales wrapped in burlap. When a footman unwrapped them, they proved to be rolls of priceless, hand-painted red Chinese silk.

She touched one reverently, then turned to Elf in horror. "You *can't!*"

"I'm going to hang it all around the ballroom."

"Elf, you can't!" Chastity wailed. "It's far too precious!"

"Oh," said Elf, "not for a Malloren."

Then Chastity saw the way Elf's lips were twitching. She looked again at the silk. It was undoubtedly very valuable. She gently unrolled some. It was a cleverly constructed dummy bale. Inside she found only a coarse glazed cotton printed with the same gilded pattern. "You wretch," she declared. "Where did all this come from?"

"Rothgar acquired it in one of his more mysterious enterprises. I keep wondering what to do with the good silk, but it's too exotic for a dress . . ." She looked at Chastity. "For me, maybe."

"I'm not going to the ball in a gown that appears to be made from the hangings," said Chastity firmly.

Elf laughed. "Of course not. But for later, perhaps. Meanwhile, we'll have this unwrapped and hung." She gave the orders and swept off. "It would be effective to paint the woodwork in the ballroom in black lacquer," she mused.

"But somewhat permanent," Chastity pointed out, wondering if that would matter to a Malloren. "You could always have mock panels constructed and placed around the room." As soon as she'd said it, Chastity knew she was being infected with the Malloren outlook on life.

"Of course," said Elf delightedly, and gave more orders. The amazing thing, thought Chastity, was that the enormous staff of servants never blinked at any order, no matter how outrageous. No wonder Cyn was as he was.

With a Malloren, all things were possible.

She had begun to think of Rothgar Abbey as a miniature Versailles.

She was directing the draping of the 'silk' when Cyn returned. He walked into the ballroom and halted. " 'Struth. Is that really . . .?"

Chastity whirled. "Cyn!" Without thinking, she hurled herself into his arms under the discreet but fascinated attention of twenty servants.

She recollected herself immediately and pulled away. He almost let her go, but then suddenly, desperately, stepped back with her out of the room and into the corridor. For a moment they stood there, drinking in the sight of each other, then their mouths met in desperate communion.

Chastity knew then that life was scarcely possible for her without Cyn's presence—his touch, his voice, his love . . .

The kiss eased away but they still clung together.

"God, but I missed you," he groaned against her cheek.

"I missed you too. I was so worried . . ."

He moved away a little. "We mustn't do this. Your reputation . . ."

"I don't care . . ."

"I do." He sucked in a deep breath and separated them completely. "Stop tempting me, wench."

"Ha!" she protested. "So I'm cast as Eve, am I?" But she smiled with the joy of his return. "Come and see the ballroom."

He allowed her to pull him back into the room and gazed at the walls. "I saw. Even Rothgar wouldn't . . ."

"It is remarkably convincing, isn't it?"

He went over and studied a panel, and blew out his breath in relief. "But it's remarkable from a distance, and in candlelight . . . The Malloren reputation for doing the incredible is about to be bolstered."

"Quite apart from whatever takes place at the ball." Then the purpose of the ball hit her like a shower of cold rain. "Did you get the documents?"

"Yes," he said, and rolled his eyes. "But only by luck. Mary gave the clothes to her maid, who passed them on to her mother. When I arrived at that lady's house, she had just plunged them all into a vat of hot, soapy water."

As if unable to resist, he took her hand.

"Oh, Lord. Did the ink survive?" That tenuous contact was shattering her mind.

He grinned. "She'd taken the document out of the pocket, thinking to return it to Mary, but put it on the table near a joint of meat. It became somewhat bloodstained."

"Appropriate in a way," Chastity commented, twining her fingers with his.

"Very true. Unfortunately it then seemed a tasty treat to the lady's pet cur."

Chastity closed her eyes. "I don't want to know."

"Only slightly chewed."

She opened her eyes and smiled at him, as much in delight at his presence as at his news. "You gave the letter to Rothgar?"

"I gave it to Verity, since it is hers. I think she is taking it to Rothgar now." He raised her hand and kissed it.

She gazed at him longingly, but said, "Come on, then. I'm quite desperate to know what is in it. And if it turns out to be some carefully-thought-out last words of advice, I shall have the vapors!"

Cyn allowed himself to be dragged along. "I live to see the day!"

She flashed him a scowl that turned into laughter, and towed him along. At the door to Rothgar's study, however, he put up real resistance and captured her against the wall. "You seem happy," he said almost wistfully.

Chastity realized with surprise that she was. That she had been for days. Happy to be a woman again, in a normal house, with a family of sorts. She'd wiped away the terrible months and was refusing to contemplate the bleak future. "Do you mind?"

He shook his head. "Why should I mind, love? This is what I want for you. What I insist on giving you. If the document turns out to be useless, we'll find some other way."

"Oh, Cyn," said Chastity. "I pray you're right."

"Of course I'm right. You have the Mallorens on your side."

Chastity shook her head at him, but said, "I want to thank you for bringing me here, Cyn. And for recruiting Rothgar. I know it wasn't easy for you."

He hooted with laughter. "Recruited! Was that what I did? How bloody marvelous!"

And it was Cyn who pulled a bemused Chastity into the study.

They found Rothgar, Verity, and Nathaniel—a very sober Verity and Nathaniel. Rothgar passed the stained and slightly-chewed document over to Cyn and Chastity.

"Lud," said Chastity as they read.

It was a very incriminating document, for all that it was signed only 'Mr. Ware.' The recipient, whoever that was, had clearly demanded proof of who he was dealing with. In response, a number of details had been given which pointed clearly, for those with any knowledge of the man, to Lord Walgrave. In one sentence, the words offspring, Fortitude, Chastity, and Verity had been combined. Victor hadn't been born at that date.

Mr. Ware promised to use his influence with certain highly placed people—read the Prince and Princess of

Wales—to induce the royal family to flee once the Jacobite army arrived within thirty miles of London.

He professed unswerving allegiance to James III, citing a meeting with the 'king' during his Grand Tour in 1717.

"Could that meeting have really taken place?" Chastity asked. "I can perhaps imagine that Father allowed his ambition to control him, and took this step, thinking that the Stuarts were about to triumph. But back in his youth, and so soon after the rebellion in 1715?"

Rothgar answered. "In fact, it is the least incriminating item. A young man can be misguided, or ill-advised. Back in those days, I understand, there was a certain fashionable bravado in making contact with the Stuarts during a Grand Tour. The rest, however, is enough to make your father's position very dangerous indeed. It will certainly shatter forever his image as the Incorruptible."

Verity looked at Rothgar. "Fort must be told. He must have a say in this."

"Of course." Rothgar sent for Lord Thornhill.

Fort entered the room suspiciously, withdrawn physically and mentally from these unwelcome allies. He sent a burning glare at Cyn. Rothgar handed him the letter.

Fort read it and collapsed into a chair. "I never would have believed . . . He must have been mad!"

"Those were strange days," said Rothgar. "You were in the nursery, and doubtless remember little. I was a young man, too young to be truly torn by it, but I remember that there were a few days when it seemed as if the impossible might become true. All was rumor and disorder. The Hanoverian royalty were packed and ready to run back to their little German electorate. Many believed that hidden Jacobite sympathizers were about to crawl out of the wainscotting . . . Your father lost his nerve."

"But a Jacobite! I'd have sworn oaths he has never had Jacobite sympathies. Plague take it! In spiritual matters he's more of a Puritan than a Papist. That's why we ended up with these names."

"But more ambitious than anything else. In 1745 he was in the prime of life, remember. He was the same age, I believe, as his friend Frederick, Prince of Wales, and would have been thirty-eight. Two ambitious men waiting in the wings, impatient for power. The great Walpole had fallen a few years before, leaving no firm hand to steer England. Everything was ready, if only the king would die." Rothgar smiled derisively. "Neither of them could have dreamed old King George II would live until 1760, and outlive his greedy son . . . The ironies of fate.

"But before that turn of the wheel came this other foul blow of destiny. With Walgrave poised to take control of England as soon as Frederick became king, was he going to let the *Jacobites* wrest it from him? He struggled against them, but when it seemed they might in truth prevail, he faltered, unable to see his dream turn to dross. Perhaps they approached him, tempted him . . . Frederick, you know, was not an inspiring figure upon which to build a great new order. He was a drunkard and a libertine . . ."

He suddenly shrugged. "Forgive my speculations. Perhaps the noble earl will enlighten us when he comes."

"When he comes?" asked Fort numbly.

"Didn't Chastity tell you? I have invited him to the ball."

Fort stood, the letter still in his hands. "I could throw this in the fire."

"Perhaps," said Rothgar.

"You have the whip hand at last, don't you, Rothgar?" sneered Fort. "How you must be loving this. What are you going to do?"

"I?" said Rothgar mildly. "I am going to ensure that my brother can comfortably marry your sister. It is my sole interest in this matter. That letter plays a very small part, and only to twist your father's arm a little. For anything more, I leave it up to you, but I would not let him know you have it without safeguards."

The room was silent as Fort considered the fact that his

father would kill him to gain the document. He thrust the letter back into Rothgar's hands. "Keep it. I'll let you know when I decide what to do." He stalked out of the room.

Verity said something softly to Nathaniel and rose to her feet. She looked at Chastity. Chastity went with her sister in pursuit of their brother.

They tracked him down in his room where he was attacking a bottle of brandy. Moving in unison, they relieved him of it. "Not now, Fort," said Verity.

"This is all your fault!" he snarled.

"Well, really!" declared Chastity. "If ever I've heard a piece of injustice, it is that! Verity and I have suffered terribly, and have brought none of it on ourselves."

He turned on her. "If you hadn't debauched yourself with a damned Malloren, bloody Rothgar wouldn't have our family over a barrel!"

Chastity planted her fists on her hips and leaned forward. "If Father hadn't committed treason, none of this would have happened! Or have you forgotten that?"

He groaned and sank his head into his hands. "If this comes out, we'll all be destroyed."

Chastity and Verity sat, one on either side of him. "Fort, you heard Rothgar. It won't come out."

He looked up. "You trust *Rothgar?*"

"Yes," said Chastity. "Don't you?"

"He hates the Wares."

"Why is that, Fort?"

"It mainly hinges on a man named Russell, an adherent of the Pitts, whom Father detests. I see now—I think I see—that Father detests anyone and everyone who gets between him and power. Russell was Commissary General of the Army. He was tried and ruined for corruption, but Rothgar stood by his friend throughout. There was talk that he had shared in the spoils, of course. Father has boasted of having a part in bringing Russell to justice, of putting an end to the scandals that had our brave soldiers fighting in tawdry uniforms and using unreliable weapons ..." He sank his head in his hands once more. "Now, I don't know what to think."

Verity said, "Now you think Rothgar might want revenge?"

"He's not a man to let sleeping wrongs lie."

Chastity said quietly but firmly, "I don't believe it." When Fort looked at her, she added, "I know you think I'm besotted with love, or lust, but Rothgar's devotion to his family outweighs any other impulses he might have. To expose Father would only make my situation worse, and he won't do that to Cyn."

Fort's frown lightened a little. "I pray you are right. But when this is over, he'll still have that document, or at least the knowledge ... I don't trust him."

Chastity laid a hand over her brother's. "I'll have Rothgar's promise to return the document, and to keep silent. He'll be true to his word."

Fort shrugged her hand off. "I'll not have you groveling to a Malloren for favors. I wonder," he sneered, "what price he'll ask."

Verity's shocked "Fort!" clashed with Chastity's "Fool!"

Chastity stood and faced him. "For your information, the marquess is like a brother to me, and has been a better brother these past days than my real one has ever been!" She turned on her heels and slammed the door behind her.

Fort cursed. "That girl is out of hand. I'd like to beat her."

"No, you wouldn't," Verity said firmly.

He sighed. "I feel as if I'm in the maelstrom. Chastity's letting these Mallorens twist her inside out. She believes everything they tell her." He looked at Verity. "I'm glad you're married to Frazer, but it's another scandal in the making, especially when Vernham takes you both to court. And now there's Father."

"And you, I suppose, are pure as snow."

"No," he admitted ruefully, "but I'm beginning to look like it, the company I'm keeping."

Verity smiled at him. "I trust Rothgar too. And so does Nathaniel."

"You're all mad," said Fort.

Chapter 20

"**Y**ou're all mad," said Fort, looking around the Tapestry Room later that afternoon. Only the non-Mallorens appeared to agree with him.

"I don't think so," said Rothgar. "There is an amount of rancor that needs to be vented. Cyn wants to kill you for the abandonment of your sister. You want to kill him to protect your sister. A duel is in order."

"But I don't want either of them killed!" Chastity protested.

"You are a woman," said Rothgar dismissively, "and know nothing of these matters." But she saw the teasing amusement behind it, which reassured her, except that Rothgar's amusements were rarely harmless.

"Then you should not raise these matters before such ignorant woman, should you?" she asked pertly.

"Alas," he said with a small bow. "I was maladroit, but would it not excite you, *mignon*, to know you are to be fought over?"

"No," said Chastity, but something inside told her she was lying.

"Tell me, Lord Thornhill," said Rothgar, "how good are you with a sword?"

"Very good," snapped Fort. "But I don't intend to kill Lord Cynric. I doubt it would endear me to my family."

"It would endear you to your father," Rothgar pointed

out amiably. "But if you are very good, I think you and Cyn could fight *an naturel* with little chance of permanent damage."

"With naked swords!" exclaimed Nathaniel in deep shock. "I will have no part of it."

But Cyn was on his feet, a glint in his eyes. "I think it a wonderful idea. It is time Lord Thornhill bore some wounds of his own."

Chastity leaped to her feet too. "He's still bruised from defending me, Cyn. You're not being fair."

"He was slow to his duty." He eyed Fort challengingly. "Weren't you?"

"And you were rather precipitate to yours," sneered Fort. "Weren't you?"

They were already out the door.

Chastity turned on Rothgar. "If either of them is hurt, I'll blame you."

"I tremble," he replied, and chucked her under the chin. "I thought of putting them to fisticuffs, but then they would end up bruised and bloody. They are both harboring resentments, my dear, and I want them clearheaded tomorrow when the fun begins."

"What fun?" demanded Chastity, but he was already following his brother out of the room.

Chastity hissed between her teeth as she followed him.

She found the duel was to take place in the hall. Cyn and Fort were stripped to stocking-feet and shirts, testing light dueling rapiers. The weapons seemed almost fragile and had an eerie beauty, but they were deadly without anything to blunt the tips.

Chairs were being set out for the spectators, but Chastity went over to Rothgar. "Please, don't do this! Accidents are possible . . ."

He looked down at her. "Was your brother boasting when he said he was very good?"

"I don't think so."

"Cyn is also very good, or possibly better. It will be a

freak accident indeed that sends a blade where the user does not intend it to go. Accidents can happen anywhere, any time. Only clods avoid adventure for fear of them."

Chastity muttered about men in general, and Mallorens in particular, and flounced off to sit by Elf. "Your whole family is mad," she told her.

"So is yours," said Elf, bright-eyed with excitement.

"Aren't you the tiniest bit nervous?" Chastity demanded.

Elf looked at her in surprise. "Of course not. Cyn is really very good. I don't think he's ever been beaten, not even by Rothgar. Rothgar claims he's hampered by old age, and could have bested him in his youth, but I don't think he means it."

Chastity looked at Cyn again, surprised. Why was she constantly surprised by him? She'd seen him fence when he'd rescued her in Maidenhead, seen him in effect play with his opponent. She'd known then he was good. But very good?

As soon as the bout started, she knew it to be true. She'd witnessed fencing before, and knew some of the science of it, some of the art. She could appreciate the light spring in the men's legs, the suppleness of their bodies, the strength in their agile wrists.

She saw more here. Fort fenced well, always balanced, and very strong. Being some inches taller than Cyn, he had a reach advantage. It didn't do him much good.

Cyn's quicksilver blade tapped and slid against Fort's with an ease that seemed effortless. No matter what thrust Fort tried, Cyn's blade met it smoothly, making the engagement appear to be a dance, sweetly choreographed for harmony, rather than a perilous contest.

Chastity saw from the growing frown of concentration on Fort's face that the dance was not of his making. He broke the pattern and moved in a sharper, less graceful, but much more threatening way—straight for Cyn's heart.

Chastity gasped, but Cyn parried and controlled exactly as he had before.

Fort grinned and stepped back, dropping his sword. "Damme, but you're good."

Cyn lowered his sword too. "You are skilled too."

Fort laughed derisively, but didn't seem put out. "You could disarm me, couldn't you?"

"Perhaps," said Cyn, his lashes guarding his eyes.

"Show me." Fort took up the stance.

Cyn hesitated.

"Show me," said Fort, "and I'll support your marriage to my sister."

Cyn smiled, and raised his blade in salute.

They met again, with a slither of steel on steel. "You deserve a wound," said Cyn, and quite casually touched Fort on the jaw with his tip, so a line of crimson beads sprang forth.

Fort cursed and faltered.

There was no immediate disarm. Cyn waited until Fort settled again, then almost lazily, in three moves that Chastity saw Fort recognize and try to circumvent, sent his opponent's sword spinning neatly out of his grasp.

"Sweet heaven," said Fort. "Where did you learn?"

"Here and there," said Cyn, "but mostly from Rothgar. He's a sterner master than most hired ones. He nicked me often to teach me to keep my guard up, and I was only a boy then."

"I have never had any intention," said Rothgar with chilly precision, "of losing a brother carelessly to a braggadocian sword." He shrugged out of his coat. "Little brother, I want to test my mettle. Perhaps I can mark you again."

He swooped up the fallen sword and faced Cyn.

"Perhaps I can mark you," said Cyn, a glint in his eyes.

Rothgar laughed, actually laughed. "Try it."

The swords tapped together again, but this time one could see the similarity of styles. One could also see that

Cyn was having to extend himself completely, but so was Rothgar. Wounds were frequently only a hairsbreadth away. Once Rothgar's sword slid toward Cyn's face, and was only just deflected. Chastity found she had her hands pressed over her mouth.

A moment later Rothgar's point went for Cyn's face again, as if he really intended to put out his eye. This time it was easily controlled.

"Glad you've finally remembered that one, Cyn." Then the marquess gasped as Cyn's blade nicked his shirt over his heart and withdrew. Rothgar stepped back, smiling, and saluted with the blade. "I forget my own lessons. Never take time to gloat."

The brothers embraced, Brand and Bryght came over to comment, and soon even Fort and Nathaniel were part of a happy male coterie set upon rehashing the moves, and learning new passes.

Elf, Chastity, and Verity shared a look and went off to discuss at length the insanity of the male of the species.

The marquess' plan appeared to have worked, however. Fort was still suspicious, but he was willing to work with the Mallorens. He had also pledged his support for Chastity's marriage to Cyn.

It was only later that he said to Chastity, "I won't oppose your marriage, but I'm still not sure of Rothgar. It's not so much his honor I question, as his motives. His plan may not be completely to our advantage. Keep your wits about you, my dear. When the lines are drawn, I expect you to be on the side of the Wares."

The day of the ball dawned clear and sunny, if cold. Good traveling weather, and the moon almost full so people could return home in safety.

Chastity knew that Rothgar expected her father to come to the ball, but didn't know how he could predict that. The earl would have to be suspicious. For her part, she hoped her father wouldn't come. She didn't want to face him again. Surely it would be enough to tell him that they held the evidence that would ruin him.

She was nervous enough about this first social event since her disaster, without adding other terrors. Certainly, there was some safety in the fact that this would be a masqued ball, but Chastity shivered at the thought of moving among people who would cut her dead if they recognized her.

She also knew the ball would be a turning point. She didn't know exactly what Rothgar had planned, but her peaceful interlude was over. After tonight she would either be restored to grace—unlikely as that seemed—or forced to decide what to do with the rest of her ruined life.

She had been avoiding Cyn. He seemed to mean his vow not to take her to bed, but that just made his nearness more of a torment. The sight of him, the lightest brush of his clothing against her, could leave her breathless with longing. But reason told her they must soon part. She must prepare for that.

She hated it.

She had submerged her desire in the preparations for the ball and everything was now ready. Bright paper lanterns had come from London to give light to the ballroom while maintaining the exotic air. A cleverly illuminated pagoda had been erected there, around which clockwork Mandarins walked.

A team of boys was responsible for rewinding the automaton, but Chastity could almost believe it to be magic. There was something fey about the Abbey tonight, as if miracles could really happen. Or perhaps the coming event was just a mechanical toy, with Rothgar as the clockmaker.

Torn by fears and hopes, Chastity wrapped a fur cape about herself and escaped the last-minute preparations to walk on the West Terrace and watch the setting sun gild the Abbey. Then Cyn came to stand by her side. She should have left and sought the safety of company, but she found she could not flee from him now, so close to the end. She shivered, not with cold. "I feel something building."

"The excitement of the ball." His voice alone was enough to melt her.

"No," she said. "Everyone's wound tight." Then she thought of clock-makers and wanted, with shattering intensity, to be safe in her beloved's arms. She turned to him. "Do you think my father will come, Cyn?"

"If Rothgar sent the correct message." His eyes told her his desires matched hers. Exceeded them.

"What message could that be?"

"I don't know, but Rothgar will have found it." He smiled suddenly at her. "What will you be wearing tonight?"

"A domino and mask."

"As will everyone. Give me a hint."

She made herself stay silent.

"No matter," he said softly. "If I don't find you, Chloe, I don't deserve you." He took her hand, and that use of their private name dissolved her ability to resist.

As they strolled along the terrace, Chastity's heart and soul became focused on the contact with his elegant swordsman's hand. She twined her fingers with his. "Why didn't you tell me you fenced so well?"

He slid her a glance, his fingers responding to her play. "It's hardly the sort of thing one drops into conversation. 'By the way, I happen to have a gift for duello.' "

"Happen to have?" she echoed. "A great deal of work goes into a skill such as yours."

His thumb caressed her hand. "I enjoy it. I often have trouble finding an opponent who will test me, but in Canada I took a French prisoner who was my equal. He honed my skills."

She stopped and faced him. "You dueled with a *prisoner?*"

He raised her hand between them, still twined with his, and kissed it lingeringly. "For practice only, my heart."

Chastity shivered under the sensual power this man had over her. How could she survive without him?

"It's rapidly becoming an ornamental art, anyway," he said quite calmly, though his eyes were not calm at all. "It's true, as Rothgar said, that it's useful to be skilled, so some bully-boy can't steal your life over nothing, but if death is required, a pistol is more certain."

Death. No, please don't talk of death.

He rubbed her knuckles softly against his lips.

Chastity swayed with the need to be protected, and to protect him from all hurt. "Why do men always end up fighting?" she protested faintly.

His teeth rasped against her skin, the rough edge of danger sending a jolt of hot desire though her. "Men sometimes do other things," he reminded her softly.

"Cyn, don't," she whispered, but weakly. If he wanted her here, now, on the cold stones, she was his.

He caught his breath and collected himself. "Perhaps I should teach you swordplay," he said lightly, "in case you go masquerading again."

"I pray I never again have the need."

"Did you find no pleasure in it at all?" There seemed to be meaning behind the question.

"A little," she confessed. "I enjoyed the excitement, but not the deceptions. And certainly not the shame . . ." She turned her hands so she held his. "I enjoyed having a friend, though, a friend called Cyn."

Like shifting clouds, his expression changed from the darkness of leashed desire to the heavy darkness of regret. "Until I spoiled it by seducing you."

Chastity blushed. "I wouldn't call it spoiling . . ."

"Wouldn't you?"

She closed her eyes. Why did he always push for truth? "Things change, Cyn. It would be perfect if only we could marry . . ."

"We *will* marry," he said roughly. "I take back my word. I will never surrender you to any other man." His hands slid beneath her cloak to hold her tight against him. "I can't live without you, Chastity. These last few days have taught me that. But it's not your body I need most. If you wish, we will live as brother and sister all our days."

"Why on earth would I wish that . . . ?" she asked, her hips moving against his with a will of their own. But then a sound alerted her and brought back reality and all her fears. "I hear a coach!"

She pulled away, but his hold did not slacken. "Peace, love. It could be anyone."

She shook her head. "It won't be a guest, not this early, Cyn. It could be Father." Pure fear had every nerve trembling.

He took her hands in a firm grip. "You are free of him. He will never hurt you again." As she steadied, he kept one of her hands and led her toward the house. "Come along, love. If it is the devil himself, let us face him bravely."

They entered the marble hall to hear Henry Vernham's drawling voice demanding his ward.

Cyn hissed between his teeth and surged forward. Chastity chased after him to stop him killing the man who had ruined her, but Rothgar was there before him.

"Ah, Vernham. Your ward?" he said, placing himself effortlessly between Cyn and his target. "You mean young Sir William. You doubtless want to assure yourself of his safety, but you would hardly wish to remove him from his mother's care when he is still at the breast."

Vernham glared around uneasily at a gathering of Mallorens. Brand and Elf had followed Rothgar into the hall, and now Bryght emerged from the library. No doubt Vernham sensed malice, but he would be unaware that they knew anything of him other than that he was the baby's guardian.

He took a pinch of snuff. "Lady Vernham is welcome to accompany her child."

"But Verity is now Lady Verity Frazer, and her husband's wishes must be taken into account. Now, sir," said Rothgar with a bucolic bonhomie that would terrify anyone who knew him, "take some refreshment. If you are come in response to my note, you know we have an entertainment planned for tonight. You must stay."

Despite his protests, Vernham was drawn into the Tapestry Room and seated with a dish of tea in his hands. "I demand to see my ward!" he snapped, then he saw Chastity. He blanched.

She smiled at him.

She had never seen eyes bulge before, but now she did.

"But of course you must see your ward," said Rothgar, and sent for Verity and the baby.

By the time they arrived, accompanied by a hard-eyed Major Frazer, Vernham was on his feet, uneasily eyeing his company. He gave the babe scarcely a glance. "Good, then you will come with me now."

"Of course I won't," said Verity firmly. "And you will not take William, Henry. You will have to petition the courts, which I believe can take a very long time."

Vernham's narrow eyes flickered about the room. All the Mallorens were smiling, even Cyn, but Henry didn't seem to find that comforting, which proved Verity correct when she had described him as a shrewd man.

"I suppose that is true," he said with an attempt at an easy manner. "Nothing I can do, really, at this point if the youngster is all right. I must not take any more of your time. I apologize if I have distressed you, Verity, but I was extremely anxious about you. It was not kind of you to leave no message, no indication of where you had gone."

"But I was running away from you, sir," said Verity simply.

He was thrown off-balance. "Why, for God's sake?"

Nathaniel stepped in at that point, to prevent an annoyed

Verity from saying too much. "Her reasons may have been misguided, Vernham, but we must all rejoice that everything has turned out so well. I intend to apply to be the child's guardian, which I am sure you must see to be proper, and thus administer the property."

Vernham flashed him a look of pure hate, but smiled. "I will contest, as you must expect. I am sure the courts will uphold my brother's will." He drew on his gloves, still glancing uneasily around, as if expecting to be prevented from leaving. "Which reminds me," he added with strained casualness. "A document is missing, Lady Verity, one which my brother had in safekeeping. Did you by any chance take it with you? It is a codicil to the will, I believe, and should be delivered to the solicitors."

Chastity held her breath and worked hard at not giving anything away.

"Oh, that," said Verity vaguely. "Yes, I did take it for safe-keeping. I wonder where I put it. I believe it must be in one of my pockets."

Chastity could almost see Henry Vernham gnashing his teeth behind his smile. The trouble was that she could also see the amusement in Verity's eyes. At any moment she would give the game away by giggling. She never had been able to carry a lie.

"Do you think you could look?" asked Vernham tightly.

A distraction came in the shape of Fort, who burst into the room. "They said . . . It *is* you. I have a score to settle with you, you wretched cur!"

He had Vernham by the throat, and it took three Mallorens to get him off. At least one Malloren was not being philanthropic. "You'll have to wait in line, Thornhill," said Cyn. "He's mine."

"You'll have to fight me for it," snarled Fort.

Cyn just raised a brow, and Fort cursed.

Vernham held his hands to his bruised throat. "I offered to marry the slut!"

Fort knocked him out.

"How crude," murmured Rothgar. He rang a bell. A footman came in and was ordered to take away the unconscious gentleman and care for him.

When Vernham had been removed, Rothgar said, "I confess, though, that I was a little perplexed as to how to prevail upon him to stay in this lion's den. You would all persist in licking your chops over him. My felicitations, Thornhill."

"Felicitations be damned," said Fort. "I want to gut him."

"Later," said Rothgar. "First I want a confrontation between him and Walgrave, preferably before witnesses."

The first guests began to arrive in the evening, uncomplicated local people thrilled by an invitation to the Abbey. Some arrived already masked—mostly the younger guests; others put on their disguises after they had shed coats and cloaks. For some, the disguise was just a face mask, but most also wore the encompassing hooded silken cloaks called dominoes. In most cases little attempt was made to truly disguise their identity, and they were constantly greeting each other.

Chastity, on the other hand, had gone to great lengths to be sure she would not be recognized. A rose silk domino and a pearl half-mask were moderately concealing, but in addition she'd powdered her wig heavily with silver-gray.

When she'd looked in the mirror in her room, she'd been sure even Cyn would never recognize her. She remembered his words. Would the eyes of love penetrate even this disguise?

As she observed the scene, watching mainly for the appearance of her father, Chastity absorbed the chatter of the local people. They talked of children and crops and—with amusement rather than passion—the latest fashion. Her lips began to quiver, and she realized how much she wanted this for herself. An ordinary life, wrapped up in matters of extraordinary importance.

These people took an interest in politics, but would not kill for power; an interest in fashion, but would not beggar themselves over it.

She heard two portly gentlemen grumbling about Lord Bute and the influx of greedy Scots into England, but even that topic didn't stir great heat. Whitehall could go hang as long as the squires were left to care for their land.

Then she realized that the topic had been raised by the presence of the man himself. Lord Bute's slender mask could not conceal—was not intended to conceal—one of the handsomest men in England. He was accompanied by a woman in full-face mask and red domino. Another Society lady out adventuring?

He smilingly accepted the attention of the small court about him, and of the local people inclined to brush against the great. Chastity shook her head. He was handsome, amiable, and quite well-intentioned, but not of the caliber to lead England to greatness. She could quite see how his holding power had driven her father to extremes.

She began to search the arriving guests for her father. Surely she would know him. Would he even bother with a mask? It was not in his style.

She was distracted by a gentleman bowing before her. "Sweet rose, will you walk with me?"

The voice and the blue velvet tickled at her memory. "Perhaps I am waiting for someone, sir," she said.

"Then wait no longer, my charming bud. He is here."

Now she had it. It was Lord Heatherington! What was he doing here? She tapped him gently on the wrist with her fan. "Wretched deceiver. He has not your height."

"Then you do not want him. Will you not allow me an opportunity to persuade you of my charms?"

He was not an unattractive man, but knowing what she did, Chastity would not go apart with this man for the Crown of England. "I fear not, sir," she said. "You must find another blossom."

He took her rejection gracefully, bowed, and moved away.

That interruption meant that a number of people had arrived without her scrutinizing them. A gentleman in gold silk and a mask passed by, stopped, turned, and eyed her. He came forward. "My pretty chameleon," Cyn murmured. "I see the worry has turned you gray."

"How did you know me?"

"How could I not? Come," he said, holding out a hand, "I have to find Rothgar."

"Why?" asked Chastity, suddenly nervous.

"Merely to tell him Brand has persuaded Vernham to join the throng."

Chastity could not resist. She placed her hand in his and they wove through the growing crowd in search of the marquess. "How on earth did Brand manage that?"

"Told him it was the only way he'd get any food and drink. Extremely fond of his drink, is Vernham. Been calling for brandy ever since he came around."

"Has Rothgar told you his plans?"

"No. Don't worry. I won't let anything, or anyone, hurt you." It was as if he knew she was filled with fear.

Rothgar was not in the hall, and so they moved toward the first reception room. A sudden crush near the door made Chastity aware that Cyn was wearing a sword. "Will it come to violence then?" she whispered anxiously.

He smiled, all Malloren. "I hope so."

The cheerful uproar of happy people, without a care in their head beyond crops and children, became almost macabre to Chastity as she contemplated the coming horrors.

They found Rothgar in the room arranged for gaming, settling Bute at a table. He was being particularly attentive to Bute's masked partner. Chastity realized that she had to be Augusta, Princess of Wales, the mother of King George.

Her throat seized up. Was this just chance, or was Rothgar playing for incredibly high stakes? Was the fact that Princess Augusta and the Earl of Walgrave were vicious enemies part of the web he was weaving? Augusta had always been jealous of the closeness between Walgrave and her husband, the Prince of Wales. When Prince Frederick died, she had turned her son—the present king—against the earl.

Cyn gave Rothgar the message that Vernham had joined the party, and Rothgar nodded. His hair was powdered white, and he wore a light maquillage that emphasized a wickedness in him, but he was not disguised except for a slender black mask. Anyone would know him, and know him to be dangerous. Chastity had grown used to him as he was with his family, relaxed in country clothes. Now, grand enough for court in deep-blue satin and silver, she feared him once again.

Had Fort been right? Would Rothgar take this chance to destroy an enemy at any cost?

Perhaps he guessed her thoughts. He smiled, and captured a hand to kiss it. "Begin planning your wedding, *mignon.*"

"You can't be sure . . ."

He raised his brows. "All is falling so beautifully into place."

Chastity knew then that she was right. They were all moving at his direction. She cast an alarmed look at the queen. "I am not going to unmask," she said firmly.

"You will do as you are told. Cyn, stay with her, and control her as a good husband should."

"We're not married yet," said Cyn levelly, "and even if we were, I would not force her to unmask here."

Rothgar did not seem particularly put out. "Then at least stay with her."

"That accords with my wishes perfectly." Cyn led Chastity away.

"I'm scared to death," she whispered. "I've been so happy, and it's all going to shatter."

"To open the gateway to yet greater happiness. I've

never known Rothgar to be confident and fail." He drew her into a quiet room and faced her. "He has agreed that I am fit for service now. He will not stand in my way."

Chastity felt as if the world had become an empty husk. "When will you go?" she asked, trying to be brave.

"After we're wed. Or perhaps not at all." He trapped her gently against the wall. "I'm not sure you will like military life."

Her feelings in turmoil, Chastity protested, "Cyn, you can't give up your career for me!"

"But I can't give up you for my career." His fingers traced the edges of her mask. "There are other things," he reminded her, and her body instantly responded.

"You love being a soldier." Chastity was proud of the firmness in her voice, especially when his body against hers was dissolving her into pure need.

"I've been thinking about that, Chastity," he said softly as his hand wandered—seemingly uncontrollably—down her neck to loose the fastening of her cloak and lay it open. "I'm not sure it's true. I love travel and adventure." His fingers traveled to the swell of her breasts beneath the silken shift.

"I love doing something significant," he said, and the heel of his hand found the significant spot beneath the stomacher where her nipples swelled with sensitivity. He pressed just enough to steal her breath. His lashes shadowed his cheeks as he thoughtfully studied her reactions.

"But there are other things," he murmured. "If the war is ending, soldiering will be dull, but there will be interesting work in the Canadas—establishing government, mapping and exploring, what more could any man want than to explore a place so beautiful and mysterious." His hand explored the dip between her breasts.

Chastity leaned her head helplessly against his shoulder. "You're confusing me. You don't really want that."

His fingers slid behind the stomacher. "I delight in confusing you, and there are no words in the language to express the depth of my need." He found her sensitive flesh and captured it.

"Ah!" The cry of desire escaped Chastity and Cyn caught it in his mouth. He used his tongue fiercely to promise other delights, stroking in and out as she shuddered and melted. Her flimsy hoops were pressed flat and his thigh came between hers to both comfort and torment her.

Chastity's legs ached to uselessness and she clung to him. Her heart deafened her. Fiery heat engulfed her, dizzying her beyond a scrap of reason.

His mouth released her and she gazed at him, dying with a need that he surely would not assuage.

Then his hand left her bodice and conquered her skirts to find the heated ache and stroke her there, speeding her rampaging body to impossible heights.

"Cyn!" she gasped, clutching him. "Dear God! Dear God!"

"Melt for me, Chastity," he whispered. "Here, now."

She had no choice. She clung to him as shudders racked her, and muffled her own cries of release against his velvet shoulder. Then calm settled.

Chastity was dizzy and sticky and her legs still felt like stuffed rags. Even as her heart slowed, his mouth played a soothing message against her neck.

She sucked in a breath. "Why?"

He drew back to smile at her and she could see the passion that marked him. "Because I desire you to the point of insanity."

"But . . ."

"But I have a vow, and one I intend to keep. I hope," he said, resting his head against hers, "not for much longer."

"Oh, Cyn . . ." She stroked his hair gently. "I did not need that. Not really."

"But I did." He moved back and grinned. "Do you think me a noble martyr? Sweet Chastity, there is only one pleasure in the world greater than making you dissolve in ecstasy."

She had to believe him honest. "I had no idea . . ." And the halting phrase expressed a world of ignorance.

"We will explore it together, along with a new land. Will you, beloved?"

She searched his masked features. "You really want to give up soldiering?"

"Yes."

She surrendered to the dream. "And what would I do?"

"Explore with me . . . in and out of bed." He began to deftly reorder her clothing. "We could have a home, perhaps in Montreal. Or there is a promising town being built called Halifax. It's in Acadia on the east coat. You could stay there when you had to, and travel with me when you could."

She captured his head and kissed him. "It sounds wonderful. Do you know, I have never much relished a life lived in drawing rooms." She was wondering what would happen if she tested his vow.

"I do indeed know. I recognized a kindred spirit when we first met." He removed himself from her hold. "A bold piece of goods."

"It was probably the pistols that gave you the hint," she murmured, moving toward him again.

He shook his head. "Doubtless. Give me your left hand, stealer of hearts."

Chastity halted and held out her hand. He slipped a ring onto her finger, a gold *fede* ring made up of two clasped hands. She stared at it. "Oh, Cyn—"

He slid another ring on top, a hoop of diamonds. "It's called a keeper ring," he said. "King George has just set the fashion by giving one to his new bride. It sits on top, to guard the ring and the relationship from all harm. Do you know a diamond is the hardest stone?"

Chastity touched the beautiful rings and tears escaped

the mask to roll down her cheeks. "Oh, Cyn, I'm so afraid. I'm afraid to hope. I'm still the Notorious Chastity Ware."

He kissed the tears away. "Come and dance, my lady Notorious. It'll chase away care."

Chastity lost herself in the dancing—the first time she had danced with Cyn—until she saw Nerissa Trelyn in her set.

This was Nerissa Trelyn the leader of Society, and she had done little to disguise herself. Her beautiful blonde hair was unpowdered, and a small feather mask did not disguise her features. Instead of a domino, she wore a flowing sacque gown of pristine white silk.

Chastity thought bitterly that she would look positively virginal if it weren't for the wide, low neckline which made the most of her magnificent figure. If her identity was in the smallest doubt, she wore the magnificent Trelyn diamonds, given by her doting husband.

She partnered her husband with almost regal dignity, the Queen of Society. Lord Trelyn was not an old man—he must be about Rothgar's age—but he acted as if he were sixty, while at the same time preening himself on the possession of this glorious creature.

Chastity felt some sympathy for Nerissa, until she remembered that this marriage had been the lady's own choice, and that she had apparently jilted Bryght Malloren in the process, and was now the mistress of Lord Heatherington.

Chastity began again to scan the guests for her father, but in the dim atmosphere of the Chinese ballroom it was impossible to see far. There were even spices burning—incense or some such—and the silvery smoke from them and the candles fogged the air.

When the dance ended, she moved with Cyn into the refreshment room and drank some wine. "It is a magnificent affair, especially for one prepared in such a hurry."

"The household is accustomed, and can do this at the drop of a hat."

"And with a great deal of work," Chastity pointed out.

"Of course. Rothgar is immensely rich. He considers it his duty to employ people."

"My father is even richer, I believe. He counts the candles and checks the meals served in the servants' hall."

"Well, have some sympathy," said Cyn with a twinkle of amusement. "He's had to support the greedy Vernhams all these years."

That was bringing matters to mind with a vengeance. Chastity shivered. "When are things to happen?"

"When the time is right. Why don't we go and watch the gaming?"

"I thought you didn't like gambling."

He guided her out of the room. "I said I don't like to gamble for money. It is very relaxing to see fools who can afford it throwing money away."

They watched as Bute calmly lost thousands, then won some of it back; as Princess Augusta almost lost a bracelet worth a great deal more. Chastity was not surprised to see old Lady Fanshaw hunched over her cards like a vulture. She had doubtless been invited, but if not she would have turned up anyway, drawn by the rumor of play like a carrion-eater lured by the smell of a rotting corpse.

A footman presented a note to Cyn. He read it, then slipped it into his pocket. "The Garden Room," he said.

Chastity's heart started pounding as he led her from the room. "Father?" she whispered.

"It doesn't say." He stopped in a quiet corner to kiss her. "Be brave, Charles. This time, you are not alone."

Chapter 21

The Garden Room was merely a small saloon decorated with wallpaper featuring trellises covered with flowering vines. Through wide glass doors, it could open into the conservatory, which itself led to an outside terrace and the knot garden. At this chilly time of year, the glass doors were covered by a curtain and a fire warmed the room.

Cyn and Chastity entered the small room to find Henry Vernham sitting in a chair guarded by Brand Malloren. Vernham started nervously.

Cyn ignored him to seat Chastity on the sofa and take a place beside her. "Mr. Vernham," he said amiably, "I hope you are being well cared for. Been given all you require?"

"I suppose so." Despite the betraying glitter in his eyes, the man was able to form his words correctly. Clearly Rothgar had been right as always, and Vernham was a hardened drinker. "Surprised you care, though," Vernham said with a sneer. "Your big brother reined you in, has he?"

Cyn smiled. "The condemned prisoner should always be served a hearty meal."

Vernham paled and tried to get to his feet, but Brand pushed him down. Before it came to a fight, the door opened and the Earl of Walgrave stalked in with Lindle and two hefty attendants trailing them. Rothgar and Fort entered behind them.

Despite Cyn's reassuring presence, Chastity's heart started to pound.

The small room was crowded, but her father created a space around himself as if by natural right. Chastity noticed he had a new cane, ebony with gold decoration, and rather more solid than was his habit. He showed no nervousness. His eyes passed over her as if she were a stranger. Defiantly, she took off her mask and pushed back the hood of her domino.

"Well, Rothgar?" Walgrave demanded. "May I know the reason behind this? I am displeased, most displeased, to find you have meddled in my family's affairs."

Rothgar took a stand by the glowing fire. "But our families are to be felicitously joined."

The earl's eyes impaled Chastity. "That shameless trollop? You are welcome to her, but she's no child of mine."

Cyn's hand comforted Chastity's and she met her father's sneering gaze. He looked away—at Henry Vernham.

Stark terror marked Vernham's face. Chastity realized that without the crucial evidence, Vernham was naked to Walgrave's malice. However, she noted something guarded in her father's glance at Vernham. Perhaps the earl was not entirely sure that Henry Vernham was helpless.

"So be it," said Rothgar equably. "I merely thought to do you a kindness for family's sake." He took a contemplative pinch of snuff. "In fact, I insist. My own generosity at times astonishes me. I believe Mr. Vernham has something you want."

"I believe he has," said Walgrave with a malignant smile. "Do I understand you will allow me to retrieve it?"

Rothgar gestured. "Please."

"Damme," cried Vernham, again trying to struggle to his feet. "I have nothing. Nothing!"

The earl, however, had focused again on Rothgar. "Perhaps I should beware of Mallorens bearing gifts."

Chastity suddenly realized the numbers were in her father's favor. There were three Mallorens here and four in her father's party, including the two attendants. There was Fort, but she could not be sure how he would side when the future of the earldom hung in the balance. Vernham would fight for himself.

If it came to it, she would do her part, but she feared she would be a lightweight in this company.

Rothgar took another delicate pinch of snuff and brushed away a few specks. "It is always wise to be wary, Walgrave. In this case, however, I have reason to be generous. I cannot allow a taint to come into my family with your daughter."

The earl let out a crack of laughter. "Gads, man, you're taking in a gutter-full!"

"Father!" exclaimed Fort. Cyn surged to his feet.

Walgrave turned on his son. "Are you on their side, boy? You're a fool then. If the chit wasn't debauched by Vernham, then she was debauched by Malloren."

Cyn's sword hissed from its scabbard, but Rothgar raised his hand. Cyn froze, cold eyes on the earl.

Rothgar turned to Vernham. "My dear sir, are you an innocent after all? Did you not have your wicked way with Lady Chastity?"

Vernham was clearly terrified out of his wits. His eyes were fixed on Cyn's drawn sword, even though it was not pointed at him. "No, of course not! Hardly touched her."

"It must have been a prank gone awry. And you nobly offered to wed her to repair the damage you had so inadvertently caused."

"Yes, yes. If she was a virgin when I climbed into her bed, she was one when I climbed out."

"If?" demanded Cyn, and now the rapier did point at Vernham, inches from his terrified eyes.

"She was. She was!" he babbled. "He had her hymen broken to stop her proving her innocence. But that was later!"

All eyes turned to Walgrave.

He was unmoved. "Gibberish. If you seek to whitewash the girl this way, Rothgar, you'll fail." He looked down his nose at Vernham. "I'll have the paper, wretch, and let you live."

Vernham shrank back. "I don't have it, I tell you!"

"Then we'll take you apart piece by piece to make sure—"

The door opened.

Everyone in the room turned to stare as a woman entered. Cyn even lowered his sword from Vernham's face. A stranger. No, not a stranger, thought Chastity. She gasped with horror when she recognized the woman who had stolen her proof of virtue.

She was tall and handsome, if one did not note the hardness of her eyes and mouth. She was dressed as richly as any lady in the house.

"Ah, Mirabelle," said Rothgar. "Welcome."

Mirabelle gazed around the room with infinite cynicism. "I was paid by the Earl of Walgrave," she said clearly, "to break the maidenhead of Lady Chastity, his daughter. All the evidence spoke of her being completely untouched by man." A slight smile curved her pointed lips. "I am more in the business of repairing what has been inconveniently been broken . . ."

"Is this supposed to count for anything?" asked the earl. "A woman such as that can be bought for a few guineas."

"On the contrary, my lord," said Mirabelle. "I do not so much as blow a gentleman's nose for less than twenty." With that, she nodded to Rothgar and swept out of the room.

Rothgar turned to Vernham. "As you are innocent, why not give the earl his document, then you may leave."

"I don't have it, I tell you!" Vernham exclaimed. "Verity has it in one of her damn pockets."

"Then perhaps we should send for Lady Verity and the letter. Lord Thornhill, would you oblige?"

Chastity saw her father react to the word "letter," which told him Rothgar knew what the document was. He turned to sneer at his son. "Go and be Rothgar's lackey, boy. It's all you're good for."

Fort's lips tightened, but he left the room.

"While we wait," said Rothgar, "why don't you tell us, Mr. Vernham, how you came to be in Lady Chastity's bed without her consent, and without her raising the alarm? It's a trick I could use on occasion."

Vernham's wits were clearly scrambled by drink and fear, and he didn't see the strange turn the conversation had taken. He laughed. "She sleeps like the dead. An army could get in the bed with her and she'd scarce stir. I had to pinch her to wake her when the witnesses arrived."

"You can't have counted on her deep sleep, surely?" Rothgar inquired mildly.

"Walgrave told me," said Vernham, and then looked nervously at the earl.

The earl looked death back at him but said nothing. If Rothgar hoped to force him into an incriminating admission, he was failing.

Chastity wondered if she could break her father's control again.

She rose, dodging Cyn's restraining hand. "And my father didn't care a fig for me, did you, you monster?" She took an insolent stance in front of Walgrave and laughed at him. "You must have thought it would all be so easy, but I've thwarted you at every turn!"

She saw his lips form a snarl.

"If I'd married Henry Vernham, none of this would have happened, would it? But I laughed in your face! So you decided to force me. You gave that man the key to my room, then brought the cream of Society to be witnesses. You as good as debauched me yourself, you stinking hypocrite!"

She was ready for his use of the slashing cane and danced out of the way. Cyn stepped forward, sword ready.

The earl grasped his cane and twisted it to unsheathe a blade. He tossed it to his henchman. "Lindle!"

Cyn smiled lovingly. "Ah, so you are Lindle. You really don't want to do this, you know."

Lindle came at him. Cyn danced back. "You are badly outmatched," said Cyn, "and cannot possibly prevail. Is it worth death to do that man's bidding?"

Lindle's expression did not change, and he wore that strange smile. "Stop crowing, cockerel, and fight."

The swords clicked briefly, then—almost idly—Cyn gashed Lindle's cheek. The man cried out and pressed a hand to the wound. Blood welled between his fingers.

Cyn's point now rested at his neck. "I don't think your smile will ever be quite the same." He pushed with the sword and the man staggered back, until he was against a wall and had nowhere else to go. "Now," said Cyn, "did Mistress Mirabelle break Lady Chastity's hymen on the earl's orders?"

Truly Lindle must have some deformity of the mouth, for he was still smiling in a ghastly way as he flashed a desperate look at his master.

The earl ignored him as if none of this had anything to do with him at all.

"Yes," Lindle choked.

"You were there?" asked Cyn.

"Yes." Blood still poured through his fingers. That casual cut had been deep and the man looked ready to collapse.

"And did the earl arrange for Mr. Vernham to be caught in his daughter's bed?"

"Yes!" gasped Lindle. "On the earl's orders, I let him in, I encouraged him. The paltry worm didn't think it would work. But once he realized how deep she slept, he had a merry time touching her up."

Chastity felt sick. Cyn snarled, and for a moment it looked as if he would skewer the man, but he moved back and lowered his sword. He bowed slightly to his brother. "My apologies for interrupting your discussion."

"Not at all," said Rothgar. "Walgrave? Why not admit it? You doubtless had your reasons."

But Walgrave held firm. "I deny all of it. I thought Lindle had more courage than to spew lies on command, but I was mistaken."

Verity came in with Nathaniel and Fort. She paled at the sight of her father, and gasped to see Lindle covered in blood.

"Lady Verity," said Rothgar, "have you retrieved the paper mentioned earlier?"

"Yes," said Verity, and produced the folded, sealed paper, walking forward to give it to Rothgar.

Walgrave snatched it, and in one move threw it into the fire and pulled out a pistol. "Keep back!" he cried. "No one try to snatch that out!"

They all watched as the paper blackened and then caught, to flame into ash.

Walgrave started to laugh. "At last! Free! Ha, Rothgar, for all your clever tricks, you've cleared my way. You can have my damned family, every plague-ridden one of them. May they make your life hell as they've made mine!"

"Hell surely comes from the company there," said Rothgar, looking thoughtfully at the ashes of the evidence. "You appear, however, to have won. Perhaps you could be noble in victory and admit that your daughter did not lose her maidenhead to a man."

The earl was giddy with liberation. "Certainly," he declared. "Though what the devil good it will do you I can't imagine."

"Perhaps in writing," said Rothgar, indicating a desk where paper and ink stood ready.

The earl hesitated, but he was still grinning madly. It was as if success had succeeded where threats had failed, and tipped him into insanity. "Why not? But I'll write that I did it to force her into a necessary marriage. It doesn't alter the fact that Vernham was in her bed, and I deny any part in that."

Chastity was weighed by a dull sense of failure. Rothgar was making the best of things, but without the evidence of treason, nothing could be done. Nathaniel could soon be under attack, and nothing that had happened here could do her any good.

"What?" cried Vernham, leaping to his feet. "You won't put the blame on me, you devil! It was all your plan, every bit of it, just to stop my brother from using that letter. It may have gone, but I know it word for word. I can still tell the world—"

Walgrave turned and shot him.

The crack of the pistol reverberated in the small room and Chastity clapped her hands over her ringing ears. Vernham crashed back into his chair, a look of amazement on his face, blood spreading over his chest. He tried to speak, then grimaced in sudden agony as he died.

Cyn dropped his sword to pull Chastity into his arms, as Verity was held by Nathaniel. Chastity clung to him, but then pushed away to stare at her father. "That was cold-blooded murder." She looked around at all the men. "You can't let him get away with cold-blooded murder."

Her father dusted his sheet of paper with fine sand and delicately tapped it clean, then held it out. "Here, girl. Take this and hold your tongue. Learn to keep out of men's affairs."

Chastity grabbed the paper, but threw it aside. "Men's affairs? Men's affairs have ruined me!"

"I'm pleased you at least realize the finality of that."

"And you don't care. You, my father, don't *care* that I am unjustly vilified. How can you think you can serve England when you cannot serve your family?"

"My family exists to serve me," he said, rising. He shoved her carelessly out of the way.

She grabbed Lindle's sword from the floor, and despite the outcry, lunged at her father. He deflected the blade with the pistol, but the point slashed into his sleeve, gashing his arm. He snarled, and swung the pistol viciously at her head. Chastity felt it brush her temple as Cyn tackled her to the ground and safety.

". . . in the noble house of Stuart we see fortitude and verity, accompanied by noble chastity, all virtues dedicated to the greatest good of England."

Everyone froze. Silence fell over the room as they all turned to where Rothgar stood, reading from a document. A bloodstained, slightly chewed document.

"No," choked Walgrave.

Lindle giggled.

"You really should have read it before you burned it, shouldn't you?" asked Rothgar mildly.

"No!" howled the earl. He raised his pistol and fired, but it was already discharged, and merely clicked. He hurled it at Rothgar. It missed.

"Kill him!" he raged at his two henchmen. Still on the floor, half under Cyn, Chastity saw that at last the earl was mad, but would he cause the deaths of all of them?

The two men had merely been goggle-eyed observers to all this mayhem. Now they looked at each other and did nothing.

"Kill him, or I'll see you hang! I'll ruin you. I'll ruin your families . . ."

The men looked to Rothgar for help.

Rothgar smiled. "Now, my lord," he said to the purple-faced earl, "you dance to my tune rather than the Vernhams'. Do you think you will like it any better?"

"Never," snarled Walgrave. He plunged a hand into the pocket of the nearest man and pulled out a pistol. The man, clearly terrified by all these goings-on, stood like a dummy and did nothing.

By the time Walgrave raised the gun to fire it, however, both Brand and Rothgar had firearms aimed at him.

"An interesting situation, isn't it?" asked Rothgar. "You

could kill me, but you will surely die. Are you ready to meet your maker?"

Walgrave's mouth twitched in a rictus of hate. "I'd rather die than give you the victory, Rothgar. You've been a thorn in my flesh for too long."

"I'm pleased to be appreciated."

"Give me that document, and no one need die."

"No," said Rothgar. "But I give you my word not to use it as long as you live quietly at Walgrave Towers, take no further part in government affairs, and do not concern yourself with your offspring anymore."

"*What?*" cried Walgrave. "Dance to your piping for the rest of my life. Never, you fiend!" He waved his pistol around the room wildly.

Would he shoot Rothgar?

Brand?

Fort?

Herself?

With a cackle of insane amusement, Walgrave backed toward the door. "Don't try to stop me!"

"You may leave," said Rothgar calmly. "Just remember my conditions. Unlike Vernham, I will lose nothing by making this paper public."

"Public," Walgrave crowed. "Yes, public ..." He opened the door and ran cumbersomely into the hall.

Cyn leaped to his feet. "He's mad. He'll hurt someone." He ran after him.

Chastity struggled up too, hampered by skirts and domino, and followed with all the others.

She heard Walgrave howling something about treason and Rothgar. He was trying to incriminate Rothgar ...

She dashed into the marble hall to see her father waving his pistol and ranting about traitors and fornicators like a mad preacher. Guests cowered behind chairs and pedestals. Chastity saw Fort enter the far side of the hall and move swiftly to control the earl.

It happened so quickly.

The earl's demented eyes focused on someone in the gaming room. "You . . . !" he snarled. "You! The author of all my woes . . . !"

Fort whipped out a pistol. "Father, no!"

The earl aimed.

Fort shot him.

The earl's arm jerked, and his own ball ricocheted harmlessly off a marble pillar. He crumbled in an ungainly heap. Chastity had the peculiar thought that he would hate to be seen in such an undignified position.

She ran forward, but her father was quite dead. Shot through the heart. She looked up and saw Princess Augusta sprawled inelegantly unconscious in her chair, cards spilled from her hands. She had been the target and had fainted from terror.

Chastity looked up at Fort, where he stood white and frozen, staring at what he had done. Then Verity and Nathaniel were at his side.

Excited chatter, shot through with weeping, built all around them. Cyn pulled Chastity into his arms and away from the body.

Brand and Rothgar's pistols had disappeared from view. Rothgar moved smoothly to calm alarmed guests, but Chastity noted that he did nothing to prevent people from gathering in the hall. Elf appeared and ran forward to tend to the princess, untying Augusta's mask and applying smelling salts.

Word immediately spread as to who the mysterious lady was, exciting the gentry rather more than the corpse.

Rothgar passed by and quietly instructed Cyn to take Chastity away from the center of the action. They accordingly moved back through the crowd. What now? How many of those events had been part of the clock-maker's design? Surely even Rothgar would not have planned for a son to shoot his father.

Would he?

She looked over, but Fort had disappeared from view.

"Cyn," she said, "I must go to Fort. He must feel so terrible."

But Cyn grasped her arm. "Not yet. Verity is with him." He edged them around the back of the crowd to a place where they could see and hear what went on in the card room.

August had regained her senses and was being tenderly assisted to a chaise. Rothgar bowed solicitously over her, assuring himself of her health.

The princess pressed a cool cloth to her head. "That man. Walgrave," she said in her German-accented English. "I have never liked him. He was a bad influence on my darling Frederick."

"I fear he went mad, your highness," said Rothgar.

Augusta moved the cloth slightly, clearly coming to terms with the situation. "He was shouting about treason. I think he accused you of treason, my lord marquess."

"Said you'd been a Jacobite in the '45," said Lady Fanshaw. "Man was crazed. You couldn't have been out of the schoolroom in that year."

"True," said the princess. "And you are so loyal, you Mallorens." Chastity saw the flick Augusta's eyes toward Lord Bute, who had tactfully moved away. It would not be desirable for the rather conventional gentry to realize the mother of the king had come to this affair without attendants other than the man reputed to be her lover.

"Completely loyal," said Rothgar, pouring her some wine. "I cannot tell you how distressed I am to have had this happen while you were a guest in my house, your highness. We must find your lady-in-waiting." He looked around. "Where is Lady Trelyn?"

Nerissa Trelyn was a lady-in-waiting, but Chastity knew she hadn't come with Princess Augusta tonight. The suggestion, however, neatly conveyed the impression of propriety. But how would Rothgar make the Trelyns dance to his tune?

The princess relaxed and sipped her wine. "I'm sure this

fiasco was none of your fault, my lord. I wonder what turned the poor earl's wits."

"I fear he was consumed with remorse, your highness."

"Remorse?"

"Yes, your highness. You see, at this affair he met the scoundrel who brought about his daughter's disgrace earlier in the year. He discovered, since the man was in his cups, that his poor child was innocent of all wrongdoing."

"You speak of Chastity Ware?" asked Augusta in amazed disbelief.

"Indeed. It appears that Henry Vernham obtained the key to the lady's room and slipped into her bed. He knew from family gossip that she is an extraordinarily heavy sleeper. He deliberately shamed Lady Chastity in order to gain her hand, and her large dowry."

"The scoundrel," muttered someone in the crowd. "Horsewhip the wretch."

"I fear," said Rothgar, "that is impossible. The earl's anguish was so great, he shot the man."

There was a distinct murmur of approval.

The princess was a little skeptical. "It is a strange story, my lord."

"Extremely strange," agreed Rothgar, "but the earl insisted on recording one crucial aspect of the truth."

The princess took the paper Rothgar gave her and read it. "Extraordinary," she remarked. "This does make it clear that poor Lady Chastity was more virtuous than it appeared. Perhaps her name suits her rather better than we had supposed."

"And I would like to add my word," came a voice. Nerissa Trelyn walked forward. Chastity noted that though he faded away, Bryght appeared to have been with her, and for once he looked amused.

Nerissa was composed, but she was as pale as her pristine gown. She curtsied low to the princess. "I apologize for being from your side when this dreadful event occurred, your highness."

Augusta could play a part, too. She waved a hand. "I gave you permission to absent yourself. But what word do you have to add, Lady Trelyn? Were you not one of those who reported Lady Chastity's shame?"

"Indeed, your highness," said Nerissa demurely, "which makes it all the more important that I now right the wrong. Lord Trelyn and I—" The beauty directed her doe-like eyes at her doting husband, and he hurried forward to stand at her side. "—we hesitated to support the story, for we knew Lady Chastity a little and thought her to be virtuous. We felt that at the worst she had been guilty of an indiscretion. It was only when she appeared unrepentant that we were obliged to speak."

"And now you know better?" asked Augusta.

"Indeed." Nerissa was the picture of a beautiful, virtuous woman. "After your highness so kindly permitted me to dance with my husband, I was taken faint by the heat and perfumes in the ballroom." She lowered her head coyly. "Your highness will understand. I am in an interesting condition . . ."

"Ah," said Augusta. "Of course."

Trelyn preened with pride.

"I went into the cool of the conservatory. While I was there, people entered the small saloon off the conservatory, leaving me no way to depart other than by going outside. I could not risk a chill. I heard all that took place. Mr. Vernham confessed his wicked plot, and that he did not . . . did not sully Lady Chastity. The earl was distraught to think that he had so misjudged his daughter, as am I."

Augusta was no fool, and Chastity could see that she smelled a rat in all this, but she had nothing to gain by opposing it, and risked scandal if her presence here with Lord Bute were revealed.

"A sad case," she said. "I wonder what became of the unfortunate girl. Perhaps she can be found and we can do something to restore her good name. A respectable marriage would be in order."

Rothgar's eyes found Chastity. She stood frozen to the spot, hating the thought of baring herself before this crowd, who were standing around as if watching a play.

But Cyn's hand firmly pushed her forward. Heart pounding, she walked shakily over to Rothgar. "This is she, your highness. May I present Lady Chastity Ware?"

It was the telling moment, for presentation to royalty was the *sine qua non* of respectability.

Augusta stared at Chastity for a long moment. Then she smiled, if a little thinly, and held out her hand. Chastity sank into a deep curtsy to kiss it.

"You appear to have been hard done to, my dear," said the princess. "Do you swear now before witnesses that you are pure?"

Chastity rose, knowing her face had flamed. She prayed it be taken for embarrassment and sought words of truth. "I vow before heaven that I was a virgin when Henry Vernham sneaked into my bed, your highness, and that I did not invite him there. Thanks to Divine Providence he did not have opportunity to despoil me before I was rescued." She turned to Nerissa Trelyn. "You cannot know how grateful I was that you came at that time, my lady. I do understand how hard it must have been to believe me virtuous."

Nerissa managed to squeeze real tears from her big eyes, and embraced Chastity in a cloud of familiar rose perfume. "You poor dear innocent!" She turned to Augusta and knelt theatrically. "Your highness. We must do all in our power to correct this wrong, or my conscience will never be at ease."

"Of course we must," said the princess, though with a jaundiced air. She considered, then said, "This event has been a sad shock to my nerves. I will rest here a few days, Lord Rothgar, if that is possible."

"Rothgar Abbey will be honored, your highness."

"And as Lady Trelyn is in a delicate condition, I will

need additional ladies-in-waiting. Perhaps Lady Chastity and Lady Elfled will fill those posts pro-tem."

Both ladies curtsied deeply. "It will be a great honor, your highness," said Elf.

"Information about this revelation must be sent to the news-sheets which have delighted in spreading the scurrilous falsehoods." Augusta looked at Chastity and her eyes did seem to soften. "Lady Chastity, I'm sure your experiences have been shocking, but a marriage would be wise, especially one that would keep you away from London for some time."

Chastity wished she knew her lines in this play. She curtsied again. "I am willing to be guided by you, your highness." She saw Augusta's brows rise and realized her rings were visible. Oh, Lord.

Rothgar stepped forward. "I believe my brother, Captain Lord Cynric Malloren, would be willing to marry Lady Chastity. He has served the country well in the army, and is, I think, now interested in doing so in the administration of the Canadas."

"The Canadas," said Augusta dryly as Cyn came forward. "An excellent notion, and so very *convenient*, my lords. It could almost have been planned."

Chastity wanted the earth to swallow her. Cyn took her hand and squeezed it.

"As the lady is recently bereaved," said Augusta, "it would be as well to have the marriage performed privately and soon. I assume that too presents no problem."

"It will be as you command," said Rothgar, admirably straight-faced. A sparkling look flashed between him and Augusta.

The princess' lips twitched with genuine humor. "Rogue," she said reprovingly. "I suppose you intend that I crown all this by standing witness to the match. Why not? I'm sure my son can be brought to attend too."

Chastity stared at the princess in shock. The king as

well. Rothgar lost not one whit of his calm. "Your highness is, as always, supremely gracious."

"Indeed," said Augusta. "You will remember that, my lord. Now, after such drama, I require a room in which to rest."

She sailed toward the door but halted near the cloak-shrouded body, eyes fixed on a distant point. The corpse was hastily dragged out of the way and a small carpet flung on top to cover the blood. The queen then continued, Elf and Chastity in her wake.

"Good," said Lady Fanshaw. "Now can we get on with the damn game?"

Later, much later, the Mallorens, Frazers, and Wares gathered to celebrate and wonder. Except Fort. Fort—silent and deeply anguished—was with his father's body.

"My lord," demanded Chastity of Rothgar, "how much of that was planned?"

He smiled slightly. "Shall I claim all of it, and supernatural powers to boot? No, but the secret of genius is to be ready to grasp opportunity. I confess I hoped to push your father into more damning admissions, but then I did not expect to push him into madness and violence. I am sorry for it."

"I'm not, except for Fort's part." Chastity faced their shock. "Not because of what he did to me, but because of what he was capable of doing. I knew he was mad, but he could conceal it so well. No matter what sword hung over him, he would never have ceased to weave his plots, and he cared nothing for anyone else. Think if he had gained power over England."

"I fear you are right," said Rothgar. "The business of the false letter was planned, of course. I hoped that, if all else failed, it would throw him off-balance. As it did."

"And Henry Vernham?" asked Verity.

Rothgar shook his head. "A greedy fool, but I hadn't expected such an end. I must confess that at that moment,

I began to think as Chastity does. The earl shot him like a dog. That is a very dangerous man to leave loose upon the world."

"And Fort shot Father in turn," said Chastity. "He is heartsick over it."

Cyn took her hand. "It had to be done, love, and he was the only one with a clear shot."

Chastity wasn't sure about that, but she let it pass. "What of the princess?" she asked. "Why did you invite her?"

"Acceptance by royalty was essential to my plans," said Rothgar. "I admit that I did not forget the deep enmity between her and Walgrave. I hoped that she would support us if she saw it as a means to thwart him. I did not, you see, expect him to die."

Chastity shook her head admiringly. "Now tell me, my lord. How was Nerissa Trelyn brought to act? The letter?"

"That is Bryght's story."

Bryght Malloren smiled wryly. "Dear Nerissa was delighted to seduce me in the conservatory. I didn't have to do a thing but lie back and enjoy it. Then, as planned, we were trapped. She became rather worried, for I am the one man of whom her stupid husband is jealous. We listened, but she had no urge to clear Chastity's name until I showed her the letter. I'm afraid Nerissa is not at all pleased with any of us."

"I'm not sure the princess is either," said Verity.

"True, but she is a sensible woman overall," said Rothgar. "She is annoyed to be embroiled, but rather grateful to me for casting a cloak of respectability over this jaunt." He raised a brow at Chastity. "I understand Cyn promised that if you were restored to honor, he would not insist upon marriage, but we have rather forced your hand."

Chastity looked at her rings. "For once, my lord, he had already broken a promise."

"Yes," said Rothgar somewhat severely, "and those

rings could have ruined all. In future, you will kindly not embellish my plots."

Cyn kissed Chastity's hand by the rings. "In future, we hope to be free of your plots."

"Now that's gratitude for you," said Rothgar, but he was smiling.

Soon Chastity and Cyn found themselves alone in a house, resting deeply after the excitement. Most of the public rooms were still being cleaned after the ball, and all the spare bedrooms were full of guests who had elected to stay. So they ended up in Cyn's bedroom, in each other's arms on the bed.

"But no impropriety until we're married," he said.

"In two days," Chastity said in wonder.

"As long as your brother keeps his word and consents."

"Why would he object?"

Cyn's tone turned wry. "Because the Mallorens are once again at odds with the Wares. He thinks Rothgar forced him to pull the trigger."

"How could he think that? No one even knew my father would try to shoot the princess."

"No, but Rothgar told Fort to be in the hall, in case your father should create trouble there. When the moment came, either Rothgar or Brand could have fired at your father, but they didn't, forcing Fort to it."

"I saw Rothgar hold Brand back," said Chastity. "I did wonder."

She could tell Cyn was troubled too. "I think it was because no one would think Fort inspired by malice, whereas the enmity between Rothgar and Walgrave is well known."

Chastity shivered. "I quite like Rothgar, but at times he makes my blood run cold. Poor Fort."

"Poor everyone. I hope this doesn't mean continued bitterness, but if your brother and mine are going to show their teeth, I thank God that we, at least, will be far away. You'll like Acadia, love."

Chastity leaned back with a contented sigh. "I'm sure I will. It should be called Arcadia—a perfect place." She rolled and reached up for a kiss. "Our own special heaven."

Cyn kissed her but said wryly, "Have I misled you? It's a beautiful place, but wild and rough."

"You'll be there," she said simply.

The next kiss grew dangerously deep, but Cyn found the strength to end it and push her to her feet. "Come on. To your room. After all this, we're not going to start again by having you found in a compromising situation."

"Ah," said Chastity mischievously, as he steered her toward the door, "but at least I could be persuaded to marry *you*, sir . . ."

Chapter 22

❦

The wedding was of startling magnificence.

Many of the guests had stayed after the dramatic ball; others had been invited especially for the wedding—people of social importance, and a sprinkling of avid gossips.

Prodded by Princess Augusta, the king and his new bride arrived to take part. George's ostensible reason was to make sure that his beloved mother was recovered from her ordeal, but he and his plain German bride were quite obviously pleased to be present at the event of the year.

After careful consideration—for he was rather dull but very conscientious—George agreed to allow the Notorious Chastity Ware to be presented to him, and then laboriously quipped that she was clearly notorious for her beauty and virtue. His shy wife appeared agreeable, and commented on the keeper ring so like her own.

Chastity's wedding gown was a cloud of purest white. She had hesitated about this, but Rothgar had firmly overruled her. Due to the shortness of time there was not a great deal of fancy needlework on the gown, but since it was composed of the most expensive silk Valenciennes lace, festooned with pearls and diamonds, that hardly mattered.

Rothgar had ordered it. Fort had paid for it, which could be another reason for enmity. It would have bankrupted a

372

less wealthy family. Fort had returned—in severest black—to give his sister away. His manner to all the Mallorens was frigid. By comparison, Bryght Malloren was positively jovial, for he seemed to be recovering at last from Nerissa Trelyn's spell.

Elf and Verity were Chastity's attendants, but the mother and wife of the king insisted on sitting by for the robing. Chastity had the feeling that Princess Augusta hoped to see some sign of wantonness. She was deeply relieved that the stain had finally worn off her nipples.

Chastity's very anxiety, her feeling that at any moment this bubble would burst and leave her naked again before the malice of the world, appeared to convince Augusta that she was a suitably nervous bride.

Augusta tapped her cheek as she left. "Perhaps you feel hurried into this match, my dear, but it is for the best. Some of the damage has been repaired, but as a well-married woman you will be safer, especially when part of the Malloren family. Few would risk offending there. And out of the country you will have time to settle into your new state. My son has appointed your husband aide to General Lawrence, the Governor of Acadia. I have included a message with the dispatches to reassure his lady in case any unfortunate rumors might have traveled there."

The younger queen accepted the curtsies of all the ladies as she rose to leave. She raised Chastity and leaned close. "Truly," she said in her heavy German accent, "you must not be afraid." She turned pink. "It is all . . . it is rather nice, actually!" She then hurried off.

Chastity shared a hilarious look with her sister, but in truth, she was touched by the queen's attempt to soothe her fears. If only someone would soothe her real fears.

That this would all turn out to be dream.

That her father would appear again to torment her.

That someone would stand at the ceremony to denounce her.

That someone would face her with the question—*Have*

you ever made love to a man? She would not be able to lie convincingly.

She trembled slightly as Fort led her to the chapel in Rothgar Abbey.

He sensed her tension and stopped, frowning. "Do you not want to do this, Chastity? God knows, by any right you should marry him, but I failed you once, and I won't a second time. If you wish, I'll prevent it, Rothgar and all the Mallorens be damned."

Chastity knew he'd be glad of a fight. She found a reassuring smile. "I want it, Fort. Truly. I'm just terrified something will prevent it."

He smiled back, though bleakly. "Come on, then. Let's have it done with."

Cyn wore dull gold velvet trimmed with glittering braid. His hair was unpowdered. The gold seemed to leap into his eyes at the sight of her, as if he too had been afraid this event would never take place.

They had been busy these past few days and seen all too little of each other. In some ways that had been as well, however, as it had demanded less of their willpower.

Fort hesitated as he handed Chastity over to Cyn. "Hurt her, Malloren," he said softly, "and I'll destroy you."

Cyn merely raised his brows. "The protective brother? A new tack for you."

Chastity hastily put her hand in Cyn's and moved between them. He smiled lazily down at her and kissed her hand. "Hello, Charles."

Chastity felt the blush and turned her attention to the Abbey's chaplain.

She hardly followed the ceremony for stretching every sense she possessed in search of the first sign of disruption, disruption that would indicate that someone was going to stop this marriage. She spoke by rote as prompted, and suddenly found herself facing Cyn, her husband.

"Oh," she said. "But I didn't do it right! Can we do it again?"

Laughter rippled through the chapel. Cyn's lips twitched. "Why not?"

So they said their vows again, and this time they looked at each other, and made their vows solemnly to each other. Then they kissed, the lightest touching of lips.

Hand in hand, they mingled as the guests took wine and cake. Chastity saw some close and even cynical looks—especially at her waistline—but in view of the overwhelming acceptance, especially by royalty, none turned their back.

Already, she knew, coyly in news-sheet, frankly in letters and gossip, the story of poor Chastity Ware flew about the country, made even more sensational by the scandalous deaths of Henry Vernham and the Earl of Walgrave.

Then Cyn drew her into the hall. Even though it was still afternoon and daylight, Chastity looked toward the stairs.

"No," said Cyn. "I have something else in mind. Your portmanteaux are in the coach." He held out a beautiful white velvet cloak, lined with white ermine. "Will you come, wife?"

"Anywhere," she said, and he wrapped it around her.

They climbed into the handsome coach, one she knew rather well. She noted the escutcheon was restored to glory, and Hoskins and a groom were on the box.

A plain coach was following.

"Jerome and your new maid," Cyn said in explanation. "We are a respectable married couple, and must act as such."

"Respectable?" she teased. "That sounds dull."

He grinned. "O ye of little faith."

They passed the journey remembering their strange adventures, retasting the pain and joy, confirming for each other that this dream was true. Chastity paid little attention to the road until they entered a busy town. She looked out. "But this is . . ." She looked at him. "Winchester?"

They pulled into the Three Balls.

Chastity glowed at Cyn. "The same room?"

He nodded.

"When we were there, I thought . . . I wanted it to be our wedding night."

"So did I."

He handed her down and led her into the inn. The innkeeper bowed low, and it soon became clear Lord Cynric Malloren had taken the whole inn for his use. They were shown up to the familiar, small, beautiful room. Someone had found fresh roses and a bowl of them sat before the window, scenting the air.

The servants brought up their baggage, but were then dismissed. A cold collation and wine were laid on the table. A fire made the room cozy.

Cyn shrugged out of his greatcoat. Chastity removed her cloak. She stroked the fur. "This is a lovely thing. It must have cost the earth."

"Rothgar's wedding present to you. I couldn't have afforded it. Do you mind marrying the poorer end of the family?"

She could see the twinkle in his eyes, and sighed. "Alas, I had no choice, sir."

He held out his hand and she walked forward to put hers trustingly into it. He kissed her palms, by now unblemished, then pulled her closer to kiss her lips, his hands on her sides.

"Whalebone and hoops," he commented. "I warned you. Off with 'em."

"But sir," she protested, "you threatened . . . er, promised to strip them off me."

He assessed her expensive gown and found it was in one piece and fastened down the back. Soon it was pooled carelessly on the floor. He smiled at her hoop-frame. "These things look damn silly with nothing over them." Then it too was gone, and her laced corset followed.

She turned to face him, clad only in her sheer silk chemise and her clocked stockings. She pushed his coat off his shoulders and unbuttoned his brocade waistcoat. This time her fingers made it to the end without failing. She even managed to unknot his cravat and slowly pull it off.

Soon he wore only his gold velvet breeches and open-necked shirt. Chastity waited, her mouth dry with anticipation.

He looked at the table. "Food," he said.

"Cyn!"

He took her hand and pulled her to the table, sat down, and tugged her into his lap. His nimble fingers found her garters and untied them. He looked at them and grinned. They were a pair they knew well. "Do you remember . . . ?" he asked.

Trembling, she hid her face in his shoulder. "Yes."

He slid the silk stockings off her legs, then his hand traveled up her naked leg, but up the outside, all the way to her hip. She twisted, but he wouldn't touch where she wanted him to touch.

Instead, his hand came out from under her chemise and picked up a tart, a golden apple tart with a frill of rich cream.

"Do you remember?" he asked.

She laughed. "I remember! Heavens above, Cyn, are we to relive our time together, moment by moment, meal by meal?"

"What a lovely idea," he said. "I wonder where I can find some Shrewsbury biscuits . . ."

Chastity grabbed the pie and took a large bite.

"A wench of truly ferocious appetites," he said, and licked some cream and crumbs from around her mouth. When she swallowed, he kissed her, full and deep. "Mmm," he said. "Delicious."

"You only love me for my apples."

With a hoot of laughter, he set his lips to first one nipple and then the other. "And your cherries," he murmured.

His hand traveled lightly over her chemise, exciting

where it touched. He produced a vial she remembered and tenderly anointed secret places.

"I wondered where that had gone," she whispered.

"I bought it with this moment in mind, though perhaps I did not know it then . . ."

Chastity snatched the vial and anointed him in turn. After a laughing struggle, he recaptured it. The musky perfume swirled around them as they wrestled for it. As her hand ran down his body, she found something else. "Cucumber!" she declared, and they dissolved into laughter.

Then he slid from under her so she sat alone in the chair. He put the remains of the tart in her hand and slowly stripped off his clothes, watching her with darkened eyes.

Chastity was frozen in breathless delight, the tart ignored in her hand. He was so beautiful, her husband, that tears sprang to her eyes.

"I thought you were hungry," he said.

She looked at the tart, then threw it at him. He just stood there as golden fruit and juices and rich yellow cream slid slowly down his lithe torso. It landed on his penis, hovered there for a moment, then dropped off, leaving him well decorated.

He looked down and grinned. "I do believe dinner is served, milady."

Chastity felt somehow this wasn't the way a proper married couple was supposed to behave, but she rose and advanced on him. He retreated until he fell back across the bed. "I surrender!" he declared. "Have your wicked way with me, wench."

Chastity was mesmerized by a big blob of cream on the tip of his penis and she leant down and sucked it off. He bucked. " 'Struth!"

When she looked up, though, it was clear he wasn't angry. She slowly but gently cleaned him with her tongue. She could see his chest moving with mighty breaths, hear his breathing, sense the tremors running through him. She slid on top and impaled herself on him.

"No!" he gasped, but then rolled them and surrendered, loving her with fevered intensity. Chastity burned with joy to be able to do this to him, for him, with him. They roared into flame.

They were damp with sweet-odored sweat when Cyn pushed himself up from her, frowning. "I didn't mean our first time to be like that."

Chastity's heart sank. She'd known, hadn't she, that proper married people didn't behave like that. "I'm sorry . . ."

He silenced her with a kiss, a long drowning kiss. "I'm not," he assured her. "I just wanted it to be perfect for you this first time."

"It *was* perfect, but I'm sorry . . ."

He covered her lips gently with his hand. "Don't be. You can ravish me anytime you want. But now, dear wife, let me ravish you . . ."

Through silk, then under silk, he teased her pleasure points to heat, until she writhed under his hands and lips, longing for release. Then he entered her with infinite, tantalizing slowness and set her free.

The next day Cyn and Chastity wandered the ancient streets of Winchester in a private world of joy. But in time they came to a certain crossing-boy.

"I remember you, Captain," the lad said with a grin, then quickly added, "Milord."

Cyn laughed and tossed him a golden guinea. "That for your memory, and because I'm newly wed."

The boy whooped, then remembered to make a bow. "And best wishes to you both."

As they strolled on, though, Chastity's smile faded and she pulled her fur cloak closer around her. "People do have long memories, don't they?"

Cyn glanced at her then steered her toward a familiar building—Darby's Bank.

They walked in and were both quickly ushered into Mr. Darby's paneled sanctum and plied with sherry.

"And what can I do for you, Lord Cynric?" the banker asked.

"I am here to make financial arrangements for my bride, Darby," said Cyn. He turned to Chastity. "My dear, this is Mr. Darby. I will arrange for you to draw funds here while we are in England."

Mr. Darby bowed and kissed her hand. "Lady Cynric, this is indeed an honor. Please accept my warmest felicitations . . ."

Soon they emerged into the crisp air again and Cyn smiled at Chastity. "You see? The reputation of the Notorious Chastity Ware is being put to right, but she has also disappeared. From now on you are Lady Cynric Malloren and safe, I assure you, from all distress."

Chastity turned with a shining smile. "I was new-born from the day I met you . . . Oh, Cyn! It's really going to be all right, isn't it?"

He pulled her into his arms, there on the street. "It is, and always will be perfect, my beloved. But I think we should create a new notoriety. Let's become notorious for our unfashionable contentment and fidelity. And for the amount of time we spend in private. As I recall," he said, his eyes already darkening with desire, "we have a delightful private room awaiting us . . ."

Chastity's happy laughter lingered as they hurried back to the sweet privacy of the room at the Three Balls.